lit
8/17

Libidan

P.J.Goddard

First published in the United Kingdom in 2001
by Hilltop Publishing Limited

The author and publishers are grateful for permission to quote from "Sex
Kills" by Joni Mitchell.

ISBN 0 9536850 1 2

Printed and bound in Great Britain by Biddles Ltd,
Guildford and King's Lynn.

Typeset in Bembo by Avocet Typeset, Brill, Bucks.

Hilltop Publishing Limited
Brill
Buckinghamshire
U.K.
www.hilltoppublishing.co.uk

For A.S.
And all our future captains

Author's note

My thanks and appreciation to...

Joni Mitchell, for her Thucydidean inspiration; the United States National Organization for Rare Disorders, for allowing me to access their database and construct the (entirely fictional) syndrome Bullman-Sachs; Roger D'Arcy of D'Arcy Computers Oxford, for fixing my Mac when it blew up and without whom this novel would start somewhere in the middle of page 14; Mark Auty of the Crown Prosecution Service, York, for advice on the police and matters legal; John Stevenson, for his observations on DNA and One Life; Susan Hill, for her enthusiasm and encouragement; Catherine Croydon, for her ever astute criticism and ceaseless labours in correcting my prose – those errors and infelicities that remain are entirely my responsibility; Hilltop Publishing, for backing the novel; and, finally, my son Julius, for lighting my every day.

P.J.G.
Ipso nocte pervigilii veneris - 30th April 2001

I pulled up behind a Cadillac;
We were waiting for the light;
I took a look at his license plate –
It said 'JUST ICE'.
Is justice just ice?
Governed by greed and lust?
Just the strong doing what they can,
And the weak suffering what they must?

And the gas leaks,
And the oil spills,
And sex sells everything,
And sex kills.

Joni Mitchell
- *Sex Kills* -

Part One

The Gas Leaks

Prologue

Just before Squire's Park roundabout, where the A634 meets the Harledge New Town bypass, holy charity lay murdered in a ditch. An immense refrigerated truck, carrying meat pies and sausages to the town's supermarkets, had snapped an axle directly in front of the traffic lights that controlled entry to the roundabout, and, in the mile long tail-back that had formed behind, no one was conceding an inch.

That Squire's Park could one day come to witness such rush hour congestion would have horrified Sir Henry MacKinnell, FRIA, the architect who drew up the road system for Harledge New Town in the late nineteen fifties: he had considered himself almost lavish in the provision of twin-laned dual carriageways for this and the other major approach roads to the city. Indeed, a water colour sketch from the time, one of a series commissioned by the Borough Council to attract new residents and stapled up on stiff hardboard panels in the foyer of County Hall, had depicted precisely this stretch of the A634 running from the motorway down towards Squire's Park. Between lush, grassy slopes a line of uniformly spaced saloon cars glided purposefully forward like the first wagon train of forty-niners to have made it over the mountains and down into the valley beyond. In the main, subsequent events proved this optimism well founded. The businesses so critical to the development of the new town sprang up in even greater numbers than predicted and almost without exception decided to stay. The increase in car ownership they brought with them, however, exceeded all expectations, and, as the years passed, distances between vehicles on the A634 became ever shorter. So it was, that at eight o'clock on this spring morning, the last day in April two thousand and one, the gaps finally closed up altogether, stranding our latter day pioneers tantalizingly short of their destination and no less desperate to get their wagons through the pass up ahead than if the surrounding hills were discovered, after all, to be crawling with hostile redskins.

Had the tow truck that had been summoned shortly after seven itself not suffered a broken fan belt, all perhaps might have ended well; in anticipation of its imminent arrival two police motorway patrol vehicles had diligently kept the hard shoulder clear for over an hour. By the time another was found, though, Harledge was already embarking upon a turning point in its civic history – albeit one whose true import went unrecognized even by those commuters who were actually involved in the incident that was to follow. The one or two who did later take the time to reflect mistook it all for some sort of ghastly graduation ceremony as their town finally experienced the standstills that were commonplace throughout other cities the length and breadth of the nation. Perhaps only Sir Henry himself would have understood the deeper significance of those next fateful twenty minutes – which went far beyond the simple logistics of gridlock. For he and his team of planners had been genuinely inspired by a vision of the city they were to design, leading the human race forwards towards a bright, utopian future, not backwards into its murky, primordial past.

A change in the timing of the traffic lights proved to be the catalyst. At 08:12 precisely, programmed to regulate a normal morning's peak vehicle flow, the signals on the westbound carriageway began switching back from green to red every eighteen seconds instead of every twenty-six. Up until then, the queue had at least been progressing at a crawl, but from that point onwards, it began inexorably to slow towards a standstill. And that was when it started. From just behind the lead six or seven vehicles, a deep subliminal wave of claustrophobic anxiety began to pulse its way backward along the queue. One after another – in a mile-long mental chain reaction – each driver's frontal lobes crackled, sparked and then fused out altogether. Within a few short minutes, the jam was no longer composed of individuals, but of so many inautonomous drones, whose every sensory neurone hummed in unison with those around them, utterly enslaved to the task of detecting any factor that might influence their collective chances of a successful escape. Even Bill Kennedy, who routinely arrived for work at least ten minutes late every day, found himself rudely plugged into this neural network as he edged around the back of the stranded juggernaut to take up fifth position from the lights. Up until then, he had more or less been day-dreaming, but pulling up the handbrake and staring through the windscreen ahead, he suddenly became conscious of the peculiar atmosphere of nervous tension all around him. So it was, that a full two seconds before anyone else that morning, it was he who spotted the first unmistakable sign of the event that would bring an end to Sir Henry's Arcadian dream.

What Bill saw was the driver at the front of the queue pursing her lips in her rear-view mirror. By itself, this slight facial movement was not enough to attract the attention of the other drivers who had their eyes very much fixed on the signal that at any moment was due to turn green again. However, when she extracted a lipstick from her handbag and actually applied it to her mouth, they began frantically scrutinizing every aspect of the vehicle that had found its way into the all important pole position. Their assessment was rapidly made and its conclusions were dire indeed. Everything about the stately, azure-blue Range Rover exuded independence and freedom from the anxieties of the common herd: the personalized number plate; the plush, acoustically-proofed interior; the two children on the back seat arraigned in smart, private-school uniforms. More worrying still was the distinct air of idiosyncrasy about the woman herself: her ludicrously tall velveteen hat would have made the Mad Hatter gasp and the lipstick she applied so unhurriedly was uncompromisingly mauve. Somehow, though, the lights stayed red long enough for her to finish her cosmetic fine-tuning, pop the lipstick back in her handbag and place both hands on the wheel again and, for a single, agonizing moment, there seemed an almost better than evens chance that she would engage the powerful 4.6 litre engine and liberate her fellow commuters behind from their torment. But it was not to be. A fraction of a second before the lights turned green, she undid her seat belt and leaned around to retrieve an object from the floor. The response was instantaneous. A sonic shock wave of car horns, vitriol and threats of death surged forwards along the queue towards her Range Rover, whilst a thunderbolt of nervous panic went arcing backwards, practically blowing the final driver a mile behind right out of his seat.

Handing her daughter's fallen boater back to her, Mrs Gabriella Zelig wondered what on earth the appalling hubbub behind might possibly be about. Belting herself back into her seat, she was about to pull away when she at last connected the green light up ahead with the rowdy commotion behind. Peeved by this vulgar display of impatience, she pressed the button to wind down the driver's window, fully intending to issue her most withering glare of reproof. On looking back down the queue the first thing she saw was the face of the driver directly behind. Only he didn't look impatient. He looked insane. As did the seemingly innumerable host of motorists lined up behind him.

Had this same burst of exasperation been directed at anyone else at the front of the queue that morning, it would have immediately achieved its objective and sent the offender flying off towards Squire's Park. Such were the peculiar dynamics of Gabriella Zelig's temperament, though, that what should have been a powerful following wind acted instead like a blast of turbulence, disastrously flipping her into an uncontrollable tailspin. For now completely terrified by the raw emotion with which the atmosphere outside was charged, Gabriella's instinctive reaction was to try somehow to shut it all back out again. This she did by throwing out her left hand and slamming down on what she thought was the control to rewind the window. The button she hit, however, and hit so hard as to jam it right under the lip of the dashboard's walnut veneer, was not in fact driver's window rewind, but the next one to it – driver's seat readjust. By the time she realized her error the car's silky internal hydraulics were already collapsing the front seat inwards on itself, folding her body in two like a sliver of salami between the jaws of a baguette. Nor was her virtuoso display to end there, for, lungs squeezed of oxygen, feet hoisted off the pedals and face coming ever closer to the steering wheel, there was nothing Gabriella could then do to stop herself from stalling the car.

Although the queue was still entirely stationary at this point, a number of drivers began bouncing around inside their vehicles like crash test dummies rammed at ninety miles per hour. Their cavortings were brought to a halt but two seconds later when the lights could finally wait no longer and changed from green back to amber. So it was, that at the exact moment the tip of Gabriella Zelig's nose came to rest on the perspex plinth of her speedometer dial, Harledge's municipal innocence was lost. For, in that instant, Gabriella sensed with absolute certainty that she must either make it through the lights up ahead in the next half second or be torn limb from limb by her fellow residents behind. Grasping the ignition key with her left hand and stabbing out

12

with her right foot, she gunned the engine back into life and, with all four wheels skidding, went screeching out in first gear on to Squire's Park. Engulfed in the rush of traffic that poured onto the island from the southern approach road, her Range Rover then proceeded, within a few short moments, to all but disappear from sight.

Thus unaware of the illusion left lying in ruins behind her – that human wit can ever for long impose itself on human nature – Gabriella Zelig passes both from these pages and the pages of history.

Chapter 1

The journey from Squire's Park roundabout into the centre of town is widely regarded by the residents of Harledge as something of a mystery tour: the mystery element coming from the fact that no one has ever really been sure where the centre actually is. There are two reasons for this. Firstly, being a new town, Harledge has no historical central hub – a market square, river or bridge around which the community originally formed. Secondly, a series of decisions were taken during the early planning stages for the town which, although individually sensible, nevertheless later collectively conspired to deprive it of any semblance of an urban core. To spread the transport load, Harledge was given two railway stations – yet neither of them was located in the city's geographical centre. In an attempt to create a uniformly spacious atmosphere, all the pavements, roads and grass reservations were made to exactly the same size and specification throughout the town – with the result that no one area appears any more or less architecturally dense than any other. Most disorientating of all, though, is the effect created by utterly separating the people of Harledge from the motorized vehicle by means of endless pedestrian precincts and the concealment of every residential estate behind a line of trees: namely that, to the motorist, Harledge appears permanently to be stuck in a time warp of nine o'clock on a Sunday morning: the few souls one does glimpse are neither able implicitly to suggest one's location in the town, nor, short of a megaphone on the passenger seat, explicitly likely to do so either. As a result, many a hapless traveller has been known not just to miss the middle of Harledge, but to drive all the way into the town and then right out of the other side in anticipation of some defining feature that was never to materialize.

No such sense of uncertainty afflicted Bill Kennedy, however, as he was finally able to make his way out on to Squire's Park roundabout. For almost six years he had been travelling to work along this same route from his home five miles away in the village of Wyburn and routinely undertook the journey in a state of complete mental torpor. Because of the drama at the traffic lights, though, he was much more alert this morning, and, as he accelerated away from the roundabout, he noticed some schoolchildren up ahead. They were making their way in twos and threes towards the High School at the end of Boulevard 12. Normally, when Bill cruised along this stretch of road, these same students were little more than a blur of green and grey flannel, but he now found himself staring across at their faces. What would the world bring them this day? He shook his head pensively. He could not possibly imagine. Within a few moments the familiar features of his daily commute began to reassert their customary deadening effect on his senses, and five minutes later, as he approached the main gates of Asper Pharmaceuticals, the children were far from his thoughts.

Swerving past the 'Full' sign at the entrance to the employees' car park, Bill came to a halt by the gatehouse and then wound down his window, waiting for the gatekeeper to appear.

'Here, Derek, you couldn't let us into the visitors' car park for an hour or so could you, mate?' he asked, flashing the gatekeeper his best naughty-boy grin.

'Nah, sorry, Bill. Not enough spaces left. You'll have to go round the back to the contractors'.'

'What!'

'What's the matter, forgot your wellies?' replied the gatekeeper, with a laugh.

'Ah, come on, have a heart ...' pleaded Bill, but the gatekeeper had already turned on his heel and was smartly making his way back to the gatehouse.

Frowning, Bill shifted his car into reverse and for the second time that morning cursed the traffic jam that had delayed his arrival. Not that he was concerned about finding the employees' car park already full. On the contrary, it usually ranked as a first-rate start to the working day. For, in such circumstances, Derek normally let him use one of the visitors' parking spaces for a couple of hours, thus furnishing him with the opportunity to slink away from his desk mid-morning to reposition his car in an employee's space that had later become vacant. This ruse worked well when he was ten minutes late, but he now realized it was five past nine, some thirty-five minutes after the site's official clocking-in time, and the gatekeeper had already bestowed his favours elsewhere. Left with no alternative, Bill drove around to the contractors' car park at the back of the site, squeezing his Mondeo in between two HGV's piled high with scaffolding. Slamming the driver's door, he locked the car and, with a resentful grunt, began the long trudge along the muddy, potholed service road back towards the main gate; being late was not supposed to be about incurring effort, but avoiding it – he of all people knew that.

Outside the gate Derek was waiting for him – only this time, it was he who wore the naughty-boy grin.

'Over here, quick!' hissed Derek, beckoning him into the gatehouse.

Wondering what intrigue lay in wait for him, Bill followed the burly gatekeeper through the door. Inside, Derek had taken up position next to a large black box that appeared recently to have been bolted onto one of the gatehouse's internal walls. A connector attached to a clutch of ribbon cable dangled down from a duct in the ceiling above – seemingly soon to be connected to the box in a final wiring-up operation.

'The electricians put this in yesterday morning, apparently – I was on my day off,' explained Derek, with a mixture of awe and amusement, as though beholding a coffin that had fallen off the back of an undertaker's lorry and landed in the middle of his front lawn.

'What is it?' asked Bill, staring at the box's sinister, unmarked graphite surface.

'I reckon it's an SDSU.'

'What's an SDSU?' asked Bill.

'A Secure Data Storage Unit. Like a flight recorder – you know, a black box.'

'What's it for?'

'Come here. I'll show you.'

Taking a clipboard down from the wall, Derek flicked through the dozen or so crumpled delivery notes attached to it and, having made certain they were not being observed from outside the gatehouse, pulled one out and surreptitiously showed it to Bill.

'Eleven infrared scanner units,' read Bill from the manifest.

16

'I signed this lot in last week,' said Derek. 'They took 'em straight down to main stores.'

'So?'

'Eleven buildings on site, right?'

'Yeah …' replied Bill, smiling at the conspiratorial look on Derek's face.

'Have you been to the United States lately? To one of their new airports? They check your palms with infra red scanners now – they've mostly done away with passports. All the records for 'em are stored in SDSU's … like this one.'

'So, d'you reckon this is all some sort of palm-activated entry system, then?' replied Bill, looking nervously across at the black box and then back at the manifest again.

'You're dead right, I do. I know the old bastard's game. Inside a month he'll have all our palm prints stored inside this thing and one of these scanners at the entrance to each of the research buildings. Ha ! You'll be for it, then, won't you?' taunted Derek, clipping the advice note back on to the clipboard and stretching across to hang it up on the wall. 'Swannin' in 'ere every mornin' whenever you feel like it.'

'Bah! I don't believe you,' scoffed Bill, walking over to inspect the box again. 'Who says it's not just another piece of switch gear, anyway? A junction box or something.'

'You mark my words, son,' responded Derek, sagely. 'No one'll be able to go anywhere on this site without him knowing – he'll have a complete record of every individual entry to each of the buildings.'

'What for? We've already got a swipe card system.'

'Yeah, but swipe cards don't tell you exactly where everyone is. Besides, people swap 'em, don't they? Eh? All the time. Can't swap your hands, though, can you? Total control he'll have. Just you wait.'

'Ah, come off it.'

'And then before you know it there'll be a scanner at the end of every corridor, in every lift. In six months you won't be able to lean down and scratch your arse without a bell goin' off somewhere in the old man's penthouse. "Hello, hello, hello! What have we here? Bill Kennedy with his hands in his pants again. That's the third time this morning. Write it down in the book, quick!"'

'I can't stand here listening to this paranoia all day,' laughed Bill, turning towards the door. 'I'm off.'

'Paranoia? Paranoia??' responded Derek, taking up the challenge. 'So put me a fiver on it then, son! Eh? Come on.'

Walking off towards the employees' entrance, Bill could see Derek gesticulating at him through the window of the gatehouse, still trying to goad him into the wager. Shaking his head in amused disbelief, Bill went through the turnstile and began strolling down the central avenue of the site. As he walked past the main reception, though, he could not stop himself from peering through at a bronze sculpture within of the old man to whom Derek had referred. Could it be true? Was Sir Paul Giulani, Chairman and Chief Executive Officer of Asper Pharmaceuticals, really intending to take his notorious obsession with security and management intelligence as far as tracking each of his employee's movements around the site? Bill shuddered. Certainly, in the three years since Giulani had acquired Asper in his now infamous leveraged buyout, his bold restructuring programme had transformed the company from a sprawling, over-diversified conglomerate into a highly focused pharmaceutical major. So far all the heads that had rolled had been at the top. If Sir Paul was now about to start directing his particular brand of ruthless, autocratic management towards ordinary researchers like Bill Kennedy, then life on the Harledge site was going to become altogether much more uncomfortable.

'Here! What time d'you call this, then?'

Snapping out of his reverie, Bill looked around to see Peter Layford waiting for him up ahead, staring at his watch in a gesture of mock reproof. Even before the two had fallen into step together, Bill had his riposte ready – he was not going to let his buyer friend get away with a comment like that.

'Never mind what time it is – where's my hormone fragment?'

'What hormone fragment?'

'What d'you mean what hormone fragment? It's the only thing I've got on order with you at the moment.'

'Oh, that thing.'

'Yeah, that thing. Instead of loafing around the site slagging off hard working researchers like me, why aren't you at your desk chasing up your overdue orders?'

'Overdue! You only ordered it three weeks ago – give us chance! What's the hurry, anyway?'

'Well, I need it today, don't I?'

'Today! You'll be lucky! We've had to ask a specialist synthesis house to make it up as a custom job – it's not a catalogue chemical, you know.'

'Isn't it?' replied Bill, his bravura suddenly faltering.

'Of course not. Didn't you check before you sent the requisition through to purchasing?'

'Er, no, no. I didn't think to …'

'Well, I can certainly give 'em a call for you, but don't expect miracles. A complex peptide like that takes time to synthesize. What d'you need it today for, anyway?'

'Oh, I've got Martindale on my back.'

'Don't tell me he's giving you any stick. He wouldn't be head of the Minority Diseases Unit if it wasn't for you – everyone knows that. Besides, I didn't think he was the bolshie type.'

'Well, its not so much he's on my back – I just sort of promised him I'd have all my projects up to date by today, that's all,' replied Bill, cheering up slightly at the reference to Phosphopenim – the antibiotic which he had discovered five years previously and which was widely held to have saved his boss's department from closure.

'I bet he's bidding for one of the new labs, y'know.'

'What new labs?'

'God, you do keep your head down, don't you? You've seen those fancy new laboratories they're putting up at the back of building 3, haven't you?'

'Yeah.'

'He's probably trying to get one of them earmarked for your unit.'

'D'you reckon?'

'Well just about every other section leader's busting a gut to get their hands on one – I don't see why he should be any different.'

'Oh, you're probably right,' replied Bill looking across at the buyer's bright, intelligent face. Three years his senior and widely held to be destined for the top, Peter Layford was far more au fait with what was going on around the site than he.

'Listen,' asked Bill, confidentially, 'is it true about the new security arrangements?'

'What new security arrangements?'

'The palm-activated scanners they're supposed to be putting in.'

'Palm-activated scanners!' laughed Peter. ' This is Asper, not NASA! Who told you we're getting palm-activated scanners for God's sake?'

19

'Derek, on the gate.'

'You don't wanna listen to him.'

'I thought it all sounded a bit far fetched.'

'Ah, it's just another Giulani scare story,' scoffed Peter. 'There's a new one every week. You know the new CCTV system?'

'Yeah …'

'The other day, one of the blokes in engineering swore blind to me the old man's got it wired up to a stack of TV monitors in his penthouse! Hah! Could you believe that? What a joke! Anyway, what's the matter? Worried he might catch you sneaking in here at half nine every day?'

'It's quality that counts, sunshine – not quantity,' replied Bill, enjoying the banter once more. 'Just you get my hormone fragment in here quick so I can discover the next blockbuster. Otherwise it just might be your guts Giulani's after, not mine.'

'Yeah, OK, mate – I'll see what I can do,' laughed Peter, giving Bill a good-natured wave as the two men went their separate ways.

Crossing the main avenue and walking up to the entrance to Building 7, Bill found himself staring into the lens of one of the CCTV cameras that Peter had just described. The site had indeed recently become littered with such devices, although in this particular case its installation had been more a matter of compliance with the latest FDA directives than Sir Paul's indulging his commercial paranoia: the Infectious Diseases Unit on the third floor carried out research into some of the world's most contagious micro-organisms and entrance controls grew stricter every year. Nevertheless, with the exception of the new entry camera, Building 7 had undergone very few changes since its construction five years previously and, as the electronic bolt shot back into its lock, the reception area that Bill entered was as impressively immaculate as the day the Queen had cut the red tape and glided squeakily forward over its epoxydised flooring. On that occasion, the organizers had estimated that her Royal Highness would require between twelve and fifteen minutes to complete a circuit of the ground floor. This morning, however, Bill took nearly the same amount of time to make a much shorter journey along the silent, aseptic corridors from the researchers' locker room up to the second floor via the lift. For, although Building 7 was very much a state-of-the-art R&D facility, it still suffered from one fundamental weakness: the labyrinth of walls, doors and isolation vestibules which was so effective in frustrating contact between humans and microbes similarly ensured that for most of the time the humans did not get to see a great deal of each other either – a state of affairs Bill Kennedy exploited by sauntering around the building at visiting royalty pace, unobserved and uncensured.

As he emerged from the second floor lifts and began walking towards his laboratory Bill was suddenly right on his guard: the door at the far end of the corridor was slightly ajar. Pressing himself as closely up against the left-hand wall as possible, he began padding silently towards his lab – with a bit of luck he might just be able to get in there without being observed.

'William, my boy!' came a booming voice. 'Well met! Well met! Can you, er … ?'

Bill released the door handle with a groan – just two seconds more and he would have made it. Certain of the sight that would now greet him, but praying all the same that just this once he might be spared, Bill turned around. His hope was in vain. At the end of the corridor – exactly as he had expected – stood Dr Edward Martindale, knees bent, the forefingers of both hands extended, swinging his arms to and fro in the peculiar Charleston-like gesture that Bill had come to recognize as an invitation from his boss to enter his office.

'Oh, hi, Edward. Did you want me?'

As though one of twenty, rather than the only person in the corridor, Bill pointed a quizzical finger at his chest. This attempt at avoiding the inevitable quickly drew the response it deserved, however, as, propelling his arms still more vigorously in a blur of nervous energy, Martindale span around on his heel and disappeared back inside his room. Shaking his head in resignation, Bill followed after him.

'Shut the door and, er, take a seat, William – please, please.'

'Thanks,' said Bill, gingerly lowering himself into the decrepit armchair that Martindale somehow still managed to maintain for visitors to his office. Looking down at its grimy, moth-eaten arm rests, Bill wondered why site services hadn't had the thing incinerated years ago: it probably harboured more dangerous micro-organisms than the Infectious Diseases Laboratory on the third floor.

'I'm so glad I spotted you just now in the corridor,' began Martindale, confidentially. 'I've been, er, wanting to share a little scheme of mine with you for some time now.'

'You're trying to get the unit transferred to the new laboratories at the back of Building 3, yes?' asked Bill, flatly.

'Good lord, how did you know?' replied Martindale, his eyebrows rising above the top of his ancient, gold-rimmed bifocals by a good six inches.

'Just a guess. What d'you think our chances are?' replied Bill, trying to hurry the conversation along. Much as deep down he liked and admired Martindale, today, somehow, he could feel his patience with the older man wearing rather thin.

'Good, very good. I've been asked to submit a report tomorrow to the subcommittee in charge.'

'Oh, great. Well, there we go, then. Let me know how you get on ...' said Bill, half rising out of the chair.

'And it was for that reason,' continued Martindale, undeterred, 'that I asked you to have all your projects up to date by today. Do you think you could let me have a summary of your results to put before the committee to help press our case?'

'Er, yes ... yes, of course, Edward,' replied Bill, his voice wavering slightly – to get his results properly up to date would take more like eight weeks than eight hours.

'Thank you, thank you. As our star researcher on the Minority Diseases Unit I knew I could rely on you. I've asked Lester to do the same, by the way. He tells me he has been making some very exciting progress recently – very exciting!'

'Oh ... right,' responded Bill, flinching at the mention of his fellow researcher's name.

'Yes, in particular with his novel therapy for Bullman-Sachs.'

'Bullman-Sachs? How interesting. Yes, yes, I remember that condition, it's the, er, what is it again, now ... ?' enquired Bill, feigning a temporary memory lapse. This was getting serious. The prospect of a frantic day's work throwing together a report for Martindale was disturbing enough, but the suggestion that his archrival Lester Mold had somehow managed to steal an edge on him was alarming in the extreme.

'It's similar to precocious puberty – and is very often misdiagnosed as such, I understand – but its actually one of the alpha-hydroxylase deficiency syndromes. It's very rare, too – even by our standards.'

'And, er, Lester's found out what, exactly ... ?'

'I'm not sure. But he's certainly been very busy lately – locked up in his laboratory from dawn till dusk. He's prepared a presentation for us tomorrow morning – you can ask him all about it, then.'

'Oh, right, I'll look forward to that,' replied Bill, his eyes narrowing. That devious bastard Mold had obviously been keeping his results close to his chest.

'And, er, yes – talking of hours and timekeeping.'

'Yes, Edward?' replied Bill, switching instantly to his most innocent-looking expression.

'Well, er, it's just that. It's just that …'

Mercilessly, Bill watched his boss squirm in discomfort. Peter Layford's evaluation had been completely correct. Martindale's section had indeed been facing the threat of closure when, for six months during 1996, the Asper graduate induction scheme placed Dr William Kennedy Ph.D. amongst its ranks. The rest was history. At the age of just twenty-three, through a combination of meticulous screening and inspired biochemistry, Bill achieved a breakthrough that had eluded scores of researchers in academic institutions and competitive organisations around the world for decades. Phosphopenim. A fast onset *Stapholococcus Aureus* antibiotic, over eight times more potent than any other compound in its class. Overnight, the discovery rescued Martindale from an enforced early retirement and transformed him into the manager of a genuinely productive team. A year later, he was promoted to chief scientist on the newly formed Minority Diseases Unit, the post that he still occupied today.

'It's just that, what, Edward?' asked Bill.

'That if abnormal factors were in some way to be, er, brought to the attention of the committee, this unit's otherwise perfectly legitimate claim to take up one of the new laboratories might be, er, put in jeopardy.'

Suddenly, Bill felt tired with the whole discussion: the sooner he brought it to a conclusion the better.

'OK, I understand. Get here in the mornings on time. I know.'

'If it were up to me, William, you could come and go as you please. I have always had confidence in your abilities as a researcher.'

'Yes, yes, I know …'

'It's just that this is a rather sensitive time and, of course, well, you did have that, er, warning last year – didn't you?'

Bill looked up and frowned at Martindale. There had been no need for him to refer to that.

'I said OK, Edward, I understand,' repeated Bill emphatically, recalling with a shiver their painfully embarrassing visit to the Human Resources Department together the previous June.

'Thank you, thank you, William. Right, then! See you in the canteen at, er, eight-thirty tomorrow.'

'When?' exclaimed Bill.

'Eight-thirty. My meeting with the subcommittee is at eleven, so Lester thought it would be a good idea if we started early.'

Frowning, Bill left Martindale's office and began to wander back down the corridor towards his lab. So, the eight-thirty meeting had been Mold's idea, had it? Talentless little shit. He probably thought that breakfast meetings made him look like some sort of highflying executive – and he knew Bill hated early mornings. Bill scratched the side of his head in irritation. How was he going to list up the results of his projects when he hadn't even done half of the experiments for them yet? Still pondering this predicament, he suddenly became conscious of someone else moving in the corridor, and, looking up, saw a maintenance engineer in dark blue overalls standing outside his lab. From the way the man was wiping his brow on his forearm he was obviously in some sort of distress..

'Oh, Jesus, no …' cursed Bill, under his breath, 'not today, please.'

Taking a few steps forwards, he gave the engineer a hopeful nod of greeting, but in response the man merely shook his head in pained disbelief, picked up the tool case at his feet and walked off towards the lifts. Staring up at the ceiling, Bill exhaled in despair. Certain now of what the engineer had just had to go through, and wincing in anticipation of it being his turn next, Bill opened the door and, sure enough, standing there at the work bench, holding a test-tube up to the light, was the cause of the engineer's discomfort.

Angela Marks had started work at Asper two weeks previously on a Government-sponsored Vocational Training Scheme. A keen javelin thrower whose abilities had taken her well beyond county level almost to the heights of the English national team, she had thought it prudent at twenty-six to acquire some qualifications which, while standing her in good stead for later life, would not in the short term interfere with her still vigorous round of training and competition. The three-year day-release scheme leading to laboratory technician grade II that she had seen advertised in the Harledge Gazette seemed to fit the bill admirably, requiring her merely to attend college one day a week and Asper on any two others of her choice. What perplexed Bill and just about every other male on the Harledge site, however, was how a woman like Angela Marks could somehow come to imagine that the onus was on her to pursue a career, rather than the other way round. For, in terms of her physical appearance, at least, Angela Marks was quite simply the most magnificent specimen of womankind that any of them had ever seen. If there were an institution or an organization on the planet which, having once beheld those long muscular legs, that magnificently proportioned torso and those fine, aquiline features would want to do anything other than reorganize itself immediately to accommodate their holder within its ranks, Bill, for one, could not imagine what it might be. At first, he had been thrilled to learn he would be granted his very own assistant, especially when he discovered that she shared his interest in sport – he himself had been a fanatically keen soccer player in his younger days. However, the actual experience of meeting Angela, he was later to conclude, was probably the closest he would ever come to asphyxiation in his life. On the day that she had come for her interview, his lungs simply went into seizure the moment Martindale escorted her into the lab and only began to function again some forty seconds later once his boss had taken her back out of the room to continue with the round of introductions. The unusual events of the morning's traffic jam had caused Bill to forget that Angela would be with him in the lab until four that afternoon, and, as he closed the door behind him, he groaned inwardly at the prospect of another day of wrestling with his carnal imaginings.

'Was that man supposed to be in here?' asked Angela, continuing to examine the test tube she held aloft and not looking across at Bill. She had dispensed with everyday greetings from the afternoon of their second day together on account of the state of confusion into which phrases like 'Hi, how are you?' seemed to propel him.

'Er, yeah,' replied Bill, scratching the side of his head awkwardly.

'Who was he, then?'

'A maintenance engineer. We use an outside contractor. They, er, come round and calibrate the measuring equipment every couple of months.'

'Did the equipment need calibration?'

'Er, probably not. But they do it anyway. It's a sort of FDA thing.'

Sensing there was something of use to be learnt about the subject, Angela lowered the test tube and at last deigned to look across at Bill.

'What sort of an FDA thing?' she asked, crisply.

'GLP. Good Laboratory Practice. The FDA can inspect us, I mean, audit us, at any time. It doesn't matter whether the equipment's working properly or not, if they don't find calibration records then it's curtains. We could lose our approval status and everything. That'd be it.'

'Well, he was rather quick in that case,' said Angela, reproachfully.

'Probably wanted to get back out for some air.'

Angela stared hard at Bill and then gave a slow, studied blink, her long eyelashes gently brushing the inside of her perspex goggles. The laboratory's ventilation system pumped in purified air, and, whilst doubting that Bill's comment could possibly be some oblique reference to her personal freshness, she could not imagine to what else he might be referring. Realizing how she may have interpreted the comment Bill reddened and laughed nervously, but Angela was already swishing the test tube around again and no longer seemed to be aware of his presence.

Turning to the cupboards above the nearside bench, Bill extracted his project folder and began flicking through the pages. The situation was far worse than he had thought – even those few experiments he had bothered to carry out were only partially written up. Dismayed by the magnitude of the task, Bill soon found himself stealing a series of glances across at Angela, each time becoming ever more captivated by the perfection of her deportment and physique. Over the years he had seen literally thousands of women walk around the Harledge site in white overalls. Once draped about Angela's frame, however, the standard issue, size 12 Asper Pharma lab coat seemed to undergo a miraculous transformation from functional industrial protective garment to seductive item of boudoir apparel. The button spacing alone was wickedly salacious, the top one being positioned at the exact distance from the shoulder to stretch the front lapels taut over the top of her chest and allow tantalizing glimpses of what reposed beneath, and the bottom one being just so far above the hem as to offer a different view of her legs each time she made even the slightest shift in position. In between these furtive gazes, Bill started to wonder just what effect prolonged exposure to Angela might have on his physiology. It was now only ten minutes into their fifth day together and already he felt close to endocrinological melt down. How was it all going to end? He almost dared not think. Perhaps, after months of chronic over-stimulation, and with no means of dissipating the streams of chemical and kinetic energies generated along its biochemical pathways, his body would be left with no option

26

but to unleash these pent-up forces on itself. One summer afternoon, Angela would turn her back to take a fresh conical flask down from the store cupboard and that would be it. As she stretched upwards, the sight of her calf, or perhaps a section of inner thigh, would catalyze a disintegrative reaction through the William Kennedy genome, bursting every nucleotide bond in his being, and when, seconds later, the ruptured helixes rushed to realign themselves his entire DNA structure would be recast. Alerted by the strange, squelching noises behind her, Angela would turn around like some sci-fi B-film heroine, no longer to see the inspired young scientist who had been there moments before, but the suppurating blob of goo into which he had now metamorphosed. And, as he lumbered pathetically towards her, saliva dribbling from the open gash that had once been his mouth, she would let the conical flask fall to the floor and smash, clasping her hands to her cheeks and screaming out in abject terror.

'What would be the pH of magnesium hydroxide in methanol?' asked Angela quizzically, carefully examining the litmus strip she held over the rim of the test tube. When no answer was forthcoming she tried again: 'I've made up a solution according to the instructions, but …'

Her words trailed off as she looked up to see Bill staring glassily but fixedly back at her, his whole body rocking backwards and forwards in a gentle swaying motion, his head inclined at an angle of around seventy degrees to his right shoulder. Inhaling deeply, Angela decided to give up and consult her Merck index, resigning herself to the prospect of being able only to conduct one or possibly two complete conversations a week with this peculiar character. The thud of her opening the heavy book on the bench top snapped Bill back into consciousness and with it came an awareness of his protracted stare.

'What did you say? In ethanol? Er, sorry, Angela, it's er, er …'

'Not ethanol,' intoned Angela, more in observation than response. 'Methanol.'

'Er, nine something – nine point …'

'Forget it,' she interrupted. 'I've already found it.'

Closing his eyes momentarily, Bill leaned wearily back against his work bench. The traffic jam, the alarming news about Mold and now Angela sex-bomb Marks – he was definitely having a bad, bad day. Opening his eyes again, he looked across the room at the laboratory clock. 09:50. Officially, he wasn't supposed to go off for his morning break until 10:15, but if he hung around the lab any longer who knows what disaster might befall him next? Despite the pressing need to get on with collating his results, perhaps the best thing to do on a day like this would be to go off to the canteen, get a cup of coffee and then start all over again.

'Er, Angela. I'm just off to despatch. There's a hormone fragment I've been waiting for – I want to see if it's arrived yet. See you later.'

As the door swung to behind him, Bill caught a fleeting glimpse of Angela hunched over her work bench, clearly oblivious of his departure. Taking the long way around to the lift so that he could avoid Martindale's office, Bill decided to take a peek inside Mold's lab, only to find that he had sellotaped a sheet of heavy brown paper over the inspection panel of the door to prevent anyone seeing in from the outside. Desperately, Bill racked his brains as to how he might extricate himself from his worsening predicament. If the Minority Diseases Unit did move to the new laboratories, and if Mold really had made a breakthrough on Bullman-Sachs, Asper might end up promoting him ahead of Bill. No sooner had this frightening eventuality occurred to him than he realized he had the answer. He would forge his test results. Not to make it appear as though he had discovered any promising new drug candidates – that would be foolhardy in the extreme – but simply to suggest that he had correctly carried out all the experimentation for those candidates which had failed. At tomorrow's meeting he would hand over a perfectly tabulated set of results; as long as they were credibly presented there was no way that Martindale or anyone else inside Asper would ever want to go back and check them. To all who cared to read his summary, Bill Kennedy would appear the assiduous researcher, patiently and professionally moving from project to project, working his way inexorably towards his next breakthrough.

Not bothering to wait for the lift, Bill took the staircase to the ground floor, happily skipping down the steps two at a time. It was a brilliant plan. So what if Mold had found a treatment for Bullman-Sachs? It was such a rare disorder that even by the standards of the Minority Diseases Unit it would scarcely be classed as a major new product development – and compared with Bill's achievement with Phosphopenim it was insignificant. He'd see Mold's challenge off yet. Emerging from the entrance to Building 7, Bill smiled broadly as yet another benefit of his plan occurred to him: because his results were going to be entirely spurious, it would only take a few minutes to type them up – all the more time to enjoy his coffee break. As he started to walk towards the canteen, though, he felt an ice-cold breeze brush across his face. Puzzled, he looked up and around. What was happening? It was a warm summer's day. There shouldn't be a wind like this. And it was at this moment, just as an unexpected shiver ran down his spine, that by one of those peculiar interactions between body and brain, Bill suddenly found himself recalling a dream. It was a recurring dream. One that came to him in the early hours of the morning between sleep and waking. One that he had had perhaps a half dozen times since, just under a year ago, he and Martindale had been summoned to the Human Resources Department together.

It was a winter's day.

Above him the sky was a churning black mass of cloud that lashed rain against his face like a flail. He was in a soccer match, the striker at the spearhead of his team, a position he had occupied times beyond count during his school days and at College. With only fifteen minutes of the match played, and against mediocre opposition, his side had managed to let themselves go two-nil down. Gritting his teeth, he was trying to force himself to be patient – to give the skills he knew he possessed a chance – but somehow his game seemed to have become infected by a terrible recklessness and the harder he tried to fight against it the more wayward it became. Horrified at what he was doing, but completely unable to stop himself, he tugged at one opponent's shirt after another, lashed out at their ribs with his elbows and threw himself to the ground feigning the very fouls that he himself was committing. The breeze dropped and Bill snapped back out of his recollection. With a shrug of the shoulders, he pushed the memory of the dream from his mind and hurried on his way.

Two floors above, Dr Edward Martindale looked momentarily up from his British Medical Journal to see the fast-retreating back of the gifted researcher whom he had once held in such high esteem as he sped off towards the canteen. Looking at his watch and seeing that it was not even ten o'clock, Martindale put the periodical down and sadly shook his head, wondering for the thousandth time how a scientist of William Kennedy's extraordinary talent could have come to hold so cheaply an occupation which once had meant more to him than anything else in the world.

Chapter 2

Euston, it seemed, was destined to become Louise's bogey station. For the second time in six weeks, horribly late for an appointment, she found herself running up the escalator from the Underground and dashing out on to the main concourse. Darting and weaving through the stream of evening commuters she reached the telephone stands where Gail stood waiting.

'Oh, God! I'm so sorry. Have you been here ages?'

'No, no, not long, don't worry,' replied Gail, giving Louise one of her enormous, expressive smiles and placing a reassuring hand on her forearm.

'I don't know what it is about this place. It must be spooked or some-thing. The brakes went on the train. I've just been sitting there in the tunnel ten yards away from the platform for over twenty minutes!'

'Oh, no! You poor thing! But, look, no problem: I've already bought the tickets and we've still got five minutes till the train goes,' responded Gail brightly, trying her best to ease her friend's distress.

'Oh, great. How much were they? I'll …' Louise made a movement as though to take out her wallet, but Gail reached across and squeezed her arm again warmly.

'Relax, relax. We'll sort it out later, OK? I'll just phone my brother – he said he'll pick us up at the other end.'

Still smiling, Gail turned around to the telephone behind and, as well organised as ever, inserted the phone card she had been holding ready for the moment when her friend would eventually appear. Welcoming the opportunity to regain her breath, Louise slipped the heavy weekend bag from her shoulder and leant against the other side of the phone, although with the station's bustle and Gail's thick black hair covering the receiver, she was only able to catch one side of the conversation.

'Hi. It's me ... At Euston ... Yeah, we're coming home a day early ... Louise ... The girl I told you about.' Exasperated, Gail raised her eyes heavenwards. 'Lou-ise! From the TAG thingee! ... In Mum's room ... No, it's all right, you don't have to look rightaway.'

Cradling the receiver to her shoulder, Gail slapped the palm of her free hand against her forehead.

'God, he gets in such a flap. He's gone to see if we've got the right clean sheets now.'

'Are you sure it's all right?' asked Louise, guilty at seemingly now having inconvenienced both sister and brother.

'Yeah, yeah. Don't worry. He's dying to meet you. Honest.' Gail had the receiver back at her ear again. 'What? Good ... No. No! Don't go off again! The train's just about to leave ... Yes ... On the platform, OK? ... See you in an hour. Bye'.

Replacing the receiver, Gail turned and looked gravely at her friend.

'OK Lou. I'm going to ask you one last time. Are you really sure you want to do this? Because, if not, this is your last chance to pull out. I mean, there's ordinary guys, right? And then there's what we're gonna find at the other end of that train line.'

'What, you mean, there are men up there even worse than Eddie Best?' whispered Louise, feigning an equally serious response.

'Eddie Best!' laughed Gail, out loud. 'Ha! I'd forgotten all about him. God, if the men back home were anywhere near as bad as him I would-n't let you near the place! C'mon. Let's go!'

The weekend mood now well upon her, Louise slung her bag back over her shoulder and ran off across the station after Gail. Their sprint soon turned into something of a race and laughing uncontrollably the two young women were only just able to pull up at the ticket barrier in time. Almost bowling the ticket inspector completely over – an experi-ence the veteran railway employee was later to remark ranked as one of the most pleasurable in his thirty-seven years of service – it was Gail's turn to pour out an apology, her infectious humour spreading a grin wider and wider across the man's face as he clipped their tickets. Louise, meanwhile, having caught a glimpse of the station's Melton Street exit out of the corner of her eye, found herself reflecting on how much more enjoyable life had become for her since six weeks previously she had passed through that same exit on her last mad dash across Euston. Moving leisurely down the ramp towards the waiting train, she felt a fount of affection well up inside her for the new-found companion by her side who was the reason for this improvement and, as she turned to look admiringly at Gail, her friend was somehow sensitive to her thoughts and returned her gaze with an unusually shy and gentle smile that seemed to say, 'Me too'. All the while at the top of the ramp, deaf to the sundry clatters and rattles that echoed between the platforms, the inspector stood with his elbows resting on the cold metal surface of his gate, staring thoughtfully down at what he was certain were the two most charming women ever to have passed through it until long after the train had taken them out of the station.

It had been a two-day course entitled 'Effective Negotiation Skills' that had brought Louise to Euston Station on the previous occasion. By running the full half mile from the station to the surprisingly shabby, prefabricated concrete building that housed the headquarters of the TAG Training Organization, she had managed to claw back some lost time. Glancing at her watch as she finally scampered up the front steps she took scant relief from the fact that she was arriving only twelve minutes late. In a cursory flick through the course notes the previous evening, she had noted three attendees from a company based to the north of Leeds, and it offended her professional pride to think that this group of individuals would now be treated to the spectacle of Louise Mary-Ann Schreiber, resident a mere three-quarters of a mile away in Marylebone, arriving later than they.

Having entered the foyer, Louise followed a series of arrowed signs down several murky corridors to the half-open door of the room in which the course was being held. A dozen or so dreg-filled cups on a table at the back suggested that she had missed the introductory coffee. At the front, a distinguished-looking grey-haired gentleman – undoubtedly the course lecturer, Mr Vasela – had just taken off the jacket of his three-piece suit and was carefully folding it over a chair next to his lecture podium. Louise breathed a sigh of relief: clearly, they hadn't actually started yet.

The main body of the room was filled with two ranks of regularly spaced and extremely solid three-seater wooden desks, the first two rows of which were occupied by the other eleven delegates to the course. Walking as unobtrusively as she could down the side of the room to the single empty space remaining on the front bench, Louise felt an antisocial twinge of relief at being able to get straight into the course itself without having gone through the doubtless awkward introductions.

More out of politeness than because she seriously expected anything other than an affirmative response, Louise gave a brief, questioning nod at the powerfully built man who occupied the middle seat of the bench next to the vacant place. Instead of the assenting shake of the head she had expected in reply, much to her surprise the man responded by spreading his large, muscular hand over the empty stool and leaning forward towards her with an uncompromisingly dour expression on his face.

'Oh, I dunno 'bout that, luv,' he drawled.

It was not just the underlying tone of threat with which this answer was charged, but the appearance of the man himself that caused Louise to pull up with a start: in all her twenty-three years she could not recall ever having seen a shirt, suit and tie so crisply pressed. However, although the folds and curves of his button down collar were so exact and creaseless that the article might almost have been sculptured from marble, the blotchy, moon shaped face above it sat perched in monstrous contrast to the sartorial elegance below. It was as though some saucy Hallowe'en reveller had sneaked into the most expensive men's boutique in town, unscrewed the head of the mannequin in the front window and replaced it with a grinning pumpkin jack-o'-lantern. The grin then broadened into a leer of truly awesome vulgarity as the man removed his hand from the stool.

'Naw, you're all right, petal. I'm used to 'aving a couple of lasses around me most of the time.' Saying which, he nodded dismissively in the direction of the female delegate seated on his other side. With a cackling laugh, he then inclined his head around to two men on the bench behind who tittered appreciatively back at him.

'Good morning! Miss Schreiber, I presume!' announced Mr Vasela from the front, clasping his hands cordially and smiling at Louise.

'Oh, er … good morning,' stammered Louise, sitting down nervously.

'You've missed the coffee, I'm afraid, but there's still time for you to introduce yourself before we get started. Don't need to know every last one of your GCSE's – just a bit of general background'll do.'

'Oh, er, right …' Standing back up again and wishing, after all, that she had been in time for the coffee session to see how all the others had introduced themselves, Louise did her best to compose her thoughts.

'Er, my name's Louise Schreiber. I am a Marketing Consultant for Thomas Radley & Co. I, er, studied Latin and History at University, and ...'

'Bit of Latin comes in right useful when you're sellin' I've 'eard,' announced the man out of the side of his mouth with a chuckle.

Louise had no idea why this oaf had chosen her to become the butt of his humour and, completely distracted by the interruption, found herself tripping over her own words.

' ... and, Radley's have sent me on, I mean, I've come on this course to learn about negotiation techniques for, er, my job.'

Louise did not actually hear Mr Vasela's thank you as, sitting down again, she delved into the depths of her bag for her file and pen, all the time fighting the impulse to climb inside it and hide at the bottom. Regretting her naiveté in for a moment assuming that the course would necessarily be composed of individuals in circumstances more or less similar to her own, she extracted the course notes and read through the list of delegates again with a degree of care she sorely wished she had exercised the previous evening. Thomas Radley may well have been one of the top three marketing organisations in the country, and, eighteen months previously, Louise Schreiber may well have beaten several hundred other candidates to a coveted place on its graduate recruitment scheme, but as she ran her finger down the names of the companies on the course list and saw the almost uniform job descriptions of their delegates, she quickly realized that this achievement would afford her no prestige here. A fine chemical giant, a textile manufacturer, a printed circuit board design company – the catalogue of industrial concerns ran on and on. Not for these individuals the intellectual challenge of product conceptualization, the interpretation of focus group responses and the formation of elegant brand management strategies. Long after the Louises of this world had applied their multi-disciplinary talents to launching the commercial cycle, these were the men and women who day after grueling day would be out there wrestling with its final stage, a task for which one skill, and one skill alone, was required. A freak storm, Louise realized, had carried her ship to the island of the professional salesmen. Like some nineteenth century naturalist jumping down from the prow of the landing party's rowboat, she at first recoiled in horror from the fearsome-looking reptiles parading up and down on its hot, sandy beach, but her adventurous and inquiring mind soon began to sense that this strange place might, after all, furnish a wealth of insights into a broader world she desired so avidly to understand. To what adaptive extremes had these creatures been driven by the forces of evolution, living in such brutal, daily competition with each other in an environment so altogether isolated from the outside world? Slowly raising her head so as not to cause any undue alarm, Louise applied herself to the task of classifying each of the species.

The first clue was to be found on the far table at the front. The young man nearest to her had a silver pen-shaped object clipped outwards rather than inwards over the lip of his inside jacket pocket. If it were a micrometer, that would surely make him some sort of engineer. The printed circuit board salesman, she decided. Although the two men next to him exhibited no immediately identifying features, the clear similarities in their fixed stares and straight-backed posture marked out all three individuals on that table as being of the same genus. Leaning forward, she ticked off the two aerospace sales engineers on the list. The desk behind them was much more difficult and, even after several seconds, Louise was not able to place either of the two neutral-looking men. As there were only two other women delegates on the course beside her, however, she knew that the woman seated in between them must be either designer textiles or petrochemicals. Her suit, although well cut, was last year's colour. The fashion pack would never tolerate that – must be petrochemicals. Not wanting to turn around and stare openly at the table directly behind, Louise instead tried to work out who the man next to her might be. His accent, and those of his two cronies, suggested that they were the three delegates from the north of Leeds car-component company for whom she had earlier so mistakenly felt such concern. She ran her finger down their names. Eddie Best – this must surely be the beast next to her. Placing her bag on the floor, she decided to risk another look at him. Thankfully, he now seemed to be ignoring her completely and was instead gazing blankly at Mr Vasela, all the while masticating furiously on some foul smelling gum. Before Louise had time once more to marvel at his astonishing attire, he exhaled heavily and leaned back on his haunches, giving Louise her first full view of the woman who sat on his other side.

Clutching to her chest two chicken salad sandwiches, two perspex beakers and a half bottle of wine, this same woman was now making

35

her way back towards Louise from the dining car.

'That was quick,' said Louise, closing her magazine.

'Well, alcohol in transit. Gotta get a move on,' laughed Gail in a singsong voice, twisting on her heels and landing neatly in the seat opposite. 'Actually, the train's almost empty – probably 'cos it's a Thursday.'

'How long does it take?' asked Louise.

'About an hour,' answered Gail, unscrewing the top of the wine bottle and pouring for them both. 'Long enough to drink this, anyway. Cheers.'

They clicked beakers. Having taken a swig, Gail rolled her eyes in ecstatic appreciation and fell back luxuriously into her seat. Louise leaned forward and began peeling the plastic film off the sandwiches.

'When was the last time you were back, then?

'What, home? Oh, about three months ago, I suppose. I used to go back every other weekend before Mum went off to Australia, but I seem to have dropped off a bit lately. Thanks.' Taking the proffered sandwich from Louise, Gail took a deep bite. 'God, I needed this. I had to miss lunch again today.'

'You'll fade away.'

'Huh, some chance,' laughed Gail, ironically.

'So, does he live in this great big house of yours all by himself then, your brother?'

'Yeah, yeah. He thought about renting a couple of rooms out once but he never did anything about it, or at least I don't think he did.'

'Not married, then?' quizzed Louise.

'Nah!' exhaled Gail in disgust, grabbing the second half of her sandwich. 'He always says he loves his work too much. I mean he's totally brilliant at what he does and everything, but if you ask me he could do with a good woman around the place. Or better still a bad one, come to that.'

'Does he ever come down and see you?'

'A couple of times a year. Not as often as I ask him, though.'

'And all the men in your family always have to be pushed, right?'

'Yeah, how did you know that?' asked Gail with a surprised laugh, a tiny shred of lettuce falling unnoticed from her sandwich on to her lap.

'You told me,' replied Louise.

'Did I?'

'Yes. Well, at least, I thought you did.'

'Oh. I suppose I must have done, then.'

Even before the conversation had started, it had stalled – just as it always did when Gail got on to the subject of her family. Something was wrong at home: Louise had felt as much ever since her friend had invited her to spend the weekend there. Sensing that Gail was still not yet ready to discuss the reason, and imagining that whatever it was would anyway be revealed soon enough, Louise decided to change the subject. Before she could, Gail began speaking again.

'I bet you never have that problem with your dad, do you?'

'What problem?'

'You know, get up and go.'

Over dinner at Louise's house the previous weekend, her father had casually referred to his planned trip to Tibet the following year – a pronouncement that had drawn an open-mouthed gaze of admiration from Gail.

'No, just the opposite. Sometimes, Mum and I think we should put something in his tea.'

'I do worry about him, you know.'

'What, my dad?' Louise's response was deliberately specious – the injection of humour being an attempt to help ease the passage of what, after all, appeared to be the imminent disclosure.

'No, silly! My brother. I mean, I know he's got his job, but when he's not at work, he just sort of, well, mopes around the house. He never seems to do anything.'

'Well, does he have to? I mean, the gay social whirl's not everybody's cup ...'

'No, it's not that, it's not that,' interrupted Gail. 'I don't mean he hasn't got a social life – although actually he hasn't as it happens – it's more that he seems to be sort of, well, just existing, rather than living. D'you know what I mean? It's like everything's there, everything's in place; talented bloke, good job, fantastic house – all the bits and pieces – but it's like ... like an engine that just goes dead on you one day. You open up the bonnet and it all should work, only there's no spark, nothing to get the whole thing moving.'

'Was there ever?' replied Louise, after a moment's pause.

'Yeah,' responded Gail quietly, 'there was. Or at least, I think there was. It's so hard to tell. I mean, I was younger then, but he seemed a different person when we all lived together – more ... animated.'

'Did your mother notice it? She was back at Christmas for a few weeks, wasn't she?' asked Louise, with half an eye on the guard who was approaching from the next carriage.

'No, he pepped up, then. And several times since on the phone he's sounded OK. It's just something I can't quite put my finger on. I don't know. Maybe it's me who's changed.'

Sensing the presence of the guard in the aisle beside her, Louise turned her head to find him waving his grimy ticket-clipping machine to and fro in front of her face. Flashing an apologetic smile, she opened up her wallet to extract her ticket but it appeared to have gone. Across the seat, Gail handed over her own ticket and smiled indulgently back at Louise as she ransacked her coat and bag in search of the elusive piece of card. Having squeezed Gail's ticket between the jaws of his mottled, plastic contraption – producing in the process a rasping noise that would have graced any medieval thumbscrew – the guard returned it to her before turning his attention back to Louise again.

'Erm ... it is here somewhere,' mumbled Louise unconvincingly.

'Passengers should 'ave their tickets available for inspection at any time. It's a bye law y'know,' retorted the guard.

'Hey, it's all right, Lou,' volunteered Gail, springing loyally to her friend's defence. 'I've got the credit card receipt here: I paid for both tickets together, you see.'

'That won't do, I'm afraid, Madam. I have to see the original ...'

'Here you are,' interrupted Louise, whisking the ticket out of her top pocket. Having carefully examined first one side then the other, the guard finally clipped the ticket and marched briskly away.

'What a prat!' said Louise indignantly after he had gone, looking across at her friend, who somehow seemed to have found the whole event highly amusing. 'Well, don't you think so?'

'Yeah!'

'So what are you laughing for, then?'

'No, no! It's just for a minute there I was certain you were going to give him one of your acid put-downs.'

'Acid put-downs?' asked Louise, who had very much felt herself on the defensive during the encounter.

'Yeah, you know ...'

'I don't give people acid put-downs.'

'Yes, you do!'

'No, I don't!'

'Well, what about what you did to Eddie Best? What was that, then?'

Louise paused thoughtfully for a moment and then her face also broadened into a smile.

'Yeah, well, that was an exception. And anyway you joined in soon enough.'

As the course progressed, Louise found Eddie Best ever more obnoxious. From the constant, restless shifting of his corpulent frame back and forth, to the unending stream of asides and non-sequiturs with which he sought to pepper the proceedings, his every word and action seemed solely directed towards self-advertisement. More than anything, Louise felt embarrassed for Mr Vasela. Even though the measured, deliberate pace of the old man's delivery never once faltered and on a couple of occasions he even skillfully wove one or two of Eddie's retorts back into his own dialogue, all the same, she imagined it must have been intensely irritating for him to have this obscene subtext grafted on to his lecture. In the end, she surmised that his long experience had probably taught him that every course has its clown and he would be best advised just to play along. Had she watched his eyes, though, and noted the constant scrutiny under which they held not just Eddie but every other delegate including herself, she might have come closer to discerning Mr Vasela's real objective, which was not to play along with any single one of the personalities before him, but rather to play around with them all.

Where the first day of the course had been given over to theory, the second was purely practical. Mr Vasela began day two by explaining that it would be made up of a series of role-playing sessions, in which three or four of the delegates would act out a negotiation scenario for the rest of the group to observe and comment upon afterwards. On day one Louise had merely disliked Eddie Best; by mid-afternoon on day two, she utterly detested him. When she partnered him in one negotiation in the morning, he not only crowded her out of the discussion, but then went on single-handedly to trounce the two engineers with whom they were negotiating for a fictional construction deal. Later, when she acted out the role of what she thought was a most prudent buyer, his guffaw from the sidelines when she capitulated on payment terms sent a blush all the way down to her neck. Looking angrily across at Mr Vasela she wondered why he did not remonstrate with Eddie over this heckling. But, although the old man held her gaze for several moments in unequivocal acknowledgement of her embarrassment, his stony expression seemed mercilessly to imply that she should furnish her own remedy for the predicament. Worse was to follow. At three-thirty, her self-confidence already severely dented, Louise groaned in disbelief to discover that she was to be put through the ordeal a third time. Mr Vasela announced that she and Gail were to round off the day's proceedings by acting out the part of two salespeople from Atmospheric Controls Ltd. quoting the owner of a small printing company for a new air-conditioning system. Picking up the single page of instructions, Louise adjourned with Gail to the adjacent anteroom for the two meagre minutes of preparation allowed them.

'What does it say, what does it say?' asked Gail eagerly, closing the door behind her and sprinting across the room to where Louise was hurriedly unfolding the brief.

'You have assessed the printer's facilities,' read Louise, aloud. 'A standard unit costing £10,000 will meet his needs. You have just such a unit in your van. Try and negotiate a higher sale price. Everything above £10,000 counts as your personal commission.'

'Oh, great!' groaned Gail. 'What's the betting he's only got eight thousand to spend?'

'I don't think so,' replied Louise, thoughtfully. 'None of the other briefs were impossible to negotiate or anything – if we can't go below ten grand then that's that, isn't it? Somewhere in all of this we have to have a strong point, too, although God knows where. Oh, hang on. There's a bit at the bottom of the page as well. 'P.S. The workshop is very hot and stuffy.'

'That's got to be a help,' said Gail, quickly.

'Or then again, it might just be Eddie's cue to tell us to strip off if we don't like the heat.'

'I bet his mates'd love that.'

'I bet they would,' replied Louise, bitterly. 'But come on, let's think! There are two of us and only one of him – we've got to be able to work out some sort of strategy!'

As they walked back into the lecture room, Louise could see that Eddie had gleefully risen to the challenge by rearranging the benches around the perimeter of the room, leaving a single one positioned in the middle to act as his desk. Having taken off his jacket and tie, he had rolled up his sleeves and was sitting reading a tabloid newspaper. By his right elbow, in crude representation of a desk plaque, he had folded up a sheet of A4 paper and daubed across it in thick felt-tip pen 'Mr E. Best – Boss'. Along the left-hand wall, Louise could see the other delegates standing in a line, like seconds morbidly waiting for the duel to start. They were probably right to stand well clear. Any moment now, someone's head was going to be blown off. Undaunted, Gail marched smartly forwards, and even before Eddie looked up from his newspaper, launched straight into the opening pitch that she and Louise had agreed upon.

'Good morning, Mr Best. I'm sure you're a busy man, so let me get right to the point, if I may. We've finished our evaluation and would estimate total equipment needs of around fifteen thousand pounds. What's more, we have all the machinery you need with us in our van.'

Eddie took several seconds to close his newspaper, before looking up and replying in a quiet, deadpan voice.

'Whose needs mart they be, young lady?'

'Your printing company's,' answered Gail. 'To fit your factory and offices out with a new air-conditioning system'

Again Eddie paused before responding.

'You have me at summit of a disadvantage.'

A deafening silence followed. Eddie showed no sign of wishing to break it.

'Well, you are in need of a new system, aren't you?' replied Gail, her voice starting to falter.

'Who says I am?'

'Well, if you'll excuse me, we thought your company …' began Gail.

'Never mind what you thought, young lady!' bellowed Eddie, crash-ing his clenched fist down on to the surface of the table. 'The first I heard about all this is my secretary comes in 'ere an' tells me you two've been caught wandrin' round my factory! I've gotta ask you who the 'ell you think you are turnin' up like this uninvited. This approach of yours is totally unsolicited and I'm of a good mind to have you escorted off the premises forthwith!'

Rooted to the spot, Louise stood cursing herself. She cursed her stu-pidity in assuming that their quotation had been solicited, thus allowing herself to be outmanoeuvred in this way. She cursed her timidity in

41

letting Eddie's male bluster deprive her of the power of speech. But most of all she cursed her imagination, which seemed incapable of providing anything by way of assistance, save the vivid mental image of leaping forwards, grabbing that fat head by the ears and smashing it down repeatedly into the table top until all that was left was so much pumpkin puree. Gail was talking again.

'Well, er, I apologize about that Mr Best, we should have made an appointment, of course. But, on the other hand, you do need an air-conditioning system. I mean, it's very hot and stuffy in here, isn't it?'

'Maybe so,' replied Eddie, 'and maybe I am thinking about getting a new system, but what makes you think I'm gonna hand over fifteen grand to two people I've never even seen before?'

He glared viciously at each of them in turn. Out of the corner of her eye, Louise could see her fellow delegates wincing – one of them was even covering his eyes with his hand. The atmosphere of humiliation was excruciating.

'Well, I, er …' began Gail.

'Seven and a half grand,' said Eddie suddenly, opening the newspaper and beginning to read again. 'Not interested if it's any more. I've got loads of quotes at that price.'

Gail turned and looked nervously at Louise.

'Well, we, er, might be able to manage a reduction, say, down to twelve.'

'Seven and a half or you can forget it,' said Eddie, his voice utterly bored.

'OK, in that case, I think we could manage …'

Finally, Louise could take no more. Taking hold of Gail's arm, she began guiding her friend back towards the anteroom. Why should she care if afterwards Mr Vasela accused them of inept negotiation? Why should she worry if word got back to her company that she had performed hopelessly on the course? She was not going to give Eddie the satisfaction of dropping down to ten thousand, and that was that. Stopping momentarily at the door to the anteroom, she turned around and announced.

'We withdraw our offer. The equipment's not for sale anymore.'

By her side she could see Gail's face brighten. Good. It was nice to know her newfound friend was just as prepared to stand on her dignity. However, before either of them could turn and go back inside the anteroom, a worried voice behind them announced.

'Well, now, er, ladies – let's not be too hasty about this, shall we?'

It took a little over three minutes for the delegates to put the desks and benches back in position. As Mr Vasela resumed his position at the podium, a tense air of expectancy settled over the room. When finally he spoke, his eyes stared pitilessly into Eddie's face.

'So, Edward. Eighteen thousand pounds. You paid eighteen thousand pounds for something you could have purchased for, how much, Miss Schreiber?'

'We probably would have settled at ten and a half,' called out Louise, not looking around at Eddie, but sensing him seething with anger next to her.

'Negotiation is not a boxing match, Edward,' continued Mr Vasela, gravely. 'The final objective is not to beat the other party senseless and then knock them to the ground. Of course, you can go on the offensive. But that is a means to an end, not an end in itself – you should never confuse the two. Ten thousand was the price below which their brief would not allow them to go. By insisting on seven and a half you forced them away from the negotiation table and that was when they found out your weakness. Perhaps you would read out your brief for everyone's benefit?'

'You 'ave purchased an air conditioning system for fifteen thousand pounds,' mumbled Eddie, resentfully, 'but 'ave been let down by your supplier. You 'ave a health and safety inspection in twenty-four hours and risk the closure of your company without an adequate system in place.'

'Once you had revealed that you had to purchase the system in their van, you were utterly defenceless – they could charge what they wanted.' Although now addressing the other delegates, Mr Vasela kept his eyes fixed firmly on Eddie. 'Ladies and gentlemen, when you get back to your companies tomorrow or next week, please remember as you go about your daily business, that there is no one in the world of negotiation more vulnerable than a buyer who has shown his hand – and I mean absolutely no one. And always, always, always, when you are the purchaser in a negotiating situation, be ever mindful of that wise and ancient nostrum – "caveat emptor" – "let the buyer beware."'

Whether this was deliberately intended as a feed or not, Louise would never know, but when Mr Vasela finally looked away from Eddie, he turned his gaze directly upon her. The short pause that followed was all she needed. Leaning forward over the desk, she coolly addressed not Eddie, but Gail.

'Bit of Latin comes in right useful when you're selling.'

'Oh, touché,' replied Gail, before turning to Eddie, now gawping like a dynamited fish, and adding helpfully, 'That's French, by the way, not Latin.'

The first thing that struck Louise about Bill Kennedy was his tie. Not so much its episcopal purple colour, or even its old-fashioned woollen weave – although they in themselves were remarkable enough – but rather the fact that he had somehow felt the need to wear one at all on picking up his sister from Harledge East railway station. After he had somewhat formally shaken her hand, and then twice on the way to the car offered to carry her bag, it occurred to Louise that he may have donned it in her own, rather than Gail's honour. Flattered by this display of formality, she nonetheless found herself a little taken aback by Bill's polite, nervous reserve which could scarcely have been further removed from his younger sister's manic gaiety.

'So, shall we go into Harledge for a drink?' suggested Gail, tossing her bag into the boot of Bill's car.

'Oh. Don't you want to go straight back to Wyburn, then?' asked Bill.

'I thought we'd do Wyburn tomorrow night.'

'Er, yeah, yeah, OK, then, if you want to.'

'What about that club – why don't we go there?'

Bill looked at his sister uncertainly.

'Well, there still is only one, isn't there? The big sort of complex place, with the car park on the roof.'

'Joe Bananas, d'you mean?'

'Yeah, that's it – let's go there.'

Gail looked across at Louise for approval.

'Wherever,' she shrugged. 'I'm easy.'

'Great, let's go, then! My round!' announced Gail, flashing them both a smile.

Joe Bananas had originally started life as an office building but during the early eighties an enterprising property developer had managed to sweet talk the County Council into granting planning permission to convert it into a nightclub. It was an instant success. Suffocated by years of country pub claustrophobia, the youth of Harledge and its surrounding villages had been flocking to the broad expanses of its laser-lit dance floors ever since. Although it was a Thursday night, and not yet eight o'clock, there was already a queue leading up to the front entrance, and Bill, Gail and Louise had to wait several minutes to be frisked by the burly security guards outside.

'Hey, they've got a seventies disco on tonight!' exclaimed Gail, as finally they were able to make their way into the darkened foyer. 'What do you think?'

'You never stop, do you?' replied Louise, laughing as she watched Gail starting to swing her hips from side to side. For his part, Bill made no reply to this suggestion but simply took his sister by the arm and began leading her towards the downstairs bar.

'Well, it was just an idea ...' protested Gail.

The downstairs bar was very large and very full. Luckily, Bill managed to spot the only free alcove and, quickly despatching his sister and Louise towards it, went off to buy the drinks.

'What d'you think of my brother, then?' asked Gail eagerly as they sat down around the upturned barrel that formed their table.

'I've only just met him!'

'Oh, come on, Lou,' entreated Gail.

'What do I think? Well, to be honest, I think you don't know how lucky you are.'

'Really?'

'Yeah. I haven't got any brothers or sisters. I'd've done anything to have a big brother like him when I was growing up. Even now, I would.'

'Yeah?'

'Yeah.'

'Oh, great. I'm so glad you like him. He's a bit quiet at first, but he'll open up a bit once he's got to know you.'

Bill returned with the drinks a few moments later. After they had chatted about the TAG negotiation course at which they had first met, Louise decided to put Gail's assertion to the test.

'So, what are you working on at the moment, then, Bill?'

'Sorry?'

'In your lab. Gail tells me you're a pharmaceutical researcher.'

'Oh, right, yes. Er, hormone analogues, actually.'

'Yeah? God, I feel so ignorant about science. I had to give up Biology and all that at school. Come on, then. Give me a crash course. Hormone analogues for beginners.'

'Well, I don't know whether you'll find them very interesting, actually,' replied Bill shyly, glancing uncertainly across at Gail.

'No, go on. I'd love to know. Honest.'

'Are you sure?'

'Yeah, yeah.'

'Oh, OK, if you really want to …' said Bill, clearly flattered that Louise was taking an interest in his work. 'Well, I don't know where to start, really. D'you know what ordinary hormones do?'

'Er, yes. Er, no …' replied Louise.

'Well, basically, hormones regulate biochemical processes in your body – your blood pressure, how much energy you've got – a whole range of things. Sometimes, you make too much of one of them, or, like in say, diabetes, you don't make enough – in that case insulin – and you get sick. OK, so far?'

Louise nodded. Gathering together four beer mats, Bill laid them end to end on the table top, lining their patterns up in sequence.

'Hormones are chains, right? Chains of amino acids – all linked together, like this. Chonk, chonk, chonk. What I do is make a chain that looks exactly like the original hormone, but with one of the links substituted or reversed or whatever.'

So saying, Bill turned the end mat over, revealing its obverse face.

'And that's a hormone analogue?'

'Got it in one.'

'So, how does it work?'

'Well, it fools the body into thinking it's made something it hasn't and in that way switches off all the bad side-effects.'

'Is that it?'

'Yeah, basically.'

'Oh quite simple, really, then!' said Louise smiling. 'So what will the ones you're working on cure, then?'

'Well I started off with LHRH,' replied Bill, now well into his stride 'It's the big success story in hormone analogues. It's a sex hormone, really. All tied up with testosterone and oestrogen – I'll spare you the gory details. Anyway, last month I read this paper on a couple of really weird LHRH fragments and I'm thinking of tinkering about with …'

'Talking of sex hormones …' interrupted Gail, suddenly.

46

Louise looked round to see two young men, each clutching a bottle of iced lager, angling their way along the perimeter of the room to try and get a better view of herself and Gail. Seeing Louise look up and face them, they smiled and seemed to find the courage to come across to the table. Before they could, however, Bill, whom they had not yet seen inside the alcove, leaned forwards to see what was going on. Catching sight of him the two men hesitated, then nodded politely and returned to their drinks.

'This place hasn't changed,' remarked Gail, dryly. 'Sorry, Bill, you were saying?'

'Er, well, that's it really.'

'No, do carry on, Bill, its really interesting,' urged Louise.

'Well, there's not much more to add – not without going into loads of detail,' said Bill, who appeared to have been distracted by the incident.

'Oh, OK, then,' said Gail, seeing that Bill wished to leave the subject there. 'D'you want another drink?'

'No, I'd better not. I'm driving. And, anyway, come to think of it, I'd better be getting off.'

'What!' exclaimed Gail. 'What do you mean getting off? We've only just got here!'

'No, you two should stay, of course!' added Bill quickly. 'Stay here and enjoy yourselves. I'll take the bags back to Wyburn and you get a cab back when you're ready.'

'Bill!'

'Oh, look, sorry to be a killjoy, Gail,' continued Bill sheepishly. 'If I'd known you were coming back today I'd've taken tomorrow off. As it is I've got a breakfast presentation with my boss and I've got to be out really early. If I stay here drinking all night with you I'll be wrecked. You don't mind do you?'

'Oh, all right, I suppose not.'

'I'll make it up to you tomorrow night, I promise. It's Friday then and I haven't got to go to work the next day or anything. We can all go out to dinner together in Wyburn.'

'All right then, we'll let you go, you old fuddy-duddy,' said Gail, pecking her brother on the cheek.

'Thanks. Erm, nice to meet you Louise,' said Bill, slipping his jacket back on again. 'I'll probably be gone in the morning by the time you get up, so I'll see you tomorrow night.'

'OK, Bill, nice to meet you. Take care.'

'We'll try not to make a noise when we come in, OK?' added Gail.

'Oh, thanks. Bye then,' said Bill, turning to make his way to the exit.

'See what I mean,' said Gail with a frown as she watched her brother slinking through the door.

'Well, we did sort of turn up at short notice tonight, didn't we?'

'Yeah, I suppose so. And this place probably isn't his scene, anyway.'

'I'm not so sure its mine, either.'

'So you didn't fancy those two blokes, then?'

'Gail!'

'Don't play the innocent with me,' said Gail with a smile. 'I saw you looking at them.'

'I wasn't looking at them at all!' exclaimed Louise, hotly.

'Did you fancy them – yes or no?'

'Yeah, they were all right, I suppose,' replied Louise, finally.

'Well, in that case, we'd better see if we can find them, then. Perhaps they're upstairs in the disco …'

Even the slight twinge of regret that Gail and Louise had felt on Bill's behalf at his early departure was more than a little misplaced as, returning to the car park, he exhaled a titanic sigh of relief at having at last escaped from the club. Although he had never been one for theatrical gestures, as he climbed into his car Bill felt an almost irresistible urge to smash his forehead into the steering wheel, in the hope of dislodging the disturbing array of interconnected images that were flashing uncontrollably through his mind: Angela Marks's exquisite fingers curled around a test-tube; Louise Schreiber, so wonderfully lithe and intelligent, gliding along the platform and placing her impossibly gentle hand in his; the two Harledge Lotharios, putting down their bottles of lager to move in on Louise and his sister. Worrying that the impact of his cranium might set off the steering wheel's airbag, Bill contented himself with merely shaking his head and, having put his car in reverse, set off for Wyburn. Within a half an hour he was in his bed and sound asleep.

It was to be the last undisturbed night's sleep he would have in a very long time.

Chapter 3

Night after night, all manner of unrecognizable sounds reverberated through Louise Schreiber's Marylebone flat, yet none of them had ever caused her to awaken in the grip of such nervous anticipation as she now felt in the chill soundlessness of the darkened, unfamiliar bedroom. Eyes fully open, she quickly lifted herself up on her elbow to peer into its murky corners, but immediately found herself staring back down at the heavily starched linen sheets that her sudden movement had caused to crackle like Christmas wrapping paper all around her. Remembering at last where she was, Louise sat upright in the bed, only to find the tips of her fingers brushing against something knotty, yet luxuriously silky to the touch. Leaning forward and squinting by the single chink of light that slipped between the bedchamber's heavy velvet drapes, she was able to make out the line of intertwined scarlet roses that had been painstakingly embroidered along the hem of the sheet. Her brow furrowed as she examined the dense, intricate stitching and she recalled Gail's comment the previous evening about Bill finding the right clean sheets. Now accustomed to the light, Louise looked slowly around, realizing that the huge, darkened room in which she had wearily collapsed at two a.m. that morning was, in fact, nothing short of a perfectly restored Victorian bedchamber.

Swinging her feet out of the bed on to the cool surface of the parquet floor, Louise switched on the light and then stretched across to touch the waist-height dado rail that separated the upper and lower portions of the wall. She had seen attempts at achieving a similar effect in modern houses using strips of narrow, lividly patterned wallpaper, but

49

had always thought them crude. This rail, however, was genuine hardwood, and moreover had been engraved with the same delicate rose motif that embellished the sheets. Standing up, she walked across to the broad marble mantelpiece. The pair of matching cranberry lustres positioned at either end was original Bohemian glass. They must be worth a fortune. No wonder Gail moved so comfortably through the world of art and design – her parents' house would almost pass for a stately home. Catching her reflection in the broad looking-glass, Louise gave herself a smile – she was beginning to feel at home in this bedroom after all. At that moment a rich, familiar odour came wafting into the room. Quickly slipping a dressing gown over her nightdress, she turned on her heel and went downstairs.

'Hiya!' sang out Gail brightly, looking up from the grill pan. 'Found your way down all right, then?'

'Finally.'

'Oh, dear, sorry,' laughed Gail cheerily, nodding at Louise to take a seat at the enormous oak table in the centre of the kitchen. 'You're not the first one to get a bit lost – don't worry. Did you sleep OK, anyway?'

'Oh, yes. I went out like a light.'

'Great,' said Gail, rearranging the rashers of bacon with a fork and then sliding the pan back under the grill. 'D'you want some orange juice?'

'Please,' answered Louise. 'Hey. It really is a fantastic house, this.'

'Oh, thanks. D'you like it?'

'Is everything original? It all looks so authentic.'

'Well, sort of yes and no,' replied Gail, pouring a glass of orange juice and sliding it across the table. 'I mean it's mostly modern materials, but made using the original techniques, if you know what I mean.'

'Who did it all, then?' asked Louise, gazing around the room in admiration.

'My Dad, mainly.' Raising her hand, Gail described the line of the kitchen's elaborate plaster-moulded cornice. 'He did the structural stuff – the woodwork, the plastering. Mum did all the fabrics, wall coverings, what have you …'

'Must've taken them years.'

'Dad mostly worked on it at weekends – he was a builder, anyway, so he knew what he was doing. It was part sort of hobby, I suppose, part creating the dream home for his wife and children. Sad thing was, he'd not long got it finished when the leukemia set in. He was dead a few months later.'

'Oh, God. How awful.'

'Yeah, I know. Ironic really. All that work and then no chance to enjoy the fruits of it. Life's like that sometimes, though, isn't it?'

'How old was he when he died?'

'Forty-nine.'

'Oh, you poor things.'

'Thanks. Well, it was ten years ago. Time goes on. Me and Mum took it in our stride, I suppose, but it hit Bill really badly. Sixteen's supposed to be when you get all independent, but I think men really need a Dad then.'

'Oh, I'm sure.'

'Damn! It's burning!' Leaping out of her seat, Gail pulled the grill pan quickly away from the heat and began carefully to lay out the strips of bacon on to several slices of buttered bread on the work surface next to the stove.

'So, anyway, who owns the house now, if you don't mind my asking?'

'Half, half – Bill and me,' responded Gail, passing a sandwich across to her friend. 'Mum just basically gave it to us outright when she met this Australian bloke.'

'This is Alan, yes?'

'Yeah, that's him. She went through agonies of conscience, apparently, not wanting to leave us here on our own. But once we'd found out he'd asked her to go, that was it. I mean, she was only fifty-two. We both told her – you have to grab your chances when they come.' Taking a deep philosophical bite from her bacon sandwich, Gail smiled across at her friend as she munched.

'D'you think you'll ever move back here?' asked Louise

'Me?' asked Gail – her mouth half full. 'No, I don't think so. I love this house, but Harledge isn't exactly bursting with career opportunities in the world of fashion, is it? Coffee?'

'Oh, please.'

'Shall we take it out the back?'

'Er, yeah, sure.'

Finishing off the remains of her sandwich, Gail placed the coffeepot on a tray with a couple of mugs and then made her way across the kitchen to a side door.

'Follow me. And mind the steps down, OK?' she warned. 'It's easy to slip if you're not used to it.'

Following Gail through the door, Louise carefully steadied herself on the handrail as she went down the three steep, stone steps. Sensing a slight decrease in temperature and an increase in light, she imagined they must be walking into a conservatory, although nothing in her experience prepared for the quite beautiful sight that greeted her when, having found her balance, she was able to look up.

Even in the first few eager months after joining Asper from University, Bill had rarely arrived on site much before the official opening time of eight-thirty. Yet, today, thanks to Lester Mold, he found himself trudging along its deserted walkways towards the staff canteen at 07:52. Hunching his shoulders resentfully against the early morning cold, Bill began turning over in his mind the history of his dislike for his fellow researcher. Ominously, it had started even before they had actually met. When Martindale had first shown him Mold's C.V., as a possible recruit to the newly formed Minority Diseases Unit, a peculiar sense of disquiet seemed to creep over him. Lester Mold? What sort of a name was that? It sounded like one of the rare diseases the Unit had been set up to try and cure. Not that his name should have counted against him – nor his looks, for that matter. Nevertheless, when Bill first clapped eyes on Mold, the combination of his wiry black beard and straight-backed, beanpole frame immediately put him in mind of bristles at the end of a cleaning implement, and he had never been able to look at him since without thinking of a toilet brush. Hanging up his coat on the line of hooks outside the canteen, Bill's eyes became drawn to Mold's bright yellow kagool gleaming like a beacon on the peg next to the door. How was it possible to feel anything other than contempt for a man who wore the same coat three hundred and sixty five days a year, come rain or shine? Who parked his scurvy green Skoda in the same spot in the car park every morning? Who picked his teeth after every meal with the same toothpick? The man was cheapness personified. Bill frowned as he took hold of the door to the canteen. However distasteful he might normally find Mold's company, today he had to control himself and think clearly. If there were even the slightest flaw in the clinical data supporting Mold's Bullman-Sachs therapy, this would probably be his one and only opportunity to bring it to Martindale's attention.

His colleagues had chosen a table just behind the door. Beaming violently, Martindale bounded forward and shook Bill by the hand. Behind him, Bill could see Mold gawkily balancing three cups of coffee on a plastic tray.

'William, my boy! Well met! Well met! Sit yourself down and let's talk a little before we order breakfast, shall we?'

'Oh, right, Edward, thank you,' replied Bill, flashing a smile at his boss and ignoring Mold completely. 'I dropped my results in last thing yesterday evening, by the way – did you get them OK?'

'Yes, yes, I did. I have them here,' replied Martindale, pointing to the two sheets of A4 spread out on the tabletop. 'You have been busy, haven't you?'

'Well, science marches on,' replied Bill, looking down at the neatly tabulated yet utterly fraudulent results he had typed up ten minutes before going home the previous day.

'If you don't mind, perhaps we could take a look at them later. What I'd really like to do first of all is get a progress report from Lester on the pre-clinical trials of his Bullman-Sachs drug. If, er, that's OK by you, that is.'

'Sure, sure, fine by me!' answered Bill cheerily, neatly removing one of the cups of coffee off Mold's tray and leaning back in his seat.

'Over to you then, Lester,' said Martindale.

Squinting suspiciously at Bill, Mold took a battered leather briefcase out from under the table and unlocked it slowly.

'Right, er, Dr Martindale. I've, er, taken the liberty of preparing some presentation materials for you for your meeting with the committee this afternoon.'

'Oh, thank you, Lester! I'm sure they'll be of great help in the Unit's bid for one of the new labs.'

Bill stared enviously at the overhead projection slides; each one a skillful combination of text, graphics and photographs, each one absolutely razor sharp in definition. The bastard must have been up all night preparing them.

'On the first slide I've given an overview of Bullman-Sachs,' continued Mold, 'for those on the committee not familiar with the syndrome – or anyone else who should know but may have forgotten.'

Mold paused and looked fixedly at Bill before continuing. Bill bit his tongue. We'll see what I do and don't know about treating rare disorders, smart arse.

'The bullet points down here outline the principal symptoms,' said Mold, his finger pointing to each of the asterisks in turn. 'Innate genetic disorder caused by the absence of the enzyme alpha-hydroxylase. Patients enter puberty early but continue to suffer from its symptoms during adulthood. Dwarfism common, along with various psychological and emotional disorders. Death premature, around twenty-five to thirty, usually from cancerous melanoma of the …'

'How big's the patient population?' interrupted Bill.

'I beg your pardon?'

'Bullman-Sachs. How many people have got it?'

'Estimates vary. Perhaps around eight hundred to a thousand.'

'What, in the U.K?'

'No, in Europe. Maybe a similar number in the U.S.'

'A thousand people in the whole of Europe! So, it's a minority disorder amongst minority disorders, you might say, then?'

'Yes, but …'

'Sorry, do carry on – don't let me interrupt.'

Mold's eyes narrowed. Bill smiled acidly and took a sip of his coffee. Martindale, seemingly oblivious to the jousting of his two juniors, was busily scanning the next slide.

'What's this here about the trials being prematurely terminated on humanitarian grounds, Lester? I don't understand that …'

Unable to control his excitement, Bill quickly put his coffee down again and twisted around to try and see the slide. This was getting better and better. When Mold began speaking, though, his voice was anything but disappointed.

'As you rightly point out, Dr Kennedy, it is an extremely rare condition and very often misdiagnosed, too. So far the clinic's only been able to recruit five patients. They're desperate to find more.'

'So … ?' queried Bill, cautiously.

'Well, where the patient population is so abnormally small, it's recently become possible to circumvent some of the more severe restrictions that usually govern clinical trials.'

'Has it?'

'Yes. If the results for a novel minority disorder therapy are particularly encouraging, the clinician in charge of the trial may ask for it to be terminated prematurely so that the placebo patients can quickly be switched to the active compound.'

54

'Oh,' gulped Bill, 'is this some sort of new ruling?'

'Last month, actually. There were some guidelines published. I'll let you have a copy if you like.'

'And are the results encouraging?' asked Martindale.

'Exceptionally so,' replied Mold smoothly, slipping out the next slide and turning it around for Martindale to see. 'All three patients on the active began demonstrating remission in all the principal disease criteria within five weeks.'

'Five weeks!' gasped Martindale.

'Yes, five weeks,' responded Mold, quietly. 'Professor Heinbold of the London Hospital – the clinician in charge of the trial – is going to propose to the Committee of Safety of Medicines next month that the two placebo patients receive the therapy itself as soon as possible. And, if they accept, it will automatically accelerate drug launch, too. Assuming satisfactory toxicological studies, it could be made available under the new guidelines within two to three years.'

'Two to three years!' exclaimed Martindale, 'that would make it one of the Unit's very first compounds to market!'

'Exactly.'

'But … but … this is fantastic news, Lester!'

'Yes, it is, isn't it?'

'What if they refuse?' cut in Bill, desperately.

'What if who refuse?'

'The Committee on Safety of Medicines. What if they refuse Professor Heinbold's request?'

Mold smiled slowly.

'As Professor Heinbold is himself Chairman of the Committee of Safety of Medicines, I think it highly unlikely. Shall we order the breakfast, now? I'm rather hungry.'

Bill could feel his jaw drop. This was even worse than he had expected. If the therapy indeed proved to be so successful, Mold would be promoted ahead of him to senior researcher within six months, if not sooner. Asper always rewarded its successful researchers – it was a standing instruction from Sir Paul Giulani himself. On the other side of the table, he watched Mold lean forward and take a deep slurp from his coffee. The white cappuccino froth formed a thick circle in his whiskers like lipstick around the mouth of a clown.

Six months. Possibly only three.

★

It was indeed a conservatory. Not a box of PVC panels, bracketed together and then tacked on to the back of the kitchen, but a discrete structure in its own right, formed of a series of fluted glass arches that ran in a colonnade across the entire rear of the house.

'Wow! This is fantastic!' gasped Louise.

'Oh, d'you like it?'

'It's beautiful.'

'Another one of Dad's creations.'

'It's like … it's like a church or something,' said Louise, craning her head to look up at the roof.

'Ha. Funny you should say that.'

'Why?'

'See those insets up there?' said Gail, pointing to a row of geometrically patterned glass squares, alternately red and amber, which bordered the pinnacle of each arch.

'Yes.'

'They're acid etched. Dad had seen them in an old church but couldn't track down a glass merchant anywhere who knew how to achieve the effect. The technique had all but died out, apparently. He ended up rediscovering it in some Edwardian glazier's reference manual. We had canisters of acid round the house for months afterwards. It drove Mum mental.'

'He must've been so talented your father – I can see where you two get it from.'

Gail smiled at the compliment.

'Oh, he was talented all right – but very happy-go-lucky, and with absolutely no ambition.'

'Yeah, you said.'

'Mum was always on at him to expand the business. He could've made a fortune if he'd branched out.'

'More to life than money.'

'That's what he always used to say … and he was right, of course.' Leading her friend towards one of the two large cane rocking chairs at the end of the conservatory, Gail placed the tray on a table and looked back at the rows of glass arches.

'This'll be the only bit I'll miss – if we ever sell up – this conservatory.'

'You wouldn't do that, would you?' asked Louise in surprise.

'If Bill wanted to, I don't think I'd be against it.'

'What? I thought you said you loved this place.'

'I've got a certain sentimental attachment to it, of course, but, I don't know …' Sighing deeply, Gail stared up at the conservatory's vaulted ceiling. 'These big old houses, they can take you over if you're not careful. Too many memories, too much history. They need … reinventing with each new generation or they just end up like some sort of a mausoleum.'

'I don't know what you mean.'

'Well, you've met Bill. Can't you imagine him just withdrawing inside this place, becoming more and more of a recluse? In a few years' time he'll end up just living in his bedroom and the kitchen. All the other rooms'll be covered in dust sheets like something out of Dickens.'

'I could think of a lot worse places to end up.'

'I can imagine why you say that. I mean, I can sort of see the house through your eyes, for the first time, and I'm sure it appears very seductive. But as a home, believe you me, it's all past and no future. Daughter gone. Mother emigrated. Father dead. The garden's about the only place with any life left in it.'

'You know the only time you're ever pessimistic is when you talk about your brother.'

'Yeah, yeah, I know. You're right. I'm back on my hobby horse again.' Slapping her palms on her thighs Gail brightened up instantly. 'Ha! That gives me an idea!'

'What?'

'Well, see those buildings over there?' Half standing out of her chair, Gail pointed beyond the wall of the house's long, extended garden.

'Yes.'

'They're stables. We've known the owner for years. If you fancy, we could go riding later.'

'Oh, that's a great idea!' replied Louise. 'I haven't been riding for ages.'

'Your package has arrived. I think it's that hormone fragment thingee you were waiting for.'

Glancing up from her workbook as Bill entered the room, Angela nodded in the direction of a slim, aluplastic pack protruding out from amongst the various items of morning post in his in-tray.

'Oh, great,' replied Bill, dully – some quick wizard chemistry in the morning, rustle up a blockbuster drug by lunch time and then he might not have to spend the rest of his life washing Mold's test tubes after all.

'I thought you'd be pleased,' huffed Angela, returning once more to her calculations.

'Yeah, sorry, Angela. That was rude. It's just I've had a bit of a disappointment this morning, that's all. Sorry.'

Angela looked up from her workbook and smiled sympathetically at Bill. This must be the first occasion since they had met that he had actually addressed her like a normal human being. If this was how he reacted to disappointments, a few more might not go amiss.

'Oh, I'm sorry to hear that,' she said.

'Thanks,' replied Bill, walking across to his desk and then muttering to himself wearily, 'Life goes on though, I suppose.'

Sitting down, he stared at the package for several seconds and then finally decided to open it. There wasn't really anything else to do. Having just come from the canteen, he could scarcely wander off back there again. And if he went for a stroll around the corridors, he might bump into Martindale, or worse still, Mold. Tearing apart the zip seal, he extracted first the paperwork and then the small glass phial wrapped in a protective sheath of bubble pack.

'Huh. Cheeky bastards,' he exclaimed in amusement, flicking through the wad of documents.

'What's that?' asked Angela, curiously.

'I ordered a hundred milligrams and they've sent a thousand.'

'Really?'

'Yeah, look.'

Angela walked across the room and examined the packing note.

'Oh, yeah. It must be a mistake.'

'Mistake my foot,' laughed Bill, tossing the paperwork back on to his desk. 'They're trying it on. Bloody suppliers – must think we're daft.'

'What do you mean?'

'Well, it's the oldest trick in the book, isn't it? Sending the customer more than he needs. They probably figure we won't spot it. Or even if we do, with our overheads it'll cost us an arm and a leg in administration costs to reject it.'

'Would they do that?'

'Yeah, of course they would. Do it all the time, in fact.'

'But what if we complained?'

'They'll just say it's a mistake. Offer us a discount on the extra nine hundred mills or something – we might even need it next week, for all they know.'

'Cor, what a con,' exclaimed Angela. 'What are you going to do, then?'

'Oh, God, I dunno. Have a word with my mate in purchasing, I suppose. Let him sort it out.'

'Hmph. I think that's so dishonest – I really do.'

'I guess you could call it that,' chuckled Bill – amused that Angela had somehow managed to take the matter personally.

'Well, don't you think so?'

'Yeah, yeah. You're right. Of course.' Bill smiled at Angela. 'I guess I've just got cynical about these things – too long in the tooth, I suppose.'

Convinced that Bill had not, after all, being laughing at her naiveté, Angela cautiously returned his smile and went back to her work.

Lifting the phial up to the light, Bill examined the white crystalline powder inside. Even though the contract synthesis-company chemists were obviously trying to pull a fast one with the quantity of hormone fragment they had supplied, they had done more than was required of them in terms of quality. In its natural state the fragment decomposed in a matter of minutes and usually had to be shipped in special refrigerated packaging. Somehow, though, they had devised a means of keeping it stable at room temperature, although Bill could not immediately imagine how. Sitting down, he began to read through the paperwork again carefully.

'Oh, I see,' he said to himself, 'interesting.'

Clipped to the back of the Certificate of Analysis was a handwritten note detailing a chemical protection system they had developed that involved coupling one end of the amino acid chain to a sugar and then esterifying the other. Nodding his head in admiration, Bill decided to go ahead and carry out the two experiments on the fragment that he had been planning. Although a biochemist by training, he had always enjoyed dabbling in organic synthesis and the supplier's elegant chemistry was whetting his own appetite for a little experimentation.

The first thing to do was to deprotect the fragment. The preparation of the reagents for dual deblocking turned out to be very tricky and he had still not completed it by the time he went off for lunch.

Nevertheless, it was an absorbing task, and, as he made his way back to the lab at two o'clock, he found himself looking forward to carrying out the final reaction. Having donned his goggles and put the fragment into a flask with the reagent solution, Bill opened up the fume hood of the reaction chamber and placed it on the heating apparatus inside.

'Angela, have you used this heating element lately?' he called out after several seconds.

'No. Why?' replied Angela, over her shoulder.

'Nothing seems to be happening, that's all.'

'That calibration man was in here yesterday. Perhaps he did something.'

'Hm, could be.'

Removing his goggles and inserting his arm into the reaction chamber, Bill gave the heating apparatus a tap. The LCD display immediately flickered and began to register a steady increase in temperature.

'Oh, it's all right – it's working now,' he called out, and then moved across to his desk to begin rechecking the protocol for the later stages of the experiment.

After he had been reading for about a minute, he gradually became aware of a deep, low rumble behind him – a noise that seemed not so much to travel to his ears through the air, as transmit itself up through the floor in the form of a steady vibration. Alarmed, Bill turned and looked around, fully expecting to see one of the laboratory instruments in a dangerous state of overheating. The sight that greeted him, though, was far, far more disturbing. The noise was coming from Angela. Seemingly in the grip of a terrible stab of pain and about to collapse at any moment, she was lying doubled up over her work bench.

'Angela! What's the matter?' cried Bill..

Instead of falling to the floor, Angela suddenly stood violently upright. Visibly trembling – as though reacting to a blast of extreme cold – she then exhaled deeply, the air whistling through her clenched teeth like gas escaping from a pressure valve.

'Jesus Christ, are you OK?'

Bill sprang across to the room towards Angela, but, before he could reach her, she shook her head ferociously in a gesture that seemed to deter him from coming any closer.

'What's up?' he exclaimed, stopping just short of her shoulder. 'Are … are … you hurt or something?'

Still pressed right up against her work bench, and without turning to look at Bill, Angela seemed to have to squeeze out the words of reply one by one.

'Give ... me ... your ... hand.'

Her voice was almost inaudible. She sounded in complete agony.

'What?'

'Your ha ... hand'

'Wha ... ?'

'Pleeeease!!!'

At a complete loss as to what she might possibly want with his hand, yet desperate to assist, Bill extended his right arm. Grasping it by the wrist, Angela then pulled it firmly downwards and wedged it up against her crotch, gripping his fingers between the tops of her legs.

'Holy ...' gasped Bill in a mixture of consternation and pain, as she jammed his forearm between herself and the desk and started to rub her abdomen up against the flat of his trapped hand.

'What the bloody hell are you ... ?' Instinctively, Bill tried to jerk his hand away, but found himself unable to move it even a single inch, so tight was Angela's grip on his forearm.

'Angela! What ... what ...' exclaimed Bill, fighting the rising panic whilst at the same time registering the delicious warmth of Angela's body.

'Harder,' responded Angela – her eyes now closed and her hips starting to gyrate in a firm, rhythmical motion.

Realizing that he was not going to get his hand away by simply pulling at it, Bill swung his left arm around Angela's shoulder, bent himself at the knees and, having physically lifted her whole body into the air, pivoted on his heel to swing both himself and her away from the bench. A measure of his composure then seemed to return to him with the blood that he could now feel running back into his fingers, and, sensing that Angela's feet were now firmly back on the ground, he released her and took a step backwards.

'Angela, I don't know what that was all about, but, really ...'

Turning around, Angela extended her arms, clasped Bill's face between her outstretched palms and kissed him fully on the mouth. Surprised by the speed of the action, Bill was only able to withdraw after a couple of seconds, but not before her smell, the softness of her fingers and the silky, wetness of her tongue had discharged into his bloodstream the greatest single adrenaline shot of his entire life.

'I'm not sure if this is a good ...'

She kissed him again. This time he did not resist. With her hands now freed, she then grabbed either side of his lab coat by the lapels and ripped. Withdrawing from the kiss, Bill stared down at his exposed chest in disbelief. Even at this point, heart pumping and knee joints buckling, he still felt both compelled, and able, to bring an end to what was happening. But when Angela spread her hand over his right pectoral and then dug her strong, manicured nails deeply into it, his resistance shattered – so powerfully physical was her action, so plainly erotic was its intent. Pushing her several steps backwards against the wall of the lab, Bill slammed his face into hers, forcing her mouth open with the full weight of his jaw. With her arms now raised and wrapped around the back of his head, Angela's breasts were fully accessible and he brought up his hands to squeeze them both with all his strength.

Angela orgasmed.

There was no doubting it. Bill was a man of fairly limited sexual experience, but the involuntary manner in which her whole body shuddered, the totality of her reaction, could only mean one thing. Almost in horror at what he had done, Bill took a step backwards.

'What, what is this?'

Having regained her breath and opened her eyes, Angela merely stared at Bill for several seconds and then, arching a single eyebrow, slipped her hands inside her lab coat, undid her skirt and let it fall to the ground. This time, when she propelled herself forward, Bill put up no opposition and within a few, blurred half moments he found himself mounted on her back. No sooner had he begun the methodical pumping motion, than he saw a head and shoulders in the corridor outside float past the lab's glass inspection panel.

'Someone's going to see us!' he hissed.

Even from the oblique angle at which he was now able to view Angela's face, he could see this eventuality caused her absolutely no concern whatsoever. He tried again, with more urgency.

'There's a storeroom place down the corridor, we'll have to go down there!'

Angela's response to this slacking was to extend her hands behind her body and grasp Bill's buttocks in an attempt to force him more deeply into her.

'Oh, Christ!' winced Bill in pain. Realizing that once again he had been caught in Angela's fearsomely strong grip and that for the moment, at least, she was beyond all reason, Bill decided his only option was to push her across to the far wall of the lab where the two of them could not be seen by anyone going past in the corridor. Physically lifting first one side of Angela's body then the other, he began to move her forward in a slow waddling, frog-march across the laboratory. Contrary to his intent, however, this action only served to draw attention to their activity.

'Oh, yes, oh yes … oh, Jesus!' screamed Angela loudly, as the angling, left to right motion forced the head of his penis backwards and forwards between the sides of her vaginal wall. Quickly placing his hand over Angela's mouth, Bill succeeded in gagging her moans but then realized he no longer had the purchase on both sides of her hips to continue to move her.

'For God's sake Angela, not here!'

'Do that again. Oh, do that again!' groaned Angela, now limp in his arms.

Positioned squarely in the centre of the room, a mere six feet from the inspection panel, Bill could fight down the panic no longer. Like a moulting caterpillar stranded in the middle of a leaf, bound to its sloughed-off skin by a sinewy, mucal strand that just would not break, he began frantically wiggling this way and that before a passing predator might catch sight of his soft, vulnerable flesh. With still three feet to go to the wall, though, and unable to steady himself any longer, Bill finally lost his balance, and he and Angela then crashed to the floor in a mass of tangled limbs.

'Oh great, oh great … ohhh.'

Angela began climaxing again. No sooner had Bill extricated his leg from underneath her and begun to rub his twisted foot, than once again she turned to him and, raising that same, sardonic eyebrow, inquired:

'Where's this storeroom, then?'

A little over four hours later, Bill parked his car in the drive of his house and, sensing the presence of aches and pains in muscles that he did not previously know that he even possessed, lifted himself gingerly out of the front seat to make his way to the front door. During the last dozen or so of his twenty-seven years, he had often wondered why life had chosen to deny him his fair share of sexual liaisons. Now, as the motion of twisting his front door key sent a pain searing through his chest, he found himself even more mystified that it had somehow sought to redress the entire balance in the space of a single afternoon.

'Hello! Welcome home!' called out Gail as Bill entered the kitchen.

'Oh, er, hi …'

His sister and Louise were sitting at the kitchen table, cosily warming their hands on two large mugs of coffee.

'Good day at the office?'

'Er, yeah, all right, I suppose. What about you?'

'Yeah, brilliant! We've been riding all afternoon'.

'Oh, er, good …' replied Bill, an image of Angela Marks's naked bosom springing uncontrollably to mind.

'D'you want some coffee … what's that on your shirt?' asked Gail in surprise, as Bill leaned over and placed his briefcase next to the dresser.

'Sorry?' Looking down, Bill could see a small blood stain on his shirt-front. It was from the wound caused by Angela's fingernails. He must have missed it whilst scrabbling around for his scattered clothing in the gloom of the storeroom.

'Oh, I, er, I cut myself shaving. I've been walking round with this on my shirt all day.'

'Oooh, nasty. I can see,' consoled Gail, looking up at Bill's neck. 'Just under your chin, there. It almost looks like a bite mark or something …'

'Excuse me, I'll just, er …' Squeezing behind his sister, Bill made his way to the fridge and took out the single can of lager that, mercifully, still remained within. Ripping back the ring-pull he let the cold liquid stream down his throat, certain that he had never felt so much like a drink in his whole life. Gail and Louise simultaneously broke into smiles at his exaggerated gesture.

'Well,' laughed Gail, 'now we know what you get up to in the evenings. Streuth!'

'Oh, er, sorry,' replied Bill.

Conscious that what he was about to do would seem rude, but completely unable to stop himself, Bill then wiped the lager from the side of his mouth with the back of his hand.

'Charming,' said Gail.

'Yeah, sorry, I'm a bit thirsty.'

'That's all right, just make sure you leave some room for later!'

'Later?'

'Yeah, you know. We're going out to dinner.'

Bill's face twitched. He felt faint enough now. God knows what he would be like in a couple of hour's time if he continued to stay on his feet.

'Oh, don't say you're pulling out! Oh, Bill, you fink!'

'Yeah, er, sorry, it's just …'

'Bill you promised. You promised me last night.'

'Yes, I know, but …'

'What could be more important than going out with us? Come on. We've come all this way from London and everything!'

'Oh, er, yeah, but actually I'm not feeling too grand – I'm really knackered. I need a bit of an early night.'

'An early night! You had an early night last night!' cried Gail.

'I'll make it up to you tomorrow. Honestly. I will,' replied Bill weakly, rubbing his forehead up against his left hand in a feverish gesture that he was certain must have looked utterly fake.

'Oh, all right then, go to bed. I'll see you tomorrow, if you can spare the time!' said Gail, folding her arms and staring truculently at the wall.

'Er, right. Sorry again. Have a nice, er …' With a nod at both Gail and Louise, Bill turned and made his way out of the kitchen door.

'I told you. Didn't I? I told you!' seethed Gail, as soon as her brother had left the room. 'He's a lost cause. I don't know why I bother!'

Easing himself into the bath, Bill was at last able to give some undisturbed thought to how the whole incident with Angela might possibly have occurred. Running over their morning's conversation again, he recalled her cool indifference giving way to a warm friendliness, although not at such a rate as to reach steamy passion by mid-afternoon. On the other hand, if his personality was not responsible, then his sexual charisma seemed an even less likely candidate. He looked down at his stocky, soap-covered limbs: they had never driven a single female wild before – there was little reason to assume that they could do so now. Nymphomania? Bill turned the concept over in his mind for several minutes before finally deciding that the condition probably did not exist. Or certainly not in such a dramatic form, anyway. On the other hand, Angela had clearly been driven by something and, in all modesty, he knew it was something that by the end of the afternoon he had been well and truly able to satisfy. Perhaps it had all been some sort of extreme behavioural reaction. Perhaps Angela was normally sexed, but just highly repressed. This seemed to Bill to make a lot more sense. A cold, disciplinarian father, maybe, who neither routinely demonstrated any affection, nor would accept any from his daughter. This would tie in with her fanatical obsession with sport: all that physical exertion was a way of working off her frustrated urges. That must be it. The icy, aloof exterior was the dreadful legacy of a strict and loveless upbringing, and the harder she attempted to maintain it, the more violently her true nature compelled her to reject it.

Despite the awesome battering Bill's penis had suffered that afternoon, he felt it begin to stiffen a little. For if his analysis were true, today might not be an isolated incident and Angela Marks could soon be back for more. Next time he would make sure it would not be in a storeroom, but at her place, or even his. Wrapping the bath towel around him, Bill padded across the corridor to his bedroom and stared at the huge four poster in the middle of the room. More of the same with Angela Marks, but in comfortable surroundings?

Bloody hell.

Chapter 4

Bill awoke on Saturday morning aching but in high spirits and absolutely determined to find a way of making things up to Gail for having treated her so shabbily the previous night. He didn't have long to wait for inspiration. Over breakfast, Louise casually mentioned that in six weeks' time she was due to attend a marketing course at nearby Warwick University, whereupon Bill immediately suggested driving over there for the day. Louise could reconnoitre the campus, they could then visit the castle perhaps, do a little shopping and return back to Wyburn in time for dinner – which he, of course, would be delighted to prepare for them. The proposal was unanimously agreed and within an hour they were on their way. For Bill, by far the most satisfying feature of the day was being able to observe at close hand the rapport between his sister and her new-found companion. And, that evening, as he cooked his old faithful – special-occasion pasta – he found himself both charmed and relaxed by the laughter that every now and then floated into the kitchen from the conservatory where Gail and Louise sat lazily drinking their sherry aperitifs. No sooner had he started to enjoy the girls' company, though, than the weekend seemed to come to a close. They slept late on Sunday morning and, almost before he realized it, lunch was finished and once again all three of them were making their way along the underground walkways of Harledge East Station.

Having agreed that they should all meet up again in six weeks' time when Louise came to Warwick, Bill found himself on the exact same spot that he had stood three days previously, once again waving to his sister. It had been an excellent weekend, but as the train finally disappeared out of sight, a frown passed over Bill's face. Now, at last, he had to decide what to do about Angela. Several times over the weekend he had recalled their frenzied Friday afternoon encounter, but on each occasion had straightaway pushed it to the back of his mind. With Gail and Louise now departed, the decision as to whether next to meet Angela in or out of work could not be postponed any further. When he returned home he was no closer to a decision. Finally, after an uncomfortable half-hour pacing the living room like a nervous teenager plucking up the courage to ask for his first date, Bill picked up the Harledge phone directory. He would phone, drive around to her house and they would go out for an early-evening drink. What could be more normal? Phone, drive, drink. Intoning the words like a mantra, Bill ran his finger down the list of Marks in the directory. Angela came in to work from South Harledge where, he recalled hearing from Martindale, she still lived with her parents. Mr David Marks, Rosehill Avenue – that would probably be the one. Placing the opened directory on the arm of the sofa, he picked up the receiver and, as the clock in the hall struck four, dialled the number.

'Hello?' A male voice.

'Hello, can I speak to Angela, please?'

'Certainly. Hang on a moment.' Good – the right house.

'Angela, darling!'

'What is it?' Angela. Somewhere inside the house

'Telephone for you …' sang out the voice. For a strict disciplinarian, her father's tone seemed remarkably pleasant. Feet coming down the stairs.

'Hello?'

'Oh, hi, Angela, it's Bill. Bill Kennedy.'

'Wait a moment,' replied Angela sharply. A muffled sound. She was covering the receiver with her hand, although he was still able to hear her calling out to her father that she would take the call in the study. Bill swallowed down the lump forming in his throat. He should have expected that frigid exterior to have reasserted itself by now. After several clicks and the sound of a door closing, she returned to the phone.

'Hello?'

'Oh, hello, Angela, it's me. I hope it's OK to call now, I was …'

'Are you clean?' interrupted Angela.

'What?'

'Are you clean. That's all I want to know.' Her words hissed out like coolant escaping from a punctured refrigerator.

'What are you talking about, clean?'

'What do you think I'm talking about? Diseases, of course. Diseases, from doing … that.'

'I most certainly am!' replied Bill indignantly.

'Because if you're not, and I get whatever you've got, I'll smash your shitty little face in.'

'What?' said Bill

'And another thing. My boyfriend's prop forward for the Saracens. If you breathe a word of what happened to anyone and he gets to hear about it, or you so much as ever come near me again – and I mean ever – you'll need an army. Got it?'

With a harsh crackle, the line went dead. Bill looked numbly down at the handset – the very worst he had expected of the conversation had been, well, he wasn't sure, but certainly nothing like this. Still holding the receiver he stared out of his front window to the road outside. What possible explanation could there be for such dramatic shifts in her attitude towards him? From indifference to intimacy to detestation in under three days? After several seconds, a droning pitch from the handset told him he should replace the phone, but as he did so, his right pectoral gave an unashamedly psychosomatic twinge of pain from the spot into which she had dug her fingernails. Life in the lab with Angela had been uncomfortable enough even before last Friday; what on earth was it going to be like now?

Rather than risk having to find out, Bill phoned in sick at nine o'clock the next morning, but then spent the rest of the day brooding over his cowardice – he had to face the woman some time. He awoke early on Tuesday, and, after cooking a breakfast he did not eat, walked out into the drive to make his way to Asper. Clicking on his safety belt, he locked the driver's door from the inside, but then changed his mind and unlocked it again. If Angela's boyfriend was even half as fearsome as he sounded, a locked door would afford him little protection – the brute would probably just bite the handle off with his teeth.

Once on his way to work, the old familiarities soon began to reassert themselves and Bill began to feel a little more blasé about the situation.

Angela was obviously keen to cover things up – she plainly needed her job as much as he needed his – so all that they had to do now was carry on as though nothing had happened. At the front gate, Derek was writing out security passes for a couple of visitors, but still found time to wink at Bill as he walked past the gatehouse. Bill waved jovially back. So cheerful did Bill's mood become, in fact, that by the time he met Martindale at the door to his lab he had almost forgotten that anything remotely unusual had taken place there the previous Friday afternoon.

'Good Morning, Edward!'

'Er, yes. Er, could you come, er …' Martindale was charlestoning again. Smiling to himself at his boss's customary idiosyncrasy, Bill followed him into his office.

'Sorry about yesterday, Edward.' said Bill, brightly. 'I had a bit of a head cold'.

'What have you got in your schedule this morning, William?' asked Martindale.

'Nothing particular. Why?'

'It's just that I've had a note from, er, Mr Welwyn, asking the two of us to go and see him as a matter of urgency.'

At the mention of the Head of Human Resource's name, Bill's heart missed a beat, the memory of that wet afternoon the previous June springing uncomfortably back to mind. It had been Welwyn himself who had handed Bill the official Asper letter warning him about his latecoming.

'What does he want?' asked Bill, cautiously.

'I suppose it must be about our move to the new laboratories,' replied Martindale nervously, 'although I must say Personnel are rarely so quick off the mark. Unless there's some other reason you can think of why he might want to see you.'

'No. None,' replied Bill flatly.

'Right, well, I'll call him and we can make our way over there, er, forthwith.'

As they paced across the site together in silence, Bill racked his brains for an explanation as to the reason for the urgent summons. Had the Human Resources Department received a complaint? No one had seen them – he was certain of that – and Angela herself clearly wanted things kept quiet. There must, therefore, be some other reason. But what? Unable to think of one, yet finding the coincidence altogether too

70

great, Bill began preparing a response, should he be faced with the charge. Seeing Martindale's perplexed expression as they entered the Human Resources Building, he finally decided he would front it out. After all, if he still found it difficult to believe that the most gorgeous woman on site had forced him into repeated acts of copulation with her, why should anybody else credit the charge?

Mr Welwyn's office had changed little since Bill's last visit – the only addition being a television and video recorder that appeared recently to have been installed in the corner of the room. Mr Welwyn himself, unfortunately, also appeared no different. Seated straight-backed behind the same massive mahogany desk, he glared fixedly at Bill and Martindale as they entered the room, like a rooster eyeballing a couple of hens nervously returning to their positions in the coop.

'Dr Kennedy, Dr Martindale.'

Welwyn did not stand up to shake hands, but merely nodded at the two men to be seated and then began examining the contents of the single buff file on the desk in front of him. It was close on a minute before he finally chose to break the silence.

'So, Dr Kennedy,' he observed, in a matter-of-fact voice, 'you have been working in Building 7 ever since its inauguration. For some reason, I had forgotten that.'

'Yes, that's right,' replied Bill, in a croaking voice.

'And your current laboratory is RM-3. I am correct?'

'Yes.'

'Good – we are indeed talking about the same place.' Closing the file, Welwyn rested his forearms on the table and looked directly at Bill. 'Dr Kennedy, would you please therefore describe to me, in your own words and in your own time, the events that took place in that laboratory, last Friday afternoon, May the first.'

No three minute warning – just the bombshell hurtling down towards him out of the sky.

'Nothing happened,' replied Bill quickly, wincing inwardly at the way his denial had come blurting out.

'Nothing happened?' repeated Welwyn in a deadpan voice.

'No, nothing particular.'

Welwyn began examining his pen, seemingly turning this reply over in his mind. Out of the corner of his eye, Bill could see Martindale's lip puckered in surprise: he had obviously expected the interview to revolve around Bill's absence from the laboratory, not his presence in it.

'Much as I dislike having to repeat myself, Dr Kennedy, all the same, I'm going to put that question to you again. What happened in RM-3 on Friday afternoon?'

Bill blinked and could feel himself blushing. Angela had talked. The woman must be completely mad.

'Absolutely nothing, I don't know what you're referring to.'

'Right. If that's the way you want to play it. But I must tell you that it is now a matter of record that despite having twice been given the opportunity to volunteer information, you completely refused to do so.'

With an expression of pained reluctance, Welwyn opened up a side drawer of his desk and took out a remote control for the video. Pointing the device across the room, he pressed the play button firmly once and nodded at Bill and Martindale to start watching.

As soon as the screen sprang to life, Bill straightaway recognized RM-3, although not viewed from any angle he had ever seen it before. The scratchy black and white images of Angela and he working away in the lab seemed to have been taken from on high, almost as though from a camera mounted somewhere in the ceiling. The ceiling! The blood began to drain from Bill's face. His mind's eye quickly conjured up an image of the door of his laboratory. Above the glass inspection panel was the lintel and, above that, a full twelve feet up from the floor … was a clear pane of glass. Now he remembered. On the other side of the glass, fixed discreetly into the corridor's false ceiling, there was a triple-lensed security camera.

'My question still stands,' said Welwyn softly, pressing the pause button.

Looking first at Martindale, then at Welwyn, Bill exhaled deeply.

'That's from the security camera outside the lab, right?'

'Indeed.'

'OK – I admit it. I know what you've got there,' said Bill, looking shamefacedly down at the floor.

'Thank you, Dr Kennedy,' said Welwyn, frowning gravely. 'Now, you can no doubt imagine the view the company takes of such flagrant misconduct. A junior colleague, albeit a highly attractive young woman, in your charge …'

'Yes, yes,' said Bill contritely. 'There was no excuse for what we did.'

'Am I to understand, then, that in mitigation you are claiming that

72

you and Miss Marks are engaged in some kind of ongoing ... relationship?' Welwyn accentuated the final word as though describing a grotesque form of deviancy.

'No, nothing of the sort.'

'So, you admit you took advantage of her?'

'I don't admit anything of the kind!' said Bill, looking up in alarm. 'She threw herself at me!'

'Come now, Dr Kennedy,' responded Welwyn quickly, 'you don't really expect us to believe that, do you?'

'Too right, I do.'

'You are not seriously suggesting that Miss Marks invited your attentions?'

'Of course she bloody did!' exclaimed Bill hotly. 'Ask her – she'll tell you!'

'I did ask her. I spoke to her yesterday, in fact.'

'And what did she say?'

'Well, whilst not seeking even for a moment to deny that the events took place, she has almost no recollection of them. Comparing this with your own attempts at denial and the evidence of the videotape, I'm afraid the company can only really come to one conclusion.'

'Which is what?'

'That you abused your position of authority in order to perpetrate an act of sexual harassment.'

'What! That's total crap!'

'Dr Kennedy ...'

'You've got the rest of the tape there, have you?'.

'Yes.'

'Well, go on then. Play it! It's obvious what happened!"

'If you insist, Dr Kennedy, I can, but ...'

'Yeah, I do insist.'

Certain that the tape would exonerate him, Bill folded his arms and sat back in his seat. To his right he could see that Martindale was gazing fixedly at the screen, for once not experiencing any difficulty in deciding whether he should look below, through or over the top of his bifocals. The recording began with Angela bent over her desk and Bill quickly approaching her from behind. He saw once again the two violent shakes of the head that she had given that seemed to tell him to keep his distance. However, although the next shot clearly showed Bill slowly extending his hand towards her, the camera's elevation and situation were such that the sight of her grasping it was obscured by his own right shoulder. Worse was to follow. For, moments later, Bill could be seen wrapping both his arms around her and then lifting her bodily into the air. The place where he had deposited her, though, was just off camera and the kiss that she had given him there and her loosening and removing her skirt had not been captured for posterity. When Angela next came back into shot, Bill was firmly mounted on her back. Welwyn paused the tape again.

'I don't think we really need to see any more, do we, Dr Kennedy?' Once again, Welwyn began examining the documents in the buff folder in front of him. 'Now, referring to the conditions of employment signed by you in June 1995, under the provisions of article six, clause three – 'Dismissal and Severance' – employees charged with acts of gross misconduct …'

'No way!' interrupted Bill. 'You can't pin all of this on me. I'll, I'll … go to an industrial tribunal!'

'If you'll allow me to finish, Dr Kennedy. Employees charged with gross misconduct have recourse to independent arbitration – the industrial tribunal to which you refer – a process which …'

'And don't think I won't, either!' interrupted Bill again

' … a process which in some cases can take months, even years, and which Asper consequently makes the most strenuous efforts to avoid. And that is why, in your case,' added Welwyn, bitingly, 'we are thankful that you have already forfeited your right to it.'

'What d'you mean?'

'I refer once again to your contract of employment. Article seven, clause two point four: the section entitled "Disciplinary Action". I quote " … Asper Pharmaceuticals shall issue the employee with a written warning within twenty-eight days of the incident. Should the employee within one calendar year of issue repeat such an offence, *or any other offence similarly occasioning a written warning*" – that's the relevant part, I feel – "Asper Pharmaceuticals may at its absolute discretion dismiss the employee forthwith."'

Bill stared numbly at Welwyn. His latecoming. Eleven months ago, Asper had served him with an official warning letter about his time-keeping. It had been his yellow card.

And now, Welwyn was reaching into his top pocket for the red.

'You mean, you're … you're sacking me?' asked Bill, incredulously.

'No. Actually, you're going to resign. It works like this. You receive three months salary; we keep the details of your disciplinary record here. Should you subsequently be so ill-advised as to attempt to sue for unfair dismissal,' said Welwyn, resting his palms on the file affectionately, 'we can use it to demonstrate due process before any court in the land. Our sincere hope, however, is that it never comes to that, and you depart forthwith to pursue your career elsewhere, regarding what you have been offered as, in the circumstances, a fair and equitable severance package. Here. Please take the cheque. Now, your pension …'

Bill carried on watching Welwyn's mouth moving, but his mind ceased to process the literal sense of what the Human Resources Manager was saying. Out of the corner of his eye, he could see that Martindale had taken off his spectacles and was wearily cleaning one of the lenses. There was nothing he could do for Bill now – his career at Asper was finished and they both knew it. If the company really had been so outraged, of course, they would have hauled him and Angela in together and fired them both on the spot. But the truth was they had grown tired of his contrariness and indolence and just wanted him out. Deep down Bill knew he could not blame them for that, but all the same he could not help finding the final chapter bizarre in the extreme. Sexual harassment? He would never have imagined it ending this way. Despite the sickening, empty feeling in his stomach, Bill allowed himself a smile. They were definitely going to let Angela off. He could feel it in his bones. With looks like that you could get away with anything. Allowing himself a final, laconic glimpse of the scene of his downfall, Bill turned once more towards the screen, which still remained paused on freeze-frame.

And that was when he saw it.

The gap.

The little, four-inch gap that he knew, in an instant, was going to change his life forever.

'Are you sure you don't want to stay until the end of the month? I'm certain Mr Welwyn will be discreet.'

'I've no doubt he will, Edward,' replied Bill, as the two men came to a halt outside the door of RM-3, 'but other people won't. These sorts of things always find their way out by one means or another. It'll be all round the site by tomorrow morning. I just couldn't face it.'

Much as Bill genuinely appreciated his boss's concern, every fibre in his being was screaming for Martindale to get himself back into his own office.

'But there must be so many people you'd like to say goodbye to …'

'Yeah, well, there you go. You can't choose how these things happen. Just give me a half-hour to clear my things. I'll pop my head in before I go.'

With a stoical smile at his boss, Bill turned to unlock the lab door. Mournfully, Martindale began moving off towards his office. At last, thought Bill. At last!

'I just want to say, you know, that I believe you.' Stopping at the door to his office, Martindale turned to address Bill. 'I'm sure you're not the sort of man who, well, would force himself on a woman.'

'That's kind of you, Edward. Thanks.'

Martindale opened his mouth as though to say something more, but changed his mind and walked sadly into his room. Heaving a sigh of relief, Bill took his keys out of his lab coat pocket. For the last twenty minutes he had thought of nothing else but getting back to RM-3 to check that what he had seen on the screen was really true and now, finally, here he was. With shaking hands and fumbling fingers, he inserted the key in the lock. Closing the door quietly behind him, he rested his head up against the inspection panel and looked across the room at the experimental reaction chamber.

'Jesus Christ …' he exclaimed, under his breath.

He had not imagined it. The fume hood that was supposed to seal up the reaction chamber during experiments was still ajar, just as it must have been prior to Angela having gone so completely wild. Obviously, he had failed to clip it back on properly after he had put his hand into the chamber to chivvy along the heating element. The hormone fragment must have undergone a chemical alteration during deprotection: only that could account for Angela's otherwise entirely inexplicable advances. Moving away from the door into the centre of the room, Bill looked inside the reaction chamber. The flask containing the hormone fragment in solution was still there, sitting on top of the heating element.

Before he and Angela had hurriedly departed for the storeroom on Friday afternoon, he recalled flicking off the power switch at the wall to cut the electricity supply to all the instrumentation in the chamber. Gingerly, he now removed the flask from the heating element, and then turned the switch back on again. Just as before, the LCD display on the heating element flickered and then went blank. He tapped the side of the machine. It came back on again after a moment, indicating a temperature of twenty-two degrees. Bill watched the display for several seconds more, but it did not change. It must be faulty – that was well below freezing.

'Centigrade!' whispered Bill to himself, suddenly. 'The stupid bugger went and calibrated it at centigrade!'

Sitting back on his stool, Bill realized that he now had all the parts of the jigsaw. A maintenance engineer distracted by a gorgeous lab assistant. A hormone fragment unnaturally protected and then zapped at upwards of 100 degrees centigrade. A thermal rupturing of its delicate amino acid chain, resulting in the release of a gaseous fragment into the air. A four-inch gap through which the gas had then passed into the atmosphere. Through such a series of coincidences, in room RM-3 of the Harledge laboratories of Asper Pharmaceuticals Inc., a new drug substance had been discovered. A substance that stimulated the female sexual response, but of whose existence Asper was totally unaware.

Leaping off the stool, Bill resolved to make sure it stayed that way.

Moving quickly across to his desk, he picked up the glass phial containing the nine hundred milligrams of the protected hormone fragment that he had not used and slipped it into his shirt pocket. Turning to the wash basin, he then ripped off several lengths of paper towel and hastily sellotaped them over the inspection panel and the glass panel above the door. He was not going to get caught that way twice. Having scrawled 'Do not disturb' on a sheet of blank paper and affixed it on the outside of the lab door, he then locked the room from the inside and began a systematic search of every document that related to the existence of the hormone fragment. He knew he had only minutes.

'So, I guess it's goodbye, then.'

Martindale looked up from his desk. Bill was standing in the doorway to his office. Under one arm he held a large leather briefcase, under the other a couple of bulky reference books and some files.

'Oh, er, yes right.' Martindale stood up and moved around to the other side of his desk.

'I hope you don't mind – I'm taking some things with me. Some odds bit of work and a few old reference books; nothing that'll be missed. Well, I don't think so, anyway.'

'Fine, fine …' said Martindale, his voice beginning to choke. The combination of Bill's strangely enthusiastic expression and the sight of him struggling to carry the books had poignantly brought back to mind a day six years ago. The day that as a young graduate, this bright, talented young man had first stood before him on this very same threshold.

'There's a bit of internal post here.' Bill slowly put down his briefcase and slipped a brown package out from in between the books under his other arm. 'Can I put it in your tray?'

'Yes, er, please do.'

'Nothing too important. It's just some stuff I didn't get time to do on Fri … , er, last week.'

'Thank you. Thank you. I'll make sure it gets sent.'

Martindale watched Bill deposit the envelope in his post tray and then turn around and extend his hand for him to shake. More than anything in the world, the older man wanted to tell him that for all his late-comings and lame excuses, he had always recognized Bill as a kindred spirit, who shared his love of scientific investigation. He wanted to tell him of the affection that he had only this very day come to realize he truly felt for Bill, looking upon him, in a way, as the son that nature had denied him. But Martindale recognized his limitations all too well by now. He knew himself to be a shy man, poorly able to articulate his emotions, and so, instead of words that would be doomed to failure, he reached out and clasped Bill's hand with both of his own, hoping somehow that the gesture might transmit even some small fraction of the warmth of his feelings.

'Good luck, my boy.'

'Yeah, thanks Edward. Thanks for everything. And, goodbye …'

Overcome by emotion, Martindale released Bill's hand and, with eyes averted, moved back around to his seat. Staring blankly at the lines of journals on his bookshelf, he listened as Bill picked up his briefcase and then made his way out of the door and down the corridor. What a waste. What an appalling waste.

Suddenly, though, after a few seconds, the footsteps stopped. Martindale turned around to see that Bill had paused for a moment, and was looking back down the corridor at him through the still open door.

'Edward. Don't worry about me. OK?'

There was something in Bill's smile, some enigmatic quality, that Martindale imagined would stay fresh in his recollection for many years, but which he doubted he would ever be able properly to fathom. What he did know in that moment, as he watched Bill turn assuredly on his heel, was that if the look and those words had been intended to gladden an old man's heart, then they had more than succeeded. Perhaps, after all, this day did not mark an end for William Kennedy, but a beginning.

With less than twenty yards to go to the front gate, Bill felt close to fainting. Without having consumed so much as a cup of coffee all morning, he had already been backwards and forwards across the entire length of the site four times. Hastily stuffing the papers and reference books into two polythene bags, Bill fought back the hypoglycemic haze and tried to concentrate on the last, all-important step. So far, everything had gone to plan. He had wiped every file on his PC clean, even down to the machine's internal cache memory, so that no reference to the hormone fragment or the deprotection procedure he had developed remained in existence. In their place, he had fabricated an experimental protocol for another hormone fragment of the same family, and then carefully doctored the filed copy of the supplier's Certificate of Analysis such that even to the trained eye it would appear as though he had been working on a related, but dissimilar compound. In Martindale's internal post tray was a memo to Peter Layford, fraudulently predated to the previous Friday, requesting he arrange to pay for the excess quantity so that no invoice queries would subsequently raise the spectre of the hormone fragment again. All that was now left was to get through the main gate without being searched. Bill prayed it would be Derek in the gatehouse. Were one of the other guards to ask him to open his briefcase and discover the flask concealed inside, he would be finished.

'What's this? A half-day holiday?' asked Derek, poking his head out of the gatehouse door.

'Shh!' hissed Bill, nudging Derek back into the doorway. 'Keep your voice down.'

'What's the matter?'

'I've just had a right bollockin' from Human Resources. I'm in deep shit.'

'What for?' replied Derek, his eyes opening wide.

'They've got something on me, apparently. On camera. Something from the lab.'

'I told you! Didn't I? I told you!! They're keeping records of what everybody does.'

'You were right. You were right,' cried Bill, raising his eyes to the sky. 'God, how I wish I'd listened to you!'

'What have they got on you, then?'

'I'm not sure,' whispered Bill. 'But I'm just nipping off site for a couple of hours. I've got to dump this lot. It's a few bits of work I should've tidied up but never got around to.' With a nod at the polythene bags, Bill winked at Derek. 'If Giulani rings up and asks – you haven't see me, right?'

'Mum's the word,' replied Derek, with a tap on the side of his nose.

'Cheers, Derek. Mind how you go, mate,' said Bill, picking up the bags and moving off towards the car park.

A rush of elation mixed with relief surged through Bill as he watched the Asper site gradually recede in his rear-view mirror. Standing outside the gatehouse he could see Derek staring pointedly in the exact opposite direction to avoid looking at his car. Breaking into laughter at the sight of the gatekeeper's theatricality, all Bill's pent-up nervous energy came flooding out, and he banged the flats of his hands against the rim of the steering wheel.

'I bloody did it!' he shouted. 'I bloody did it!!'

Wiping his brow and loosening his tie, Bill forced himself to calm down and concentrate on the task of driving safely back to Wyburn. To his left, strapped into the passenger seat, was the black leather briefcase containing the hormone fragment. Except, it wasn't the hormone fragment anymore – it was something else. Some hybrid compound or compounds that had been created from it. He glanced at the briefcase nervously. The flask was stoppered so the mixture would not spill, but what if it responded in some way to agitation? He had to slow down. Bill instantly broke into a cold sweat as he pondered the significance of the fact that he knew virtually nothing about the chemical nature of what was now contained in the flask. The thermal shock could have imparted a thousand different characteristics to the fragment and any decomposition products that may have been simultaneously created in the reaction. An explosion would probably be unlikely, but what about toxicity? Mutagenicity? Carcinogenicity? If it produced such a dramatic effect in women, what did it do to men? Angela had breathed in lung-fulls of the stuff – he must have done so, too. A sickening, nauseous sensation began to spread though Bill's groin, as though his testicles had turned to water. God knows, if the compound had some sort of steroidal properties, that was exactly what might be happening to them.

'I need food,' said Bill to himself. There was a burger bar up ahead and Bill flicked his indicator to move into the nearside lane. No sooner had he done so, though, than he turned it off again. He couldn't risk taking the flask into the restaurant and he certainly couldn't leave the damn thing in the car – what if the briefcase were to be stolen? He would have to wait until he got back to Wyburn.

Pulling into his driveway, Bill got out of his car, opened up the passenger door and took out the briefcase. Despite the nearest neighbour being over a hundred feet away, he tried his best to act nonchalantly, as though having just popped home for some early lunch. Once inside though, he raced into the kitchen and hurled every single item of food out of the fridge. Chemical reactions take place more slowly at lower temperatures: whatever the hormone fragment had now become it had to obey that law. Taking out the top two shelves, he gently placed the flask on the single remaining shelf, closed the door and then sat on the kitchen table. Without taking his eyes off the fridge door, he let his hands explore to his left and right amongst the mound of food. Finding a loaf of wholemeal bread, he began tearing pieces off and stuffing them into his mouth. Three minutes later, slowly averting his eyes, he looked down at the scatter of crumbs on his knees and realized he had eaten the entire loaf. At that moment, a sudden noise sent him leaping off the kitchen table high into the air. Rushing into the living room he stood staring crazily at the ringing telephone. It was Asper. They had found out that he had smuggled the hormone fragment off-site. How could they have known so quickly? After six rings, the answering machine finally clicked in.

'Hi, Bill. It's me. Calling at … half past eleven. Hey, you never guess what? I just rang you at Asper to say thanks for the weekend and everything, and they put me through to some strange woman or other. She says you've left. Ha! What a laugh – unless there's something you haven't told me, that is! Anyway, thanks again. We really had a brilliant, brilliant time. Look forward to seeing you again when Louise goes up to Warwick. Anyway, I've got to dash now. See you soon. Give me a call when you can. Byeee!'

Bill stood by the answering machine, watching its miniature tape rewind and its red message indicator flick metronomically on and off.

'Gail,' he said finally, listening to the words echo around the room, 'the fridge is full of sex.'

His sister was right: telling her would be difficult.

'Bloody hell!' exclaimed Peter Layford, almost dropping his glass in surprise. 'It really is true about you and Angela, isn't it? You look terrible ...'

It was the following evening. Actually, Bill didn't feel too bad, but having spent most of the afternoon asleep he had then gone straight to the pub to meet Peter and no doubt still looked a little dishevelled.

'Yes, it's true. What're you having, anyway?'

'No, no, let me!' said Peter, hastily calling across to the barman. 'A double whisky, please!'

'Oh, thanks, Pete.'

'My pleasure, mate. It's the least you deserve. God, she must've shagged you within an inch of your life! Why you got the push I'll never know – they should've given you a medal.'

'So, the story's out, then, is it?'

'Nobody's talked about anything else for the last two days. Pirate copies of the video are goin' for fifty quid a time, apparently.'

'What? Where did they come from?'

'Joke. Joke. Come on, come over here and tell me about it.'

Laughing, Peter paid for the drinks and escorted Bill across the pub to a quiet alcove.

'There isn't an awful lot to tell, really.'

'What d'you mean, there isn't a lot to tell? God! And I always had you down as such a quiet one. You're a dark horse, you are. But what a way to get yourself fired! Listen, I've just gotta do this.' Peter extended his hand for Bill to shake. 'On behalf of every red-blooded male at Asper Harledge, William Kennedy, congratulations. Your name'll go down in company history.'

'That makes me feel much better,' said Bill dryly, wincing as he took a swig of his whisky.

'This won't. She's working for Mold now.'

'What! That was quick.'

'I heard just before I came out. The Unit's landed one of the new laboratories because of his Bullman–Sachs drug. She's gonna be assigned to him permanently now, apparently.'

'Well, good. The two of them deserve each other.'

'That's the spirit! You're better off out of Asper, anyway. You've done your apprenticeship – you ought to set up in the drug discovery business yourself. There are loads of people out there with no more talent than you making fortunes for themselves right now.'

'Are there?'

'Yeah! Of course.'

'Oh, really, I didn't know that …'

As Bill leant forward and took another swig of his drink, his heart leapt. Peter was one of the most knowledgeable people that he knew in the pharmaceutical industry, and, without prompting, he had already got straight on to the exact subject that Bill wanted to discuss.

'I had one of them in only yesterday, actually. They're a sort of technology brokerage. 5Z Pharma they're called. Down in Greenhill. Started with nothing eight years ago – absolutely nothing, right? They just filed their third product licence last week.'

'Three drugs? In eight years? That was quick!'

'Wasn't it just? And they've no manufacturing facilities either. No analytical labs, no R&D. They're just a marketing organisation.'

'How on earth did they do it, then?' asked Bill.

'Well, basically, they concentrated on their core marketing skills and bought in everything else as a service. People have always thought that big company-type ventures – like launching a drug, or opening a bank or something – are beyond the capabilities of small companies. But it's just not true any more. Not with IT and the internet and all that. As long as you can get your hands on some decent intellectual property, and as long as you can stay solvent, small organisations or even individuals can handle just about any undertaking. Virtual companies, they call 'em.'

'Yeah, well, that all sounds very grand, but I think I'll just try and get myself a job in another research lab somewhere,' replied Bill, hoping that none of his excitement or interest was showing.

'What! Well, you do whatever you think's best, but I'd give my right arm to be in your position, honestly I would. As I think I probably would've been last Friday afternoon 'n' all,' added Peter, archly. 'So, come on, you're not getting out of it. Tell me what happened. The rumours have you and her in that storeroom for over four hours …'

★

Four double whiskies, three pints and a taxi ride later, Bill eased himself luxuriously into his bed. His conversation with Peter had absolutely clinched it. A virtual company. He was going to form his own virtual company. Head of R&D, Director of Marketing, Chief Executive Officer and tea boy – he would single-handedly develop his discovery and realize it as a merchandisable product. Having turned the question of the possible toxicity of the compound over in his mind during the day, he had come to the conclusion that his initial worries were probably unfounded. It was much more likely that the compound was safe, but that it would take years to perfect. He didn't care, though. He was up for it. Up for the challenge like no other in his life before. Despite the alcohol, Bill remained awake for over an hour, basking in the glow of the decision he had made. Whether it was during this time, or in those moments of half consciousness just before his mind finally succumbed to sleep, he was not able later to recall. All he knew, when he awoke the next morning, refreshed, invigorated and raring to get to grips with the task of characterizing the molecule he had discovered, was that there was one name, and one name only, he could ever consider calling it.

Libidan.

Part Two
The Oil Spills

Chapter 5

'Right. Just stay here and keep your eyes peeled.' Jabbing his finger emphatically, Ray pointed through the rusty security bars to the dimly lit street outside. 'If you see anything, don't shout. Come down and get us.'

Una nodded nervously at him through the gloom of the darkened staircase. Moving swiftly down to the landing below, Ray went back through the door into the main office area. Inside, he could see that Len had already managed to open up both of the large, metal filing cabinets and was running his fingers through the folders in one of the top drawers. Ray wondered if there was a lock on the planet that Len couldn't pick.

'Is she gonna be all right?' muttered Len, mistrustfully, examining a typed document by the light of a pencil-torch that he gripped between his teeth.

'What have you got?' replied Ray, ignoring the question.

'Invoice,' said Len, deftly letting the torch fall into his gloved hand. 'Export order. Big one.'

'Where?'

'France.'

Taking a notebook out of his jacket pocket, Ray carefully recorded the name of the French importer and then returned the invoice to the folder. Within ten minutes the two men had worked their way through both cabinets, their search yielding the names of the company's seven major trading partners and four principal suppliers. Carefully ensuring that none of the papers they had examined were left dog-eared or protruding from their folders, Len firmly pushed the drawers closed and re-locked each cabinet in turn with a thin, metal micro-file.

'Desks,' said Ray simply, turning quickly to examine the large secre-tarial bureau behind him.

Raids like these were as much about information as anything else.

'Nothin',' said Len five minutes later, cuffing a gold-framed photograph of two smiling school children, the glass shattering as it connected with the edge of the radiator.

'Forget it,' said Ray irritably – as annoyed as his partner that the desks had failed to reveal a single employee's address. 'Let's do the workshop.'

At the top of the stairs, Una had moved away from the window and was looking anxiously back down the staircase towards them as they emerged from the office.

'I told you to watch the window,' hissed Ray.

'I was, but I heard something breaking. Are you all right?'

'Je-sus,' exhaled Len in disgust.

'Come on downstairs with us,' said Ray, frowning as he made his way towards the rear of the building.

The workshop was small, intimate and extremely well equipped. Moonlight flooded through two broad skylights in the ceiling. Ray looked at the seven tailor's benches, each equipped with a state-of-the-art industrial sewing machine. This was no rag-trade sweatshop, with immigrant labour churning out fake designer jeans for a pound an hour, but a highly organized industrial venture, dedicated to crafting the finest in leather haute couture. These people knew how to make money, all right – the whole place reeked of it.

'Yes!' exclaimed Len gleefully, running to the back of the room where a dozen calf skin coats, completed that day, hung invitingly on a rack. Sliding to a halt in front of them, Len turned his lapel around to take out the razor blade hidden beneath.

'Do the machines first,' said Ray sharply.

'OK.' said Len, still hungrily eyeing the coats as he unscrewed the protective casing of the nearest sewing machine. The workings inside were intricate and precisely engineered, but there would be a weak point, there always was. A rustling sound up above him. Then another. Ray had located the blinds over the skylights and was closing them for him. Good. He would need strong artificial light if he were going to do the job properly. Flicking on the standard lamp next to the machine, Len took the two tubes of superglue out from his shirt pocket and laid them on the table. He had picked them up that morning in the market for a pound. Len smiled to himself. The havoc you could wreak for just a quid.

'Here,' said Len curtly to Una. He had found what he was looking for. She approached uncertainly. 'Hold this.'

Whilst she held the casing open for him, Len used the tungsten tipped micro-file to jemmy open the tiniest of gaps in the jacket of the machine's central motor. Inserting the nozzle of the tube, he then slowly and patiently began to squeeze. Within a minute the motor was full – a line of the transparent glue trickling down its metal jacket like spit running down a mouthpiece.

The other machines took less than ten minutes. When the last one was finished, Una leaned her back against the wall, exhausted by the effort of holding up the heavy casings. Like a dog at the feet of its indulgent master, Len gave Ray an excited, begging look. Let me off the leash now – it's got to be time. Ray nodded. Sliding the razor blade back out again, Len stepped forward and slashed each of the coats in turn.

'Shh!'

It was a police siren. Ray held his finger aloft for several seconds. Una closed her eyes in dread. The car sped past without stopping and disappeared into the night.

'Come on. Let's split,' said Ray purposefully.

'What about the poster?' replied Len.

'Quick, then …'

Len had the poster stuffed between his T-shirt and chest, folded four ways. He had picked it up on an anti-vivisection rally in London a year ago. A beagle lay helplessly sprawled out on an operating table, an array of electrodes affixed to its brain. A long way from the leather trade perhaps, but they'd get the message. Besides, it was better than a spray can – daubed slogans always looked crude. Len laid the poster out face down and ran a line of superglue around its perimeter.

'Hold it up against the wall.'

Una stepped forward and held the poster flat against the wall while Len smoothed down the glued surfaces at the sides and bottom.

'OK. Let go.'

Una stood back. Len then extracted the razor blade and sealed it, cutting edge uppermost, between the top edge of the poster and the wall.

'What's that for?' asked Una.

'Give 'em a surprise when they pull it down.'

Len clenched his fingers, making a gesture of tearing the poster down from the wall, and then shook his hand violently, as though the razor blade had scythed deep beneath his own fingernails.

'Oh, no,' said Una. 'I'm not having anything to do with that.'

Len moved towards her menacingly. 'Listen to me, you soft bitch …'

'Leave it out!' interrupted Ray. 'We've gotta get movin'.'

Una dropped them off in the city centre. The pubs had long since closed but she could sense they'd got somewhere lined up to go. Returning to her flat, she switched on the light and looked around the cold, empty room. She had found the whole experience distasteful. No, worse than that, repugnant. Much as she and Ray held objectives in common, she knew he thought of her as little better than a skivvy. And as for Len, she just felt corrupted by his malevolence. Boiling the kettle, she went to make herself a cup of tea, but deciding it might keep her awake, put all the water in her hot water bottle instead. All the same, she could not sleep and her feet still felt cold an hour later.

As Bill parked his car in front of Sykes and Garnier Storage and Distribution Ltd., he looked across the pot-holed courtyard at the vehicles in the depot opposite. There were several articulated lorries, a dozen or so transits and a whole squad of light delivery vans. He had assumed from their name that the firm would be nothing more than a two-man band, but judging from the size of their fleet, they were in fact quite a substantial operation.

The reception area was sparse and functional. On top of the only chair sat a ten kilo metal drum of olive oil with a 'Damaged in Transit' sticker plastered across it.

'I've got an appointment to see the Site Manager, Mr Beckett – at ten o'clock,' said Bill.

'What's it in connection with?' asked the receptionist, who, by the look of her microphone and headset, was also the firm's switchboard operator.

'Er, about the job,' he replied, taking out of his pocket the advertisement he had cut from the Harledge Gazette.

'Oh, right, well, he's just popped off site for a few minutes, actually. Erm, would you like to wait in the canteen? I'll come and get you when he's back. It's just down the end there ...'

'Oh, OK, thanks.'

Walking through the battered swing doors, Bill smiled to himself as he recalled the plush grey and turquoise decor of the Asper staff canteen. By comparison this place was nothing short of a transport café, complete with bare Formica tables and an all male clientele staring up at every stranger who came through the door. Not that he felt intimidated. On the contrary, the smell of fried food and tobacco vividly brought back memories of the bricklayers and labourers his father had employed, in whose company he had spent many happy childhood hours, running errands or helping in the workshop. Having got himself a mug of tea, Bill sat down at the nearest table. The man opposite wordlessly offered him his newspaper. Bill nodded his thanks and turned to the sports pages. Just as he finished reading them, the receptionist appeared and took him to the door of Mr Beckett's office.

'Sorry to have kept you waiting, Mr, er ...'

'Kennedy.'

'Mr Kennedy, that's right. I've got your letter here somewhere ...'

Bill's first impression on entering the office was less of the boss than his room, which seemed crammed to the ceiling with all manner of papers, dockets and advice notes. Computerized documentation systems had obviously not reached this particular corner of the transport industry yet.

'Sit down, sit down.'

'Thanks.'

Beckett was a portly, benign-looking man in his late fifties. The pointed tips of his mustard-coloured waistcoat stuck upwards like a Scotty dog's ears. Bill instantly took to him.

'It's here somewhere,' said Beckett continuing to look through the mass of papers on his desk. 'No. Oh, well, never mind. I'm sure it'll turn up later. Anyway, have you done any drivin' before?'

'No.'

'You got a clean licence?'

'Yeah.'

'References?' Bill handed over the envelope Asper Human Resources had sent him. Beckett nodded his thanks and placed the letter on the edge of his desk, from which it almost straightaway fell off onto the floor. 'You know some of the hours are, like, antisocial, don't you? I mean, you get overtime and days off in lieu and everythin', but ...'

'Yeah, it said in the advert.'

'Missus won't mind, will she? Give you any stick, or anythin'?' enquired Beckett, mildly.

'Not married.'

'Sensible man, sensible man.' Beckett had obviously intended the comment to put Bill at his ease, but his own reference to marriage seemed to unnerve him and he began anxiously hunting around the table for his cigarettes. 'All right. We'll get you doin' some light stuff first. D'you know your way around Harledge?'

'Yeah, yeah. Lived here all my life.'

'Good.' Drawing deeply on the cigarette, Beckett depressed a button on the intercom. 'Irene. Is Brummie in today?'

'Yeah. He's out the back,' came the voice in reply.

'Send him in, will you?' Through the clouds of tobacco smoke, Bill could see Beckett giving him a reassuring smile. 'Brummie'll go round with you for the first week or so. Till you learn the ropes and what have you. The forms don't take much gettin' used to – I'm sure you'll be all right'.

'OK.'

'Just make sure you always get a signature, right? It's the golden rule.'

A slightly uncomfortable silence followed, with Beckett appearing to imply that the interview had come to a close.

'Erm, how much is the, er ... pay?' ventured Bill, after a few moments.

'Oh, right, sorry! Five forty an hour. Double time nights and weekends.'

'That's great. When can I start?'

'Er, I dunno,' said Beckett, scratching his head, 'Tomorrow, if you want to, I suppose. Ah, good. Here comes Brummie. He'll sort you out.'

Bill was delighted with the interview. Anonymous, with flexible working hours and plenty of overtime – Sykes and Garnier was exactly the employer he needed. Walking back towards his car across the courtyard, he felt a wave of awed excitement run through him. Now that he had sorted himself out a full-time job, he could actually start putting his plans into practice. Ever since the inspirational night out with Peter Layford five days previously, he had been wrestling with the question of where best to start. As he climbed in his car to drive back to Harledge, he realized that the decision had now more or less been made for him. Much as it ran contrary to all his experience to start examining the effects of a new chemical entity when he had virtually no idea of its molecular make-up, he simply could not pursue the task of characterizing Libidan's exact chemical structure. For the time being at least, the flask he had smuggled out of Asper would just have to stay in his fridge. He was not an analytical chemist and, if he employed an outside laboratory to attempt the task of identification, the fifteen thousand pounds severance pay from Asper and his modest income from Sykes would be eaten away in no time at all. Instead, he would just have to content himself with reconstructing the reaction conditions that had first produced Libidan back in RM-3, and then testing the isolated product for reproducibility of effect. He was a biochemist and he had a big empty house – those were his strengths and he had to play to them. He would convert his father's old study into a small-scale chemical synthesis unit and the large, unused cloakroom under the stairs into a laboratory for a placebo-controlled study in mice or rats.

Parking in a multi-storey car park in the centre of Harledge, Bill decided to stop in one of the supermarket cafés for brunch. As he walked down the grimy concrete staircase towards the shopping centre, he was still deep in thought. Chemical synthesis had always come naturally to him, so setting up the equipment to isolate the Libidan molecule should be relatively simple. On the other hand, although he understood the principles of placebo-controlled trials well enough and had injected plenty of rats and mice at University, because Asper subcontracted all their animal studies, he had no first-hand experience of either equipping or running an animal laboratory. Passing by Boots the Chemist, he began to wonder whether one or two high street consumables might be pressed into service. So far, he had only thought of ordering what he needed from a medical supplies catalogue, but they would be bound to make a small, private customer pay through the nose, and absolutely every penny of his meagre budget counted. Deciding there was nothing to be lost by looking, he walked through the main entrance into the store. The front half was mostly food and cosmetics, and nothing really caught his eye. The rear section proved altogether more interesting, though, with the first article he saw immediately attracting his attention.

'Have you got a microwave oven, luv?' said the shop assistant pointing to the bottle of sterilising fluid he held in his hand.

'Er, yes, yes,' replied Bill.

'Well, you don't wanna bother with that stuff, then; boiling pans of water 'n' all. I mean, I did with my three. But, oh, it was so much trouble. You're forever scalding yourself on the saucepans, too. Come over here. I'll show you what you want.'

Replacing the bottle on the shelf, Bill followed the assistant deeper into the baby section.

'These things are life-savers,' she confided, with sage authority, 'believe you me.'

The shop assistant was holding up a large, circular plastic box.

'What is it?' asked Bill, curiously.

'It's a microwave steriliser.' She took off the lid. Inside, elevated half an inch above the base, was a moulded plastic grill. 'They're dead easy. You put your bottles on here, half a cup of water in the bottom, three minutes in the microwave, and there you are. Everythin' done.'

Bill looked dumbly down at the price tag. Eight pounds fifty-nine. Industrial autoclaves came in at well over a thousand.

'Erm, do you know if they kill all strains of germs?'

'Yeah! Of course they do! Well, it's the steam, isn't it? They're completely safe, too. Not just for bottles. You can put your teats in there, spoons, even syringes – although they say you're not supposed to re-use them, but everyone does.'

'Do you sell syringes here, too?'

'Hm, for Calpol and the like.'

'What's Calpol?'

The woman threw back her head and let out a whoop of laughter.

'Ooh, you'll soon find out what Calpol is, luv. Half past three in the mornin' when the little blighter's screamin' the house down.' Her laughter quickly abated and she returned to her crooning litany of observation and advice. 'But I suppose you don't know anythin' about that yet. If it's your first one and you're only just buyin' bottles 'n' all. How old's your little one, anyway?'

'Oh, er, only a couple of weeks, but he's growing fast.'

'Oh, bless him,' cooed the woman. 'The syringes are there, but I wouldn't go buyin' any just now if I were you. You can get 'em on prescription.'

'Oh, er, no, I will take a couple, actually. Better to be safe than sorry.' Bill stepped forward and took two syringes off the peg – they were without needles, but seemed extremely sturdy and were marked with very clear gradations.

'As you like. It never hurts to have a few going spare, I suppose. And will you be wanting the steriliser, too?'

'Er, yes, definitely.'

'There are a couple of designs, but they're all basically the same, I'd say ...'

The woman's voice trailed off, leaving Bill to decide. The nearest to hand had a line of toy soldiers across the front. On the bottom shelf, however, was a chunky, mauve-coloured one with the silhouettes of three tailless mice stencilled on the base – no doubt, thought Bill, after the nursery rhyme.

'I'll take that one.'

Bill did not regard his choice as in the least bit macabre. He wasn't going to do anything revolting like cutting off their tails. All the mice on the active compound had to do was copulate – which rodents spend most of their lives doing, anyway – and as for the placebo group, hell, they just had to run around the cage for a couple of weeks. After that, as far as Bill was concerned, they were all free to go.

'Shall I wrap them up for you?'

'Please,' replied Bill,

Winding his way around the rest of the ground floor, Bill proceeded to pick up supplies of rubber gloves and antiseptic wipes as well as two digital thermometers that he was sure could effectively be used to monitor reaction temperatures. By the time he reached the pharmacy he was almost euphoric – the place was simply an Aladdin's cave of consumables. At this rate he could complete the trials for under a hundred pounds. Behind the counter a young Indian shop assistant smiled at him as he approached.

'Hello, may I help you?'

'Yes, I'd like some needles, please.'

'Needles?' replied the woman impassively.

'Yes, hypodermic needles. I got the syringes over there, but they didn't have any needles'

'Just wait a moment, sir, please'

The assistant pressed a buzzer under the counter and a few seconds later a woman, whom Bill took to be the chief pharmacist, came briskly towards them. The combination of her starched white coat and pretty, yet uncompromising features immediately reminded him of Angela.

'This gentleman wants some hypodermic needles.'

'Are you registered with your GP?'

'Yes,' said Bill, wondering what that might have to do with it.

'Well, if you are a registered methadone user you'll understand that it's his responsibility to supply you with needles – or your local rehab clinic. I mean, I can under certain circumstances …'

'No, no!' interrupted Bill, hastily 'I don't want them for that!'

'Oh.' replied the pharmacist, surprised.

'No, no. I'm not a drug addict or anything.'

A moment's pause whilst the two women exchanged a puzzled look.

'So, what do you want them for, then?' asked the pharmacist with apparently genuine interest.

'Er, well …' Bill stared blankly at the two women, 'Nothing really, I, er …'

The pharmacist continued to stare enquiringly at Bill, but he could see that the Indian woman's eyes were beginning to stray towards the burly security guard who stood at the rear entrance to the store.

'No, it's all right. I'll leave it. Sorry to waste your time.'

Lowering his head, Bill scuttled off back towards the front of the store, executing a quick right turn behind the refrigerated sandwich display in the hope of getting out of sight as soon as possible. His heart was pumping as he reached the street outside. Fighting back the impulse to break into a run, he slipped down a side alley that eventually led into a square, deserted save for an old woman feeding the pigeons. Sitting down on a bench, he looked back down the alley. He had not been followed but, nevertheless, his behaviour had been stupid and careless in the extreme. Running through the events in his mind again, he tried to calculate whether he had acted suspiciously enough for the pharmacists to want to check with any of the other sections in the store where he had made a purchase. They had his credit card number, so effectively they had his address. Deciding he had probably got away with it, Bill stood up and began to make his way back to the car. The trials he intended to conduct in his house were illegal for a whole variety of reasons. Next time, he really was going to have to be more careful.

'D'you want some toy?'

'Pardon?' asked Bill.

'A cuppa toy,' replied Brummie, changing down into third gear and pointing at the still-bolted gates up ahead. 'Looks loike we're twirly for goods inwards.'

'Er, yeah, why not?'

Ignoring the no-U-turn sign on the central reservation, Brummie swung the van around on to the opposite side of the dual carriageway, causing the six copper water tanks in the back of the truck to bounce around like so many fairground skittles.

'Are those things OK?' asked Bill, righting himself from the G force of the turn.

'I dunno. I s'pose so,' replied Brummie, seemingly a little startled by the question, as though the connection between the way he drove the van and the condition of the articles he had to deliver was being brought to his attention for the first time.

'What time's the place supposed to open, then?' asked Bill, looking back across the road at the as yet unopened DIY superstore.

'Noyne, usually.' Although his right indicator was still blinking, Brummie suddenly moved into the left-hand lane, cutting up several drivers behind in the process. The man clearly drove as he spoke, with a considerable degree of ambiguity. Turning into the Leys Industrial Estate, he then slowed down and pulled into a lay-by, at the far end of which was a small and surprisingly hygienic-looking tea wagon.

'How d'you take it?' asked Bill, conscious that the onus was on him, as the novice, to do the fetching and carrying.

'Oooh, tar. Woite with,' said Brummie, switching off the engine and taking a tabloid newspaper out from between the windscreen and the top of the dashboard.

'So, you was at Asper before, then?'

'Yeah, yeah.'

'What did you do?'

'I was a chemist.'

'Ooh, ah?' Brummie took another sip from the large polystyrene cup and then slid down a little in his seat to get more comfortable. 'Must be a bit of a comedown, though, this. Wor'appened?'

Coming from many people, such a question would probably have seemed prying or even confrontational. Looking across at his new found partner's shaggy beard and teddy bear face, Bill was surprised at how genuinely considerate the enquiry sounded.

'A woman,' said Bill simply.

'Well, if you're lookin' for a choinge you've come to the royte plice,' smiled Brummie, ruefully 'Not much bint on this job.'

'No?'

'Nah!' said Brummie, before pausing and then observing casually, 'There's other perks, loike, though.'

'Yeah?'

'Yeah, from the deliveries. If you know wor' I mean..'

Bill turned to look at Brummie – it was plain to what he was referring.

'Oh, right,' said Bill.

'Yeah. We all look afta each other. The droivers. If you need anythin', just let me know.'

Bill thought for several seconds, then decided to follow the voice of his instinct.

'Ha, well, it's funny you should mention that ...'

'Hm?'

'I'm sort of, well, in need of some ... hypodermic needles.'

'How many?'

'A couple of boxes ...' Inwardly Bill winced at how this might sound. Brummie merely nonchalantly swigged down the last of his tea and switched the engine back on again.

'No problem, kidda.'

Ever since Gail's message on his answering machine, Bill had given a good deal of thought as to the reasons that he should cite for his departure from Asper. With Brummie – or anyone else at Sykes' who might care to enquire – he had decided simply to come clean: deliverymen got around, and if it was discovered Bill had fabricated an excuse, suspicions could well be aroused. Returning from his first full day's work at Sykes' to find yet another message from his sister, however, he resolved, in her case, to be somewhat more economical with the truth. Apart from Bill himself, Gail no longer had any friends or connections in Harledge who might inadvertently cast doubt on his story.

'Hi, it's me.'

'Bill! Where the devil are you?'

So charged with urgency was her voice that the receiver seemed almost to want to leap out of his hand. Same old Gail.

'At home.'

'I've been trying to get you all week. What's happened? I mean, is it true? Have you really left Asper?'

'Yeah, last Tuesday,' replied Bill, doing his best to sound offhand.

'What on earth for?'

'They promoted Mold ahead of me. And then they were going to kick me out of my lab, too – stick me in some new building or other.'

'When did you decide this, then? You never mentioned anything when we were down.'

'I didn't know they were going to do it when you were down. They just dumped it on me on Tuesday morning. I walked out on the spot. Thin end of the wedge, I reckon.'

'Bill, I'm amazed.'

'What, didn't think I had it in me? I didn't either, I suppose.'

'What are you going to do?'

'Oh, don't worry, I'm not going to starve. I've got another job already.'

'Thank God for that. Is it research again or what?'

'No. Driving a van.'

'What!'

'Yeah, a place called Sykes'.'

'Bill, you're a biochemist, not a …'

'I know, I know!' interrupted Bill, 'But don't worry. It's only temporary. I'll find something better soon. Although, I must say I'm quite enjoying the work all the same …'

Replacing the receiver several minutes later, his sister's anxieties duly calmed, Bill felt a warm feeling of satisfaction spread through him. Despite the fact that she was several years his junior, he had always been slightly in awe of Gail, and this was the first conversation they had had in years where he felt able to assert his own opinions. Of course, he had felt obliged to omit one crucial and overwhelming fact, but the main thrust of what he had said was completely true. He did resent Asper's not allowing him to conduct his research in the manner he felt appropriate. He was engaged in the pursuit of something better. On the crest of this wave of self-confidence, Bill made his way into the study. He had moved his computer in there before leaving for work that morning and, as he entered the room and switched on the lights, he felt a thrill of satisfaction at how it made the room look like a real laboratory. Within moments his sister was far from his thoughts, as he connected up to the Medibase Internet search engine, entering the double key words 'human reproduction' and 'animal models'.

Albertstown had effectively become part of Harledge during a period of urban sprawl in the nineteen eighties, but its pre-war architecture still made it look very different from the rest of the city. Nothing like the parade of shops, with its slip-road at the front and two storeys of residential flats above, existed anywhere else in Harledge, and, as Bill parked his car amongst the first of the Monday morning shoppers, he very much felt himself in terra incognita. The pet shop itself was one of those old-fashioned retail outlets, with a long, angled window extending into its interior to create a greater frontage. Shoppers would sometimes shelter from the rain in the porch this created. On his guard after the Boots experience, he peered suspiciously through the condensation that had formed on the window in the early morning cold. It was a small, local affair – just like he had thought. A faded yellow sign, suspended on the inside of the door, had a monkey holding up a banana on which was written 'Everypet is open.'

'Good morning, can I help you?'

The shop assistant was bending over cleaning out a cage, whilst its occupant – a scaly, green reptile of some sort that Bill took to be a gecko – rested in brooding quiescence on top of her head. Bill was immediately struck by the similarity between their long, pointed noses. He wondered if such resemblances were an occupational hazard for pet shop owners.

'Oh, er yes, I'd like to buy some guinea-pigs, please.'

'Come on then, Pete, let's get you back inside.' Flicking out its tongue in a token gesture of annoyance, the reptile then obediently let itself be put back through the cage door. 'Right, if you'd like to come this way …'

Wiping her hands on her blue, chequered overall the woman gave Bill a restive smile and moved deeper into the shop. Following her,

100

Bill looked around. Crammed with animals from floor to ceiling, Everypet was indeed a most appropriately named establishment. He wondered what the place would sound like if they all started to screech at once.

'We've got a pair over here, actually. Are they for your children?'

'Er, no, I don't want to buy any of the ones you've got in stock. I want you to order some for me.'

'The woman turned and raised her eyebrows in surprise.

'Oh … ?'

'Yes, I want a particular breed you see. And a particular number of males and females of certain ages.'

'Well, I'm sure we can make some enquiries for you, but …'

'Thanks,' added Bill hurriedly, 'I thought a small shop like you might help me. I mean, there's one of those pet superstores in town but I reckoned they'd just want to sell me what they'd got.'

'Yes, well, that's them all over,' said the woman with sudden, unexpected vehemence. 'They treat their animals just like … just like commodities. Shuffle 'em around the place like so many tins of baked beans!'

'Well, exactly,' said Bill – imagining the impact the superstore must have had on this small family business – 'that's why I came to you.'

'Yes … well …' The woman gradually began to calm herself down. 'What type of guinea-pig did you want?'

'*Cavia Porcellus* – Peruvian Satin,' said Bill, taking a sheet of paper, on which he had carefully written the name, from his raincoat pocket. 'Six months to a year old.' The optimum age for a robust pharmacological study, thought Bill to himself. The woman squinted a little at the paper and then nodded her head in recognition.

'I know the ones you mean. How many did you say you wanted?'

'Eight.'

'Eight!'

'Two males, six females.'

'You're not thinking of putting them all in the same cage, are you?' asked the woman, her brow furling in concern. 'They'll tear each other to pieces.'

'No, no!' replied Bill quickly, 'they'd go bonkers, I know that; the males especially.'

'We're very concerned about the homes our animals go to, you know.'

'I'm sure you are. No, I'll be needing eight separate cages, too. The biggest ones you've got.'

'Oh, well. OK. You do realize all this is going to cost a pretty penny, don't you?'

'How much would you say?' replied Bill. 'Roughly.'

Bill looked at the woman's face as she totalled up the amounts in her head. He wouldn't be surprised if she ended up closing the shop early today – this was probably the biggest order she had had all year.

'Eight or nine hundred pounds at least. I'll have to talk to our supplier, though.'

'Could you give me a call? I mean, that sounds about right, but I'd just like to know,' said Bill, handing the sheet of paper over to the woman and pointing to his name and phone number at the top. 'Leave a message on the machine if I'm not there.'

'Well, all right.'

'How long before you can get them, do you think?'

'Well, as I say, they're not unusual, so I guess we're looking at about a week. Ten days.'

'Brilliant,' said Bill nodding cheerfully.

'Have you got many other pets?' asked the woman, quizzically.

'No.' replied Bill, casually moving into his prepared spiel, 'but I've always wanted to keep guinea-pigs since I was a kid, and I just came into a bit of money recently, so I thought, why not?'

It must have sounded plausible. For, although the woman blinked crankily, seeming to turn the whole thing over in her mind for several seconds, she then moved behind the counter to pick up the telephone.

'Well, I'll give my suppliers a call now, then.'

Climbing back into his car, Bill hastily checked the time. He had rung and ordered a scientific supplies catalogue two days previously, but the post had still not arrived by the time he had left to go to Everypet. Would he have time to nip back home and still be able to clock on at Sykes' at ten? He decided to give it a try.

Leaving the engine running, Bill jumped out of the car and opened up the front porch. Excellent. It had arrived. Ripping the polythene wrapper open with his teeth, Bill flicked through the catalogue as he drove to Sykes'. The evaporation temperature was clearly a critical control parameter, so a top-of-the-range heating unit would be essential

– it would certainly have to be more reliable than the one in RM-3. In addition, to separate out the peptide fragments he was going to need a reverse phase chromatographic column. Pulling into the main gate at Sykes', Bill parked and switched off the engine. He still had five minutes to spare. The heating unit was no problem and he found a suitable model straightaway. However, the chromatographic systems all proved to be way beyond his budget and Bill groaned as he ran his finger down the price list. Just as he was beginning to despair, though, he found the schools and colleges section at the back of the catalogue. There was a kit. A budget priced, self-assembly system designed especially for the young chemist. It was perfect. He didn't need the bells and whistles on the expensive systems anyway – just a functioning column would do. Locking the catalogue in his glove compartment, Bill made his way across to the front entrance. After a few paces, Brummie approached from the other side of the car park and fell into step with him.

'Ulroyt?' asked Brummie, cheerily.

'Yeah, great, you?'

'Foyne. 'Ere, I got them needles you was afta.'

'Did you? Oh thanks. How much do I owe you?'

'Forget it,' said Brummie with a shake of the head. 'Dain't cost me nothin'.'

'Cheers, mate.'

'I'll bring 'em in tomorra. Fancy a nose bag?'

'A what?'

'Y'know – food.'

'Have we got time?'

'Yeah. 'Course.'

Following Brummie into the main entrance, Bill smiled to himself happily. Hypodermics for free. Thirty quid in Boots. Thirteen hundred pounds for the instruments and glassware. Add in, say, nine hundred for the guinea pigs and that would still only make just over two thousand pounds. With a smile at Irene, the receptionist, Bill made his way down the corridor with Brummie towards the welcoming warmth of the canteen. The spending was mounting up, all right, but was still well under control.

Una did decide to close the shop early that evening, but not because of the day's takings. There was an Animal Liberation Army meeting at six o'clock, but it was over an hour's drive away and she had promised to pick up Ray and Len in plenty of time. Closing the blinds and retreating into the shop, she examined the piece of paper the man had given her and wondered if she should mention him that night. Finally, she decided against it. Not that his behaviour hadn't been desperately suspicious. The way he had peered in through the window, for a start. She had seen dozens of men doing exactly the same at that horrid Sex Shop at the other end of the parade. And then eight Peruvian Satins? No one buys eight pedigree guinea-pigs all at one go unless they're up to something. Besides, she knew a fellow animal-lover when she saw one, and he definitely was not in the class. No. The problem was she didn't have a clue what he might be up to and Ray was a stickler for evidence. Switching off the lights and checking the thermostat a second time, Una made her way up the stairs to her flat above.

For the time being at least, she would just have to content herself with keeping an eye on the sinister Dr William Kennedy.

Chapter 6

The equipment was delivered a week later. Bill had just completed a five-day shift – returning in the small hours from an overnight to Leeds – and was still asleep when the van arrived mid-morning. Having slid the two bulky boxes down the hall and into the lab, he fetched a carving knife from the kitchen and began eagerly, but carefully, to scythe through the layers of brown masking tape. The first box contained the glassware and the heating unit, which he straightaway took out and plugged in at the wall – it had arrived in perfect working order. As he levered the chromatographic column out of the polystyrene packing of the second box, however, it suddenly occurred to him that it only func-tioned in an upright position and that he had neither the framework nor the clamps required to achieve this.

'Damn,' he cursed, under his breath. At Asper he just rang central stores whenever he needed any rigging.

Pushing the column safely back into place, Bill went off to look for something suitable in the house. He could find nothing and, after ten minutes, returned somewhat disappointed to the lab. Looking through the rest of the box, he was pleased to discover that the suppliers had included a thick, free-of-charge instruction booklet. It had been years since he had set up a chromatographic system from scratch and the book appeared to provide an ideal refresher course. Walking through to the kitchen, he began to read it while he fixed himself a cup of tea. Just as the kettle boiled, the telephone rang

'Hallo?' A woman's voice. Loud.

'Hallo.'

'Dr Kennedy?'

'Yes.'

'It's Una Arnold. From Everypet.'

'Oh, hallo, Mrs Arnold, how are you today?' said Bill, wincing and holding the receiver a couple of inches away from his ear.

'It's Miss Arnold, actually, and I'm all right. I want to bring the guinea-pigs around on Friday.'

'Oh, yes, great. What time?'

'Lunch-time. If that's convenient.'

'Yeah, sure.'

'Now. Tell me. Have you got your alfalfa yet?'

'My what?'

'Your alfalfa.'

'Er, no, what's that?'

A long, mistrustful silence followed. Mentally, Bill kicked himself: he was going to have to be quicker off the mark than that if he didn't want a repeat of the Boots incident.

'Do you know anything about keeping guinea-pigs, Dr Kennedy?'

'Yes, of course, I do,' lied Bill.

'Have you bought any food for them? Anything at all?'

'Yes.' said Bill quickly, in an attempt to sound convincing. The ensuing silence, however, merely challenged him to describe precisely what.

'Erm … biscuits and nuts …' Still no response. What did the damn things eat? ' … and some fruit.'

The sound of Miss Arnold exhaling – fruit must have been the right answer.

'All right, Dr Kennedy,' she said, begrudgingly. 'I'll bring some alfalfa with me – guinea-pigs do thrive on fruit but they also require plenty of natural fibre. I'll let you have some hay, too, for the cages. I hope the room you intend to put them in is not too hot or stuffy. Guinea-pigs are extremely susceptible to heat exhaustion, you know.'

'Yes, yes. They live in burrows in the wild, don't they?' replied Bill, a flash of secondary-school Biology suddenly returning to him. 'Which is how they stay out of the sun most of the time,' he added, feebly.

'See you on Friday lunch-time,' came Miss Arnold's stony response.

Frowning, Bill replaced the telephone. So far, he had given plenty of thought to experimental protocol for the guinea-pigs, but none to their general welfare. The nosey pet shop woman had a point – these were living creatures and as such warranted his full respect. Besides, they were not going to generate valid experimental data in unhealthy conditions. The first thing he would do that afternoon was visit Harledge Library – there was bound to be a book on keeping guinea-pigs somewhere in the pets section. After that, he would stop by the ironmongers his father had always used to pick up some clamps and steel tubing. Deciding to forego the cup of tea, Bill made his way back upstairs to catch up on the rest of his sleep. Setting up the equipment that evening was going to be quite a task.

In the end, it took him just under three hours. Hands on hips, Bill stared with satisfaction at the chromatographic column and its array of distil-lation feeder pipes, now soundly supported by a custom-built metal framework. Unlocking the cupboard in the corner of the room, he extracted the phial containing the hormone fragment and began to measure out a hundred grams, just as he had done on that Friday after-noon at Asper a little over three weeks previously. As he added the sol-vents to the reaction vessel, his thoughts again turned to the likely molecular structure of the compound that the deprotection procedure had somehow gone on to produce. The fragment itself was made up of eight amino acids in a chain. Up until now, he had assumed that heating had snapped the chain in two, one half of which had then undergone a further chemical reaction with the solvents. But what if the thermal shock had been so severe that the chain had ruptured in several places, the individual links reforming into a variety of smaller chains, only one of which was pharmacologically active? If that was so, he might have to effect the deprotection reaction dozens of times and then carry out numerous separations before the active compound could be isolated. Bill looked at his watch. He was tired. The likelihood of this first run producing anything conclusive was fairly remote. Maybe he would be better off facing the disappointment in the morning.

'Nah. Let's do it now,' he said to himself – after all, he had the whole of the next day free and could sleep late if necessary.

Sealing the reaction vessel as tightly as he could, Bill placed it on top of the heating element. For several seconds he stared at the upward pointing triangle on the green, soft-touch switch and then, finally, placed his finger on it and pressed. The digits on the LCD dial strobed rapidly upwards. At ninety-four degrees he stopped and stood back. In a little under two minutes the mixture began to bubble and he watched, fascinated, as vapour began to form, rise and then creep along the condenser towards the column. After five minutes, a time more or less equivalent, he guessed, to that which had elapsed before he had turned off the equipment in the Asper lab, Bill cut the power from the heating element.

'Yes!'

Slowly, and one by one, beads of a clear, colourless liquid began to drop into the column. Something had evidently passed through the vapour phase and was condensing as a liquid, although Bill had no proof that it was the same substance that had escaped in RM-3: what he was witnessing now might simply be the evaporation of the two solvents. After staring at the chromatograph for a further fifteen minutes, Bill rubbed his eyes, leaned forward and unscrewed the tiny receiver vessel containing several millilitres of elute. Stoppering it tightly, he marked it 0001 with a black stylo pen and then placed it on top of the fridge.

'Go again, I guess. But first … cleaning.'

It took twenty minutes to disassemble and clean the feeder pipes, dousing them firstly with an ethanol, and then a water wash. He had one batch – of something – but now he had to perform the deprotection reaction again, and then compare the two elutes. As far as Bill could tell from the temperature probes and visual observation, the second reaction proceeded in an identical fashion. He looked at his watch. Five past midnight. He would mark the second test tube 0002, put it in the refrigerator and then get some sleep.

'Holy shit!'

Throwing out a hand and grabbing the standard lamp, Bill swung it around and shone it on the first test tube, 0001, which all the while had been gradually cooling on top of the refrigerator.

'Wow …'

His eyes had not deceived him. There, around the tube's meniscus, where the curved upper surface of the liquid met the glass wall, a fine white line had formed. The experiment had not produced solvent alone – that was now absolutely certain.

Something inside had begun to crystallise.

The cages were enormous and the pet shop woman was only able to ferry them from her van one at a time. Under normal circumstances,

Bill would have offered to do this, but the last thing he wanted was to give her half a chance to poke her head inside the house. Taking each cage off her at the porch, he lined them up along the hallway, resolving to transfer them to the cloakroom under the stairs as soon as he was able to get rid of her.

'Right, well, that's the last one, Mrs, er, Miss Arnold. Thank you very much.'

'Did you, er, phew …' steadying herself against the porch, she fought to regain her breath, '..did you check the temperature of the room where you're going to … ?'

'Thermostatically maintained at twenty five degrees C,' interrupted Bill, rattling off one of several passages he had memorised from *The Essential Guide to Guinea-Pigs*. 'With the lights left on at night more closely to mimic the natural sleeping environment.'

Miss Arnold was unable to hide her surprise. Ha! Got you, thought Bill, gleefully.

'And what about ventilation?'

'Ammonia from their urine can cause respiratory distress – I know. The room is fully ventilated. Also, I've bought some vitamins to ensure a balanced diet. Oh, and talking of balances, here's the outstanding payment I owe you,' saying which, Bill thrust towards Miss Arnold the envelope he had prepared in advance containing seven hundred and seventy pounds in cash. 'Do please count it.'

'No, I'm sure it's all there,' replied Una, now even more certain that this smarmy youth was hiding something inside his sinister, gothic mansion.

'Right, well, thanks again …' said Bill, slowly closing the door.

'Er, Dr Kennedy …'

'Yes?'

'You will call me if you need anything, won't you?'

'Oh, rest assured,' replied Bill, with a smile as sweet as lemons.

After peering through the curtains to make certain her van actually did drive away, Bill moved the guinea-pigs one by one into the cloakroom. Even without the advice in 'The Essential Guide', he had guessed they would need a while to settle in and so, having arranged their cages in two sets of four along the broad shelving on the left side of the room, he topped up each of the animal's gravity-fed water dispensers and retired to let them acclimatize in peace.

Returning later that afternoon, Bill found them all asleep save for one of the males, who waddled across the cage at his approach and poked his nose inquisitively through the bars. Bill had already decided to place this particular guinea-pig in the active group, for although he was the same age as the other male, he appeared considerably larger and more muscular.

'I bet you could stand up to anything in the bonking department, couldn't you?' said Bill, tickling the animal's soft pink nose. 'A regular little Hercules, aren't you, eh?' As though in confirmation, the guinea-pig inclined his head at an angle and began vigorously to gnaw at Bill's fingertip.

'Well, that's you christened for a start,' observed Bill, allowing Hercules to continue his chewing. 'What about your wives?' He looked around at the six sleeping females. What had been his history teacher's aide memoire? Divorced, beheaded, died. Divorced, beheaded, survived. Bill smiled to himself. Nice one. He could even name them in the chronological order that he introduced them into Hercules' cage.

'But don't worry girls. Absolutely no one gets their heads cut off in this household ... which just leaves you.' Bill moved his face closer to the second male's cage and was surprised to find that although seemingly coiled up asleep in a ball of hay, he was, in fact, eagerly eyeing the female in the next cage.

'Ooh, you bender. And you're supposed to have been neutered.'

Folding his arms, Bill stood back and looked at the cages. Although he had already made up the trial syringes that morning, the advice in 'The Essential Guide' was very clear. Guinea-pigs formed complex social hierarchies in the wild, and even though spaying and neutering stopped the production of hormones that resulted in serious fights, suddenly thrusting one into another's cage could still produce a tussle. The next few days, therefore, would have to be taken up with carefully introducing each of the animals to the others until a natural pecking order emerged. Then, and only then, when all animosities had been removed, could Bill see whether Libidan reawakened the female's desire to breed.

'Here, Brummie. Have you got a minute?'

'Hey! Ulroyt, boss? How you gooin?' called out Brummie, his happy, booming voice echoing around the warehouse. 'Just gissa sec and oil come royt down.'

'Shh! Not so loud!' hissed Beckett, looking nervously up and down the darkened aisles. Thankfully, no one else seemed to be about. 'It's all right, I'll come up to you.'

'Oh, OK, boss,' replied Brummie.

Heaving himself the ten feet up the aluminium ladder, Beckett joined Brummie on the second tier of racking.

'What you doing up here anyway? I've been looking for you everywhere.'

'Covering up the markings on this lot. There's been a right cock-up.'

'Yeah?' Easing himself off the ladder, Beckett walked forward and examined the sturdy blue plastic drums that Brummie had positioned out of sight right up against the warehouse wall. 'What is this stuff, anyway?'

'It's supposed to be acetone, but the customer sent it out as benzyl cyanide by mistake,' replied Brummie, peeling off a large, orange label and slapping it over the stencilled markings on the side of the keg.

'Isn't that explosive?'

'Nah, its just class one caustic.'

'Yeah?'

'The bloke's shittin' himself all the same. He sent these masking labels around half an hour agoo by courier. Paperwork don't match the goods. Transport police'd 'ave his bollocks off if they caught him on a spot check.'

'So, what're we gonna do with the stuff?'

'Hang on to it for a couple of days. Till he can get it marked up proper. There we go!' Slapping on the last of the labels, Brummie turned and grinned at his boss. 'Saved his bacon.'

'Well done, Brummie. Keep 'em sweet, eh?.'

'No problem, boss. Besoides, I've got him payin' double warehouse charges, anyway.'

'Ha! Great. Now listen, I've got a favour to ask you.'

'Oh, ah?'

With another furtive glance around the warehouse, Beckett leaned forward to within a few inches of Brummie's face.

'It's Mrs Beckett,' he whispered. 'I was home a bit, like, late last night. She's gone all suspicious on me again.'

'Oh, God, no. Not again. It was terrible last toyme.'

'I know! I know!' replied Beckett, fearfully wiping the flat of his hand across his stubbled chin. 'But look, I, er, told her that I was out with you. So, if she asks you about it, I mean, would you back me up? Like you did before.'

'No problem, boss. Where was we and what did we do?'

'Drinking at the Prince, in Harledge – till half nine.'

'Oh.' replied Brummie – his face dropping slightly in concern, 'I ain't never been in there. It's supposed to be dead posh insoide, innit?'

'Well, if she quizzes you on the place, just use your imagination. Or, or, pop in one lunch-time or something.'

'Yeah, yeah. OK, boss. I'll think of summit.'

'You're a mate, Brummie. Listen, I won't forget this, all right?'

Lowering himself back down to floor level again, Beckett straightened his tie and with a final wink at Brummie walked briskly off towards the main goods–inwards area. Heaving a heavy tarpaulin over the twelve plastic drums, Brummie then rested up against one of the uprights of the metal shelving and smiled to himself. Lying for the boss. Lying to the boss. Same difference.

Benzyl cyanide was indeed caustic. But, more to the point, as a precursor in the synthesis of amphetamines, it was also a controlled substance.

'I name thee … Catherine of Aragon.'

Bill had been thinking of this line for days, but now that he was actually going to inject the female and put her inside Hercules' cage, it didn't seem quite so funny any more. In truth, he was scared of hurting either of these two little bundles of fur whose friendship he had been fostering so assiduously for nearly a week. Dousing her belly with an antiseptic wipe, Bill forced himself to concentrate. The very least he owed this creature was the steady hand of clinical diligence. The needle slipped in easily and Catherine did not even flinch. Thank God for that. Bill stroked her head. At less than 0.1 of a milligram – almost the lowest limit of sensitivity of his newly acquired vacuum weighing machine – this was just the first experiment in an ascending dose study. It was highly unlikely anything would happen until he increased the concentration of Libidan at least a hundredfold.

Wiping her stomach for a second time to be absolutely sure to avoid infection, Bill let Catherine into Hercules' cage and closed the door. Turning around, he quickly picked up the yellow plastic water pistol he had purchased from his local newsagents in case anything untoward should happen. According to 'The Essential Guide', there was nothing like a quick blast of cold water to separate a pair of fighting guinea-pigs, and nothing as effective as a child's water pistol for administering it. At first, Catherine stood stock-still, as though sensing some difference between this visit to Hercules' cage and those she had made hitherto. By way of greeting, Hercules brushed his nose against hers, but receiving no response wandered off to play with the toilet roll in the corner of the cage.

Suddenly, and without any hint of what she intended, Catherine raised herself up on to her haunches and jumped a full five inches into the air. Dropping the water pistol in disbelief, Bill watched her purposefully walk towards Hercules, who, with his head now firmly stuffed inside the cardboard spool, remained completely oblivious to her approach. Snapping out of his surprised trance, Bill quickly reached down to pick up the pistol, but changing his mind mid-movement, stretched across instead to grab 'The Essential Guide'.

'What did it say, what did it say?'

There was a paragraph about leaping in there somewhere – he was certain he had seen it. Here! Eyes flicking backwards and forwards between the book and Catherine's slow, inexorable advance, Bill read aloud. 'The term jumping for joy could well have been coined by a guinea-pig owner because this is a typical expression of happiness. Young guinea-pigs are especially known for "popcorning" where they leap upwards and …'

Bill was not able to read any further. With all the abandon of a wedding-night bride, Catherine launched herself at the exposed haunches of the male guinea-pig who immediately pulled himself back out of the toilet roll, whiskers twitching in consternation. Cooing furiously, she gambolled backwards and forwards over his back, but, finding this produced no result, then started to thrust her groin up against his. Bill pointed the water pistol at the cage and aimed – this was surely going to turn into the ugly territorial scrap he had feared. Hercules, however, seemed very quickly to become indifferent to Catherine's attentions and, within the space of just a few moments, resumed his investigations of the toilet roll, like the coolest hunk on the beach brushing off the babes to concentrate on his surf board.

Lowering the water pistol, Bill stood and stared at the cage, remaining unmoved even when several seconds later droplets of water began to drip from the nozzle and wet the front of his trousers.

Point one of a milligram, even for a guinea-pig, was a microscopically small dosage.

'Hiya, it's me.'

'Gail! How are you?' replied Louise, happily clutching the receiver more tightly to her ear.

'Oh, I'm all right. Everyone else in the office is dying of flu, mind you, but I'm OK.'

'Is that where you are now?'

'Yeah, there's only me and two of the secretaries in, so I thought I'd give you a call. Are you still on for the weekend?'

'Oh, you bet.'

'When are you off to Warwick?'

'After lunch – about an hour or so.'

'Yeah? Oh, it's just as well I called. Are you looking forward to the course, then?'

'Yes,' answered Louise, dropping her voice, 'not least to get out of the office – the place is driving me mad.'

'What's the matter?'

'Well, you know that new project I told you about?'

'Yeah?'

'All gone belly up, hasn't it?'

'Oh, no … and you said it was going so well.'

'Well, it was as long as I was in charge of it. As soon as it started to look like a runner, though, it got hijacked, didn't it? The boss steps in and decides it was his baby after all. Until he screws up, of course, at which point the whole thing immediately reverts to me again.'

'Oh, what a drag …'

'Yeah, well. Worse things happen at sea. Anyway, have you rung Bill yet?'

'I couldn't reach him: I just left a message on his answering machine. I don't suppose he's going anywhere, though, so I guess it's all still on.'

'Hasn't he found another job yet, then?' asked Louise, her voice filling with concern as she remembered his many kindnesses towards her during the weekend at Wyburn.

'I don't think so. But I wouldn't worry. I mean, last time we spoke he sounded fine. It's amazing – if you'd told me that six months ago I'd never've believed you: he used to be mad about Asper.'

'Well, I suppose we'll get the latest on Friday. What's the arrangements, then?'

'I'm getting that same train from London we got before,' replied Gail.

'Six thirty-five?'

'Yeah, that's it – so I'll be along about half-seven. What about you?'

'Well, we're not supposed to finish until six, so, I don't know …'

'Six! On the last day!'

'Yeah.'

'Bastards!'

'Oh, they want their pound of flesh, all right. So, I guess about eight, eight-thirty. I looked up the train times – it takes about an hour and a half.'

'We'll come and pick you up at Harledge East,' replied Gail, quickly.

'Well, I tell you what, don't hang around at the station, get on home to Wyburn and I'll take a cab up.'

'No!'

'No, it's all right. It says six but it might be later; there's no point in the two of you waiting around at the station for hours.'

'OK, if you're sure.'

'Yeah, yeah, I'll be more comfortable knowing I can take my time. I'll give you a call if I'm going to be really late, though, all right?'

'Fine, fine. Well, see you then!'

'Bye.'

'Oh, bloody hell!' groaned Bill, switching off the answering machine. So much had happened in the past four weeks that Gail and Louise's planned visit had completely slipped his mind. Even though all the actual experimentation went on in the two rooms at the back of the house, the rest of it was still littered with incriminating material. He scanned the living room around him: equipment packaging stacked up behind the sofa; medical supplies catalogues strewn over the table; two bright red play balls in the middle of the carpet where he had been familiarizing Bender and Anne of Cleves ready for the first of the placebo trials. He couldn't put Gail off at only two days' notice – she'd go ballistic. There was nothing for it. He would simply have to tidy everything up. Thankfully, he finished at Sykes' at two on Friday: he would go over the place with a fine toothcomb in the afternoon before they arrived. Right now, he had one last important experiment to carry out. Wolfing down the sandwich he had bought for his lunch, he washed his hands in the kitchen and made his way to the lab.

Unscrewing the cap of a one-litre flask, he slowly began filling it with distilled water. The previous dilution had reduced the concentration of Libidan down to between one and ten parts per million, yet it had still shown activity. With the addition to the masterbatch of another nine hundred millilitres he would be moving into the realms of parts per billion. Stirring the vessel for several minutes, Bill siphoned five millilitres off into a syringe and held the colourless liquid up to the light. It couldn't possibly be effective at this level.

Ten minutes after injection, Catherine of Aragon had still not reacted in any way. Taking her gently from Hercules' cage, Bill returned her to her own and sat down on the cloakroom's single stool deep in thought. Although he had decided at the outset not to attempt the expensive practical analytical tests required to characterize the Libidan molecule, he had never given up trying to calculate its structure theoretically. It couldn't be anything but a short amino acid chain – a di or tripeptide. Similar compounds were already used quite widely in medicine and were known to be highly active. Their solubility and bioavailability, however, were generally very poor. How was Libidan able to be potent at such tremendously low levels and for such protracted periods? Those were the two key questions. For the umpteenth time, Bill took up a paper and pen and sketched out the sequence of eight amino acids that made up the hormone fragment. What on earth could be happening to it? After staring at the formula for several fruitless minutes, he screwed the paper up into a ball and threw it at the bin. It missed. He sat with his arms folded, watching the paper slowly uncrumple on the lab floor.

Whether his brain somehow related the ball of paper to the problem with which it had been wrestling for over a month, or whether it was just chance that the breakthrough came at that particular moment, Bill would never know. But at that precise instant, he finally understood with complete and total certainty the structure of the compound.

'It's not a chain, it's a bracelet …'

There could be no other explanation consistent with the facts. He had been so hung up on the idea that the chain had broken into smaller pieces that he had failed to consider the possibility that a spherical struc-

116

ture could have formed. Amino acids two and three were bonding together with seven and eight to form a cyclic ring. That was it. Walking quickly into the lab next door, he took down the Merck Index and flicked through the pages until he reached the K's.

He was right. There was the exact chemical structure. Libidan was kintamane – a quatraneuropeptide produced in the brain in response to sexual stimuli. A relatively simple, well-characterized substance, known to scientists for nearly two decades. What medical science had no reason to suspect, though, was that it possessed extra cerebral activity. He rested his hands on the desktop and stared out through the room's single window at the sky outside. Somewhere in the central nervous system, left over from the time when sexual attraction amongst the human race's distant mammalian ancestors had been effected by pheromonal means, a receptor still existed. And absolutely no one knew it was there.

Frowning, Bill scratched his chin. This explained Libidan's mode of action, but what about its bioavailability? How come onset occurred in minutes and the effects lasted for hours? No sooner had the question formed in his mind, than a second wave of revelation flooded over him, and he held on to the side of the desk, dizzy with the continuing euphoria of discovery. Having produced the cyclic ring, the heating process must then be going on to bond it to the protecting sugar released at one end of the chain. That explained why Angela had been able to absorb the substance through her lungs. Not only was Libidan extremely pharmacologically active when it reached the receptor, it also had a highly efficient delivery system to transport it there. Bill took a deep breath as the ramifications of his hypothesis began to dawn on him. If Libidan acted on the central nervous system, and if it was a struc-turally-robust cyclic peptide, then there was every reason to assume that as a drug substance it could be administered by the most universally popular method of all.

Orally.

Bill's sense of elation stayed with him for the rest of the day and, when he returned his delivery van to the depot at eight o'clock that evening, his head was still buzzing with excitement. Dropping off the day's dockets and advice notes, he caught sight of Brummie through the window of the reception loading up a truck in the main despatch area. Quickly grabbing his coat, Bill made his way across the courtyard just in time to catch him slapping the flank of the truck as it moved away.

'Hey, Brummie, d'you want a point?'

'Do I want a what?' replied Brummie, frowning.

'A point. You know, a point of beer.'

Brummie's eyes narrowed and he paused before answering.

'Are you takin' the piss out of me?'

'Yeah,' replied Bill, cheerily.

'Ulroyt. But you're buyin'.'

'Great!' replied Bill, glad to have someone with whom he could celebrate. 'Where d'you fancy going?'

'The Prince.'

'That's a bit up-market isn't it?'

'What's that mean? Too posh for a workin' class git loike me.'

'Exactly.'

'You're really sailin' close to the wind tonoyt, d'you know that?'

'Ah, I'm only kidding! If you want to go to the Prince, then the Prince it shall be.'

'D'ya moind?'

'No, no, not at all. Is the beer good, or something?'

'I dunno, I've never been.' Brummie could see Bill still staring at him quizzically. 'I've gotta check it out for someone. It's a lung story. Come on. I'll tell you in the van.'

Despite being located almost in the centre of Harledge New Town, The Prince's clientele was very much drawn from the landed gentry of the surrounding shires, and the Sykes' delivery van stood out conspicuously amongst the array of shining saloons in the car park. Although described as a pub, the greater part of The Prince was given over to a French restaurant. The single lounge the pub did possess similarly took up the French theme, being decorated with brocaded curtains and red velour upholstery. Even more bourgeois than the decor, however, were the Prince's customers, who turned their heads as one when the two uniformed deliverymen entered the room. Now both thirsty and elated, Bill paid them little attention as he went to the bar and ordered two pints. The barman wore a waist coat and bow tie and did not thank Bill when he returned his change – nor Brummie five minutes later when he went up for their second round of drinks.

'What're you up to at the weekend, then?' asked Brummie, placing the beers on the table.

'I've got my sister and her friend coming down, actually.'

'Hm. That'll be good. What you gonna do with 'em?'

'God. I dunno. We'll end up going clubbing probably – if Gail's got anything to do with it.'

'D'you want some oise, then?' replied Brummie, taking a sip of his beer.

'Ice. What in my beer? No thanks.'

'No. Oise. You know. Oise'

'What d'you mean, oise..?'

'Oise!' cried Brummie, 'God streuth! And I thought you was supposed to be the brain box around 'ere. Oise!!'

Bill stared at him, utterly mystified. With an exasperated shake of the head Brummie delved into his back pocket, pulled out a small polythene packet of white pills and dangled them in front of Bill's face.

'Oise!! So you and your sister can dance all night lung. You know!'

'Oh, E's!'

'That's worr' I said. Oise!'

Sensing, all of a sudden, that every other customer in the room was now looking at them, Bill hastily grabbed Brummie's hand and pushed the pills back into his pocket.

'No, no. I don't want any E's.'

'Well, I only asked,' replied Brummie, a little offended. 'I thought you was into all that.'

Bill's eyebrows furrowed, unable to imagine how Brummie had got that impression. Then he remembered.

'Yeah, yeah. Sorry. I see what you mean. No. Those syringes. They weren't for me.'

'Oh, OK,' said Brummie, good-naturedly taking another sip of his beer.

Bill looked around the lounge again. Something had occurred to him. The other customers were ignoring them again.

'Where, er, did you get those?' he asked in a quiet voice.

'What, the oise?'

'Sh!' said Bill, quickly raising his hands in a calming gesture. 'Yeah. The pills.'

'A mate of moine'

'And where did he get them?'

'Why do you wanna know, if you don't wanna buy 'em?' replied Brummie, cautiously.

'Well, it's just, I, er … might be looking to get my hands on a tablet press, that's all.'

'Yeah?'

'Hm.'

'Gooin' into business for yourself, are you, Professor? You should be careful.'

'Oh, no, no. Nothin' like that,' replied Bill quickly. 'God, I wouldn't touch drug-pushing with a barge pole. No, it's just something I want to try out, that's all.'

'He made 'em,' replied Brummie simply.

'Who, your mate?'

'Yeah.'

'He's got a tablet press, then, has he?'

'A tablet press, a blister-pack machine and a whole other shedful of shit, too. How many pills d'you want knockin' up?'

Bill swallowed. Today was just racing along.

'Fifty. A hundred.'

'Is that all? Nah. He wouldn't be interested. Too small.'

'Oh, pity.'

'I might be, though,' added Brummie.

'Yeah?'

'We'd 'ave to keep it quiet, though. Between you and me.'

'Oh, of course, of course.'

'I mean, not that he'd mind. He's got two tableting machines and he only uses the small one once a month or summut. All the same I wouldn't wanna get on the rung side of him. You know what I mean? And what the oi don't see 'n' all that.'

'Right, right. So, er, how much would it, er, cost, then?' asked Bill.

Brummie leaned back in the red velour chair and seemed to carry out a quick calculation in his head.

'I dunno. Shall, we say … two hundred quid.'

'It's a deal,' replied Bill quickly.

'And it's your round,' answered Brummie with a smile. 'Bring your gear in tomorrow and I'll knock you up some trial samples first of all. I'm quite a dab hand with a tablet press, y'know.'

Chapter 7

'Hallo, caller, are you still waiting?'

'Yes, unfortunately,' replied Gail wearily, too nauseated to protest her exasperation at any greater length.

'Sorry to have kept you holding for so long,' continued the switchboard operator, with genuine sympathy in her voice. 'I've found the course you mentioned, but unfortunately it's over in the Galsworthy block and they're on a different exchange from us. I'll have to ask you to ring in again.'

'What! You mean you've kept me waiting all this time just to tell me I've got the wrong number!'

'Look, I'm terribly sorry about this, but it's not a College event so there's no record of it in the ...'

The operator left the sentence unfinished as Gail erupted in a violent fit of coughing.

'All right, forget it,' said Gail, choking down the bile. 'You've been very helpful. Just give me the number of this Galsworthy place.'

'No, no, listen. You sound so unwell, let me take a message. You won't be able to speak to your friend, anyway – there are no phones in the actual lecture hall. I'll walk it over there myself in my afternoon break.'

'Would you?'

'Yeah, yeah, don't worry.'

'Oh, thank you. That's very good of you. It's for Louise Schreiber.'

'Yes, I've got the name.'

'Just tell her, Gail's got the flu and can't go, and that I've called Bill and it's all off.'

'Bill.'

'Yeah, Bill. She should go straight back to London when the course finishes tonight. I'll call her tomorrow.'

'OK, I've got that.'

'Thank you. I really appreciate it.'

'No problem. And now I think you'd better get yourself off to bed,' added the operator, kindly.

'Oh, I will, don't worry.'

Arriving home at three o'clock, Bill found himself thoroughly deflated by the cancellation. Once he had got used to the idea of having to clean up the house, he had really started to look forward to Gail and Louise's visit as being precisely the sort of break he needed after four weeks continuous work in the lab and at Sykes'. Looking glumly around the dining room and kitchen, he decided not to bother tidying up after all: he was not back at work until Monday and could do it anytime over the weekend. Having checked the guinea-pigs' water, he then ambled upstairs to take a short afternoon nap.

He woke to the sound of the doorbell ringing. The bedside alarm showed ten past six. He had obviously needed the rest more than he had thought

'Ulroyt, mate, ow's it gooin?'

'Yeah, fine, fine,' replied Bill – one hand still buttoning up the fly on his jeans. 'Do you wanna come in?'

'Nah, I won't stop. I don't wanna disturb you or nothin'.'

'No, no. Come on in, I'm all by myself. I was just getting some kip.'

'OK, just for a mo'.'

'Come on through to the kitchen. Do you wanna cup of tea or something?' said Bill, leading Brummie down the hall.

'Er, no, I'm foyne. 'Ere, it's a big 'ouse this, innit?'

'Yeah, yeah.'

'I, er, just stopped by to drop off yer samples.'

'You haven't made them up already, have you?' asked Bill, opening the kitchen door and showing Brummie through. 'That was quick!'

'Ooh, ah. I don't hang around, y'know,' replied Brummie, delving into his inside pocket. 'Here y'are, I gorrem 'ere.'

Shuffling across the room, Brummie deposited three small polythene sachets on the tabletop. Resting his elbows on the surface,

Bill peered down at them closely.

'These are them, then, are they?'

'Yeah,' replied Brummie, leaning forward himself and pointing to them one by one. 'This one's loike a straightforward tablet, just done up with lactose. This is a caplet – same blend, royt, but a smaller soize. And this one's an effervescent.'

'They look great,' said Bill. 'Ha! And you've marked each of them with an 'L', too. That's neat. How did you manage that? Has your mate got a stamping machine, too?'

'No, no, the Manesty does marking as well.'

'He's got a Manesty! Bloody hell. That's top-of-the-range kit. What on earth does he need a Manesty for?' By way of response, Brummie merely gave Bill a dubious look. 'Yeah, yeah, you're right – maybe I don't wanna know after all. Anyway, listen, do they all contain the same amount of active substance?'

'Three or four granules in each. You can turn anythin' into a tablet at that koinda level.'

Three or four granules was a highly imprecise measurement of weight. However, judging from the rather fine powder with which he had provided Brummie for the tableting trial, Bill guessed that each pill probably contained around a milligram. Picking up each of the polythene sachets in turn, he weighed the three different pills in his palm and then squeezed each of them between his thumb and forefinger. After a few moments' thought, he decided the straightforward tablets should be quite sufficient to demonstrate proof of principle.

'Just make up the rest as ordinary tablets – like this first one,' he said, finally.

'Yeah?'

'Yeah. I don't need anythin' fancier than that, really. D'you want the money now?'

'Nah, nah,' replied Brummie with a wave of the hand. 'Cash on delivery's foyne. I'll drop 'em off at the weekend, OK?'

'Yeah, that's great, any time. Thanks. Listen, are you sure you don't want a drink or something? I've got a whole load of beer in the fridge.'

'Nah, I gotta get movin'. I'm on an early tomorra …'

Closing the front door behind Brummie, Bill made his way back to the kitchen and, with a feeling of pride tinged with awe, examined the three pills once again. Thinking back over the last four weeks, he knew that his progress had been quite incredible. On a shoestring budget, he had managed to isolate, characterize and finally, it seemed, even formulate his discovery. The fact was, though, that from here on in, his resources would prove increasingly insufficient for the task of taking Libidan through to actual drug launch. Sooner rather than later, he was going to need a commercial ally – and a big one at that. There would be multinational clinical trials, toxicity studies, large-scale synthesis, marketing. Not that finding a suitable partner would be likely to prove difficult. With the samples that Brummie was going to produce he could walk into any pharmaceutical company in the world and be guaranteed a director-level audience. There was still no effective treatment for female sexual dysfunction, neither during menopause nor at any other time, and so the potential market was truly massive. Sitting down at the kitchen table, Bill imagined the scene. The company's top executives would all be gathered in the boardroom. With an air of calm confidence, he would walk to the front, take a bottle of Libidan pills from his pocket and then slide it casually across the polished surface of the huge mahogany table. What would be his asking price? Smiling, Bill gripped the three samples in his fist. He could worry about the money later; right now it was time for a well-earned celebration. He would take a long hot bath to freshen up and then drink that beer – the whole bloody lot of it. If there were no one else to celebrate with, then he'd have a party all by himself. There wasn't any champagne in the fridge, but later on, to commemorate his achievements, he might ceremoniously pop the effervescent pill into a glass of water instead. It would be interesting to see whether it actually disintegrated or not.

Two hours later, a pot of curry bubbling on the stove, Bill cracked open the first can and proudly toasted his continued good health. Seconds later, the doorbell rang again.

'Hello, Bill, how are you? Sorry I'm a bit late, the train just crawled along.'

Pecking Bill on the cheek, Louise turned around and heaved her bulky black suitcase into the porch. In the street outside, Bill could see a taxi retreating into the night.

'What time did Gail arrive, then?' she asked brightly.

'Didn't you hear?' said Bill, after several moments.

'What?'

'She's sick. She can't come. Didn't you get the message?'

'No.' Seeing Bill's open-mouthed stare, the situation began to dawn on Louise and, involuntarily, she cast a sideward glance at her suitcase. 'Oh, dear. I see.'

'Come in, come in,' said Bill quickly, a sudden blast of cold night air making him realize how rude he was being. 'Let me bring your case inside.'

'Oh, er, thanks. What's the matter with her?'

'Flu, I think,' said Bill, swinging the suitcase into the hallway. 'She said she'd already called the College and they were taking a message to you.'

'Oh, no! They changed the venue today at the last minute. We ended up about three miles away in some annex or other. Her message must've got lost.'

'Oh, dear …'

Bill and Louise looked awkwardly across the hall at each other, neither of them knowing quite who should speak next.

'Well, I, er, suppose I'd better order another cab and make my way back to the station, then,' said Louise at last.

'No, no. I wouldn't hear of it. You can't go back out in this.'

'No, it's all right,' replied Louise, recovering from the surprise at last. 'I can be back home by ten. It's only an hour from Harledge to Euston.'

'Not at this time of night it's not.'

'No?'

'The commuter services are pretty much finished by eight. You might end up having to wait ages at the station.' Bill could see Louise evaluating her options. Suddenly, an image of the mounds of polystyrene packing in his dining room flashed before his eyes. Hell's teeth! What if she decided to accept his offer and stay the night? He had better try and put her off after all. 'I can take you down to the station, though, if you like. Wait with you there – if you really do want to get back tonight, that is …'

Smelling the heavy aroma of curry in the hallway, Louise was quick to decide.

'Well, no, that's probably more bother than if I stayed, isn't it? I mean, if you're sure you don't mind, I'd really appreciate it …'

'Great!' replied Bill, desperately thinking of how best he might steer her through the science park that his house had now become. 'Would you, er, like to go upstairs and freshen up? You can stay in the same room you had before.'

125

'OK,' replied Louise.

Making sure to keep on her left side so that she had no sight of the lab door, Bill carried Louise's suitcase up to her room.

'D'you mind putting the sheets on yourself?'

'No, no, of course not.'

'I didn't bother to make up the beds when I heard.' Opening the linen cupboard with his free hand, Bill nodded at the sheets on the top shelf. Smiling, Louise took them down and folded them over her forearm. 'Come on downstairs, when you're ready.'

'OK. Thanks, Bill.'

The dining room was even worse than he remembered. Moving as quickly and silently as he could, Bill just managed to transfer all of the equipment packaging and guinea-pig paraphernalia into the lab, before hearing Louise's bedroom door close and the sound of her high heels on the oak boards of the upstairs landing. Running into the kitchen, he scooped the three pills off the tabletop, stuffed them in an empty tea caddy on the window sill, and, grabbing a ladle, began to stir the curry.

'Smells great,' said Louise as she walked into the kitchen.

'Oh, er, thanks. Let's hope it tastes so, too,' replied Bill, nervously. 'Oh, and by the way, I'm afraid I've only got beer in. There's a pub over the road – if you want to nip out and buy a bottle of wine …'

'No, beer's fine,' said Louise. 'Can I … ?'

'Yes, please sit down.'

As Bill watched Louise walk across the kitchen and pull up a chair, he could not help noticing how different she seemed since her first visit. On that occasion, he had found her attractive enough dressed merely in a baggy track suit and sneakers, but now in her tight, pinstriped business suit and carefully applied make-up, he realized just quite what a stunning woman she really was. Opening the fridge he took out a can of beer and began pouring her drink.

'Pyuu, pyyu! You're dead!!'

Bill's heart leapt into his throat and he all but dropped the glass. With one eye closed like a sharp shooter, Louise was pointing the yellow plastic water pistol at him,

'Whoops! Sorry! I didn't realize it was full!' laughed Louise, as a stream of water shot across the kitchen and doused his shoulder.

'Oh, no, don't worry,' replied Bill, wiping his arm. Once the guinea-pigs had got accustomed to each other, he had left the pistol lying on the kitchen table and promptly forgotten all about it. 'Ha! Ha! I've been having a clear-out the last few days; the place is full of rubbish.'

Handing the glass to Louise, Bill turned his back and pretended to get on with the cooking. The dining room was cleared now. The sooner he got her in there the better.

As the ten o'clock news began, Una switched off the television and walked into her bedroom. News – they called it. Huh! The real news never made the headlines. Dropping to her knees, she reached under her bed and pulled out the heavy wooden trunk beneath. Unlocking the two padlocks, she swung back the solid oak lid and began to rummage around for the things she would need. Gloves, yes. Torch, yes. Balaclava? Probably not, but she would take it anyway. As she reached deep down to the bottom of the chest, beneath even the most provocative of her cache of Animal Liberation Army pamphlets, her fingers brushed against the 'Hello' magazines she would still, on occasion, idly allow herself to read. She had no time for such trifles tonight, though.

Tonight, she had work to do.

As the evening wore on, Bill could feel himself becoming more and more captivated by Louise's company. As they ate and drank and talked, he found it hard to remember when he had so much enjoyed a woman's company – if ever. So in tune with her thoughts did Bill become, in fact, that when at the end of the meal he asked if she would like another drink, even before she began to speak, he had guessed what her response was going to be.

'Er, no, I'll just have some water if you don't mind. I haven't drunk as much alcohol as this for ages!' laughed Louise, adding bashfully, 'And I'll, er, just use the loo, as well …'

'Go ahead.' smiled Bill. 'You know where it is, don't you?'

Going through into the kitchen, Bill turned on the tap to pour her a glass of water. As he did, he suddenly remembered his earlier idea of trying out the effervescent pill. He had a few moments while Louise was powdering her nose, he might as well give it a try now. Of the three pills Brummie had supplied, it probably had the least chance of functioning properly. Effervescent tablets were notoriously difficult to formulate; instead of dissolving it would more than likely drop straight to the bottom and stay there. Bill swayed a little as he opened up the polythene sachet. He'd drunk even more than Louise had. Letting the pill fall into the water, Bill smiled as it began to fizz and break up. Not bad, Brummie! Silently, Bill clapped his hands twice. Achieving initial disintegration was of itself no mean feat, although the real challenge was complete dissolution. Within a few moments, the thick, scummy deposits that always formed just above the water-line would inevitably stain the perimeter of the glass.

Except … no deposits were forming.

Rapidly sobering up, Bill walked over to the kitchen table and put the glass beneath the electric light. The pill had completely dissolved. The water was totally transparent. And then he remembered. Brummie had only had to use three or four granules. Taking several paces backwards Bill stared at the tumbler aghast. Of course. The active ingredients in the pill, not the disintegrants, almost always formed the deposits in effervescent tablets. Added to that, Libidan was a highly soluble compound. No wonder the water was so clear.

'Oh, thanks, Bill!'

So deep in thought had Bill been, that he had failed to notice Louise enter the kitchen from the dining room, helpfully bringing in the dinner plates to be washed. Almost before he realized it, she had placed them on the table and picked up the glass.

'Louise!' said Bill quickly.

'Yes?' replied Louise, holding the glass a few inches from her lips.

Time froze. Outside the house a car door quietly shut to. Inside his head a dozen different voices all began talking at once.

'Stop her now!'

But you'll never be able to think of a reasonable explanation quickly enough …

'Stop her now!'

You knew all along that you were making up that effervescent pill for her …

'Stop her now!'

Wait a little, and then substitute the glass later when she's not looking …

'Stop her now!'

In the end, though, all the voices faded but one.

'This is the most beautiful, desirable woman in the world.' it said, 'Don't spend the rest of your life wondering what might have been.'

'Yes, Bill, what's the matter?' she asked again.

'Do you, er, want some coffee as well?'

'Oh, yes, that'd be nice,' replied Louise, smiling and walking back into the dining room, carrying the glass.

The moment Louise had gone back through the door, Bill's hands began to tremble. He had not thought about Angela for weeks, but all of a sudden the memory of her came flooding back – not of the sex, but of that excruciating Sunday-afternoon phone call. Would Louise react in the same way the morning after? What would Gail say when she found out? As the kettle came to the boil, Bill was already beginning to regret what he had done, but if he ran through the door now and pulled the glass from her hand, what would she think? Overpowered by cowardice, he stared at the two boiling cups of instant coffee and swallowed hard. He could not stay hiding in the kitchen all night. Picking them up, he inched his way towards the dining room door.

'Oh, Christ!' exclaimed Bill, his voice echoing around the empty room.

Louise wasn't in the dining room any more! Was she upstairs already, lying stark naked on the bed? Rushing through the open door and into the hall, Bill hurtled down the corridor towards the stairs.

'I didn't know you kept guinea-pigs!'

Bill pulled to a sharp halt, coffee spilling over the rims of the cups. Louise was standing at the entrance to the cloakroom, cradling Anne of Cleves to her shoulder.

'Oh, er, yes …' gasped Bill in relief – she might have discovered the guinea-pigs, but at least she still had her clothes on. Perhaps Libidan wasn't so bioavailable after all. Or perhaps she only just sipped the water. That would more likely be it.

'Oh, but they're beautiful …'

Turning back inside the cloakroom, Louise sat down on the stool and continued to stroke Anne of Cleves. Following her, Bill was grateful to be able to put the scalding coffees down beside one of the cages. Surreptitiously, he scanned the room. Thankfully, there were no syringes or anything lying about.

'This is a side of you I haven't seen before,' said Louise, smiling. 'How long have you had them, then?'

'Not long. Since I lost, er, packed in my job actually,' answered Bill, a little shyly. 'They keep me company. I'm … very fond of them.'

'They're lovely. And they're so soft, aren't they?'

'Yes, yes. They're pedigrees, actually. Peruvian Satins.'

'So, so, soft …'

Still holding the guinea-pig, Louise slid off the stool and in a slow, single movement leaned gently up against Bill, her head coming to rest in the cradle of his shoulder.

'So, so, soft …'

After a few seconds her voice seemed almost to drop away to nothing and Bill could feel that she had also stopped stroking Anne of Cleves. Unable to see her face, yet too scared to move, he began to wonder what she was doing. If the pill was working she certainly wouldn't be standing there so deadly still – he knew that all too well from his experience with Angela. Then at last, it dawned on him what was happening. She's half-asleep, he thought. Of course! It must be the drink and all that travelling. What a break! If he could just ease her up the stairs and then tip her into bed, she'd be totally dead to the world in a matter of moments. Tomorrow she would have a hangover but remember absolutely nothing. Carefully slipping his arm around her shoulders, Bill decided to angle her towards the door. However, as soon as he touched her, Louise stirred, and his relief rapidly gave way to apprehension as she slowly lifted her head. When at last he saw her face, he knew everything was lost, so filled with trust was her gaze, so open in invitation were her lips, so shimmering with desire were the deep, erotic pools of her eyes.

No sooner had their mouths met, than Louise pulled back from the kiss and smiled in coy amusement. Pressed between the two of them, Anne of Cleves was fidgeting to escape. Returning Louise's smile, Bill gently took the guinea-pig from her and carefully transferred the animal back into its cage. Bringing his hand back up again, he slipped it inside Louise's suit, unzipped her skirt and slowly pulled it down over her hips.

They made love three times – right there, first of all, up against the cloakroom shelves and then twice on his four-poster bed. Looking back on the experience two hours later, with Louise asleep on his shoulder, Bill found his thoughts once again turning to Angela. Where she had directed and demanded, Louise had merely hinted at her needs. Where Angela had used her fingers to grip or to clench, Louise had applied only the lightest of pressure, or simply stroked. Wondering all the while if there could be a more delightful partner in the world with whom to make love than Louise Schreiber, Bill breathed in the fragrance of her hair and himself drifted gently off to sleep.

Four miles away, in another darkened bedroom, her mind still reeling from what she had witnessed, Una was beginning to doubt whether she would ever sleep soundly in her life again. Cruelty for financial gain was despicable enough, but cruelty in the pursuit of that sort of physical gratification was simply vile beyond belief. She had first heard of the practice a couple of years previously, when her horrid, wastrel brother had gone and foisted himself on her for the weekend. At the time she had been almost unable to credit that civilized human beings could be capable of such an act, yet tonight, with her own eyes, she had actually seen it take place. Pulling the bedclothes up against her face, Una squirmed in discomfort as she recalled the conversation with her brother.

'You don't read this pap, do you?' he had scorned.

'Oh, I just, er, bought a copy the other day for something to look at,' she had replied – kicking herself for not hiding the 'Hello' magazine away when he had phoned to say he would be coming.

'Lord and Lady De Vere. Chez nous at their ancestral Sussex retreat. Give me a break! It's just ... just sycophancy.' Sensing her vulnerability he had pressed mercilessly on, flicking through the pages of the photo magazine one after another. 'The landed aristocracy, soccer stars, TV personalities. Puke! Oh, hang on a minute. This is a good one.'

His face had suddenly lit up. Holding the magazine open at the centre pages, he turned it towards her so that she could see the double-page spread. The film star was world famous – a household name.

'Relaxing in the grounds of his Beverly Hills mansion, eh? My arse! Or should I say his. 'Cos you know what he gets up to in his spare time, don't you? Eh? This guy.'

Una had no idea. Seeing her puzzled face, her brother had then taken great relish in explaining.

Bill awoke to the sight of Louise's naked back. It was early – not even seven o'clock. Seated at the bottom of the bed, she had just put on her bra, and was holding up her blouse in the early morning gloom, trying to work out where the armholes were. Smiling to himself, Bill switched on the bedside lamp to help her see. Louise flinched. Momentary, and in no way pronounced, her reaction was nevertheless charged with an unmistakable nervousness and all at once Bill knew that the time of reckoning had come.

'Hi.'

It was all he could think to say. By way of response, Louise half turned her head and bravely attempted a smile, although it fell apart pathetically even before it had properly formed. Lowering her eyes, she looked around the floor and then leant down to pick up her tights. Hoping that something more appropriate to say would somehow spring to mind, Bill sat upright and leant forward. However, the way she deliberately stood with her back to him, and her slow, purposeful dressing movements clearly indicated she wished him to say nothing further. A horrific, empty feeling took hold of Bill's stomach and, suddenly conscious of his own nakedness, he pulled the quilt up to his shoulders and lowered his face into it.

When he was able to bring himself to look back up again, she was standing and zipping up her skirt. Turning to take her jacket off the chair, she still could not meet his gaze.

'I'm going downstairs,' she said, slipping on her shoes and hurriedly leaving the room.

Ten minutes later, having washed and dressed, he followed her into the kitchen. Opening the door, he resolved to take command of the situation. She had had a few minutes now to get some perspective on what had happened. A cup of coffee, a quiet talk, and he would try his best to apologize for having taken such shameless advantage of her.

'Are you cold?'

She was seated at the table in her raincoat.

'A bit.'

'The heating's not on yet, I'll just, er ...

He moved across the room to switch on the thermostat. In the grey morning light of the kitchen, there seemed an almost traumatized rigidity to her posture. Oh God, he thought. What have I done to her?

'Do you want some coffee?'

'No thanks.'

'Come on – it'll warm you up ...'

Switching on the kettle, he sat down opposite her at the table. It was now or never. But before he could open his mouth, she spoke first.

'Bill.' Her face was impassive – as though in a trance. 'I have abused your hospitality terribly.'

Bill stared at her aghast. She was blaming herself.

'Don't say that! It was absolutely fantastic, it was the most ...'

A heavy knocking sound at the front door. Standing up, Bill moved in surprise to the kitchen window. Who the hell could it be at this time of the morning? On catching sight of Bill's face, the taxi driver gave a thumbs-up gesture. Louise must have rung for a cab as soon as she had come downstairs. Turning, he could see her moving slowly towards the kitchen door.

'You didn't have to call a taxi; I'd've taken you down to the station!'

'I know,' she replied, blankly.

Her eyes were looking at him now, but seemed almost not to see him, as though her consciousness had withdrawn in upon itself to some sheltered corner of her mind. Dumbstruck with guilt, Bill carried her suitcase down the hallway. Turning the latch on the front door, he had to fight down a tremendous desire to slip his arm around her shoulder to comfort her. As though sensing his intent, Louise quickly slipped through the doorway and out on to the gravel path outside.

'Just one case,' she said to the taxi driver, who, with a nod, walked across the path, took the suitcase from Bill and lifted it into the boot of the car.

As the cab pulled away, Bill strained to peer through the drizzle that flecked the passenger window. Louise seemed to have a hand raised in salute or farewell. Perhaps she couldn't bear to depart leaving any bad feelings between them. When the car turned into the street, though, and he saw her face in profile, his heart sank as he recognized both her gesture, and what it signified. Louise Schreiber was biting the curled forefinger of her right hand. Gone was the confident career woman that had arrived at his home less than twelve hours previously. In her place there was only a frightened young girl – her face stripped of make-up and white from lack of sleep – struggling to cope with the damage to her dignity and self-esteem.

As Bill closed the front door, he was overwhelmed by a tidal wave of self-loathing. So deeply had the image of Louise at the passenger window buried itself into his psyche that he knew it would stay with him for the rest of his life. Leaning with his back against the door, he looked down the hallway at the carved oak staircase – the last thing his father had completed before his death. What would that genuine and profoundly decent man think of his son if he could see him now? All at once, the pride and affection his father had always shown him, and which still formed the very bedrock of his self-respect, seemed to turn to dust. Opening the door to the lab, he looked around at the masses of empty packaging strewn around the room. In the middle stood the chromatographic column, pointing upwards like the accusing finger of truth. Only the previous night, he had stood right here, congratulating himself on everything he had achieved. Leaning backwards against the work bench, Bill let his face sink into his hands.

'Oh, Dad. Oh, Dad. What have I done?'

Libidan was no treatment for the menopause.

It was a rape drug.

Hanging her coat on the peg behind the door, Irene Carter moved across the reception area and looked at the pile of manifests on her desk. Not too bad – just enough to keep her occupied until she knocked off at twelve. Saturdays were always fairly quiet. Moving into the kitchen and filling up the kettle, she peered down the corridor towards Mr Beckett's room. No sign of the old lecher yet. Probably still sleeping off his hangover. Hearing the telephone, she decided not to hurry back down the corridor and answer it, but just to let it ring. She needed her cuppa. Besides, the overnight answering machine was still on – they could leave a message on that. Returning to her desk, she had only just taken her first sip of tea when the phone rang again. Someone was persistent today.

'Sykes and Garnier, good morning,' she sang out gaily.

'Irene? It's Bill. Bill Kennedy.'

'Oh, hi, Bill. How are you?' she replied, stretching down to place her handbag under the desk.

'Is Brummie there, Irene? Have you seen Brummie?'

'You just missed him, Bill.'

'What?'

'He's just driven off.'

'Where's he gone? On a delivery?'

'Well, it's funny you should mention that, but I've no idea.'

'What d'you mean?'

'Well, when I got here this mornin' he was packin' up some special

134

order or other. A stack of blue drums of some sort – I'd never seen them before. You know what he's like, though, always doin' favours for people. I asked him if he'd got all the paperwork but he said he didn't need any. He's supposed to log all his deliveries with me, but, honestly, I dunno what he's up to half the time.'

'Did he say when he'd be back?'

'No, I didn't ask him. Have you got his mobile number?'

'Yeah – it's switched off. Listen, the moment he gets back, get him to give me a call.'

'Yeah, all right, when I see him.'

'No, listen, Irene, it's an emergency. A real emergency.'

'Oh, gosh, Bill, what's up, luv?' asked Irene, sensing the increasing tension in Bill's voice.

'I've made a terrible mistake.'

'What? What d'you mean?'

'He's got something of mine, Irene. Something dangerous. Something I need back right away.'

Chapter 8

Even though six years had elapsed since his one and only visit to the offices of the Department of Health and Social Security, Snod had no trouble in finding the place again. Nevertheless, once inside the building, he scarcely recognized the interior, which seemed to have undergone a complete refurbishment.

'Business must be boomin',' he remarked to himself, as he strolled across the carpeted lobby towards the gleaming new lifts.

Exiting on the fourth floor – housing benefits – he pulled the buff-coloured envelope out of his pocket, and then extracted the printed form to check the details of his appointment.

'Interview suite 5,' he read aloud.

Interview suite? It sounded like some sort of swanky hotel. What were they going to do? Grill him about his benefits first and then sling him into the en-suite Jacuzzi if they caught him on the fiddle?

'Where's this?' he asked the uniformed security guard, holding up the letter to his face.

'End of the corridor,' replied the man, glaring at Snod suspiciously from beneath his peaked cap.

'Service with a smile, eh? Well, there goes your tip …' muttered Snod audibly, as he turned and walked off towards the interview rooms.

The door to suite 5 was open, but there was no one seated on the other side of the plexiglass screen and, as far as Snod could see, no button he could press to summon anyone. Resigning himself to a wait, he closed the door and sat down on one of the room's two plastic moulded chairs. After several seconds of staring around at the white, panelled walls, he lifted up on to his lap his hemp bag which contained a half dozen oranges, took one out and began to peel it.

'Mr Snodgrass?'

A woman's voice – booming, yet at the same time strangely tinny. He looked up. She was seated on the other side of the screen. Lips too close to the microphone. Black. Early thirties. Next to her sat a balding, middle-aged white man. Poker-faced – deliberately so.

'Snod, actually.'

'I beg your pardon?'

Seemingly unable to hear, the woman squinted and leaned slightly nearer to the microphone.

'Snod.' He said it louder this time. 'Call me Snod.'

Frowning, she went as though to exchange a look with the man, but then at the last moment changed her mind. Hello, thought Snod, he's the boss, isn't he? You're here to keep an eye on me, and he's here to keep an eye on you.

'We'll use your full surname today, if you don't mind.'

'Suit yourself,' replied Snod, remembering the last person who had insisted on doing that. The kid had been over fifteen and Snod was only just twelve. There had still been specks of blood on the playground a week later.

'And, er, would you mind not eating during the interview.'

She was pointing at his orange.

'It's doctor's orders, actually. My skin condition. But don't worry, I'll take all the peelings with me afterwards,' replied Snod, inoffensively holding up a coil of orange skin.

'All the same, I must insist. There is a sign, you know.'

'Oh, OK, sorry.'

Replacing the half-peeled orange back in the bag, Snod meekly folded his hands and sat waiting for the first question. This time, the woman was unable to restrain herself and cast an inquisitive look at her boss. Where was all the hostility she had been led to believe that this claimant would show?

Coming right around the corner at you, bitch.

'Anyway, thank you, for, er, coming in today, Mr Snodgrass.' As she spoke she flicked through a file of notes on the table in front of her. 'As far as I understand, you have been claiming housing benefit on your property, 52 Waltham Heights, since August 1994.'

'Right.'

'Are you the only person living at the property, Mr Snodgrass?'

'Yeah.'

'And do you use it for any other purposes – other than as your private residence?'

'Like what?'

'Answer the question please, Mr Snodgrass.'

She was glaring at him now.

Scareeey.

'No.'

'Well, Mr Snodgrass, I have to inform you that certain activities taking place at 52 Waltham Heights have been brought to the attention of this office, leading us to believe that you and/or accomplices of yours, are making use of it for criminal purposes.'

'Wouldn't know anythin' about that,' shrugged Snod.

'You wouldn't?'

'No. Haven't got a clue what you're talkin' about.'

'Do you sublet your property, Mr Snodgrass?'

'No.'

'Who are the two women that have been residing there for the last four months?'

'Friends. They're stayin' with me.'

'Not good enough, Mr Snodgrass,' said the woman, with a tense shake of the head.

'Is that a crime?'

'No, but prostitution is.'

'And you've got evidence of that, have you?'

'It's with the police. They'll be questioning you separately.'

Narrowing his eyes, Snod looked across at the man, and then back at the woman again. He hadn't lived in the flat for years, but the council still owned the place, and if the police had done a full observation number on it they could evict him just like that. The two faces were giving nothing away. He forced himself to think, to try to piece together what could have happened. The girls were careful. He was always checking up. The Johns wanted anonymity even more – they'd never had a rowdy one yet. So how had it got out? 'Certain activities have been brought to the attention of this office', she had said. Of course! That was why he was here and not down at the nick. Housing Benefits had got a sniff – a complaint from a neighbour or something – told the police and ... they'd just sat on their hands. And for at least four months, by the sound of things. Inwardly, Snod smiled. That's why these two looked so pissed-off. All this stuff about police questioning was total bollocks. The Filth never gave a toss about girls on the game except when they hung around street corners.

'So, what exactly are you tellin' me, then?'

'What we have constitutes sufficient grounds for us to withdraw your benefit, Mr Snodgrass. Do you have anything to say?'

Snod exhaled in relief, but kept his facial expression anxious: the benefit he could lose, but not the flat, nor the income from it – at least, not for the time being anyway.

'How am I gonna pay the rent if you do that?'

'Employment, perhaps?' replied the woman with a sardonic smile.

Snod's whole body tensed. He looked at the glass screen screwed tightly into its wooden frame. She'd be off down the corridor behind before he could smash it down. And, anyway, he needed the flat. The flat. The flat! Concentrate on the flat! Fighting to calm himself, he moved right up against the screen and, loosening his collar, displayed the section of his throat and neck where the scaly, red weals were at their thickest.

'It's easy for you to say get a job – you're only black.' Snod watched the woman recoil backwards in repugnance. Sitting back in his chair with a sneer, he began re-buttoning his collar. His skin condition could scare the shit out of just about anyone.

'That concludes the interview as far as we are concerned,' said the woman, closing the folder decisively in an attempt to re-impose her authority. 'Your housing benefit payments will stop as of today. You'll no doubt be hearing from the police authorities soon.'

'When they kick my bastard door down one morning, I s'pose,' replied Snod, resentfully. 'You people make me sick ...'

Turning on his heel, Snod left the room but paused at the door to look back inside. The two housing benefits officers were still rooted to their seats. They probably thought he was sizing them up one last time. In fact, he was staring at the screw-heads around the screen.

Maybe next time he'd bring a screwdriver – turn up early and loosen them a little.

In the end, Brummie did not call Bill until eight o'clock at night.

'Where the hell have you been?' gasped Bill, his voice exasperated by twelve dry-throated hours of pacing around the house waiting for his phone to ring

'Nowhere special,' replied Brummie, affably. 'How lung 'ave you been troying to get hold of me?'

'All day!'

'Woy didn't you call me mobile?'

'Because you never had it bloody switched on!!' exploded Bill.

A pause. The rustling of clothing.

'Ooh ahh, sorry.' Bill could almost see Brummie at the other end of the receiver, wistfully scratching his head. 'The battery's gone flat. What you afta, anyway? Yer gear?'

'Yeah, I want it back. Tonight. It's doesn't matter if you haven't had time to make it up into tablets yet, I'll pay you anyway.'

'Nah, yer ulroyt. I did 'em this afternoon.'

'What!

'Yeah, used up all the powder you give me – every last bit of it.'

Bill swallowed hard. He almost dared not ask.

'How many?'

'Two hundred and eight. Ten packs of twenty. The rest of 'em loose.'

'Oh, Christ!' gasped Bill, under his breath.

'Yeah, I was round my mate's ploice today anyway,' continued Brummie cheerfully, 'so I thought I might as well finish the job off for you there and then. They was a dead cinch in the end. And they slipped into the blister packs loike a dream, no problem at ...'

'OK, OK!' interrupted Bill, irritably. How was it that the thirty scientists in Asper's formulation department all swore on their mothers' graves that no new compound could ever be successfully tableted in less than a couple of weeks, yet this semi-literate van driver had managed it in an afternoon? 'Where are they now, then?'

'Still at the factory.'

'Where is it? I'll meet you there.'

'Whoa! No can do, moite,' said Brummie quickly. 'I can drop 'em round at your ploice though, if you loike.'

'No, no. I'll come and meet you halfway. In town.'

'Yeah, all right. Where d'you fancy? The Prince?'

'Oh, Christ, not there again. No, er, what about that place over the road from Sykes'?'

'The Owl?'

'Yeah.'

'Yeah, ulroyt. We can 'ave a couple of points, too, if you loike. About noyne, OK?'

'See you then.'

Bill arrived at half past eight. He had deliberately chosen the Owl because Brummie could not possibly confuse it with another pub and because the smoke-room at the rear of the building was almost always empty. Sitting alone at his table, Bill suddenly felt ravenously hungry: he realized he had not eaten all day. Thankfully, the barman still had two ham rolls left over from lunch-time, which Bill purchased and speedily devoured. Screwing up the cling-film wrapping and depositing it in a ball in the ashtray, he looked around the large, empty room and thought of Louise. Was she now by herself, too, all alone in her London flat?

'D'you wan' another point?'

Brummie was standing at the smoke-room door, nodding at Bill's half empty glass. Despite the many frustrating hours he had spent that day trying to track him down, in the end Bill found himself really glad to see the big midlander's bearded face.

'Nah, I'm all right. Have you got the pills?'

Tapping his inside pocket, Brummie winked and sat down on the opposite side of the table. A wave of relief spread over Bill.

'What d'you need 'em so quick for anywoy?' asked Brummie, unbuttoning his coat to reach inside his pocket.

'You know the three samples you knocked up for me?'

'Yeah.'

'I tried one of them out. They're bad shit, mate. Really bad shit.'

'Oh. Shime that,' replied Brummie sadly, before looking behind him at the smoke-room door and then dropping an unmarked, white cardboard box on to the table.

'Thanks,' said Bill, passing over a rolled-up wad of notes in exchange.

Leaning back in his chair, Bill opened up the box and looked inside. Brummie had indeed loaded them into ten, alu-foil blister packs. His friend obviously had packaging apparatus comparable to his top-of-the-range Manesty tableting machine.

'The eight extra ones are loose insoide.'

'Oh, cheers,' replied Bill – letting a couple of the pills slip out from the bottom of the box into his hand. 'Why did you stamp 'em with an 'E' this time?'

'What?'

'An 'E'. Why did you stamp them with an 'E'?'

'I didn't.'

'Yes, you did. Look.'

Bill passed one of the pills across to Brummie.

'Oh, ahh,' said Brummie. He squinted at the small white sphere in the centre of his huge palm, and then announced in a matter-of-fact voice. 'These must be the rung ones, then.'

'What did you say?' croaked Bill.

'I made up two lots this afternoon. Your L's, and then some E's for another mate of mine. I must've, loike, got 'em mixed up or summut. Sorry about that, Bill. Bill ? Are you ulroyt, Bill?'

Bill had slumped backwards into his chair, his eyes closed tight. When finally he spoke, his voice was slow and deliberate.

'Let me get this straight. What I've got here are the E's you made up for your friend … and he's got my L's? Is that what you're saying?'

'Yeah, I guess so,' replied Brummie, adding brightly, 'but don't worry, it's still early. He probably won't 'ave sold many of 'em yet.'

'We'll park 'ere,' said Brummie. 'There's no restrictions after seven.'

The pedestrian precinct was bustling with life. To their left, a double-decker bus had pulled up in front of Harledge's main department store and was disgorging out on to the pavement a seemingly unbroken stream of late-evening merrymakers. On the other side of the road, a group of about a dozen or so young men in leather jackets and jeans stood around joking and noisily bating each other while they waited for the last of their party to arrive. As Brummie locked the car and joined Bill on the pavement, two pretty girls in thigh-high boots and mini-skirts breezed swiftly past them, their arms happily linked against the cold. Saturday night was well under way.

'Come on, we've gotta move quick.'

'This woy,' said Brummie.

They set off at a run down the precinct, weaving their way between the crowds of revellers.

'Which pub does he work in then, your mate?'

'It's not a pub, it's a club.'

'I thought you said he was a barman?'

'He is. At Joe Bananas.'

Brummie nodded towards the end of the precinct as he spoke. Despite having been to Joe Bananas only a month previously with Gail and Louise, Bill was unable to orientate himself – on that occasion he had driven directly to the roof car park. Looking left and right as he ran, he tried to make out the yellow, neon sign that he remembered hanging down over the front door of the club. It was then that he saw them. A little over fifty yards away. Two figures pressed so tightly up against a lamppost that they almost seemed to be a part of it. Thirty yards – the man had apparently passed out and the woman was propping him up to stop him from falling. Bill's lungs were pumping strongly now but he was unable to take his eyes off the couple. Twenty yards – the man's body was completely limp, in obvious pain. Ten yards – no, wait, she wasn't supporting him against the lamppost, but ramming him up against it, tightly coiling her legs around both it and him. One yard …

As Bill at last recognized the couple's pose, memories of that fateful Friday afternoon in the draughty storeroom at Asper came flooding back to him. Coming to a halt, he stopped and stared in horror at the scene developing before him. Flicking back her long hair, the woman was forcing her hands into the man's mouth. Having prized his jaw apart, she then leaned purposefully forwards. Seconds later her tongue came curling out between her lips and in a flash disappeared down his throat like a snake slithering into a hollow log.

'This is it. Phew!' Brummie had caught up with Bill and was standing with his hands on his hips, trying to regain his breath. 'Dunno why the doors are woide open, though. And where's the bouncers? Fookin' hell! What are them two doin'?'

While Brummie stood and stared wide-eyed at the couple, Bill edged forwards towards the entrance. There were indeed no security guards at the door. A blackboard lay collapsed on the pavement proclaiming in lurid yellow chalk, '70's Disco! A Crate of Bubbly for Tonite's Disco Queen!!' Bill stepped over it and squinted through the gloom into the club's murky interior. Although the downstairs bar was full of customers and its jukebox was blaring out music, the building seemed gripped by a strange eeriness.

'Come on, we'd better go in.'

Mesmerized by what was taking place against and around the lamppost, Brummie was completely unable to move. In the end, Bill had to grab him by the sleeve and physically drag him towards the entrance. No sooner had the two of them crossed the threshold, than they were both immediately bowled back out on to the pavement again by another young couple coming hurtling through the door.

'Oh, er, sorry ...' mumbled Bill.

Despite their immaculate disco costumes, the couple had a look of hunted panic about them, like a pair of frightened foxes fleeing from a pack of hounds. Instinctively grabbing on to her partner's arm, the woman stared at Bill and Brummie in alarm and then, in an instant, whisked him quickly off into the night. As Bill watched their fast retreating backs he could see the man was holding up his torn satin trousers with his free hand.

'Where does your mate work?'

'First floor. In the disco.'

'Come on. Let's go.'

The foyer was deserted. To their right, a broad hardwood staircase swept steeply upwards into the gloom. Brummie hesitated at first, but eventually followed Bill as he gingerly began his ascent. Two steps short of the top of the stairs, Bill came to a halt. Finally plucking up his courage, he then turned into the corridor, only to be stopped dead in his tracks by the scene unfolding before him. At the end of the hallway, in front of the double doors to the disco, a huge seven-foot bouncer in coat and tails was reeling backwards and forwards, his arms flailing wildly. Mounted on his shoulders and back, three young mini-skirted women were wrestling with him, systematically stripping him of his clothing stitch by stitch. Like a giant, black beetle that has inadvertently strayed into the path of a line of soldier ants, the bouncer lumbered this way and that trying to shake off the tiny, tenacious creatures. But, despite the strength in his heavy, thrashing limbs, their mandibles probed and slashed without mercy, bringing inexorably closer the moment when they would feast on his exposed, defenceless flesh.

'Quick!' hissed Bill, as the bouncer and three girls suddenly toppled over, collapsing through the open door of the cloakroom in a tangle of arms and legs. Launching themselves the last few feet down the corridor, Bill and Brummie spilled into the disco, the heavy double doors quickly swinging to a close behind them.

'Bloody hell!' gasped Brummie 'Where is everyone?'

The circular dance floor in the centre of the room was completely empty save for a single pair of stacked heels. All of a sudden, a child-hood memory came flooding back to Bill. Once, on the way to school, he had seen a paperboy hit by a car. Although the teenager himself had been blasted off into a hedge, his sneakers had somehow remained in the middle of the road, stubbornly fixed at the point of impact. Slowly turning his head, Bill scanned the seating area around the perimeter of the room that lay unilluminated by the bright dance-floor lights. The entire area was a seething mass of bodies, vibrating with a deep, uniform groaning that somehow cut through the disco rhythms of the sound system. Bill's eyes struggled to focus and deter-mine some recognizable structures in the amorphous mass before him, but, even after staring for several seconds, all he could make out was the odd stray calf or elbow that occasionally caught a spare shaft of light.

'Over there!' said Brummie, pointing across the hall.

'Where?'

'There!'

Next to the unmanned disco console was a small bar area. Bill and Brummie exchanged a look. How were they to get across there? Reluctant to present themselves out in the open, but still more terrified of what was going on in the shadows, they both took a deep breath and then dashed across the dance floor towards the bar.

'Shit! Where is he?' gasped Bill – the bar area was completely deserted.

'I dunno,' replied Brummie.

'Pssst!'

Bill and Brummie turned and stared into the gloom together.

'Pssst! Over here!!'

From the gap between two upturned tables, a hand was summoning them. As soon as they approached, the tables parted and the hand reached out and pulled them in. Crouching down, Bill and Brummie looked around the makeshift shelter. Huddled together in terror were the barman and the other two bouncers.

'What happened, Neil?' asked Brummie.

'It was a hen party,' replied the Barman. 'From Luton. They, they … just went beserk!'

'When?'

'About ten minutes ago.'

'Did you sell 'em any of the pills?' asked Bill. 'The pills he gave you?'

'Yeah, yeah,' replied Neil.

'How many?'

'Just a strip of 'em.'

'Where's the rest?'

Before Neil could answer, one of the bouncers leaned forward and grabbed Bill's forearm.

'Did you see Graham? When you came through the door? A doorman – dressed like me. He was going downstairs for help.' The man's eyes were full of panic and he nervously clutched a fire extinguisher to his chest.

'He never made it,' replied Bill.

The bouncer's face collapsed in despondency, and he leaned backwards against the wall with a groan. Bill turned once again to Neil.

'Where's the rest of them, then? The rest of the pills.'

'In my locker. At the back of the bar.'

'Come on,' said Bill, leaning forward.

'No way!' replied Neil, hotly. 'I'm not bloody goin' out there again!'

Bill went to speak again, but Neil was obviously not going to be persuaded. Instead, he reached inside his waistcoat pocket and handed over a small silver locker key. Bill looked across at Brummie, who nodded in response and crouched forward at the ready. Opening the tables, Neil let the two men slip through.

Skirting their way around the wall as unobtrusively as they could, Bill and Brummie made their way back to the bar and quickly slid through the door at the rear to the 'Staff Only' area behind. The key opened the third locker and within a minute Bill had recovered the white cardboard box from beneath a pile of clothing. He emptied the loose pills out into his hand and then quickly counted up the foil packs.

'They're all there,' said Bill. 'Let's split.'

Launching themselves out of the bar area, Bill and Brummie hurtled across the dance floor towards the exit. But, with less than five yards to go, and just as they were beginning to think they had made their escape, the double doors suddenly burst open and a group of uniformed policemen came spilling into the room. Sliding to a desperate halt on the dance floor's parquet flooring with only inches to spare, Bill and Brummie stared at the four burly officers. Seconds later the entire room became flooded in light and a plain clothes officer walked stiffly through the door.

'Bugger me …' exhaled the man in undisguised awe, as he scanned the circle of semi-naked bodies strewn around the now illuminated seating area. 'This wouldn't be anything to do with you or your friend, would it, Brummie?'

Louise was neither alone, nor in her flat.

'Hi, thanks for coming round, Lou,' said Gail, gratefully.

'That's all right,' smiled Louise, handing her the bunch of flowers that she had brought. 'How are you feeling, anyway?'

'Well, still pretty grotty, but over the worst, I suppose. Last night was terrible – I thought I was gonna die!'

'What time did you get up this afternoon, then?' asked Louise, slipping off her jacket and taking the flowers back from Gail. 'No, I'll do these – you sit down.'

'Oh, thanks,' said Gail, flopping down into the armchair. 'About four. I had a bath just after you phoned – I was just drenched in sweat. Then I had some soup and I felt a bit better afterwards so I stayed up.'

'Great,' replied Louise, walking through to Gail's kitchenette and looking around for a vase. 'Do you want some tea?'

'Oh, yes, please,' said Gail. Pulling her dressing gown more tightly up to her neck, she sat back in convalescent contentment, listening to the sounds of her friend moving about the kitchen.

'Here you are,' said Louise, handing her a mug and then laying the flowers out on the table and slowly arranging them in the vase one by one.

'Thanks. Listen, I'm so sorry about the weekend. I know you were really looking forward to it. Did you manage to get a train back from Warwick to London?'

'No, er, not quite. I ended up going to Harledge, after all. I didn't get your message.'

'What!'

'They moved us at the last minute. Your note never quite caught up with me.'

'Oh, no! What happened? Was Bill there? He hadn't gone out, had he?'

'No, no. He was there all right,' replied Louise, fluffing up a couple of the blooms with her palm. 'I ended up staying the night and travelling back the next morning.'

'Phew! You had me worried there for a minute. How was he, anyway? OK?'

'Yeah, yeah, he was fine.'

'What was the place like?'

'A bit of a mess, frankly.'

'Well that's no surprise, I guess. Did he tell you anything about his new job – driving this van? It doesn't sound much fun to me,' enquired Gail.

'No, not much. I did most of the talking, really,' answered Louise, looking up from the vase and staring vacantly towards the window. 'He did show me his guinea-pigs, though.'

'His what?' replied Gail, almost choking on her tea.

'Guinea-pigs,' murmured Louise, her eyes slowly glazing over, ' … and his little yellow water pistol …'

'Guinea-pigs! Water pistols! Is he having a second childhood or something? Oh, my God, this is just what I thought would happen. All alone in that dead old house. I told you he'd turn into a recluse, didn't I? And now … Lou, what on earth's the matter?'

Louise's whole body had begun to shake. Hastily placing her tea on the floor, Gail stood up to move across to her friend, but before she could, Louise let out a heart-wrenching sob, dropped the flowers she was holding and burst convulsively into tears.

'Oh, Gail. I'm so sorry!'

'What is it, Lou? What's the matter?'

'I never, ever had a friend like you and now I've gone and ruined it all!'

Wrapping her arms around Louise, Gail sat her gently down and placed her mouth up against her ear.

'Don't cry, Lou, it's all right,' she whispered.

'I don't know why I did it – it was so stupid of me, so selfish. People have always said I'm cold and hardhearted, but I'm not, you know, I'm not.'

Surprised by Louise's distress, yet rapidly sensing that warm words alone would not suffice, Gail placed her hands on her friends cheeks and lifted her head up so that they could see each other face to face.

'Listen. Whatever's happened,' said Gail firmly, 'whatever's happened, you'll be my friend forever, OK?'

Louise nodded, and Gail could see that her message had got through, but, all the same, nearly a minute passed before Louise could bring herself to speak again.

'And Bill, as well. I know how much you love him, and he's been so kind to me.'

'Did you sleep with him?' asked Gail, guessing by now what might have happened.

'Yeah.'

'Is that so bad?'

'It's bad to toy with people, Gail,' replied Louise, wiping the tears from her eyes with the side of her wrist, 'To make them think you care when you don't. I mean, I do care for him, of course, but just not in that way ...'

'I can't imagine you deceiving anyone like that.'

'I can't either. Oh God! I must've been off my head!' Louise could feel her nose beginning to run and had to throw her head back. Gail passed her a tissue. She blew on it heartily. 'I mean, I know you said how much he could do with a girlfriend. And I suppose I could sort of feel it from him, too – how lonely he is. So why did I go and do it, knowing it might hurt him?'

'And is he all interested now?'

'I think so,' replied Louise, sheepishly.

'Well, you'll just have to tell him it was only a one-night stand and it's all finished now.' Although Louise raised her head sharply at this, Gail at last felt able to risk a smile. 'Oh, Lou, darling, you great big sensitive thing. You're not the first girl to do something like that and you certainly won't be the last. And he is a grown-up, you know, an adult. As for me – I don't mind, I don't mind, at all. Why should I?'

'Are you sure?' asked Louise, seemingly about to cry again although this time more out of relief.

'Of course not. Of course not,' answered Gail, folding her arms around her friend's shoulders once again.

The clock above the notice board read five to two. Nearly an hour had passed since the last time Bill had gone across to the hatch and asked the desk sergeant if there were any news of Brummie. Leaning back on the waiting room's worn wooden bench, he ran once again through the series of events that had followed their being brought to the station for questioning.

Brummie's face had remained completely impassive in the squad car and he had not said a single thing. When finally he did speak, it was obvious that he had been carefully planning both his exact words and the precise moment he would utter them. Just as the car had come to a halt in the station compound and the two officers in the front had got out, he quickly whispered to Bill between barely open lips.

'We went to Joe's for a drink. Stuff the pills down your shirt.'

No sooner had he spoken, than the rear doors of the car were opened for them and they were escorted up the ramp towards the entrance to the station. Following Brummie's example, Bill stealthily undid the top two buttons of his shirt and then slipped his hand into his trousers pocket to take hold of the box of pills. The second they passed through the police-station doors, while the two officers were unable to see them, he slipped the cardboard box inside his shirt, flattening it several seconds later by pressing up against a door lintel as the desk sergeant checked them in.

Bill and Brummie were separated straightaway. The concealment of the pills actually proved unnecessary, for the police showed no signs of wanting to charge Bill and he was not asked to turn out his pockets. It did, however, turn out to be extremely uncomfortable, for all the way through the interview – in which his innocent bystander plea was not once challenged by the young detective opposite him – his every movement seemed to cause the serrated edges of the aluminium blister packs to saw into his chest and stomach.

After the initial interview he was left alone in the room for nearly an hour. Finally, the detective reappeared and asked him to run through his story again. Just as Bill started talking though, a second detective, an older, senior man, entered the room, and with a neutral-looking expression summoned the first one outside again. As the younger detective made his way towards the door, the older detective turned and stared at Bill. Slowly, Bill began to feel the pit of his stomach begin to drop out. The grey-haired, broad-shouldered man was the very epitome of authority. Alone in the interview room once more, Bill's mind began to race. What if this were all psychological tactics? What if the police were doing a hard-man, soft-man routine on him? If the second detective were to reappear and ask Bill what had really happened that night, he would probably crack in seconds. However, ten minutes later, the younger detective came into the room once more and Bill was told he was free to go.

He had been sitting waiting for Brummie ever since.

'Are you sure there's no news about my mate?' he called out to the desk sergeant. The waiting was driving him absolutely mad.

'Hold on, I'll have a look for you,' replied the sergeant with a begrudging nod, slouching slowly through the door into the offices behind.

'They finished with him about a half hour ago,' announced the sergeant as he reappeared.

'So when's he going to come out, then?'

'He's already left. He went out the back way.'

'What! Why didn't they tell him I was waiting for him! I've been sitting here for nearly three hours!'

'They did.'

'What?'

'They did tell him you were here. Apparently, he chose to go home on his own.' The sergeant stared at Bill's bemused face for several seconds and then added wearily. 'There were no charges against him either, son. Why don't you get yourself off home now, eh?'

Standing on the steps of the station, Bill looked around the deserted Sunday morning streets and concluded that Brummie must have had very good reasons for making his own way home. Inarticulate and possessing something of a limited vocabulary, the man was nevertheless both shrewd and resourceful – his advice in the police car had, after all, been exactly right. Perhaps he had thought it would look better for his story that way. Or perhaps he was doing Bill a favour: he was obviously known to the police and maybe he was trying to ensure that Bill did not become tarnished by association. Pulling up his collar against the cold night air, Bill began the long walk towards the centre of town, but before he got there he came across an empty taxi and was back in Wyburn in less than ten minutes.

Closing the bedroom door, Bill sat down on the edge of his bed and was overcome by a tremendous sense of gratitude. His curiosity and vanity had taken him to the very edge of the abyss, but thanks to the quick thinking and magnanimity of two people he scarcely knew, he had been able to make his way back to safety. For not only had he been rescued from the tender mercies of the police by Brummie's skillful explanation of why they were at Joe Bananas, but, when he had returned home, he had found the most wonderful, heart-warming message from Louise on his answering machine. Switching off the bedside light, Bill lay back on the bed and thanked his lucky stars that what had started as the most terrible day in his life was ending so providentially. Libidan was finished. The police had stumbled across it by chance, lost interest and now he had every pill back under lock and key.

And, on top of that, Louise Schreiber wanted to see him for a drink and a chat.

It was three days later and the entire episode was already starting to seem like an unpleasant dream.

'Still no word from Brummie, then?' asked Bill, as he handed the keys of the transit van over to Irene.

'No, but he'll turn up, don't worry. He's done this before. Probably gone off on some drinking binge with his mates back in Birmingham.'

'Well, tell him to give me a call at home if he turns up.'

'Yeah, of course I will. Are you having a day off, then?'

'Two, actually. I've got a few jobs to do in the house.'

'Oh, right. Well, enjoy yourself anyway.'

'Thanks, Irene.'

With a smile at the receptionist, Bill made his way across the forecourt to his car and set off towards the DIY superstore on the other side of the Harledge ring road. Checking his watch, he realized he had more time than he had thought – the store closed at seven on Wednesdays, but it wasn't even six o'clock yet. Slowly making his way through the early evening traffic, Bill reflected on the speed with which everything had more or less gone back to normal. The previous night he had travelled down to London, called for Louise at her flat and, despite a few uncomfortable moments at first, the two of them had had a perfectly civilized drink together. On the sole occasion she had referred directly to Friday night, stating that she wished it all to go no further, he had only had to nod once and she had seemed satisfied. Working three days straight at Sykes' had also helped to settle things down, and now all that was needed was for Brummie to show up again for the whole sorry story to be brought to an end.

'Well, not entirely,' said Bill to himself, as he turned into the car park of the DIY store. There was still one last job to do, which he would start tonight and complete over his two days of holiday. With the image of Louise's face at the taxi window springing to mind every time he closed his eyes, he had come to the conclusion that it was his solemn duty to wipe all trace of Libidan from the face of the earth. Every document he had ever produced relating to its existence he would burn in the incinerator at the bottom of his garden, along with every last granule of the drug substance itself. As for the glass vessels and chromatographic column, these he would smash one by one into the tiniest of pieces and then deposit them in industrial disposal sacks from the DIY store.

Four hours later, with all the equipment disassembled and lined up neatly on the laboratory floor for breaking up the next morning, Bill switched off the downstairs lights and made his way up to bed. Wearied by the evening's work, but nevertheless satisfied with what he had achieved, he began to think for the first time of what he might possibly do with his life now that Libidan was behind him.

'Yeah, well, let's worry about that tomorrow,' he said to himself as he threw his shirt into the corner of the room and moved across the hallway to the bathroom.

No sooner had he finished cleaning his teeth, than he heard a noise coming from the back of the house. It sounded like it might be from the kitchen. Opening the bathroom door, he stood still in the hallway and listened. There it was again. Returning to his bedroom he retrieved his shirt and resolved to go downstairs and have a look.

'Is anyone there?' he called out from the stairs. If it were burglars, the best thing to do would be unequivocally to announce his presence and they would no doubt wish to make their escape as soon as possible. Gallumphing as noisily as he could down the remainder of the stairs, he switched on the light in the downstairs hallway and peered through into the kitchen. Someone was moving around. There was no doubt about it. A silhouette – it appeared to be somebody of quite slight build. Bill groaned to himself. The sound of a kitchen chair scraping on the stone floor. He was being burgled. Being burgled by some local kids.

'What do you want?' called out Bill as he entered the kitchen.

'Money,' came the response.

Bill turned on the light. The man was sitting on the kitchen table, his feet resting on one of the chairs. To Bill's complete surprise, he could see that he was holding an orange, which he had obviously brought with him, and was nonchalantly peeling off the skin. Despite the fear he felt at having his home invaded in this way, Bill found that he could not help staring in fascination at the peculiar sight before him. Poised straight backed on top of the table, with his red leathery skin and neat chewing movements, the man looked like some strange exotic monkey.

'I don't keep cash around the house. Look, can you …'

'Not your money,' interrupted the man, 'mine.'

'What d'you mean, your money? I haven't got your money.'

'Oh, yes you have,' replied the man, casting a piece of orange peel on the floor. Bill felt his hackles rise and he angrily took a step forwards.

'Who d'you think you are, coming in here … ?'

Once again the man interrupted Bill.

'I asked Brummie who'd got my money and he gave me this address. You do live here, don't you?' The man turned to look at Bill and smiled. 'I thought so. Yeah. Brummie's had to give up one or two addresses lately. Had his finger in too many pies, stupid sod. First of all, he told the police where I keep my Manesty. And then, of course, once they'd taken it away, he had to go and tell me where you live.'

'You're … you're the guy with the factory, aren't you?' said Bill after several seconds.

'That's right,' replied the man.

Shifting the chair with his foot and sliding off the table the man turned and squared up to Bill. He was a good six inches smaller than Bill, and considerably less well built, but his face … it was absolutely ter-rifying. Bill had never seen anything like it.

'Have the police raided your factory, then? Where you make your drugs … ?'

'Oh, no,' replied Snod. 'The factory's all right. Brummie wasn't that stupid. If he'd've told 'em where that was I'd have fuckin' killed him. No. He had to tell 'em something to get them off his back. So he sold 'em a dummy – gave 'em the little warehouse where I keep my Manesty.'

'Look, I'm sorry about that,' said Bill, quickly, 'but it wasn't my fault.'

'Correction – where I used to keep my Manesty. Because I haven't got it any more now, have I? Mr Plod's gone and locked it all away in his shed.'

'Look, I told you, it wasn't …'

154

'Quiet now, children!' cried Snod, putting his finger to his lips. 'Teacher's gonna tell us what we've all got to do next. Right. Tomorrow I'm gonna go away and talk to my nice friend and see if he can find me a new Manesty from somewhere. And meanwhile, you – you're gonna go off and get me the fifty grand to pay for it.'

'What?'

'You heard.'

'I haven't got fifty thousand pounds! You're mad!'

'Say that again.'

'No, look, sorry, I didn't mean that. But I can't find that sort of money! Besides it wasn't my fault. You can't expect me to ...'

The first thing Bill knew about the hemp bag was when it crashed into his sternum, blowing every last ounce of air out of his lungs and sending him careering backwards against the kitchen dresser. As he lurched forwards again, gasping for air, Bill saw Snod twist the bag around his other hand, take a step forwards and swing it upwards in an arching, underarm movement. It connected directly with his jaw. The ceiling flashed crazily before his eyes and the next thing he knew he had landed in a heap on the hard stone floor. Looking up, he watched Snod walk slowly across the kitchen and stand over his prostrate body. Even if he had seen the blow which followed he would never have been able to move out of the way in time. Savagely jabbing his fist downwards, Snod put his full weight into a punch to Bill's testicles. The bolt of pain that shot up through his groin was excruciating and Bill curled up in a paroxysm of agony.

But Snod had not finished. Raising the bag of oranges above his head, he began smashing it down repeatedly onto Bill's defenseless, doubled-up body.

'Don't ... fuckin' ... tell ... me ... I ... can't ... have ... my ... money!'

Returning to his perch on top of the kitchen table, Snod then unwound the bag, took out an orange and began to peel it. It was a full five minutes before Bill was able to move. By the time he had managed to drag himself to the table and pull himself up on to a kitchen chair, Snod had finished eating the orange and was licking his fingers clean.

'All a little bit clearer now, is it?' asked Snod.

Bill nodded.

'Good. Now, I don't care how you raise the money. Sell your house.

Do what the fuck you like. But you owe me. You owe me big time – and I'm not going anywhere till you've paid. OK?'

'OK.'

'Great – I'm glad we're makin' progress. Now, insurance. Just in case you're thinkin' of goin' awol or somethin'. There's these. Recognise 'em?'

Raising his head slowly, Bill looked down the table towards Snod. He was holding something in his hand. A piece of clothing of some sort. Bill strained to fight back the pain and nausea so that he could focus properly. Finally, he could make out what it was.

In Snod's hand was a single pair of women's panties.

'Yeah, that's right. Your little lady – in Marylebone. I followed you down to her place the other night. I haven't touched her. Yet. But I know where you are, and I know where she is, and – like I said – you owe me.'

Dropping the panties on the table, Snod gave Bill a final nod and moved off towards the back door.

'Stop,' gasped Bill – he could scarcely speak. His left-hand side, which had taken the brunt of the attack was screaming in pain – he guessed one of the blows might have ruptured his liver.

'What?'

'What's your name?'

'Snod,' replied the man cheerfully. 'Call me Snod.'

'I need time, Snod.'

'Yeah?'

'Yeah. I'll pay you. I promise. But I can't get the money just like that.'

Snod paused for a moment, seeming to make some mental calculations.

'OK. You can have four months max. But it's five grand a month interest and if you haven't found the money by then I'll come back and finish the job.'

Bill nodded in reply and then fell forward on the table, overcome by nausea.

When next he was able to look up, Snod had gone.

Part Three

Sex Sells Everything

Chapter 9

The front door was already swinging open as he walked up the drive. In a single, graceful movement his sister came out on to the step and kissed him on the cheek.

'Where did you park the artic, then?' she asked coolly, looking out at the busy street behind.

'I, er, came on the train,' replied Bill uneasily. Even the slight pressure of her hand resting on his chest had sent a painful shiver sweeping across his bruised ribs.

'Come on. You'd better come in,' responded Gail. He looked even guiltier than she had expected.

'How are you feeling, then?' asked Bill, as they walked through to the lounge.

'Oh, much better now, thanks. I was probably well enough to go in today, but the doctor said I ought to stay off until the end of the week. Make sure I'm fully recovered.'

'Oh, good idea,' replied Bill, recalling the grave-faced physician in Accident and Emergency who had told him that he would need at least a month to ensure the same.

'Aren't you going to take your coat off?'

'No, I'm all right for a bit, thanks,' answered Bill, slowly levering himself down into the nearest dining chair.

'Oh, OK. Suit yourself. I've just made some tea, do you want some?'

'Yeah, yeah, I'd love one.'

'So, there you go, lover-boy,' said Gail, smiling ironically as she passed the mug across the table.

'So, Louise told you, then?' replied Bill, leaning forward and taking a sip. Until Snod had arrived on the scene, he had lived in fear and trepidation of the moment when he would have to face his sister. Now, all that passed through his mind was how good her tea tasted.

'Yeah – and she phoned me last night too, told me all about your little tête-à-tête on Tuesday night. Really. The two of you. Cavorting around the house in drunken …'

'Where was she when she phoned?' interrupted Bill.

'At her place, I suppose.'

'What time was it?'

'Oh, I don't know – half past nine?'

'Did she sound OK?'

'Yeah, she sounded fine. Why d'you ask?'

'Oh, it's just I wondered whether she got home all right, that's all. I tried to reach her at her flat this morning but there was no answer.'

'Well, she's gone to work, hasn't she?'

'Have you got her work number? I need to call her now, if I can.'

'Yeah, of course, I have. But look, Bill – I mean, it's probably not my place to say this, but I don't think she really wants to take things any further.'

'I know,' replied Bill, simply.

'Oh,' said Gail. The expression on her brother's face was indeed anything but love-lost. 'OK, I'll get it now.'

'Thanks. Listen. Can I crash out here tonight?'

'Yeah, of course you can. Is everything all right, Bill?'

'Yeah, fine,' replied Bill, at last managing a smile. 'There's just something she ought to know about, that's all. Nothing serious.'

Standing in the hallway in front of the door to Louise's flat, Bill ran his eyes around the doorframe and lintel. There were no visible signs of entry and Louise had not mentioned anything about burglary, either to Gail or to himself when he had finally been able to reach her at work that afternoon. How would Snod have got in? Picked the lock, perhaps? Bill simply didn't have a clue. Sombrely, he shook his head and raised his hand to knock on the solid oak door.

'Hello.'

'Hi! Come on in!'

Wincing, Bill followed Louise down the hall. Of all the things

160

she could be wearing, why did it have to be that pinstriped suit again?

'Thanks for seeing me at such short notice.'

'Oh, that's all right. I wasn't doing anything tonight. Besides, well, you know – like I said – you're always welcome to pop in any time. Sit down. Please.'

'Thanks.'

'D'you want a drink or something?' asked Louise, extracting a carton of milk from a bag of shopping that was lying on the dining table. 'Sorry, I haven't been back from work long.'

'No, no. I'm fine. Unless, you want one.'

'No, I'm OK, too. So, what was it, you, er, wanted to talk about in such a hurry, then?' asked Louise, sitting down on the armchair opposite and smiling at him brightly.

'Last Friday.'

'Oh. Again? I thought we'd had all this …'

'It wasn't the alcohol,' blurted out Bill. 'And it wasn't because you were tired, either.'

'What d'you mean? I don't understand …' replied Louise, her smile quickly giving way to a look of puzzlement.

'I haven't told a soul about this, Louise. I promised myself I was going to take the secret to my grave. And I would have done as well. You'll be the only person in the world who knows.'

'Knows what?'

'Four carboxy D alanyl three propyl leucine galactate.'

'What on earth's that?'

Bill paused. This was it. He was going to tell her everything. Well, almost.

'I didn't resign from Asper on principle – I discovered something there. Accidents happen in laboratories, you know. Freak accidents. Fleming opened up his Petri dish to get a better look at the bacteria he was cultivating. A spore landed inside – a week later he'd discovered penicillin. In the 1970's a peptide researcher dropped a flask on the floor and breaking every single safety precaution in the book put his finger in the mixture and tasted it. It was two hundred times sweeter than sugar. Aspartame. I left the protective hood open on my experimental chamber. It was that day when you and Gail first came down. A gas escaped. … I've isolated it, Louise.'

161

'What sort of a gas?' asked Louise – now utterly transfixed by Bill's air of solemnity.

'It contains a quatrapeptide – four amino acids linked together. Remember the beer mats, in Joe Bananas? Only it's not a chain, it's a cyclic ring – a ball, if you like.' Extending his hand, Bill clenched it tightly into a fist. 'It's extremely structurally robust, highly resistant to protease degradation in the blood stream – and it's phenomenally bioavailable; there's a hydroxyl group in the ninth position. It'll go through any mucosal membrane – lungs, nasal passages, you name it. It's kintamane, Louise. Modified kintamane. A neuropeptide. Millions of years old.'

'Hang on, hang on a minute – you're losing me. What exactly does it do, this stuff?'

Bill swallowed hard.

'It makes you do what you did. Last Friday.'

Louise blinked twice, looked across at the wall and then back at Bill. For a moment, it appeared as though she might not have understood his explanation, but, just as he was on the point of going over it again, she stood up and walked across to the fireplace.

'Are you saying this stuff you've discovered makes you want to have sex?'

'It makes women want to have sex, Louise. You've got a receptor for it. I haven't – men haven't, that is – it just passes straight through the male physiology with no effects whatsoever.'

'And did you give it to me?'

Fixing his gaze on a spot of wall six inches above her head and hating himself for his cowardice, Bill brought out the first of the two lies he intended to tell that night.

'No. I'd been working on it ever since I left Asper. I set up a lab in my house. That's what the guinea-pigs were for. There's almost no ventilation in the place and the atmosphere was completely saturated with it. I mean, I knew it was tremendously bioavailable but I never dreamed it would be quite to that degree, and then, of course, you turned up unexpectedly, and, well, you know the rest ...'

'But I never felt anything!'

She had believed him. Absolutely. Once again he had betrayed her trust.

'No, you wouldn't. It's a naturally occurring neuropeptide, inducing

162

an absolutely normal sexual response – the biochemistry is identical.'

'That's amazing! You're not having me on, are you? God, no, of course you're not.' Sitting back down again she looked across at him in fascination. 'So, why's no one come across it before?'

'Why had no one come across penicillin before? Your brain has thousands of chemical substances running around inside it. Why should anyone have sat down and tried to check out what this one would do if you administer it directly to the lungs?'

'God! What a discovery! But hang on – go back a bit. What was it you were saying about wanting to keep it a secret?'

'After you came round, I realized what might happen if it got into the wrong hands and so I decided to destroy it – burn everything. I'd had my dreams before that – you know? A wonder drug. Libidan I called it. A sexual dysfunction therapy for menopausal women. I mean, that's the irony – it's perfectly safe. It could bring relief to thousands of women. But, I hadn't thought the abuse thing through. Seems incredible now, doesn't it?'

'So, why didn't you destroy it, then?'

'The tests backfired on me. I had some pills made, you see. A bloke at the delivery firm I work for, he got 'em knocked up on a tablet press owned by this sort of, well, drug baron, I suppose you'd call him. I didn't know any of this at the time, of course – I just thought he'd get it done on the quiet and … Well, anyway, the long and short of it is, this bloke was into all sorts of scams, and ended up doing a deal with the police to save his neck for a half a dozen other things they wanted him for. He told them where Snod's warehouse was and then did a bunk.'

'Snod's the drug baron?'

'Yeah, that's right. The police went and impounded some of his tableting equipment and now he blames me. Says I owe him.'

'Well, it wasn't your fault, was it?'

'That's what I said at first,' replied Bill, 'but if a joy rider stole your car and smashed it into a wall, who would you blame?'

'Oh. I suppose so. What does he want?'

'Fifty thousand pounds.'

'What!'

'Yeah.'

'So why don't you go to the police?'

'I can't.'

'Why not?'

Bill bit his tongue before speaking. This second lie was to be even more cowardly than the first.

'Because of what he might do to people I know. What he might do … to you.'

'To me? What have I got to do with all this?'

'He's been following me. I'm sure of it. I think he might even have followed me here when I came down to see you on Friday night. If I don't pay, I'm worried he might try to lean on you, or Gail, or someone – I don't know …'

'Oh.'

'But look, don't worry. I'd never let anything happen to anyone else because of my mistakes. Honestly. I promise that. I'm gonna pay him. Sell the house. Give him his money – all of it. But in the meantime, you've got to take care. That's what I came here to tell you. I don't think he's going to try anything, but you really ought to be on your guard all the same.'

Bill had dreaded this moment most of all, fearing how terrified Louise might be at even the oblique threat of violence. Instead, she merely stood up and walked across the room again deep in thought.

'How long have you got to pay him?'

'Four months. He's charging me five thousand pounds a month interest.'

'If you do pay, will he stay off your back – as far as you can tell?'

'Yeah. I think so. He just wants the money to buy himself a new machine.'

'And this stuff, Libidan – great name, by the way – are you sure it's safe?'

'Assuming the molecule is what I think it is – yes, completely safe.'

'And how sure are you of that?'

'Ninety-nine percent. A hundred, if I could get it x-rayed on the right equipment.'

'Hm.' Pursing her lips, Louise began pacing the room again. 'Well, it seems to me you've got two options. Firstly …'

'I have to pay him, Louise,' interrupted Bill, excitedly, 'he's a violent man. A psycho. And I'm absolutely not going to let anything happen to …'

'Yeah, yeah. I agree – you'll have to pay him,' continued Louise, holding up her hand to calm Bill down. 'But in terms of how you generate the cash – that's where you've got a couple of options. Number one – like you say – you sell your house. Or number two …'

Louise left the sentence trailing.

'What … ?' asked Bill, his mouth hanging open expectantly.

Una was surprised to find that the meeting was to be held in the home of one of the members of the group. As far as she had understood, this was entirely contrary to normal ALA procedures; certainly it was the first time she had seen anything like it in her eighteen months with them.

'Aren't we all a bit conspicuous here?' she asked Ray, as she parked her car next to the others in the driveway. Up ahead, in the beams of her headlights, she could also make out Len's motorbike, leaning against the front wall of the large Tudor-style house.

'We had another place lined up, but we had to cancel it at the last minute. This is Latitia's house. Keep your voice down.'

So, this was where the silent, sultry Latitia lived.

Walking through an ornamental gate leading to the rear garden, Ray stopped and unlocked a concealed side door. A narrow staircase ascended steeply up to a room over the house's broad double garage. Judging by the distinctive sheet-metal light shades that still hung in the centre of the room, Una could see that it had originally housed a snooker table. In place of the green baize, there was now a large pine table around which the other members of the group were already seated. There was no other lighting in the room and it was difficult to make out their faces. Una did notice Latitia at the far end of the table, though, and the look she exchanged with Ray as he sat down. The key he had used to open the side door had been on his own key ring – Una had noticed that, too.

'Sorry we're late,' said Ray. 'Traffic.'

To her left, Una could see Len's lip curling in a sneer. He always thought her incapable of performing even the simplest of tasks. Well, tonight she would show him.

'OK,' continued Ray. 'Now, if you're all in agreement, I want to get straight on to the animal testing laboratories we've been watching in …'

'I've got something to tell you first,' announced Una – surprised at how authoritative her voice sounded. 'I've been doing some observations of my own.'

A stir passed around the table. Una was the most junior of the group, and she had never spoken out like this before. She could see Ray frowning, but then checking himself. He might only pay lip-service to the notion of the equality of individuals within the group, but she was bargaining on it being enough to allow her a say. At least this once, anyway.

'OK, Una,' said Ray slowly, clearly only being able to keep the condescension out of his voice with considerable effort. 'What do you want to tell us?'

'I've found something. Some people. In Harledge. Exploiting animals in the most sickening, the most horrible way you could ever imagine.'

She herself felt touched by the emotion with which her voice was charged. She looked around the table. She had their attention, now, all right.

'Doing what?' asked Ray.

'I saw them through a window – a couple – I saw them with my own eyes. He had the poor defenceless creature in his hand one minute, and then the next minute, it was gone.'

'Come on, Una, tell us …' coaxed Ray. Could Una really be on to something?

Like a medium summoning up a spirit at a seance, Una closed her eyes tightly and, placing her palms flat on the table top, gathered up all her spiritual energy for the dreadful, climactic invocation.

'I believe I may have found a group of … felchers.'

Several seconds of silence followed. When Una finally opened her eyes, however, she could see that none of the other members of the group had moved so much as an inch or had altered their facial expressions in the slightest.

'What's a, er, felcher, exactly?' asked Ray, slowly.

A feeling of horror crept over Una. These were all worldly people. She had assumed that they would know. Now she was going to have to explain. In detail.

'Well, it's when people … when people are having, er, sex … they put a sort of soft plastic tube up their … and then let animals, mice or guinea-pigs or whatever, run up and down it.'

'Sorry, Una. They put a tube where?' asked Ray.

'Up their, you know, up their …'

166

'Up their arseholes!' shouted Len, suddenly, smashing his fist down on the table. 'Jesus Christ, what is this! We've got a bloody multinational drugs giant right on our doorstep, dissecting twenty-five beagles a week – industrialised slaughter – and all she's worried about is some randy suburban couple trying to spice up their Saturday night sex life!'

'Leave it out, Len,' said Ray.

'Did they have a leopard-skin rug in front of the fire as well, Una? Eh? I suppose you thought that was real, too, didn't you?'

'Len!' shouted Ray.

Slamming his fist down on the table one more time, Len leaned resentfully back in his chair. Ray turned to Una. Even before he spoke, she knew the condescension would be back.

'Una. We value your contribution. We all do. But Len has a point. Much as we abhor individual acts of cruelty, our targets are organized, institutionalized groupings that condone or subsist by animal exploitation. Individuals. Institutions. Try and focus on that difference, if you can, please. Thank you.'

Mortified with humiliation, Una nodded once and then dropped her head, trying to lean back into the shadows while Ray continued talking about the plans for the strike on the laboratories.

When next she dared look up at the other members of the group, she could see that Latitia had rolled up a piece of scrap paper into a tube and, whilst trying to catch Ray's attention with a pouting stare, was slowly running her manicured forefinger around its rim.

The one part of the Biochemistry Building that Bill had forgotten was the reception. As a student he had been so used to walking straight past the desk that when the uniformed Guard called out to him from behind its glass partition, Bill took several seconds to locate the source of the voice.

'Er, excuse me, sir? Sir! Can I help you?'

'Oh, sorry, yes, I've come to see Professor Castle.'

'And you are?'

'Bill Kennedy.'

'Mr … Bill … Kennedy,' repeated the Guard, writing Bill's name in the visitors book. 'Of … ?'

'Pardon?'

'Of which company, sir?'

'Oh, er, er, Kennedy Associates,' replied Bill. It was as good a name as any to be going on with. Not that he was yet anywhere near convinced that Louise's idea was really going to work.

'There you are, sir,' said the Guard, passing the lapel badge across to Bill. 'Do you know your way up?'

'Is she still on the third floor?'

'Yes – she hasn't moved,' responded the Guard cheerily.

As the lift doors opened, Bill folded his arms over his chest. The central corridor that ran through the Biochemistry labs was renowned throughout the entire University as a veritable obstacle course of filing cabinets and redundant pieces of equipment – painful on elbows or knees at the best of times, never mind a set of severely bruised ribs. Once in the corridor itself, though, he was surprised to discover that not only had all the mechanical clutter been removed, but also someone had even seen fit to brighten it up with some high-quality strip-lighting.

Wandering slowly along, Bill stared in nostalgia at the array of homemade posters affixed to the plasterboard walls, outlining the theses being carried out by the department's various Ph.D. students. Smiling to himself, he remembered how proud he had been when the project for his own Doctorate had been put up. What would he have said then, if he could have known that seven years later one of his discoveries was going to be satellited through cyberspace to every corner of the globe?

'Bill? Is that you?'

'Yes, Professor Castle, it's me.'

'Good Lord, you haven't changed a bit!' exclaimed the Professor, leaning forward and kissing him on the cheek. 'How long has it been?'

'Seven years.'

'Seven years! My word. Do come in, do come in.'

'Thanks.'

For the second time that morning Bill pulled up in surprise, for although the Professor still had the same room, it was absolutely unrecognizable from his student days. Gone were the precariously stacked columns of books, each topped by a half-empty mug of coffee. Gone were the museum piece reaction vessels, the yards of rubber tubing and the tincture bottles of a thousand hues. Gone, in fact, was the whole mysterious labyrinth into which he had been accustomed to crawl for his tutorials, like a child worming his way through the bushes at the bottom of the garden into a secret den. Instead, there was nothing but a sweeping bleached pine desk, surmounted by just about the largest VDU Bill had ever seen.

'Wow, this has changed!'

'Yes, yes,' replied the Professor, laconically tying back a whisp of ginger hair behind her ear. 'Progress of sorts, I suppose you'd call it.'

'It's just as well I met you in the corridor; I'd never have recognized it otherwise.'

'Well, five minutes later and you'd have missed me – I've got another one of these lunch appointments with which I seem to be plagued these days. So, quick, tell me. What brings you here, then, Bill? Are you still with Asper?'

'No, not any more. I've gone to an independent start-up.'

'Really? How enterprising!'

'Yeah, well, we're small, but we've got big ideas.'

'Great!'

'So, anyway, we need a bit of x-ray crystallography doing, and I remembered the machine you had here so I thought I'd ask you if you could do it for us.'

'Oh, you bet we can, Bill. How wonderful of you to think of the college. Bringing back the dollars to the old alma mater, eh?'

'Well, it was more in the line of a sort of favour than ...'

'So, let me see,' interrupted the Professor opening the desk drawer to her left and then thrusting a series of documents across at him. 'You'll need a confidentiality agreement, a contract for external services package, a set of our standard terms and conditions and, of course, a current price list – doesn't include VAT but talk to us nicely and we'll see if we can't fix something up for you.'

'Oh, er, thanks.'

'You'll find us very competitive against the commercial labs. We have to be nowadays. It's all money, money, money! So, who do I talk to about the follow-up?' asked the Professor avidly, her pen poised to record the name in her personal organizer. 'Is it you, or does your firm have a commercial director?'

'It's quite a small job, actually,' said Bill, by now feeling decidedly uncomfortable with the direction that the conversation had taken.

'Small, medium, large – we'll bid for 'em all. Oh, excuse me. This damn thing never gives me a minute's peace.'

As she extracted the mobile phone from her handbag and began to discuss details of her lunch appointment, Bill could feel his enthusiasm for Louise's idea rapidly begin to wane. It was obvious the Professor was not going to sanction the department doing the tests for free and the prices on the list she had given him were all in four figures. How could he have been so stupid as to imply that he was working for a company who could pay for them? He was supposed to be adding to the fund to pay Snod off, not taking away from it.

'Listen, Bill, I know you've only just arrived but I've just got to dash,' said the Professor, taking her coat down from the back of the door. 'Take a look at the contracts while I'm out. And have a look around the labs. We've got some tremendous new equipment!'

Wandering dejectedly back down the corridor towards the lift, Bill peered through the inspection panels on the doors either side; the department had indeed acquired some prestige new equipment. But this was all a waste of time. Not just his time, but Louise's as well. The sooner he got back to Harledge, sold the house and got out of her life the better. Stopping at the room which had previously housed the x-ray crystallograph, but which was now obviously quite empty, Bill shook his head and then marched off in the direction of the lift.

'It's Bill Kennedy, isn't it?'

Bill did not even need to turn around, for he immediately recognized the voice as that of Ray Gillmartin, the department's chief analytical chemist, with whom he had worked during his Ph.D.

'Hello, how are you?'

'Yeah, great! You?' replied Bill

'Fine. Did you come to see Linda?'

'Yeah. God, she's shaken this place up, hasn't she?'

'Oh, too right. Just as well she did 'n' all. It'd've been curtains for us otherwise. Listen, what are you doin' for lunch?'

'Nothing.'

'Me neither. Fancy a pint?'

'Yeah, sure.'

'I'll get my coat.'

As Ray smiled and turned to make his way down the corridor, Bill was astonished to find his vocal chords starting to generate sounds and his lips forming them into words.

'Here, Ray …'

'What?'

170

'You, er, couldn't run this through the crystallograph for me could you?'

'What, now?'

'Erm, yes, please.'

'Yeah, OK. No problem,' replied Ray.

'I sort of asked the Prof, but she, er, well, gave me a load of contracts.'

'Oh, she's a right hustler nowadays,' replied Ray with a smile. 'But don't worry. I'll do it for you for nothing – for old times sake. Besides, we've got a new machine now. Only takes a couple of minutes to set up. It's a brilliant piece of kit. The results might even be ready by the time we get back from lunch.'

Taking the phial of white powder from Bill, Ray turned and walked quickly off down the corridor

'Now, just how on earth did I manage that?' thought Bill.

Louise was extremely impressed with the seven glossy prints, each depicting the compound's three-dimensional molecular structure in a different plane of elevation. The last of these computer-enhanced images in particular fired her imagination. Represented against a black background as a dozen or so spherical nodules interconnected by a matrix of silver-coloured carbon bonds, the molecule seemed almost like a space-station floating in some distant interstellar void. After staring at the picture for several moments, Louise found herself having to look away to counteract the peculiar vertiginous feeling that was beginning to creep over her.

'And this is exactly what you thought it would be?' she said, carefully sliding the prints back inside the yellow cardboard envelope.

Bill momentarily looked up from uncorking the wine and gave a quick nod. Although her own scientific background was limited, Louise could imagine how enormously knowledgeable Bill must be to have theoretically calculated this complex structure with such absolute accuracy.

'Right. Well, I guess it's my turn to show you what I've found out, then,' she said, making a space amongst the hastily prepared plates of hoummos and olives.

'Is this what you got from work?' asked Bill, passing her some wine.

'Yeah,' replied Louise, taking a quick sip from the glass and then lifting her briefcase up on to the table. 'Radley's have got a whole library of stuff on legislation and marketing regulations. I hadn't realized it was there before.'

'It won't get you into trouble, will it – doing all this on the side?'

'On the contrary, it'll probably get me promoted,' answered Louise, dryly. 'As long as I'm beavering away on Libidan, I'm not showing up all the other amateurs I'm forced to work with, am I?'

'Oh, I suppose not,' replied Bill, recalling the frustrations with the lack of challenge at Radley's she had expressed so vigorously the previous Friday evening.

'Right,' said Louise, taking out the two pages of handwritten notes and placing them on the table. 'The bad news is that it looks like oral administration is a complete no-no. So, no pills and no tucking it away in a herbal tonic like you suggested.'

'Why not?' replied Bill vehemently. 'I mean, they'll never find it at five parts per million. Not even with the most sophisticated ...'

'It's not a question of what's inside the bottle,' interrupted Louise, ' it's what on the outside that counts.'

'How d'you mean?'

'All orally-administered compounds, with the exception of licensed medicines, are covered by the food labelling regulations of 1996. Where's the passage I'm looking for? Oh, yes, here we are: "A claim that a food has the property of preventing, treating or curing a human disease or any reference to such a property is forbidden". We even so much as hint that our product restores the libido and the authorities'll be down on us like a ton of bricks.'

'So, what can we do, then? It takes years to get a product licence for a medicine!'

'We go for nasal administration.'

'What?'

'You did say it'll go in through the nose, didn't you?'

'Yeah, but that still makes it a medicine. Inhalers, nasal drops, what have you – they all need a product licence.'

'Perfumes don't.'

'A perfume?'

'Yeah. It's a cosmetic then. All we have to declare are the ingredients. And, like you say, at five parts per million, nobody'd ever find the active substance even if they could be bothered to look for it.'

'But you can't make a claim for a cosmetic, can you?'

'No, but we don't have to – not directly. I mean, perfumes are all about auto-suggestion anyway, aren't they? You know, implied product benefits.'

'I hadn't thought of a perfume.'

'I've been thinking about nothing else all day. And there are a load of other plus-points for a perfume, too. Mainly to do with association. Women associate perfume with sex – in an oblique sort of way, maybe, but certainly much more than they do with pills or herbal tonics. And also they're very sensitive about their bodies during the menopause. It's a big life-change. Because a perfume is applied externally, they won't get all neurotic about filling themselves up with androgens and oestrogens and what have you. All they have to do is just spray it on once before they go to bed.'

'What about dosage compliance?'

'What d'you mean – they spray on too much?

'Or not enough.'

'Can't we use one of those one-shot thingees?'

'You mean a metered-dose dispenser?'

'Yeah, exactly. We'll have to make it quite strong-smelling, to make sure they don't put on too much. That's a bit of a disadvantage, I suppose, but it's still probably the best way of doing it. '

Bill went to say something, but stopped and then looked pensively out of the window for several seconds.

'You're right,' he said finally. 'A perfume's definitely best. There's just one practical problem though.'

'What's that?'

'The vapour dynamics.'

'Which are what, exactly?'

'Perfumes are basically solutions of alcohol. It's the action of the alcohol evaporating that transports the aromatic compounds up into the nasal cavities – along with the drug substance, of course.'

'And …'

'The trouble is, I don't know what the characteristics of Libidan are in an alcohol solution. I mean, it might not even be soluble in HFC's or whatever they use nowadays. And even if it is, I don't know how it'll perform once you start squirting it around. I imagine the big problem's going to be timing the release exactly right.'

'What d'you mean?'

'Perfumes normally evaporate over hours. If the patients are going to spray it on just before they go to bed we'll have to bring about complete evaporation in, I don't know, ten to fifteen minutes or something.'

Louise frowned. Obviously Bill's knowledge was not as all-embracing as she had imagined.

'Can't you work it out? In your lab.'

'I don't think I've got time – in fact, I'm sure I haven't got time. I mean, there are bound to be specialists out there who spend their whole lives doing this sort of thing, but they certainly don't operate in the pharmaceutical industry. I wouldn't have a clue who to ask.'

'Oh, I see …'

They sat in silence for several seconds, but before Louise had time to become really despondent, Bill suddenly leant forward and smiled.

'Hang on, though. Wait a minute … I've just remembered something.'

Having scraped the remains of her half-eaten evening meal into the waste bin, Una washed up the plates and cutlery. Hanging the tea towel on the radiator she surveyed her lonely, narrow kitchen. It wasn't about animals for them. Not really. It was politics. And not even politics in Latitia's case – all she wanted was the thrills. Well, she would show them yet. All those class warriors and their ghoulish hangers on. She would get evidence – incontrovertible evidence to put paid to their disbelief and shame them into action. Moving into the bedroom, she slipped on her nightie quickly so as not to get cold, and then curled up underneath the quilt. She knew she had right on her side. She had seen that poor, tortured creature in Bill Kennedy's hand. The image was before her eyes every time she closed them.

Ten minutes later, on the verge of sleep, the image was still there, but its focal point was starting to shift – just as it did at this same time every night. Away from Bill. Away from the guinea-pig in his hand and down towards Louise's backside. Naked. Gyrating. Grinding. And, in a deep, dark corner of her mind, in a dungeon from which she had thought all escape impossible, Una heard the wailing of a lonely, tormented creature of her own as it strained to break free from its shackles. A creature that she had been able ruthlessly to deny all sustenance.

Until now.

Chapter 10

Situated halfway between London and the coastal resort of Brighton, the village of Greenhill had for most of its eight-hundred-year history led a fairly sequestered existence, being generally regarded by travellers down the ages as too small or too rural to be worthy of even the briefest of stop-overs. In the middle of the nineteenth century however, the Great Southern Railway Company recognized Greenhill's strategic location and purchased a large tract of land adjoining the village. Within a generation the sleepy settlement was transformed into a bustling railway town. Families who for centuries had sent their sons into the fields now watched them march off to labour in the steelyards, or take up apprenticeships in the carriage shops. No sooner had the mighty network been built, though, than one by one the anvils and riveting guns fell silent, and modern day Greenhill is little more than a satellite town of Greater London. So it was that as Bill made his way around its featureless one-way system, he travelled in ignorance of the railwaymen whose industry and endeavour had built the town. For today no civic monument recalls their labour, no commemorative plaque pays homage to their toil.

Passing under a low bridge, Bill kept his eyes peeled for the large red-brick building that Peter Layford had described as housing the offices of 5ZPharma. Frowning, he remembered the elation he had felt when his ex-colleague had agreed to arrange a meeting with the Managing Director, Mr Winston Dougal: now that he had actually arrived for it – five minutes late and sweating inside his best suit – the whole venture was growing more and more forbidding by the moment. Five weeks ago, when Bill had gone drinking with Peter, it had been the example of this very company's entrepreneurial spirit that had inspired him to start developing Libidan. But what if 5ZPharma chose not to deal with him? And, even if they were prepared to put him in touch with a specialist company in the field of metered-dose aerosols, how much would they charge for the service? Snapping out of his reverie a half a second too late, Bill saw the entrance go drifting past on the left-hand side.

'Damn!'

He would have to go all the way around the one-way system again. With a grimace, Bill leaned closer to the steering wheel: the butterflies in his stomach which he had vainly been trying to ignore all morning were now going completely frantic and he hadn't even met the man yet. According to Peter, Dougal and a fellow entrepreneur had started out brokering penicillin-purification technology from a rented office above a travel agent. Twenty years later they had built a diversified life-sciences corporation with an annual turnover in the hundreds of millions. Cadging a favour off an old mate like Ray Gillmartin with a pie and a pint was one thing. Getting a shark like Dougal – the veteran, no doubt, of a thousand blood-spattered commercial encounters – to hand over industrial intelligence for a song was going to be quite another. Approaching the slip-road at the side of 5ZPharma's offices, Bill had to fight down the temptation to drive right past. But there was to be no turning back now. Louise's idea of a perfume-dispenser had been absolutely inspired and he had to do his best to see how he could develop it – it was the very least he owed her.

The car park was completely full. Having driven around three times, Bill decided to leave his car on the street outside. It was a single yellow line, but he was now a full ten minutes late and would just have to risk the parking ticket. Springing up the steps of the building, he flashed a nervous smile at the receptionist seated on the other side of the smoked-glass doors. Even as he did so, he realized he had forgotten his briefcase and would have to go back down the steps to get it from the car. Slamming down the boot, he cursed his lack of concentration. Who ever heard of a businessman without a briefcase?

'I've got an appointment to see Mr Dougal. At half past one,' said Bill, hoping he didn't appear to the receptionist even half as nervous as he felt.

'Would you like to go straight up?' she replied pleasantly. 'You'll have to use the stairs, as the lifts aren't working today. Third floor.'

'Oh, thanks, right.'

Spying the men's room on the way to the stairs, Bill thought about nipping in and quickly sprucing himself up but, deciding it was worse form to turn up late than untidy, began straightening his tie and hair as he ascended the stairs. Hurried and confused, he realized after several flights that he was no longer sure of which floor he was on.

Bracing himself for a further excruciating display of his own amateurism, Bill crossed his fingers and walked through the stair door that was now in front of him and into the offices beyond. However, instead of the ranks of power-suited executives he had anticipated, the entire floor turned out to be deserted. There were desks and photocopiers and computers – but seemingly no one around to use them. Reaching the end of the open-plan office, he was about to turn and go back to the stairs when he caught sight of a lone office worker reclining in his chair.

'Excuse me, could you tell me where Mr Dougal's office is?'

The man neither answered nor moved so much as an inch.

'Excuse me, I'm a bit lost, could you …'

Leaving the sentence unfinished, Bill made his way back through the deserted office to the staircase. Something was seriously wrong. Just what sort of a company was 5ZPharma? So far he had only managed to find one employee and he quite plainly had been asleep. Perhaps he should pick up one of the phones and quickly try and call Peter. He looked at his watch – fifteen minutes late. Emerging from the staircase on the next floor, Bill caught sight of a large meeting room on his left. The blinds were drawn, but he could hear the sound of raised voices and people moving about inside. Walking up to the door, he decided there was nothing for it but to knock and go in – if he didn't find Dougal quickly the meeting might end up being cancelled altogether. No sooner had he lifted his fist to knock, than he found himself jumping back in surprise. Something had just come crashing into the blinds in front of him and had wedged itself in between two of the grey plastic blades. Taking a step backwards, Bill managed to get the object in focus. It was a sandwich quarter. Tuna and cucumber. On wholemeal.

'Hello! Dr Kennedy?'

Bill jumped in alarm and turned to his right. Striding down the corridor towards him was a large, extremely red-faced man with just about the broadest Father Christmas grin he had ever seen.

'Yes, that's right,' he replied, shaking the man's hand. 'How d'you do?'

'Winston Dougal. Pleased to meet you. Sorry about the commotion,' said Dougal, nodding at the meeting room sheepishly. 'We closed on a rather large contract this morning and everyone's gone a bit crazy.'

'Oh, right,' said Bill, flinching again as a salvo of champagne corks went off inside the room.

'Come this way – down the corridor to my little island of tranquility here …'

Dougal's office was large, but sparsely decorated: two desks, four chairs and a laptop computer. There were no books or files in sight. On the wall hung a single picture – an autographed, black and white photograph of a professional cricketer. Bill knew almost as much about cricket as he did about soccer, but was nevertheless unable to recognise the bowler concerned. Judging from the photo's blurred edges and sepia tones, the man was in all likelihood a sporting hero from Dougal's youth.

'Take a seat, Dr Kennedy. I'll just go off and track us down some coffee.'

Seating himself behind the larger of the two desks, Bill racked his brains to try to make some sense out of what he had seen. 5ZPharma was clearly the antithesis of everything he had so far experienced inside the pharmaceutical industry. Apart from the receptionist, its employees seemed to be either sound asleep or engaged in some mass, company-sponsored food fight. As he craned his head around the door of the office, to where Dougal was smiling and joking with an elegant, intelligent-looking woman whom Bill took to be his secretary, he found an idea for the coming discussions beginning to form in his mind. For no one played this hard without working even harder.

And no one worked as hard as that without a dream.

'Well, I'm very glad to see you here today, Dr Kennedy,' said Dougal, placing his coffee cup on the tabletop. 'Peter Layford's been a great friend of 5ZPharma's down the years and we're more than happy to help out a colleague of his where we can. So, tell me, what can we do for you?'

This was it. The pleasantries were over now. The time had come for Bill to make his pitch.

'I'm looking for a company with specialist expertise in metered-dose aerosol dispensers. I wondered if you could help me locate one.'

'May I ask why? Are you consulting on behalf of a client, or … ?'

For a moment Bill was tempted to say that he was – consultancy would be a very plausible cover story.

'Er, no, no, actually not. I'm working in an independent capacity. I have been ever since I left Asper.'

'And what is it exactly that you want this aerosol to do?' asked Douglas, his eyes narrowing. The yo-ho-ho smile was now nowhere to be seen.

'To act as a drug delivery system.'

'For what?'

'A pharmacologically active molecule.' Bill swallowed hard. 'It's a compound that I'm attempting to develop on my own.'

'Did you discover this molecule while you were working for Asper?'

They had been talking less than twenty seconds and Dougal had already got straight to the truth. Mentally Bill congratulated himself on not having tried to spin a tale about consultancy. This man would probably have seen through it in moments.

'No, and they have absolutely nothing remotely like it in their research program. Or not to my knowledge, anyway.'

'Good. That's a weight off my mind. I couldn't possibly talk to you any further if that were the case. Asper is one of our most important customers.'

'I respect that.'

'Well, now …' said Dougal, reclining back in his chair, his warm grin returning once more. 'This puts an entirely different complexion on things. I think you're very brave, by the way. Let me say that, for starters. But it won't be easy, you know. Going it on your own.'

'I know.'

'Have you got any finance?'

'A little.'

'And you understand, of course, that although you're not operating on a consultancy basis, I certainly am. It's how I pay my staff.'

'I know. And I want to pay you for your advice.'

'Always assuming I decide to give it, of course. 5ZPharma doesn't tout off-the-shelf technology any more like we used to. Nowadays we choose our customers, not the other way around.'

'Oh, I see …'

'Yes, we represent a very select group of manufacturers now. If we bring them anything other than quality enquiries, it reflects badly on us – as I'm sure you can understand.'

'Yes, yes, of course.'

Dougal stared hard at Bill for several seconds before speaking again.

'Is this invention patentable?'

'Yes, but I'm not going to pursue a patent.'

'Hm. Can you tell me roughly what it is?'

'No.'

Dougal did not flinch at this – it was obviously the response he had expected.

'All right. But I assume if you're looking at metered-dose dispensers, the active substance has to be delivered directly to the lungs or the nasal passages. Correct?'

'Correct. We're looking to formulate it as a perfume.'

'It's a cosmaceutical, then?'

'Yes. That'd be a good term to describe it.'

'Thank you, but it wasn't me who coined the phrase, you know. There are a number of companies actively working in that area already and with a lot more money at their disposal than you, I'm sure. You might be advised to do a patent search and find out whether one of them hasn't already beaten you to it with your particular application.'

'Oh, none of them will have got to this idea first, don't worry.'

'Really?'

'Really. Take my word for it.'

'So, this dispenser, is it, what, applied to the neck?'

'Basically, yes. This is what we're trying to achieve,' replied Bill, opening up his briefcase and extracting the charts he had prepared. 'We need to have the active molecule – I don't know – coated or suspended in such a way that it starts to evaporate after five minutes, with about ninety-five percent evaporation occurring in the next twenty minutes after that.'

'I see. Like a sort of fast zap,' responded Dougal, tracing his finger along the tight bell curve. 'Does the dispenser need to be pressurized?'

'Absolutely not. The atomized stream's got to be generated by pressure of the hand alone. I want to find a company that can firstly develop the formulation for me, and then let me make up a concentrate on their premises – they'll need a clean room to category three containment levels for that.'

'What sort of time lines are you looking at?'

'I need to make up the concentrate within the next two weeks or so.'

'Two weeks!'

'Yes.'

Bill could see a dark shadow of doubt beginning to spread across Dougal's face. Fighting back the image of the time-wasters who might have occupied this same seat before him, he pressed on.

'Once I've got enough concentrate made, I'll take it back to my own premises for dilution and then fill up the metered-dose dispensers myself. I'm renting some facilities on a short-term let – starting Monday for twelve weeks. I'm going to move my mixing gear in there at the weekend. Flasks. Measuring equipment. I have to get the first samples out for test-marketing before the end of the month.'

'So, these aren't proper manufacturing facilities, then?'

'No. It's a garage. At the back of a baker's.'

'They don't exactly sound ideal, Dr Kennedy.'

Recognizing the response as a likely prelude to rejection, Bill decided the time had come to try his gambit. It would be a desperate move – but it was all he had.

'Probably not, I haven't even seen them yet. I'm going around there with the estate agent this afternoon. But, then again, I don't suppose a rented office above a travel agent really seemed the right sort of place to start a life-sciences corporation either, did it, Mr Dougal? But that didn't stop you.'

This time, it was Bill who stared hard at Dougal, before pointedly turning to look at the faded, grainy print of the cricketer on the wall. Looking back at Dougal several moments later, Bill could see that his hunch had been correct. For the older man's eyes were starting to glaze over, as he, too, turned and looked at the picture. The bowler had his arms raised high into the air and his fists clenched in triumph as the bails behind the opposing batsman ricocheted in all directions. After several seconds Dougal finally stood up, walked pensively across the office and picked up a packet of cigars. Bill watched his thoughtful, impassive face, not daring to break the silence.

When finally he spoke, his voice was loud and ebullient.

'Sue!'

'Yes?' came his secretary's voice from beyond the door.

'Get me Advanced Aerosol Systems on the phone, will you? Dr Kris Rasmussen. And then go back to the boardroom and get us a bottle of champagne. In fact, no, do that first, if you wouldn't mind. Dr Kennedy and I need to toast his new venture ...'

Although he was arriving two hours earlier than any of his CID colleagues on the day-shift at Albany Road, Detective Inspector Jack Conlon nevertheless sprang smartly up the concrete steps and into the main reception area. A tall, straight-backed man, he was simply incapable of going anywhere at anything other than a sprightly pace – his father and the army had seen to that. Besides, the period between six and eight o'clock in the morning was the most productive part of his day. The previous night's crop of drunks and yobbos would be lying snoring in their cells, and the phone calls would not start in earnest until nine. He knew that some of his fellow detectives, especially the younger ones, sniped at his fiercely structured day: the sad methodicality of a lonely, teetotal widower with nothing else in his life to occupy him. In fact, he had gone about his work in just as efficient a manner when Edith had been alive. But when early evening came, and these same voices began their bleating chorus of complaint – the lack of time, the mountains of unnecessary paperwork – he would sit at the desk he had already cleared and dare one of them to look him straight in the eye. They never did. And when they caved in with the job not even half done, and trooped off en masse to drown their ill-discipline in alcohol, more often than not it was he, DI Conlon, who would be the last to leave the department, switching off the lights and closing up the office for the day.

'Mornin',' said Conlon, nodding at the desk sergeant as he made his way towards the CID offices behind.

'Good morning Mr Conlon. Oh, Sir, have you got a moment?'

'Yes?' replied Conlon, pausing at the door.

'The custody officer'd like a word. Uniform brought someone in a couple of hours ago ...'

Walking to the end of the corridor, Conlon stuck his head around custody officer McKillop's door.

'Mornin' Tom. What have you got for me?'

'Oh, hello, Jack. Bit of a queer one, actually – down in the cells now,' said the custody officer, moving around from behind his desk and handing Conlon two polythene bags of evidence.

'What is it, a burglary?' asked Conlon, looking down at the jemmy and the black balaclava.

'Well, that's the thing – she says not.'

'She?'

'Yeah. A middle-aged woman. Early forties, I'd say. PC Bryant found her just after three. Got herself impaled on some ornamental railings outside this posh house in Wyburn.'

'Has the duty solicitor seen her yet?'

'No. She's already refused legal advice twice – she says she hasn't done anything wrong. Just wants to tell her story to a detective and get off back home. Worried about some animals or other she's left unattended.'

'Is PC Bryant still around?'

'Yeah. He's been waiting for someone from CID to arrive to interview her.'

'Come on then, give him a call and we'll get it over with.'

'All right. But take a look at this first,' said the custody officer with a smile. 'She might not be much of a burglar, but she can't half knit.'

Extracting the balaclava from the bag, Conlon found himself running his fingers over the smooth, perfectly spaced stitching. That was the cruelest thing about grief. It never really left you in peace. Edith had been dead for over eight years, yet simply by the touch of this small, crocheted object he could hear the expert clicking of her needles again, just as though she were in the room with him still, seated in the armchair on the other side of the open fireplace.

With a frown, Conlon shoved the balaclava back inside the bag and resealed it.

'I did a housewife in Lymington last month. Supplying over forty pushers she was. Used to deal coke out of her kitchen when the kids were off at school. She reckoned she was innocent, too. Said she needed the money for their school uniforms.'

'I'll put her in interview room 3,' said the custody officer dourly.

He should have known better than to think that Jack Conlon would find the situation even remotely amusing.

With a final wave of thanks to the estate agent, Bill closed the heavy metal door and moved back inside the large brick-built garage. Walking slowly from one end to the other, he reviewed his would-be production facility. Although originally designed for housing delivery vehicles, the building had obviously long been used for storing foodstuffs and was absolutely spic and span. On top of that, its four frosted-glass windows supplied more than enough natural light by which to work, whilst at the same time preventing prying eyes from observing what the exact nature of that work might be. It was ideal. It would be a hard slog, but within two weeks he could reasonably expect to fill and pack all the three thousand dispensers needed to launch Libidan over the Internet. Leaning up against the stainless steel double sink, though, Bill frowned and scratched his jaw. Despite the ultra-low dosage, the detailed patient information leaflet and the careful labelling, he still had his reservations. The possibility of abuse could not be ruled out and the image of Louise at the taxi window was never far from his mind. Taking one of the three newly purchased mobile phones from his bag, he decided to call her.

'Louise Schreiber, can I help you?'

'It's me. Can you talk?'

'Yeah – no problem. How did it go with Dougal this morning, then?'

'Amazing. Better than anything we could possibly have imagined.'

'What? What happened? Tell me quick!' urged Louise.

'He came up with a company just like that. Advanced Aerosol Systems, they're called – down in Kent. I spent over half an hour with him talking to their chief formulation scientist. They do this sort of job all the time, apparently. They've got a pilot plant, computerized modeling, a full analytical lab …'

'Oh, that's marvellous news …'

'I know. But that's not the best of it, listen to this. Not only can they make up a Libidan perfume formulation in a couple of days, they've got a whole range of off-the-shelf safety dispensers we can use, too. Including one with a special time-release valve that prevents the patient from taking more than one dose at a time. We don't have to make the perfume so strong-smelling now. This thing has a four-hour delay between individual applications.'

'That's fantastic!'

'Isn't it?'

'So, how much? Go on, hit me with it.'

'Eleven grand. Plus twenty percent for 5Z. That's most of my Asper redundancy cheque gone, but it's probably cheap at five times the price.'

'Great! Where are you now, anyway?'

'At the garage.'

'I thought you said they wouldn't let you take up occupancy until next week.'

'I did, but the estate agent rang this morning to say he could give me keys this week after all. I came straight round here when I got back from 5ZPharma.'

'What's it like?'

'Well, I doubt I'll ever learn to love the lime-green walls, but apart from that it's fine.'

'Enough room for storing the finished cartons?'

'Oh, yeah, loads.'

'Not overlooked, or anything?'

'No, the bakery's over fifty yards away. And it packs up at lunch-time most days as well, apparently.'

'Right,' said Louise decisively. 'That does it. I'll come down this Saturday. Let's not hang around any more.'

'What?'

'No need to wait until the weekend after next, let's get the computer up and running straightaway.'

'Well, OK, if you want to …'

'When can you get the concentrate from, what are they called again … ?'

'Advanced Aerosol Systems.'

'Yeah, them.'

'If I take the active down tomorrow they said it should be ready by Friday.'

'That's settled then.'

'Hold on a minute, though! I thought you said the website wouldn't be ready until next week.'

'I got a lot done last night. I finished off most of the interface stuff – you know, to take credit card orders and all that. All that's left is the artwork and the text for the main page. Which is another reason for coming down this weekend. I want to talk to you about the copy you suggested.'

'What about it?'

'I'm worried it's all too … I don't know … too medical – at least to put on the front page, anyway. I wonder whether we might not be better off with a single airbrushed photo. You know, sunset, wife contentedly

185

resting head on hubby's shoulder, Libidan logo top left-hand corner, finito. People'll draw their own conclusions.'

'Maybe. I don't know. It's hard for me to say.'

'Well, don't worry. Let's talk about it on Saturday. Can you come and pick me up at the station? I'll get the eight o'clock train.'

'Yeah, sure.'

'We can go straight off to that PC superstore you told me about then. I think we should buy an extra, reserve modem – we'll have all the hardware we need then.'

'Oh, all right.'

'And then it'll be systems go, right?'

'Yeah, I suppose so.'

'You don't sound very enthusiastic.'

'Don't I?'

'No, you don't!'

'Sorry. It's just, well, I wonder whether we're doing the right thing, that's all. You know, ethically.'

'Yes, I do know what you mean. I felt a bit like that last night as well.'

'Did you?'

'Yeah. I ended up ringing my mum and asking her advice.'

'You did what?' exclaimed Bill. 'You told your mum! Jesus Christ …'

'It's all right. I said it was a product we're doing at work. I didn't tell her anything about us. I just wanted an opinion from someone I could trust – that's all.'

'Louise!'

'What?'

'OK, OK, it's done now, sorry. I didn't mean to shout. What did she say, anyway?'

'She asked me to get her some.'

'What, some Libidan?'

'Yeah.'

'You're joking!'

'No, honest. She thinks her own menopause is not very far away and she's wondering how it'll affect her relationship with Dad.'

'Wow.'

'Not exactly what you'd call comprehensive market research, but a pretty unequivocal endorsement all the same. We've got a product, Bill, I'm certain of it. We've just got to hang in there and keep the faith, OK?'

186

'Yeah. I guess you're right. Thanks, Louise.'

'See you Saturday.'

'Bye.'

An hour and a half later, Bill pulled into his driveway, brought the car to a halt and smiled to himself. Louise was simply incredible. He could see now why Gail had taken to her so much. If Libidan was going to prove a success, there was absolutely no doubt in his mind that it would be down to Louise's drive and wit. Switching off the engine, he turned around and looked at the packaging proofs for the Libidan carton lying on the back seat. The printers had been quick – he had only sent them the artwork five days ago. As far as he could tell the layouts were fine, although just to make sure he would fax a copy through to Louise's home straightaway. Once he got the green light from her he would then order an initial batch of five thousand. The printers reckoned they could run them off within forty-eight hours. It might only have taken Bill and Louise two weeks, but they had a product on their hands all right, just as she had said. She really was incredible. Locking the car, Bill turned to go into his house.

And it was then that he saw it.

Putting the polythene bags containing the proofs back in the car, he approached the ornamental railing at the side of his house. Hooked around the final rung was a strip of tape. Only three inches long, and less than an inch wide, it was nevertheless emblazoned with a distinctive yellow and black chevron pattern that left no doubt as to its origin.

Turning on the lights in interview room 3, Conlon walked across to the phone and rang through to the desk sergeant to ask him to bring Bill Kennedy in. Lowering his large sturdy frame into one of the chairs, he recalled the interview with Una Arnold, here, in this very same room, at six o'clock the previous morning. The moment he had clapped eyes on her he had known she was not a burglar. He had dealt with house-breakers and petty thieves every single day of his thirty years in the service and could spot them a mile away by now. Leaning with her elbows well forward on the table, and with her wide, staring eyes, she had exuded an aura of honesty and moral integrity. Certainly, she had been foolish – stupid even. But the clarity and forthrightness with which she ran through her story had left Conlon utterly disarmed – and he, like her, was revolted by what she had discovered. Running his eyes around the grey interview room walls, he began wondering what this Kennedy character was going to be like. Miss Arnold had described him as cunning. That would more than likely be the case: in Conlon's experience, deviants were far craftier than even the smartest villains. How many would there be in Kennedy's felching ring? A half a dozen? More? If he was going to get Kennedy on anything, it would be for running a bawdy house. Such was the appalling state of the nation's morals that prosecutions for indecent behaviour were almost impossible nowadays. Personal gratification was deemed to be sufficient justification for even the most repulsive acts of obscenity. Running his forefinger over his thick, ginger moustache, Conlon made a conscious effort to calm himself. It would be no use flying off the handle. He had to keep his nerves steady and find out as much as he could about the other members of the group: if money was changing hands, he could round up the whole lot of them.

Following the desk sergeant down the corridor towards the interview room, Bill racked his brains as to the reasons for his summons to the police station. The note that had been pushed through his letterbox had told him nothing – just asked him to call the station – and all the police officers to whom he had so far spoken had been polite but utterly uninformative. Why did they want him here? And what had been the significance of the incident tape on the railings outside his house? Knocking the door, Bill made his way into the interview room.

'Ah, Dr Kennedy, do come in and sit down! It makes our job so much easier when members of the public come on down here and help us with enquiries on a voluntary basis … Dr Kennedy, are you OK?'

Bill stood paralysed with fright. It was him! The senior detective who had come into the room the night he had been brought to the station with Brummie for questioning. But why was he being so pleasant? What the hell was going on?

'Er, yeah, yeah. I'm OK.'

'Please, then. Take a seat.'

'Oh, right, thanks.'

'Excuse me, but haven't we met before?'

'No. No – I don't think so.'

188

'Are you sure?'

'Yes.

'Your face, it looks sort of familiar … where was it, now? Sorry. I'm sure it'll come back to me …'

'No, we've never met before. But what's all this about, anyway?'

'Just a few preliminaries first, if I may, Dr Kennedy?' replied Conlon, finally taking his eyes off Bill and leaning over his notepad. 'Your address is 80 Lynhurst Drive, Wyburn. Is that correct?'

'Yes.'

As Conlon began writing, Bill's mind began to race. His summons to the station couldn't possibly be a follow-up to the Joe Bananas incident, otherwise Conlon would have recalled seeing him that fateful night. And if Advanced Aerosol Systems or 5ZPharma had alerted the authorities that he was manufacturing drug substances without a licence, there would be someone in here from the Home Office or the Medicines Control Agency, so it couldn't be that either.

'And how long have you been resident there?'

'I beg your pardon?' replied Bill.

'How long have you been resident at this address in Wyburn?'

'All my life, virtually. Apart from four years while I was away at … living somewhere else.'

Had he really been about to tell Conlon that he had done a degree in Biochemistry? Under the table, Bill pinched his thigh between his thumb and forefinger. Think, man!

'Where were you on Monday night of this week, Dr Kennedy, around three a.m.?'

'Sorry? Er, Monday, let's see …'

'Were you at your home?'

'No, I was down in London. Staying with some friends for a few days.'

'Could you give me their names and addresses perhaps?'

'No. Why should I?'

'But they will corroborate your story, if we subsequently need to contact them?'

'Of course they will.'

'Was it the same friend's house each night. Or different friends?'

'No, one night at one friend's house, and two nights at my sister's. Listen, what's this all about?'

'Your sister's!'

'Yes, my sister. What's wrong with that?'

Conlon shook his head. These people did this sort of thing with members of their own families? Maybe he shouldn't be so surprised. The nation's morals had been sinking steadily since the sixties – this must just be the next layer of filth down.

'These other friends of yours. Do they in turn sometimes stay at your house?'

'Yes. But for the last time, what on earth is this all about … ?'

'When they come, do you let them stay for free, or do they perhaps pay you rent for use of the room for a night, or whatever?'

'That's it. I'm off!' said Bill standing up quickly. 'I don't see why I should have to answer these questions about my private life without …'

'What d'you do with the animals' bodies afterwards – bury them?' interrupted Conlon, quietly.

'What?'

'The bodies. The guinea-pig carcasses. I suppose some of them do die in the process, don't they?'

Bill felt the colour draining from his face and could sense himself slowly falling back into his chair. It hadn't been 5ZPharma or Advanced Aerosol Systems contacting the authorities after all. Instead, the police must somehow have gotten wind of his pre-clinical experiments. It must have been those syringes he had tried to buy at the pharmacy in Boots.

'I don't know what you're talking about …'

'You do keep guinea-pigs, though, don't you, Dr Kennedy?'

'Yes, I do,' croaked Bill, 'but …'

'But they're pets, aren't they?' said Conlon, with a great condescending nod of the head. 'Yes, that's right, of course they are. Of course, they are, Mr Kennedy. Pets. And I'm the man in the fucking moon …'

In a flash, Conlon was around Bill's side of the table, grabbing his lapels and pinning him against the wall. His face was pressed up so close to Bill's own that he could feel the brush of his bushy moustache against his cheek.

'You think you've got it all locked away behind closed doors, don't you, sonny? Eh? All nice and private, where nobody can see what you're up to. But I know your filthy game, you pervert. You and your sick friends. I've got my eye on you – just remember that. And when you slip up – 'cos you are gonna slip up, you know – I'll be waiting. And I'll tell you something for nothing. Once you get sent down, they are just gonna love you inside, do you know that? When they find out what your game is …'

'And you're absolutely sure he's got nothing concrete on you?'

'I'm sure. I'm sure. He would never have let me out the police station if he had.'

Louise felt like slamming her fist straight through the VDU screen, but bit her lip instead and began pacing up and down the garage. She had known. She had sensed something wasn't right with Bill from the moment he had picked her up at the train station, but had pushed it to the back of her mind once everything else had started to click into place so perfectly. The website she had designed was compact and speedy, yet nicely understated. Bill had successfully diluted the concentrate to the required level of five parts per million and charged the first five hundred dispensers. The exterior packaging was subtle and the ceramic effect dispensers themselves were really quite beautiful. She stared at the neat pile of boxes stacked up against the far wall. It had taken them six and a half hours to pack them – scrupulously folding each dispenser inside its patient information leaflet. And now this. Here they were, a single keystroke away from worldwide product launch and she had unearthed the fact that three days previously he has been interviewed by the police about the pre-clinical experiments. Folding her arms, Louise glared at Bill, who shuffled uncomfortably from foot to foot. Lying really was his most unappealing characteristic. And he wasn't even any good at it, either. She had known.

'When did you buy the guinea-pigs?' she asked finally.

'About, er, six weeks ago.'

'And it's taken the police that long to search you out and interview you?'

'Yeah.'

Once again Louise congratulated herself on insisting that they operate under false names out of rented premises. If Bill kept his head down, it could well be another six weeks before Conlon came after him again. Cyberspace companies had blossomed and died in much less time than that – or so her colleagues in the small business section had assured her. Twenty pounds per dispenser. They would need to shift three thousand to generate the fifty thousand pounds. Three thousand dispensers of Libidan in six weeks? It should just be possible.

'OK, we go ahead.'

'Are you sure?'

'No,' replied Louise, tetchily. Bill continued to stand and stare at her sheepishly. In the end she took pity on him. 'We can always pack up and run if things get too hairy. Come on, you press the key.'

'Which one?' asked Bill, approaching the keyboard.

'No, second thoughts, we'll both press it. God knows, I've spent enough hours putting this bloody website together.'

With hands clasped, Bill and Louise pressed the F10 function key. On the top left-hand corner of the computer the red LED flashed once.

Libidan was launched.

'Is that it, then?' asked Bill, a few moments later.

'That's it,' replied Louise, letting go of his hand and walking slowly across the room to pick up her jacket.

'What do we do, now?'

'You can do what you like, I'm going back to bed – I'm knackered.'

Moving across to the exit, Louise stood waiting for Bill. Having checked the mobile phone and computer cables one last time, he eventually joined her. Slipping on her jacket she watched him take the padlocks out and begin locking up the garage.

'When are you thinking of coming back to check for the first orders?' she asked.

'Er, Monday, I thought. I knock off from Sykes' at six.'

'Don't come on Monday. Leave it a couple of days longer than that,' replied Louise, wearily. 'That's my advice.'

'Yeah?'

'Yeah. When's your next full day off?'

'Thursday.'

'Come in on Thursday. Give yourself a rest, and give the sales some time to gather up steam.'

With a nod, Bill opened the door and let Louise out. It was probably sound advice. They shouldn't expect too many orders to come flooding in immediately.

No sooner had he closed the door and switched off the lights, than the LED in the top left-hand corner of the computer began to flicker steadily in the darkness.

192

Chapter 11

'Oh, it's you!' exclaimed Una, lifting her hand to her face in alarm. She hated being crept up on, which was exactly what Ray, with his penchant for intrigue, always seemed to want to do.

'We've got to talk.'

'I've got a customer, hang on a few ...'

'Get rid of them,' interrupted Ray, slipping back inside the tiny kitchen at the rear of the shop.

Easy enough for you to say, thought Una, resentfully. The lady out front was Mrs Mitchener — not just any customer, but Everypet's best customer — come to pick up some fish food for her son Martin's tropical fish. Going back into the shop, Una decided to keep Ray waiting until she had fully attended to Mrs Mitchener's needs. ALA business was one thing, paying the rent on her own was another.

'Have you closed up?' asked Ray, when at last she returned.

'Yes,' replied Una, noticing that as usual he had not been slow in taking advantage of her hospitality. On the kitchen table lay a newly opened pack of her best fair-trade tea and a single, steaming mug beside it. He had not made one for her.

'Good. Listen. Some information came through last night. From a sympathizer on the inside. We've got everything we need to carry out the raid now.'

'On this animal testing place?'

'That's right. We want you to drive. Are you in?'

'Me? Why me?' replied Una. No sign of Latitia or the other hangers-on when the dirty work had to be done. Wouldn't catch one of them risking their over-privileged necks.

'We can't get out there in a car – there's too much gear. We need a van, and someone used to driving it. There'll be me and Len and two other guys from out of town – experts.'

'When?'

'Haven't fixed the date yet,' replied Ray, reclining back in his chair and taking a swig of tea.

'Well, I don't know, I, er, suppose …'

Leaning forward, Una began absent-mindedly shuffling together several invoices that were lying on the kitchen table. Only a few weeks ago she would have jumped at the chance. After their last escapade at the leather factory, though, her enthusiasm for direct action was starting to ebb away.

'Una. I hope this doesn't mean my faith in you was misplaced.'

'No, no, of course not, it's just …'

'I mean, I've always stuck up for you. Right from the beginning. But, if you don't want to remain a part of what we have in the group, well, that's your decision …' Replacing his mug on the table, Ray made as though to stand up and leave.

'No, I'll do it,' said Una quickly. 'I'll do it.'

'Are you sure?'

'Yes, yes, I'm sure.'

'Good.'

'It's just that …'

Una hesitated before continuing. For several days now, she had been wondering how best to tell Ray about the abortive raid on the house in Wyburn and her subsequent ignominious arrest. Looking into his cool, blue eyes, she finally decided to keep silent. She had never had much faith in the law, but DI Conlon was a most impressive figure and was doubtless already on the trail of that slimy Kennedy character. And besides, if Ray knew that she had had any involvement at all with the police, let alone that she might be up before the magistrate's court on a charge of burglary, he might be shy of having any further dealings with her at all.

'It's just that what, Una?'

'Nothing. Nothing. I'll be fine. Let me know when you're going to need me.'

★

Pacing up and down the garage, Bill stared at the mobile phone on the desk next to the computer. Louise had said that she would ring back in ten minutes but that had been nearly half an hour ago. Although Bill had never once smoked in his life, he found himself fighting down the urge to march right out of the door and purchase a packet of cigarettes. If he had not promised Louise to wait by the phone for her return call, he knew he would do just that. Seventy orders in five days. Fourteen hundred pounds worth of sales. At that rate it would take him over ten months to pay off Snod – he had less than three. Louise had sounded utterly crestfallen. Phoning her had felt like ringing someone to tell them of a bereavement. It wasn't that the website hadn't been repeatedly accessed, and from all over the globe, too. Cuba. Iceland. All manner of places. Several potential customers had even been back to the site two, and in one case, even three days running. But just not enough of them were buying.

Suddenly, he was snatching up the phone again.

'Hello?'

'I've got it!' Her voice was intense, animated.

'What?'

'It's not the website graphics. Not the text. Not the packaging. Nothing like that.'

'What is it, then?' asked Bill,

'It's the price!'

'The price? Well, we can't really make it much less without …'

'It's not too expensive, Bill,' interrupted Louise, excitedly, 'it's too cheap. Much, much too cheap! We have to change it quick. But, listen, it can't wait until when I come down on Sunday. You'll have to try and do it now. If I give you instructions over the phone, can you get into the on-line edit mode?'

'I suppose so, I don't know. How, do I … ?'

'Shift F6. Press Shift F6 and the edit screen'll come up.'

Hunching his shoulder to hold the mobile phone up against his ear, Bill placed his hands on the computer keyboard.

'OK – I've got it.'

'Scroll through to page three, where the pricing section is. Bottom left-hand corner. See it?'

'Yeah.'

'OK. Click on the price field with the mouse.'

'Do you want me to highlight it?'

'No, just click on it.'

'OK.'

'Now, move the cursor along to the left, delete the decimal point and then put in another decimal point between the two zeros on the right. Done it?'

'Yeah. But, hang on. It says two hundred pounds now.'

'Exactly. We've just put the price up ten times.'

'What! Two hundred pounds a bottle?'

'Yes! Yes! Can't you see?' exclaimed Louise. 'That's what the data was telling us. Hundreds of people accessed the site over the last five days. The interest's there – that's absolutely obvious. So, why weren't they buying? Why weren't they buying? Because they didn't believe anything that good could be that cheap, that's why.'

'Yeah, but hang on a minute ...'

'I was so concerned with getting the details right, I made an absolutely fundamental error. The positioning was totally wrong. Libidan isn't a mass-market product, it's a luxury item. Nobody was ever going to value it at that price.'

'Well, maybe so, but who the hell's going to want to pay two hundred pounds for ten millilitres of the stuff?'

'Listen, listen. Each dispenser has ten shots, right?'

'Yeah ...'

'That's twenty pounds a shot, right?'

'Right ...'

'Is twenty pounds too much for a Saturday night's entertainment? I don't think so. Not that it's about fun, anyway. It's the whole marital harmony thing people're buying. Feeling nice and close to their partners again. Just like they were when they first met.'

'But most people'll never be able to afford that sort of money!'

'We don't need most people. We only need two hundred and fifty people. There's your fifty grand there and then. Are you telling me there aren't a couple of hundred women out there, or couples, who won't be prepared to part with twenty quid a week to help the most important relationship in their lives through a difficult patch?'

'Well, yeah – I can see what you mean, I suppose. But what if you're wrong? What if we put the price right up like you say and nobody buys it at all?'

196

'Then you'll probably have to call it a day, Bill – I don't know, that'll be for you to decide at the time. But the one thing that's for certain now is that it's pointless to continue at twenty pounds a bottle. I mean, what are you, a charity? You're scarcely even covering your costs at that sort of income. Frankly, if you want to make the money to pay back Snod, you'd be better off driving nights at Sykes' for the next three months.'

Bill stared at the screen again and then bit his lip thoughtfully. It would be a bold move. But certainly, the logistics of shipping out two hundred and fifty dispensers would be considerably simpler than shipping out nearly three thousand.

'What d'you think?' asked Louise after several moments.

'OK. Like you say, if not enough people are buying it anyway, we haven't really got anything to lose.'

'Good on you. OK, go back one page and select the 'update' box. It's at the top somewhere. Click on 'Apply' and it'll update the site with the new price.'

'OK … I've found it. Right. There it is. I've done it. God, I hope this works.'

'Keep the faith, Bill, like I said.'

'I'll try, Louise, I'll try. Anyway, what am I going to do with these seventy orders?'

'Send a round robin e-mail to the customers. The original price was posted in error. We've received their order but are unable to accept it unless they pay the new price.'

'Can we do that?'

'Of course we can.'

'Isn't it illegal?'

'No, no. Not at all. It's just offer and acceptance. As long as we return the money we have no further obligations. Ring up the credit card company – they'll tell you how to make refunds.'

'It's not very fair, though, is it? I mean if they've ordered it in good faith and everything.'

'Listen, Bill,' said Louise, sternly. 'You're in business now – you've got to learn to be ruthless. We are going up-market, right? If these people want a quality product, then they're just going to have pay for it.'

'OK. You're right. I'll do it straightaway. Listen, are you still on for Sunday?'

'Yeah.'

'I'll pick you up at the station at twelve like last time.'

'Great. Are you going to look at the website again before then?'

'What d'you think?'

'It's your choice.'

'All right, then, if it's all the same to you, I won't. Either we come in here on Sunday lunch-time and start packing up the first orders, or ...'

He could not bring himself to finish the sentence. For they both knew that if they were to arrive at the garage and find there were none, Libidan would be finished.

'See you Sunday, Bill.'

The woman was standing under a tree. Conlon could vaguely sense that someone was there, but carried on walking when Rousseau went bounding off ahead in pursuit of a squirrel.

'Excuse me! Mr Conlon?'

He turned. He did not recognize her at first.

'I don't suppose you remember me. My name's Arnold. Una Arnold. You, er, interviewed me ten days or so ago about ...'

'Oh, Miss Arnold, yes, of course.'

'Sorry to just jump out on you like this, but I saw you walking your dog in the park here last Saturday, and, well, I hope you don't mind, but I thought you might be here again, so I, er ...'

'No, no, that's all right. What I can do for you, Miss Arnold?'

Suddenly, Conlon caught sight of Rousseau hurtling back down the path towards them, but before he had time to bark out a command to bring the young alsatian to heel, Miss Arnold dropped to her knees and was running her hands over the dog's shoulders and neck.

'There you go, boy. You're a fine strong thing aren't you? What's your name, eh?'

Standing watching her expert movements, Conlon was genuinely impressed. As a young police constable, he had spent four years in the dog squad and immediately recognized the authoritative hand of a fellow professional.

'Sorry, but I do love dogs, you know,' she said, looking up and smiling at him shyly.

'That's all right. It's nice to find someone who's not scared of him for once.'

'Oh, I'm sure there's nothing to be scared of, is there, now?' She gripped the fur around Rousseau's neck again and pulled it playfully. 'You're just a bit young and frisky that's all.'

'So, er, you were saying ...'

'Oh, yes, sorry,'

She stood up and faced him again.

'I know it's probably wrong to approach you like this, I mean, outside of the police station and everything. But I was just wondering what was happening with, er, my case ...'

'Yes, you are quite right. It is highly irregular to approach an officer when he's off-duty, Miss Arnold.'

'Sorry. I suppose I shouldn't have done ...'

'No, it's OK,' replied Conlon, quickly. Out of the corner of his eye he could see two swans on the park's ornamental lake, their long necks sensuously curling around each other. 'The short answer is, I don't know. I imagine the file's gone off to the CPS.'

'The CPS?'

'The Crown Prosecution Service.'

'Oh, oh, I see.'

He doubted she did.

'It'll be the CPS's job to advise the police as to whether to proceed with a prosecution against you or not.'

'How long will that all take?'

'Not long. I can make some enquiries for you, if you like. Find out how it's progressing.'

'Would you? That would be so kind.'

'Yes, well ...'

Kind, perhaps, thought Conlon, but, more to the point, completely contrary to CID regulations. How on earth was he allowing himself to develop a personal interest in this woman's case?

'What should I do in the meantime, then, Mr Conlon?'

'Just sit tight. We'll be in contact – well, it probably won't be me – but someone will be in contact with you soon. Good-day, now.'

'Thank you Mr Conlon,' said Miss Arnold, gratefully.

'Come on, Rousseau. Let's go.'

Conlon went to doff his hat respectfully, but, suddenly realizing he wasn't actually wearing one, hastily attempted to transform the movement into a wave of goodbye instead. No sooner had he done so, than he was immediately conscious of how familiar the gesture must seem.

Heart pumping, he dropped his hand to his side and strode away, praying that Rousseau would not take it into his head to wait around and play with his newfound friend.

A wave of self-disgust swept over Una as she stood watching the detective walk away. How could she have approached this decent, hard-working man in such a way, so dreadfully compromising his professional position? How could she have sought his help in mitigating one unlawful act in order that she might go out and commit another? Shivering, despite the fact it was a warm day, she pulled her jacket collar up over her neck and walked off back towards the shop.

'There's no need to do those, Lester: I already took a note of the results this morning.'

Dumbly, Mold replaced the rack of test tubes in the refrigerator and walked back across the laboratory towards his desk. On the way, he stopped and picked up the departmental work register. Perhaps there would be some minor task or other in there that had somehow managed to escape Angela's all-embracing scrutiny.

'Er, Angela?'

'Yes?' replied Angela, not looking across at Mold as she carefully squeezed the purple-coloured fluid up into the pipette she was holding and transferred it into a flask.

'There's something in here about ZD-4522.'

'Yes …'

'A crystallization study that Process Ops asked for.'

'Yes …'

'Would you like me to look at it, now? I mean, I don't mind. I've got a few minutes free.'

'No. It's OK. I did it on Monday,' replied Angela, patiently, 'and you were kind enough to carry the results across there for me yourself. Don't you remember?'

'Oh, yes, that's right. I did, didn't I? Sorry.'

Mold was not the least bit surprised to learn that he had forgotten about his trip to the Process Operations Building; he wouldn't be surprised if he forgot his own name next. On the four afternoons a week that Angela was now present in the laboratory, he had more or less grown accustomed to his mental faculties completely deserting him. The combination of having one's every daily task anticipated by such a ruthlessly efficient assistant, and then being left with nothing to do but gaze at her womanly perfection would be enough to addle anyone's grey matter. Giddily, Mold slumped down into his chair and, in the vain hope it might provide some temporary distraction, logged on to the Internet. God, he felt bad. Just what effect was this continuing exposure to Angela having on his physiology? They had only been in the lab together for three weeks and already he felt close to endocrinological meltdown. How was it all going to end? He almost dared not think. Perhaps, after months of chronic over-stimulation, and with no means of dissipating the streams of chemical and kinetic energies generated along its biochemical pathways, his body would be left with no option but to unleash these pent-up forces on itself. One summer afternoon, Angela would turn her back to take a fresh conical flask down from the store cupboard and that would be it. As she stretched upwards, the sight of her calf, or perhaps a section of inner thigh, would catalyze a disintegrative reaction through the Lester Mold genome, bursting every nucleotide bond in his being, and when, seconds later, the ruptured helixes rushed to realign themselves, his entire DNA structure would be recast. Alerted by the strange, squelching noises behind her, Angela would turn around like some sci-fi B-film heroine, no longer to see the inspired young scientist who had been there moments before, but the suppurating blob of goo into which he had now metamorphosed. And, as he lumbered pathetically towards her, saliva dribbling from the open gash that might once have been his mouth, she would let the conical flask fall to the floor, clasp her hands to her cheeks and let forth a scream of abject terror.

The screen flickered into life before him. Moving the mouse across to the search engine, he risked another sidelong glance at Angela and then miserably punched in the key phrase 'Sexual Frustration'.

Who knows? Perhaps someone out there in cyberspace might be able to help.

Walking across to the far side of the garage, Louise folded her arms and stared unseeing at the lime-green surface of the wall before her. Behind, she could hear the sound of Bill's fingers slowly tapping the computer keys. A full four days had passed since she had decided to increase the price so dramatically. There were precedents for such a bold move, of course – numerous precedents throughout the history of marketing. But few where the consequences of failure would be quite so grave. Breathing in deeply, she closed her eyes. It had to have worked. It had to have worked for Bill's sake.

'This can't be right,' muttered Bill.

'What?' She turned quickly. He was staring at the screen, his brow furled. 'What!'

'It must be, though.'

'What! For God's sake, Bill, don't keep me guessing.'

'It is. It's right. Forty-six. Look.'

He pointed at the screen. She sprang across the garage to join him.

'Forty-six orders?'

'Yes. That's good, isn't it?'

'My God – forty-six – you're right! Quick! Where's the calculator?' Snatching up the machine she made a speedy multiplication. 'That's not good, Bill, it's brilliant!'

He stared at the calculator's LCD in disbelief.

'Nine thousand pounds! Holy cow.'

With a whoop of glee, Louise threw her arms around Bill's neck and the two them spun around the garage.

'Hang on, hang on! Let's look where they came from.' In a second she was at the keyboard, moving the cursor through the 'orders received' field. 'UK, UK, Ireland, US, Magyar – that's Hungary, I guess – US, Qatar … isn't that in the Middle East somewhere?'

'Yeah, I think so.'

'Let's have a look at the names. Here we are …'

'Are they mostly men or women?'

'I'm not sure. Women, I think. Anyway, listen, let's get a move on and get this stuff shipped shall we?' said Louise, stretching forwards and switching on the printer. 'The quicker we get it out of the door, the quicker we get paid. This software prints off packing labels directly from the customer's order input. I'll pass them across, you stick them on the bags one by one.'

'How long before the money turns up from the credit card company, did you say?' replied Bill, tearing open a box of jiffy bags.

'About 45 days.'

'If we can finish them off this afternoon, I can get them despatched first thing tomorrow …'

★

Although Mold had thought the price utterly extortionate, he was pleased that the company had at least had the decency to send him the stuff quickly and thereby hasten the prospect of some relief from his daily torture in the lab. Hearing the sound of the door close, he furtively brought his hand up to his chest and touched the slim ceramic tube in the top pocket of his shirt. Now was definitely the best time to try it – the building was quietest of all on Friday afternoons.

'Nice lunch?'

'Yes, fine thanks,' replied Angela, leaning over the desk and sliding her handbag beneath it.

God. Those legs.

'Great. Well, excuse me a moment, will you? I've just got to pop off down the corridor. I'll be back in a few minutes.'

Angela gave Mold a sideways glance but made no reply. Why was it that all the men she worked with at Asper seemed to feel the need constantly to provide her with an inane running commentary on their every movement? That creep Bill Kennedy had been just the same.

Having checked that the three other lavatory cubicles were not occupied, Mold locked the door of his own and quickly took the container of perfume from his pocket. Shaking the bottle twice, he sprayed some on his lab coat collar and then brought it up to his nose to smell. The odour wasn't that strong at all. He could easily risk a couple more applications. Lifting up the other side of his collar, he went to spray that one too, but found that the plunger had not come back up. He tried again. It would not budge. A cold clammy sensation spread up his back and neck. The thing was defective. He had been conned.

'Two hundred quid and the bloody thing sticks after …'

Shaking the dispenser violently several times, he turned around and slammed the plastic plunger down hard on the rim of the lavatory basin. Still, it would not move. Suddenly, it dawned on him why.

'Bastards! The clever bastards …'

The unit was fitted with a slow repressurisation valve. Once the plunger had been depressed and the first dose dispensed, air could only seep back into the chamber through the valve at an extremely slow rate, thus preventing administration of a second dose for … how long? It might be hours.

'Great!'

Maybe this stuff wasn't such a rip-off, after all: they wouldn't have gone to all that trouble to prevent overdosing without a reason. However, he couldn't afford to take any chances: since he had to spray the drug on to himself, he would need a lot more to achieve any effect. Undoing his lab coat, he reached inside his trouser pocket and took out his key-ring pocket-knife. It had dropped into his lap out of a Christmas cracker at the office party two years previously. It had never cut very well, but the blade would probably be thin enough to lever the top off the dispenser.

'Shit!'

The blade slid back and forth uselessly over the seal between the container and the polypropylene unit that housed the plunger. It was chamfered inwards. He would never be able to lever it off in a month of Sundays. Panicking, Mold looked back in the direction of the laboratory. He would have to hurry. The instructions had said something about a five-minute envelope of activity. Or had it been fifteen? He regretted casting the packaging aside that morning with only a cursory glance at the carefully folded patient-information leaflet inside. There was nothing for it. He would have to smash the container completely. There was a hammer down in pilot lab.

'What's that smell?' said Angela after a few moments.

'What smell?' replied Mold, innocently.

'That strange smell. I don't know – like roses or something?'

'Oh, that! It's my aftershave.' It was now or never. In a single movement he was standing next to Angela and holding his wrist under her nose. 'Don't you like it? I got it for my birthday last month.'

Caught unawares, Angela was unable to move in time and involuntarily inhaled some of the perfume. Mold held his breath – the three or four drops of liquid that he had managed to bash out of the bottle he had put on that one wrist. The blurb had gone on about natural herb extracts, but whatever the manufacturers had put in there, it certainly seemed to be having some sort of effect for Angela's eyes were clearly glazing over. Take it slow. Take it slow. Keeping his ears pinned back for the sound of movement in the corridor, Mold slipped his arm around her shoulders.

'Oh, gosh, Angela! You look like you've gone a bit faint. Here you are, just lean back against the bench here.'

'No. It's OK, I'll be fine in a moment.'

'Of course, you will. It's very hot in here, though. Perhaps you should loosen up your coat a little.'

Sliding his arm down to rest on the bench behind Angela's back, Mold leaned forward so that his face was just a few inches from hers. For a second, he was certain that he had succeeded and was just leaning forward to bring his lips down on to hers when all of a sudden she gave a slight cough. Instantly, her retinas contracted sharply and her eyes seemed to regain their focus. Damn! What was happening? Had the agitation of the cough snapped her out of the trance? Or had she simply not inhaled a sufficient quantity of the perfume in the first place?

'Er, no, Lester,' said Angela, coolly. 'No. I can't say I do like the smell of your aftershave …'

Now completely alert again, Angela began smoothing her hands down the front of her coat. Mold closed his eyes painfully as the enormity of what he had done finally dawned on him. Two hundred pounds! That was more than he had spent on all the women he had ever known in his entire life.

'Oh, yes, and, one other thing, Lester …'

As he opened his eyes again, Mold found his entire field of vision filled with the sight of Angela's fist flying into his face. A series of extraordinary views of the lab then followed in rapid succession – a tracking shot of the ceiling, an upside down view of the rear wall and, finally, a close-up of the waste paper bin beneath his desk. Her voice was coming from somewhere. At last, he managed to locate her. There she was – framed between the underside of the desk and the top left-hand corner of his bin.

' … if you ever try anything like that again. Ever. I'll strangle you with your own limp dick.'

Breakfast started really well.

Despite not having returned from the pub until midnight the previous night, they had both woken feeling refreshed and looking forward to handling the new orders that had arrived over the last few days.

'I don't see how we can develop line extensions,' said Bill, buttering a second piece of toast. 'It's OK with, say, an alcoholic drink, where you get degrees of intoxication. But we can scarcely launch Libidan Lite, can we? It's a contradiction in terms. I mean, either the stuff makes you want to have sex or it doesn't.'

'I'm not talking about changing the strength,' replied Louise. 'What I'm saying is that there might be some benefit in elaborating on the peripheral product features, like the fragrance, or the packaging. That's the difference between us, you see. You think formulation, I think image.'

'So, do you think it would do any good, then, multiplying the packaging types?'

'People like a choice. Even if it's only between Pepsi and Coke. At the moment, they get into the website and there's just a single product. One size fits all. It's too, too … I don't know, impersonal. How would you feel if you got down to the tailors and they'd only got one style of suit?'

'But would it increase the total sales volume? Wouldn't we just end up selling five units of each of the two products, instead of ten units of one?'

'Possibly. I don't know. But, look, don't get me wrong. I don't think a line extension necessarily needs to have to have a dramatic effect to be considered a success: I mean, even if it only pushed the sales up a further five percent it'd be worth having, wouldn't it?'

'Yeah. I guess so.'

'Why don't we give it a try? This afternoon, after we've packed the orders. Sketch out a few novel designs? Have a bit of a brainstorming session.'

'Yeah, OK, I'll bring some …'

Bill found himself interrupted by a sound in the hallway.

'It's the postman,' said Louise, nodding in the direction of the window and then stretching across the table to pour herself some more tea.

The moment Bill returned to the kitchen, Louise could tell by his face that something was wrong.

'What is it?'

'It's a letter … from the Medicines Control Agency.'

'What! What does it say?'

Leaving the question unanswered, Bill sat down next to Louise and smoothed the letter out on the kitchen table. Silently, they read it through together. Finally, Bill spoke first.

'Have you heard of this MAL 8 guideline, then?'

'Yes, I have. There was something about it in that information I got from work. Hang on a minute – I think I might still have it upstairs.'

Bill watched Louise hurry from the kitchen and sprint upstairs to his mother's bedroom, which had virtually become her own since she had begun to stay over in Wyburn regularly. Seconds later, she reappeared.

'Here you are.'

Sitting down, she began to read a section out loud ' … in practice the Medicines Control Agency considers under MAL 8 any information that may have a bearing on the product's status, in particular, all claims, both explicit and implicit, that may be made for it.'

'So what are they saying? That we're making implicit claims for Libidan?'

'Yes.'

'And do we?'

'Yeah, of course we do – but they're all qualified in one way or another. You know, '..may assist in restoring the libido', 'have been reported to have beneficial effects …', that sort of thing.'

'So, our promotional literature doesn't contravene MAL 8, then?'

'No, not at all. It's all completely standard verbiage. The supplement manufacturers have been describing their products in exactly the same language for years – you know, the vitamin makers and the fish–oil pro-ducers. If we're contravening MAL 8, then ninety-five percent of the products in your average high street pharmacy are, too.'

Frowning, Bill picked up the letter. He had little experience of over-the-counter medicines, but on first reading the Medicine Control Agency's reasoning was difficult to follow.

'Where's this Dr Casey bloke from anyway?' asked Louise.

'It says at the top somewhere. Here you are. Borderline Products Section, Department of Regulatory Affairs.'

'Have you ever heard of him before?'

'No.'

'It's a very confused argument,' said Louise, picking up the letter again. 'And another thing. Although it's all written in this heavy, heavy threatening tone, they haven't told us we've got to withdraw Libidan, have they?'

'No. In fact, they haven't told us to do anything at all. There are no clear requests, or actions or anything.'

'No, absolutely nothing!' exclaimed Louise, before adding quietly, 'Is it me, or do you get the impression this Casey bloke doesn't know what he's talking about? Like he's been told to issue a warning by somebody but can't quite string a cogent argument together.'

'Hm. It sort of seems that way, doesn't it?'

'Do you think the police have been on to him?'

'What – Conlon?' Louise nodded in reply. 'I don't think so. If he thought we needed a warning, he's much more the type to come and kick the door down and give it to us himself.'

'Who then?'

'I've no idea.'

The two stared at each other for several seconds. Bill broke the silence.

'What d'you think we should do, then?'

'Are you absolutely certain that if they analysed a sample they wouldn't find the active molecule?'

'It's five parts per million, Louise. And besides they don't even know what they're looking for.'

'OK,' said Louise, taking a deep breath, 'then we tell them to get stuffed.'

'Wouldn't it be better just to ignore it? I mean, at the current rate we've only got to keep going for another three weeks and we're there, aren't we? We've got the fifty grand.'

'No, we reply. I'll type the letter this afternoon. They'll interpret it as weakness if we don't. In fact, come to think of it, we go on the attack. Accuse them of harassment. If this Dr Casey really is having his strings pulled by someone, then we should make him squirm.'

'OK, let's do it.'

Briskly they began to tidy the kitchen table. However, no sooner had Bill got halfway to the sink with the breakfast plates, than the sound of the letter box closing once more reverberated through the house.

'What was that?' asked Louise.

'Can't be the postman again.'

They entered the hallway together. There, on the doormat, was a single white envelope. Bill approached and picked it up. It was not addressed and there were no visible markings on the outside.

'Aren't you going to open it?' asked Louise.

Tearing the seal open with his thumb, Bill emptied the contents of the envelope into his open palm.

'How peculiar,' said Louise in astonishment. 'Who on earth would want to stick a piece of orange peel through your door?'

Chapter 12

As he heaved his heavy case off the back seat and then slammed the taxi door, Maruyama Hiroshi found himself overcome by tiredness. The airline companies had introduced non-stop flights from Japan to Europe over fifteen years ago, but the only route he trusted was the one he had been using ever since his first mission back in the early seventies: Osaka to Hong Kong travelling under one false passport, and then Hong Kong to London travelling under another. Swinging the case down on the pavement he felt a sharp stab of pain in his lower back. The business class seat had been comfortable enough, but, including the one-night stopover in Hong Kong, the complete journey had still amounted to well over forty hours. With a frown of resignation, he straightened up and kneaded the heels of his palms into his tender lumbar: at his age, it was only natural that journeys like this should take their toll.

'That's, er, thirty-one pounds twenty,' announced the driver, reading the total off his meter.

'Here, keep the change,' replied Maruyama, handing over two twenty-pound notes.

'Oh, ta. D'you wanna hand with your case into the lobby?'

Maruyama looked across at the hotel entrance. One thirty in the morning. Not a bellboy in sight.

'No, no. I'm fine, thank you.'

With a nod of acknowledgement, the taxi driver pocketed the money and then jabbed a series of numbers into his dashboard computer. Standing on the darkened pavement, Maruyama watched the man's fingers move over the keys. Telecommunications had made tremendous progress since that first Frankfurt Exhibition back in 1973. How conspicuous he and his six colleagues on the trade delegation had felt that day, moving from stand to stand in their identical light blue suits, the only Orientals in a hall of nearly five thousand whites. And how his heart had been beating when he had slipped his hands inside the racking of the digital telephone exchange system, a French-made prototype, and unscrewed its enormous master control board. Thirty years later, this flimsy twenty-dollar box on top of the taxi driver's dashboard probably possessed a hundred thousand times the processing power.

'Hope you enjoy your stay,' called out the driver, releasing the handbrake and pulling away.

'Thank you. Thank you,' replied Maruyama, giving the man a wave.

As the cab moved out of sight, he turned and looked through the front doors of the large intercontinental hotel into its bright, welcoming lobby. For years he had been using the place as a decoy destination, but on this occasion he was sorely tempted actually to check in there and stay the night. Perhaps he should allow himself a little luxury, just this once: well patronized by Japanese tourists, the hotel had its own in-house Shiatsu service, and his back was aching terribly. Finally, however, he lifted up his case and, gritting his teeth, walked off down the darkened alleyway that ran along the side of the building. The guesthouse was only a quarter of a mile away. He could sleep when he got there.

In Maruyama's profession, anonymity was everything.

'Sukebe?'

It was a woman's voice. Coarse. Laughing.

Maruyama stopped and looked up. There were two of them, coming out of the emergency exit at the rear of the hotel. Early twenties, stockinged legs protruding from short, vulgar skirts.

'Sukebe sometimes ... but at this particular moment, very, very tired.'

The woman laughed again – an unpleasant, jangling cackle that insinuated his fatigue was a pretext for cowardice. Maruyama stared at her sharp aquiline nose and strong, heavy features. The average western male would probably find such looks attractive. Shaking his head, he picked up the heavy case and continued walking. He would rather copulate with a dog.

Just before he reached the quiet residential street at the rear of the hotel, Maruyama quickly sidestepped behind an ornamental pine and

210

looked back along the alleyway. The two painted whores had disappeared. Moving back out of sight, he waited for over a minute, his ears attentive for even the slightest footfall. No one. Four years ago, in an effort to cheat him of his fee, one of his clients had had him followed. At the last moment, Maruyama had given the man the slip, and then promptly doubled his price. All the same, he had vowed never to be caught like that again. Picking up the case, he resumed walking. The guesthouse was just around the corner from the next block.

The twin room was dingy, but clean. Heaving his case up on to one of the single beds, Maruyama slowly eased himself down on to the other. However, despite his extreme tiredness – or possibly because of it – he did not sleep. Instead, as he stared up at the ceiling's cracked, greying plaster, he found himself finally facing up to the decision that he had been postponing for the last two years. It was time to give up. He knew it. He had made his pile. He was going to quit.

All of a sudden, he felt quite light-headed. How was he able at last to reconcile himself to the inevitable? Had it been the journey? The appalling ache in his back? Or that repulsive hooker, perhaps, taunting him that he had lost his spunk?

'No, I don't think so …'

The words came out in English. It was none of those. It was this assignment. Swinging his feet back off the bed, he opened the suitcase and stared at the plain, white envelope that he had retrieved four days previously from the left luggage locker in Ueno station. Professional thieves like himself were supposed to want to bow out with a grand finale: end their careers with the heist to end all heists, that would at one and the same time satisfy their professional vanity and provide them with sufficient cash for a long and comfortable retirement. He looked across the dimly lit room. His reflection was barely visible in the ancient mirror above the Victorian dresser. Not Maruyama Hiroshi. Centre stage was not his style. He was a bit player, waiting his cue to slip behind a piece of scenery and then discreetly disappear. Waiting, in fact, for an assignment like this. For in all his thirty-seven years of industrial espionage, he could scarcely recall a less demanding case. He opened up the envelope and read through the brief again. The instructions were simple and unequivocal. If he found the formula, there would be a substantial bonus.

But if not, the address alone would do.

Suddenly, the garage was filled with guilt.

'I talked to Gail this morning,' said Louise.

'Oh, yes? How is she?'

'Fine, fine. She sends her love.'

'What did you tell her?'

'I said I was just coming up to Wyburn for the day.'

'But I bet she thinks you're going to stay for the whole weekend, doesn't she?'

'I suppose so. I don't know what she'd say if she knew I was staying till next Wednesday.'

'Do you get to see much of her during the week now?' asked Bill, slipping a patient information leaflet inside a carton of Libidan and then carefully folding over the flaps.

'Yeah, yeah. At least once or twice – I make an effort to. Not that I'm forcing myself or anything, of course. I mean, she's my best friend, so naturally …'

'Does she think we're, er …'

'She hasn't said anything but I wouldn't be surprised if she does.'

'I don't like holding out on her either, you know.'

'I know you don't, but all the same I'm sure she feels terribly left out.'

Louise paused before speaking again, and then swung around in her chair to face Bill directly.

'Shall we tell her?'

'What, about Libidan?' said Bill, stopping his packing and looking up in alarm.

'Yeah.'

'Well, we could do, if you like. But we've only got to keep it going two more weeks and then we can call it a day – things can go back to how they were before.'

'And do you think we should call it a day – once we've got the money?'

'Yeah, of course I do. Don't you?'

'I would have said so last week, but …'

'But what … ?'

'These emails.'

'What emails?'

Putting down the half-filled pack, Bill came around the table and joined Louise at the computer. She pointed at the screen.

'There's a little, like, comment box – here, on the order form. It comes with the software. It's meant for special delivery instructions, or greetings – that sort of thing. We're starting to get repeat orders now, and three or four customers have used it to send us emails.'

'What sort of emails?'

'Thank-you messages.'

'Really?'

'Yeah.'

Moving up closer, Bill stared at the screen.

'Are they genuine?'

'I think so.'

Frowning, Bill sat down on the spare seat.

'So, what are you saying? We should carry on and not disappoint these people? Even after I've paid Snod his fifty grand?'

'I'm saying you could do, if you wanted to.'

'I don't know whether I do want to.'

'The Medicines Control Agency have gone quiet.'

'I'm not surprised, after that letter of yours.'

'If you did carry on, I'd be quite happy to continue helping you. I've had some more ideas for the line extensions that we were talking about last week. And then, of course, well, to be perfectly honest, after all this work I wouldn't mind making a bit of money out of Libidan, too. I mean, we do deserve it, don't we?'

'Yeah, yeah, of course. You more than me.'

'Thanks. But it was your discovery and the decision's really up to you. All I'm trying to say is that if you did want to continue, I wouldn't want to go on keeping Gail in the dark – that's all.'

Standing up again, Bill walked thoughtfully across the garage. Three weeks previously, strong in the knowledge that he could limit the amount of the active compound in each dispenser to five parts per million, he had decided to go ahead and launch Libidan over the Internet. Yet it had always been with the intention of quitting the moment he had raised the fifty thousand pounds for Snod. So far, the emails were all from grateful couples. But how long before someone out there caught on to Libidan's potential as a rape drug? How long before another Louise Schreiber would find herself leaving a strange house early one morning, her pride and dignity in ruins? Louise was speaking again.

'So, er, could you make more of the active, then? If you had to …'

'What, the quatrapeptide?'

'Hm.'

'Er, yes. I suppose so. It shouldn't be too difficult.'

'And if you do pack up now, what are you going to do afterwards? With your career, I mean.'

'I haven't thought about it, really. Carry on working at Sykes', I suppose.'

'Oh, right.'

'Anything wrong with that?' asked Bill quickly.

'No, no,' said Louise, swinging around on the seat and resuming her work at the console.

The atmosphere in the garage remained subdued for the rest of the day, and, despite passing the twenty-five thousand pounds mark during the afternoon, both Bill and Louise were still in a pensive mood when they left that evening. The following morning, too, although Bill had to hurry off at six o'clock to make the early shift at Sykes', Louise still had the issue of Libidan's long-term future very much on her mind when she emerged from the bath at nine. But, as she slipped into her dressing gown and opened the bathroom window to let out the steam, the matter was immediately driven from her thoughts. At the bottom of the back garden, between the far end of the lawn and the fence separating Bill's house from the one next door, someone was moving around in the bushes.

Retreating sharply several feet back from the window, Louise stood up on tiptoe and slowly scanned the garden. She spotted him again. It was a man – small and very squat – stealthily making his way towards the house. Sprinting down the corridor, she ran straight into her bedroom, and, having quickly slipped on a baggy summer dress, snatched up the telephone.

'Shit!'

Bill was not answering his mobile: he must be away from the van. Louise forced herself to think clearly. The kitchen door was locked – Bill had fitted a huge new bolt only three weeks ago – and she was certain that she had heard him slam the front door when he had left the house that morning: whoever the man might be, he wasn't going to be able to get inside the house easily. Plucking up her courage, she walked across to the bedroom window and looked out again. Perhaps he had gone away. In fact, the man was now standing right in the middle of the lawn and was staring straight up at her.

The front door bell rang a minute later.

'Yes?' asked Louise, fearfully.

'This … Kennedy house?'

Although the security chain afforded less than a two-inch gap between the door and the lintel, she could see that the man was carrying no less than three different cameras and was draped in all manner of photographic gadgetry.

'Yes.'

'You … Mrs Kennedy?'

'No.'

'Oh.' He paused and frowned. 'Mr Kennedy. He here?'

'No.'

The cameras were all Japanese. Judging by his facial features and skin colour, Louise concluded that he must be too, although he was certainly the scruffiest member of his race she had ever seen.

'I come about Poojin. You know Poojin?'

'Poojin? I'm sorry, I don't know what you mean …'

'You don't know Poojin?' asked the man mournfully, his sallow walrus moustache drooping in disappointment.

'Er, no, sorry …' replied Louise, wondering how on earth she was managing to feel guilty that she didn't.

Suddenly, the man delved into his waistcoat pocket and extracted a grimy square of paper, which he then unfolded and passed through the door.

'My company write Poojin letter … to Mr Kennedy.'

The letter, which was in perfect English, was dated two months previously. Louise began reading sections of it aloud to herself.

'" … your name has been passed to us by the Royal Society of Glaziers … interest in Gothic revivalist art in Japan … we write to ask your permission to photograph one of your outbuildings, which we understand to be a design of Augustus Pugin."'

'Poojin, yes!' repeated the man.

'Oh, Pugin! The architect! I see what you mean now. You want to photograph the conservatory.'

'Very beautiful construction,' said the man, nodding gravely, 'very beautiful.'

'Yes, it is, isn't it?' replied Louise, in a mixture of enthusiasm and relief. 'But it's not an original Pugin, or anything. Mr Kennedy's father made it.'

By way of response, the man merely shrugged and pointed a finger to the final paragraph of the letter. Louise began reading again.

'"… and we are compiling a photographic record of designs from the nineteenth century to the modern era for which we would be prepared to pay up to five thousand pounds per inclusion." Five thousand pounds!'

'Five thousand pound, OK?' asked the man, nervously.

'Er, yes, yes, that sounds fine,' replied Louise, her hand reaching up to release the security chain. 'Do you want to come in and take a closer look?'

'No, no,' said the man, extracting a business card from the pocket of his grubby green waistcoat. 'You speak Mr Kennedy. He phone my hotel. I come back, pay money. Take photo one day. One day.'

The man held up his right forefinger emphatically.

'You'll need one day for the shoot?' asked Louise.

'One day. Myself – in your house, please.'

'Well, thank you very much, Mr, er …'

'Shashin. Toru Shashin,' replied the man, handing over his name card.

'Well, thank you Mr Shashin. Your hotel number's on the back here, I see. Well, great, we'll be in touch. Thank you.'

With a nod and a woeful smile, the man was gone.

Having peeled off his moustache and unburdened himself of the junk shop cameras, Maruyama leaned back in the driver's seat and began watching the house. It had been a nice touch, leaving the letter with the girl. Later on, she would look at it again, and, finding it convincingly misaddressed, persuade herself that the original must have gone astray in the post and that Mr Toru Shashin was perfectly genuine. Within an hour, or possibly two, she would emerge and lead him straight to the factory, so greedily had she seized on the possibility of pocketing the five thousand pounds: whatever these people were up to, they were obviously desperate for money. Slowly reaching around to the back seat, Maruyama picked up the cushion he had brought from the hotel and slipped it underneath his lower back. If he were to avoid getting taken off the plane in Tokyo in a wheelchair, he had better make sure he kept his lumbar well supported. Suddenly, though, he was alert again – all thoughts of his injured back gone from his mind. The Ford disappearing out of sight in his rear-view mirror had passed in front of the house and slowed down in exactly the same way five minutes previously – he was sure of it. The hair on Maruyama's neck stood up on end. He had not managed to see the driver's face, but it didn't matter. For although his spine might be feeling the effects of age, his instincts were as sharp as ever and there was no mistaking the sensation that was now sweeping over him.

He had company.

As she placed her handbag on the kitchen table and sat down, Una realized her hands were shaking. Looking across the room to the cabinet above the fridge, she thought about the bottle of brandy inside. Terrified of the alcoholic abyss towards which the occasional tipple might lead a lonely, middle-aged spinster, she was pathologically strict with herself in keeping it solely for medicinal purposes. Standing up and walking across the kitchen, though, she decided to break her rule tonight. The meeting had really scared her. She shivered as she unscrewed the cap, remembering the empty bottles of vodka strewn around Len's filthy basement flat. Despite the scorching sensation in her throat, she found herself recalling the whole dreadful scene.

'There are some trees here,' said Ray, pointing to an area shaded green on the large, home-made map that he had spread out over the table. 'They border the laboratory grounds but they're not actually part of the complex. They belong to a local farmer. That's where we park the van. It's less than twenty yards to the main entrance, but we'll be completely out of sight.'

He looked across the table, first at Una and Len, and then at John and Callum – the two operations experts he had drafted in from the other ALA cell. The great strategist revealing his master plan to a select group of lieutenants, thought Una – Ray was really in his element here.

'After we've parked up, Len, John, you change into your overalls and then start unloading the gear. Me and Callum'll go back on to the main road and approach the gatehouse from the front.'

'Are there any street lights on the road?' asked Callum, leaning over and pointing at the map.

'All the way along.'

'What happens if the security guy clocks us?'

'He almost definitely will.'

'Won't he phone through to someone? He's an old guy, right? On his own. What's he gonna do when he sees two blokes comin' straight towards him?'

'We wear suits – businessman suits. It's ten past seven in the evening, right? His shift has just started and it won't even have got dark. As long as we don't do anything to panic him, he'll stay relaxed.'

'OK,' grunted Callum.

'We tell him our car's broken down. We want to phone for assistance. There's a toilet inside the gatehouse. You ask to go inside and use it. When you've taken him out, I'll signal two flashes on the torch to Len and John to bring our overalls across from the trees. Now, they've got pest-control logos on them to give us cover while we're walking through the complex, but once we're actually inside the animal testing area …'

'Hang on a minute,' interrupted Una. 'What do you mean, taken him out?'

A frosty silence descended on the room. From the corner of her eye, Una could see Len shaking his head contemptuously, but, resisting the temptation to turn and glare at him, she continued staring straight at Ray. His eyes flickered towards John and Callum. She knew her question implied a challenge to his authority.

'I mean, when he's unconscious, Una. Callum is going to knock the security guard unconscious.'

'What? How?'

'It doesn't matter how. All you need to know is that forty minutes later, when we come back through those trees, you need to have the van ready to move.'

'I don't know whether I like this. I mean, he's just an old man – you might really hurt him. What if nobody finds him until later and he's left all alone in that …'

Una found her words drying up. The four men's expressions had not altered, but somehow they were collectively generating an intense aura of hostility. It was as though a cage door had slipped open and a wild jungle cat had slinked into one of the room's shadowy corners. Una felt overcome by the desire to turn and flee, and, unable to stop herself, looked sideways across towards the door.

'Yeah, well,' said Ray, quietly. 'You just let us worry about that, Una.'

His words defused the tension. The moment of menace had passed. Nevertheless, in that second, Una had sensed it: the violence that these ruthless men could summon up at will and direct towards anyone who stood in their way. Direct towards a defenceless security guard. Direct towards a defenceless middle-aged woman.

Pouring herself a second glass of brandy, Una took a deep swig and began to cough. She rubbed her eyes and looked up at the ceiling. She was crying. How on earth had she got herself into all this? Taking out her handkerchief, she was about to dry her tears, but then sat bolt upright in her chair. It was after nine o'clock. Who on earth could be ringing her doorbell at this time of night?'

'Good evening, Miss Arnold.'

'Oh, oh, hello, Mr Conlon,' replied Una, trying to keep her flustered, tearstained face half hidden behind the front door.

'I'm sorry to call on you so late. If it's inconvenient, I can come back another time.'

'No, no, come in,' said Una, blowing her nose as delicately as she could. 'Please excuse my condition, its my, er, hay fever. I always get it at this time of year.'

By way of response, Conlon made a stiff, somewhat over-dignified bow and walked into the hall.

'Please, please, come through to the sitting room.'

Switching the light on, she looked around the room. Thankfully, it was not in too much of a state.

'Do take a seat. Would you like a cup of tea, or something?'

'No, no, I'm fine thank you, Miss Arnold. And, also, I'll stand if you don't mind.'

'Oh, right ...'

Having already sat down herself, Una felt a little awkward, but imagined she would feel still more so were she to stand up again. In any event, the detective began to talk almost straightaway.

'Following our last meeting – our, er, chance meeting, in the park – I made some enquiries on your behalf with my colleagues at the station and in the Crown Prosecution Service.'

'Oh, thank you, Mr Conlon,' replied Una. After the intimidating atmosphere of Len's flat, Conlon's clean-shaven formality felt absolutely luxurious.

'Despite the fact that your statement revealed allegations of certain, er, misdemeanours on the part of the householder concerned – which we are actively investigating, I might add – it's largely a question now of whether he chooses to pursue a formal complaint or not.'

'You mean Dr Kennedy?'

'Yes.'

'Oh.' Una frowned and turned this over in her mind for several seconds. 'So, if I understand you correctly, you're not going press charges against me unless he makes a fuss about things.'

'The police have a certain amount of discretion in cases such as these. But if, as the aggrieved party, he were to insist, we would have little alternative.'

'So, I'm in his hands, then?'

'More or less, Miss Arnold, yes.'

'Oh, well, thank you for telling me.'

'The injustice of this situation is not altogether lost on me, Miss Arnold. I realize you went to his house with the intention of preventing his further unlawful behaviour.'

'Will I go to jail?'

'It would be highly unlikely for a first offence. Although you will have a criminal record, of course.'

'Oh, pity,' mumbled Una to herself – Ray couldn't exactly make her go through with the raid on the laboratory if she were locked up in prison.

'I beg your pardon?'

'Nothing, nothing. Well, actually …'

Una looked up at Conlon's grave yet kindly face. Maybe trusting herself to the authorities wasn't such a bad idea after all. An image of Callum repeatedly bringing a crow bar down on the security guard's head flashed through her mind.

'Yes, Miss Arnold?'

Conlon watched as her eyes glazed over and she struggled to put her thoughts into words.

'If … if a similar situation were to happen again. If a person, like me, were to come across somebody planning something … illegal, it would be best to tell the police, wouldn't it? To tell you.'

'Of course it would.'

'Hm …'

'Is there something you want to tell me?'

'Yes, yes, there is ...' murmured Una. 'But not here. Not now. I need a little time to think ...'

Conlon felt his throat grow dry. He couldn't believe it. He had never imagined he would find the right opportunity to ask, and yet here she was, leading him straight into it.

'Well, then. Perhaps, one evening – when you feel up to having a chat about it – we could maybe, well, go out, and ...'

Snapping out of her trance, Una turned to face him.

' ... yes, Mr Conlon?'

Suddenly, Conlon felt all his self-confidence vanish. If she could only have kept her eyes averted for another half second!

'Well, anyway, you have my card. Please, just, er, call me if you need to. Goodnight.'

By the time Una had got to her feet, Conlon was already at the front door. She hurried into the hall after him. What had he been going to say?

'Mr Conlon!'

'Yes?' he turned and looked back at her.

'Thank you. Thank you very much.'

Una watched a smile start to form on Conlon's face, and then just as quickly disappear. Something seemed to have caught his attention. She followed his eyes. From his vantage point at the front door he had a perfect view of the kitchen table, situated right in the middle of which were her glass and the still open bottle of brandy.

By the time Una looked back down the hallway, Conlon had already stepped out into the night.

It was no ordinary knock at the door.

It was not simply the volume, though; as the door was metal and had been struck with the flat of a hand, the reverberations swept through the garage. It was not even that the noise was so totally unexpected – in all the many hours Bill and Louise had worked there together, no one had ever so much as approached the building, let alone knocked on its door. Rather, it was the solemn resonance of the sound, like the tolling of some fateful bell, that made Bill and Louise turn and look at each other with a terrible melancholic dread.

'Hello?'

'Mr Terret?'

'What?'

'Mr Nicholas Terret?'

'No … er, I mean, yes.'

'Sign here, please.'

Bill looked dumbly at the pen and clipboard that the motor-cycle courier was holding out for him. The mobile phones, the bank accounts, the website – everything was in the fictitious name of Terret, but all of them had been set up using Bill's home address in Wyburn. Who on earth had established the connection between Mr Terret and this address?

'Thanks,' replied the courier, turning and walking off towards his motor bike.

Bill stared down at the package and then went slowly back inside the garage.

'What is it?' asked Louise, her complexion totally white.

Bill stared around the garage: the latest batch of dispensers, filled and neatly stacked against the wall; the worktable covered with the new packaging proofs they had picked up from the printers that morning; the computer VDU displaying the modified website that Louise had toiled most of the previous night to finish.

'It's a recorded delivery. In the name of Terret.'

'What? How did they track us down here?'

'I don't know.'

'Let me open it.'

Taking the package from Bill, Louise ripped the plastic seal apart and extracted the document inside.

'It's from VISA …'

'VISA? What do they want?'

Bill watched Louise reading quickly through the letter until, suddenly, she faltered and put out a hand to support herself on the edge of the table.

'Oh, my God. They can't do it! No, no! They can't do that!'

'What is it?'

'They've withdrawn our credit facility.'

'What! Why?'

'Pending an investigation by the Medicines Control Agency.'

'Show me!'

222

No sooner had Bill taken the letter and began to read, than Louise sat down at the keyboard and began typing furiously.

'It's true! I can't access the account!' she exclaimed, banging the flat of her hand down on the tabletop. 'The bastards. The miserable bastards.'

'There's a cheque, too,' said Bill, sitting down next to her.

'What? How much?'

'Thirty-one thousand pounds,' said Bill, separating the cheque from the letter and passing it across to Louise. 'Full and final settlement of our account up until lunch-time today.'

'No. No!' she exclaimed, clenching her fist tightly and striking it against her thigh. 'We'll fight them. We'll go to another credit card company.'

'We can't,' replied Bill, shaking his head sadly. 'They talk to each other – the banks, the finance houses – they exchange information all the time. They'd pick up on us straightaway, even if we used another false name.'

'But the Medicines Control people can't prove anything, Bill. We'll appeal! It says we can, look!'

All of a sudden, Bill felt overcome by a great sense of calm. Perhaps, somehow, he had known all along that this would happen. In a way it had all been a dream – far, far too good to be true. The perfectly for-mulated product, the spectacular sales success, the wonderful working relationship that had developed between him and Louise in the garage. Leaning forward, Bill gently took hold of her hand.

'Even if we have a chance of getting the decision reversed, the hearing probably won't be for months. We have to face it, Louise. It's over.'

'But!'

'No, no listen.' As softly as he could he put his other hand up to her face to stop her speaking. 'Please. Please. We did our best, you did your best, Lou – you've been magnificent. Absolutely magnificent. But we have to face it. We've run out of time. We've just run out of time.'

Part Four

Sex Kills

Chapter 13

Stamping the floor catch down with his heel, Snod leaned his shoulder against the garage door and then pushed outwards and upwards until the rusty springs engaged and hoisted the heavy metal panel up over his head. Stepping out of the garage, he squinted in the early morning sunshine, and then scanned the dilapidated lock-ups opposite and adjacent to his own. As usual, there was no one around. It was precisely because of the isolation of these three rows of garages – tucked away down a side road at the back end of a terminally run-down industrial estate – that two years previously he had chosen to site his main drug-making operation here. During that entire period he had seen less than a half dozen people, not one of whom had directed anything more than a passing glance at his battered transit van and the unmarked drums of chemicals inside. Taking the heavy steel padlock from his pocket, he slowly surveyed the derelict railway sidings that flanked the lockups on the opposite side of the industrial estate. Ironically, he almost found himself wishing that a drugs squad SWAT team would leap out from behind the rusting carriages, megaphones blaring, and order him instantly to drop to his knees. Slamming the garage door back down and slipping the padlock through the bolt, he took out his cigarettes and looked up at the chill morning sky.

'It's all turned to shit, hasn't it, Micky, old son?'

Going downstream into manufacture had been a huge mistake – he understood that now. The moment he had started making the E's himself, after eighteen months of being ripped off by suppliers in Manchester, Leeds and London, half a dozen pushers seemed suddenly to have sprung up from nowhere peddling cheap Dutch and French-made material on his patch. By that time, of course, it had been too late to pull out – he had over two hundred grand tied up in kit. Even then, he could still have made a go of things if Brummie hadn't started pissing about. Angrily, Snod lashed out at the padlock with his boot. If he ever caught up with the bastard, he'd beat every last ounce of crap out of him. It was bad enough losing the huge network of contacts that Brummie had had for distributing the stuff. Much worse was that the man had been a chemistry wizard, and, without realizing it, Snod had become fatally dependent on his skills. The reaction from methylamine to crude MDMA seemed easy enough, but, try as he had – three times a week for the last month and a half – Snod had been completely unable to get the crude to crystallize in a form that would allow it to be properly tableted. Somewhere along the line, he was making a fundamental error. Taking a deep drag on his cigarette, Snod gave the garage door a final, resentful kick and moved off. Never again. He was finished with manufacturing. It was time to get back to doing what he did best.

As he approached the tower block, he thought at first that the four shops on its ground floor had been closed down. Bringing the van to a halt in front of them, Snod realized it was just that steel shutters now uniformly covered their windows. The shops' insurers must have insisted they put them up. Turning off the engine, he sat still in the cab for several moments, staring up at the fourteen-storey structure above.

'Home sweet home.'

Rubbing the sleep from his eyes, Snod tried to recall the last time he had actually been to the flat. He'd set the girls up sometime in ninety-seven. When was that? Four years ago? Once they'd started to bring the cash to the pub on Sunday nights, he no longer had any reason to come and check up on them – that was until they hadn't shown up for the last two weeks. Shaking his head, he got out of the van and locked it. You'd think they'd want to take any and every opportunity to get away from the estate – if only for a few hours. It was an even bigger shit-hole than he remembered.

'Look after yer van, mate?'

Turning to his left, Snod saw a young boy, about twelve years of age, holding out his hand and nodding at the van. For a second, he felt almost dizzy with recognition; the ragged clothes; the arrogance towards someone twice his age. Here he was, back on the estate on which he had been born and raised talking to … himself. Taking several steps towards the boy, Snod leaned down and stared straight into his eyes. Within seconds the boy's facial muscles began visibly to twitch as he scanned the fearsome purple and red blotches at close range. Finally, unable to bear the sight any longer, he averted his eyes and looked down at his feet.

'What's your name, kid?' asked Snod at last, his voice gravelly from the cigarettes and lack of sleep.

'Martin,' came the mumbled response.

'Here,' said Snod, taking a pound coin from his pocket and putting it into his hand.

'Thanks,' replied the boy.

'And, listen, if anyone comes near the van, hit 'em with this.'

The boy looked back up again to see Snod unwinding the hemp bag of oranges from around his wrist and passing it across to him. Nervously, he took the bag from Snod and smiled shyly back at him.

Although he had imagined the long, communal balcony would look more or less the same, he had still expected to find at least one or two noticeable differences. Yet, from the faded graffiti either side of the stair-well, down to the wooden clothes horse in front of flat 44 – draped, as always, in a half dozen threadbare tea towels – it appeared unchanged in every detail. Surely the old woman couldn't still be living there? Hadn't she died six or seven years ago? Again, Snod felt lightheaded. The walk up the five flights of stairs must have winded him. Resting against the balustrade, he went to take out his cigarettes but stopped mid-action, and knelt slowly down. It couldn't be possible. There, lying half in and half out of one of the drains, was the blue wooden trolley with which he and his elder sister Alice had used to play. Kneeling down, he picked it up, recalling how she would drag it by its string from one end of the grey, concrete balcony to the other, whilst he marched proudly along behind. He ran his fingers over the cracked paint. Actually, no. It wasn't the same toy. But why had someone left it out right next to his flat?

Why, in fact, had his whole childhood come back to haunt him this cold, lonely morning?

Dropping the toy, he stood up quickly. Someone was coming out of the next-door flat. It was a middle-aged woman, her face hard and angular, her satin dressing gown and fluffy slippers the distant echo of a glamour long since departed. Leaning down to place a milk bottle on the step, she turned and stared at him. Her right temple was a criss-cross mass of veins, purple and filamentous, like the delicate tentacles of some poisonous sea anemone.

'If you want business,' she snapped, 'they've gone.'

The woman slammed the door.

They had indeed gone. Shakily, Snod put out his arm and eased himself down on to the edge of the black plastic sofa. For the second time that morning, he found himself almost longing for his own ruin. If only the girls had exacted some revenge for the beating he had given them after the complaint to the Social Services: slashed the upholstery, broken the windows, taken a hammer to the bath. Instead, they had more or less restored the flat to its original condition. Looking around the living room, Snod shivered. The gate-leg table was back up against the far wall again, half extended in exactly the same way it had been when he was a child. An image of his father sprang irresistibly to mind. There he sat, in his string vest, stabbing at his dinner with his knife and fork. Suddenly, he stopped eating and turned to glare malevolently at Michael and Alice. Snod could feel his sister on the sofa next to him, tense with fear. The blood was pumping in his ears. Would they get a beating again tonight?

Fleeing from the recollection, Snod stumbled across the living room and went lurching down the hallway towards the rear bedroom, but the sight that was to greet him there was even worse. The night Alice had left, when she was fifteen, she had stripped the room of absolutely everything – every pop-star poster, every ornament, every last individual possession. The next morning, deaf to the sound of his father and mother screaming at each other in the kitchen, he had run to the bedroom door and stared in disbelief at these same bare grey walls. How could she have left him to face their father all by himself? He was only ten. Desperately, he scanned the bookcase and the bedside cabinet for a note. An address. Anything. She must be waiting for him somewhere. Waiting for him to follow.

Snod was suffocating. Pulling the flimsy cotton curtains apart, he tried twisting the catch to open the window. It was stuck. Again and again he slammed the heel of his hand up against the catch, until the rusting metal frame at last bent under the strain and the window burst open. Leaning out, he sucked in great gulps of the morning air, until the sense of asphyxiation eventually passed.

Five floors below, in the street in front of the flats, his van was still parked. The hemp bag lay strewn on the pavement, the oranges spilt out on to the road. There was no sign of Martin.

Finally, Maruyama could stand the waiting no more. As soon as the girl had led him to the garage, he had gone straight back to the hotel and faxed details of its location through to Tokyo. That had been over five days ago, and he had been pacing around his hotel room ever since. The staff on the desk all looked competent, and he was as certain as he could be that if Kennedy or the girl had phoned him, they would have put the call through correctly.

'Ma, yaroh!'

Standing stiffly but purposefully upright, he walked across to the wardrobe and began wrapping the cameras around his shoulders. Even if it was his last job, and even if the man in the red Ford had somehow got to Kennedy before him, he still owed himself one last shot at picking up that bonus. Perhaps five days had been too long to leave it. However, he had not wanted to call on them again until they had had every chance to phone him first: appearing too insistent would have been to run the risk of alerting their suspicions. Adjusting his moustache in the mirror, Maruyama began a minute's deep breathing exercises. Satisfied he was fully psyched back into the role again, he switched off the lights and quickly left the room. In the lobby, he mingled for several moments with the group of tourists and businessmen loosely lined up for the post-breakfast check-out, before suddenly turning on his heel and sprinting through the revolving door to the taxi rank outside.

'Wyburn, please.'

With a nod, the taxi driver engaged the engine and moved off.

Maruyama looked back at the hotel exit. Convinced that no one was following him, he gingerly swivelled around in his seat again and began planning his approach. A full day to turn over the house completely would have been ideal, but that seemed unlikely now. However, since it was just a chemical formula, and his memory, unlike his back, was still in perfect working order, all he really needed was to glimpse it once.

'Sorry. Could you drive up and down the road again, please. I know it's one of these houses, but it's been a few months and I can't remember which.'

With a frown of resignation, the driver made a second three-point turn and drove back once more along Lynhurst Drive. Leaning forwards, his face flanked on either side by the headrests of the front seats, Maruyama completed his reconnaissance of the area. The girl's car had gone from the drive and in its place was a battered Mondeo. He guessed it was probably Kennedy's car.

'OK. Fine. If you could drop me here – I think I know where I am now.'

As Maruyama silently closed the taxi door, he scanned the area one more time for good measure. There was no sign of the red Ford and every other car on the street but one – a six-seater people carrier – had been parked there on his first visit. If anyone else had Kennedy's place under surveillance, they must be doing it from inside one of the houses.

'Thirteen pounds fifty.'

'Thank you very much. Sorry to have …'

Maruyama left the sentence unfinished. Less than fifteen feet away, on the opposite side of the street, an unmarked transit van had just come to an abrupt halt. Huddling up against the side of the taxi so as not to be observed, Maruyama watched the driver emerge, cross the road and walk briskly into Kennedy's house.

'Listen, er, could you take me back to the hotel?'

'What?' cried the taxi driver, unable to hide his puzzlement.

'Yes. I've made a mistake,' replied Maruyama slowly. 'Back to the hotel, please. There'll be a tip in it for you.'

'Suit yourself,' replied the driver, philosophically. In his experience, Japanese tourists usually came armed with a suitcase full of maps and knew exactly which route they wanted to follow down to the last traffic bollard. Still, there was a first time for everything.

Leaning gently back in the seat so as not to put too much strain on his spine, Maruyama felt genuinely humbled by the tide of relief that was surging through him. Somewhere along the line he had miscalculated – and badly so. This had been no open and shut case: the red Ford, the five-day delay – his instincts should have told him earlier that something was wrong. Removing the moustache for a few seconds, he wiped the line of sweat from his upper lip. It didn't matter now if the taxi driver saw his face – by tonight, he'd be five continents away. Looking through the taxi window, he surveyed the field of wheat beyond the roadside – each stalk bent sadly over by a heavy, ripened head. In his life-

232

time he had come across some hard, unscrupulous men – some motivated by power, all motivated by money. Men who, in pursuit of their goals, would not shrink from coercion and violence. Yet none of them had remotely resembled the man he had seen emerging from that white transit van. Perhaps he was a freelance – an independent of some sort. All the same, even if there were only one individual like him operating in the world of industrial espionage, then Maruyama was glad his career was finishing today, this cold June morning on the outskirts of a small English village.

For that man had nothing but death in his eyes.

'You owe me.'

Bill felt the pen fall from his fingers as he turned and looked up at Snod, standing in the kitchen doorway.

'Yeah. I know.'

Snod's face was infinitely more fearsome than he had remembered: perhaps it was seeing it in daylight for the first time.

'Where is it? My money.'

'I've got some of it,' replied Bill, standing slowly up. 'About half.'

'No good.'

'Hang on. You said I could have some time – up to four months. It's not even two yet.'

'You owe me!' shouted Snod, slamming his fist down on the kitchen table. 'You all fuckin' owe me!'

Bill swallowed hard. Last time Snod had been cool, dispassionate almost. Now he appeared like a man possessed – his eyes wandering maniacally, aimlessly around the room.

'I told you, I've got a business. And I've made some money on that – just over twenty-five thousand pounds. The cheque is clearing now.'

'What about the rest? Huh? Huh?'

Taking several steps forward, Snod raised his first finger and thrust it viciously to within an inch of Bill's face.

'I put my house on the market today,' replied Bill, swaying backwards. 'That'll generate enough for the balance, and the interest.'

'Today! Today! You've had two fuckin' months to sell the place!'

Turning suddenly to his right, Snod rammed his forearms into the kitchen dresser and raked downwards and outwards, causing a shower of crockery to fall and smash on the stone-tiled floor.

'It's not exactly going to help things if you go and wreck the place though, is it?' shouted Bill.

They stood and stared at each other, both wondering where Bill had found the nerve to answer back like that. Bizarrely, Bill found himself assessing Snod's height; he was scarcely more than five feet tall – a good six inches shorter than himself – not that he imagined for a moment he would last more than a few seconds with him in a brawl.

'So how about I go pay your bitch a visit, then, eh? That might speed things up.'

Bill tried to compose himself. He had to keep them on the subject of the money.

'I'm making arrangements to sell the house today. That's what those documents on the table are for. The ones I was writing when you came in.'

Standing there with his chest heaving, like a raging bull with nothing to charge at, Snod seemed uncertain where next to direct his anger,.

'How much will you get for it?'

'I don't know. A hundred and fifty thousand maybe.'

'Is that all?'

'Probably. I can't exactly hold out for the best price, though, can I? It's got to be a quick sale.'

Once again Bill surprised himself by the tone of his response, although this time Snod did not seem to pick up on it. Instead, he began carrying out some calculations in his head, squinting with the effort as he did so.

'OK. So. Fifty grand plus four months interest, that makes … ninety grand. Get me the cash you've already got tonight – I'll pick up the rest when you've.'

'Hang on!' interrupted Bill. 'You said five thousand pounds a month interest – not ten.'

'Did I?'

'Yeah!'

'Well, it's changed now. I need the money.'

'That's not …'

Before he could get the words out, Snod took hold of Bill's shirt front and smashed his forehead straight into his face. Bill reeled backwards with the force of the blow, but Snod kept a firm hold and, moments later, brought their faces back close together. Through the trickle of

234

blood dripping down from his right eyebrow, Bill stared in horror at the terrifying facial psoriasis. When Snod spoke, his voice was almost inaudible. The stench of tobacco on his breath was overpowering.

'For the last time. You owe me. You started this. You made up drugs on my tablet press and you never asked me. OK?'

Thrusting Bill back down into his chair, Snod turned and, with a final glare of warning, walked slowly out of the kitchen.

Moving across to the sink, Bill ran some cold water over a flannel and put it to his eye. Throwing back his head to help stem the flow of blood, he groaned deeply. Now it was not just Louise, but Gail as well. It was bad enough that he hadn't even told his sister he intended to sell the family home, but if he were to pay Snod ninety thousand, he wouldn't even be able to give her a fair half share of the proceeds. As the significance of this situation sank in, Snod reappeared at the door.

'Here.'

He was nodding at Bill to follow him down the hallway.

'What this?' he asked, pointing through the open door of the laboratory.

'It's a column – a chromatographic column.'

Walking forwards, Snod pushed the door open and surveyed the disassembled experimental apparatus.

'If you've had kit here all along, why did you go and use mine?'

'I haven't got a tablet press. All this is just for chemical synthesis – that's all I understand, really …'

Snod squinted for a moment, seeming to turn this over in his mind.

'Have the money ready by tonight,' he grunted, finally.

He left the house without closing the front door behind him.

'Hi, it's me.'

Jumping sharply forwards on her seat, Louise pressed the receiver closely to her ear so as to blot out the sounds of the office around her.

'Gail! Oh, God, I'm so glad you've called. I've been phoning all morning – they said you were in a meeting. How are you?'

'All right, I suppose. When did you get back, then?'

'What from Bill's? Yesterday afternoon.'

'So, you went up to see him for one day and ended up staying six, then?'

'Yes, yes I did. Listen, Gail, we've got to meet up. Bill and I have been terribly unfair to you. I want to explain everything.'

'Well, I wish someone would. My only source of information at the moment is Wright and Wright, and they're not exactly liberal with the facts.'

'Who?'

'Wright and Wright – the family solicitors. They've just called to say they're sending around a load of conveyancing documents for me to sign. He's put the house up for sale, hasn't he?'

'Yes, yes. He has.'

'Well, nice of him to consult me on that – I mean, I know it's only half mine. Still never mind. Just send the forms round to dear old Gail and she'll sign 'em – don't worry.'

'Gail. He's in trouble.'

'Then why didn't he tell me?' shouted Gail.

Louise closed her eyes painfully – in all the time she had known Gail she had never once raised her voice.

'To protect you. Because he didn't want you to get dragged into it.'

'But he told you, though, didn't he?'

'Yes, yes, he did – but I'd already got involved by then and …'

'So, why didn't you tell me, then? I could've handled it, whatever it is.'

'I wanted to, but …'

'I'm used to him keeping things close to his chest, but I never thought you'd hold out on me, Lou.'

'Oh, God, I'm so sorry, Gail. You don't know how I've wanted to share it with you all along, but it's been so complicated and …'

'What's going on, Lou? Just tell me, please.'

'I will, I will – I promise – but not now – not over the phone. What are you doing tomorrow tonight?'

'Nothing.'

'I'll pick you up straight after work. Five o'clock OK?'

'OK.'

'Let's go away somewhere for the weekend, for a couple of nights, get right out of London and talk – properly.'

'All right. If you want to.'

'I do want to. I'll tell you everything, Gail. Every last single thing. Right from the beginning. And I swear I'll never, never keep anything secret from you ever again.'

236

Ten minutes after Snod's departure, when Conlon's red Ford Sierra pulled into the driveway, the front door of the house was still open. Sensing straightaway that something was amiss, Conlon instinctively leaned forward to radio for back-up but immediately stopped himself: he couldn't afford to have any other police officers present on this one. Since he had started investigating Kennedy, his objective had changed completely from one of catching the sick little pervert to ensuring that he did not pursue a burglary complaint against Una. He had told no one of his real intention, though, not even Una: he hadn't built up thirty years' worth of pension to let it slip now. However, before he could consign her bungled break-in to the station archives and let her walk free, he had to ensure that all the loose ends of the case were properly tied up. And that meant Kennedy's unequivocal agreement to letting the whole matter drop. Frowning, he turned over in his mind everything he had discovered about Kennedy since first he had interviewed him at the station six weeks previously. The man was a criminal deviant all right – no doubt about that – but by the looks of things, pretty crafty with it. If he appeared too keen on getting him to drop the burglary complaint, he or his fancy lawyer might seize on it as a negotiating tool. In no time at all they would twist everything around to make Kennedy look like the victim and drag Una right back into the frame in the process. Locking the car door, Conlon looked up at the imposing frontage of the house and wearily shook his head. The blessings of parasites.

'In above your head, son?'

Conlon felt overcome by disdain at the sight before him. Down on his knees, picking up shards of broken crockery one by one, his face swollen and streaked with blood, Kennedy cut a truly pathetic figure.

'What?' He looked up in alarm. 'Oh, it's you. What do you want?'

Sitting himself down at the kitchen table, Conlon nodded at Bill to do the same.

'Who did that to your face, then? McKenzie? I didn't think violence was his style.'

'I don't know what you're talking about,' replied Bill, nervously. 'I don't know anybody called McKenzie. I've just had an accident, that's all.'

'An accident,' echoed Conlon dryly, leaning back in the seat and slipping his hand into the inside pocket of his raincoat.

'Yes. An accident.'

'And you've never heard of Kevin McKenzie?'

'No.'

'Funny that,' said Conlon taking a notebook out of his pocket and flicking through the pages. 'Because according to my information, you and Mr McKenzie were arrested together on the evening of ... the 14th June, following a public disorder incident at a night club in Harledge. Joe Bananas by name.'

'Oh, right, yes. I know who you mean, now,' replied Bill, his face twitching uncomfortably. 'I just didn't know that McKenzie was his real name, that's all.'

'You didn't know his real name? Hm. And so neither, presumably, are you an accomplice of his in the manufacture and distribution of illegal substances.'

'No, of course not.'

'Of course not, of course not,' intoned Conlon, ironically. 'And that lot out there's just the chemistry set daddy bought for you last Christmas, right?'

'I'm not saying any more until I've spoken ...'

Bill was unable to finish the sentence because Conlon grabbed him by his shirt.

'I'm gonna have you, you little shit. Have you got that? I am gonna have you. And do you wanna know why? Because the stuff you peddle is filth. Because you are filth. And because decent, hardworking people need to be protected from your ever getting a hold over them.'

Releasing the limp, crestfallen figure, Conlon was again overcome with disgust. Clearly, he had completely overestimated Kennedy. The man was a wreck. From the kitchen doorway, he took one final look at him, seated at the table, head in hands and then, with a shake of the head, turned and walked off down the hall. He was certain now that Kennedy was no threat to Una – although, strangely, he found himself deriving little pleasure from the realization. Perhaps Kennedy was just one stooge too many – and God knows, in his thirty years on the force, Conlon had seen enough of them. Men like Kennedy only ever ended up one of two ways: at the station, confessing to everything and anything the police cared to throw at them, or dumped in a ditch somewhere, after whoever had beaten them up in the first place came back and finished the job.

In either case, Conlon need only wait. One way or another, the burglary complaint was dead.

Emerging from the front door, Conlon looked around him. The day had warmed up a little but the breeze was still nicely cool. Taking in a deep lungful of air, he put all thoughts of Kennedy behind him and turned his mind to the evening to come. The previous day, with shaking hands, he had phoned Una and asked her to dinner at his house this very evening. Even thinking about their conversation again made his heart beat faster. He had better get some flowers and things – make the place look really nice. Getting into the car, he finally radioed in.

The WPC at the other end was dumbfounded: no one in the station could remember the last time DI Conlon had taken an afternoon off.

Snod awoke at half past three that afternoon feeling clear-headed and refreshed. Leaving the van parked in front his house, he walked out into the afternoon sunshine and within twenty minutes had taken a seat in the lounge at The Black Dog. Over the top of his pint glass he surveyed the half dozen customers dotted around its huge, cavernous lounge. Late afternoon was the ideal time. Placing the glass back on the table, he took the newspaper out from under his arm and turned to the sports pages. Everyone knew what went on at the Dog. All he had to do was sit there and be patient.

He did not have to wait long. Twenty minutes later, a West Indian youth entered the pub and sidled over to a group of workmen in the far corner.

'Hello ...' observed Snod to himself, under his breath.

He was right. From the corner of his eye he could see the workmen shaking their heads and the youth turning to walk in his direction. Concentrating on his newspaper again, he waited for the inevitable approach.

'You want doves, man?' asked the youth, quietly.

'What?' replied Snod – feigning surprise. The West Indian youth was half-kneeling, half-crouching next to him.

'Doves? Speed?'

'Yeah, er, yeah,' answered Snod, putting down the newspaper and making a move as though to take out his wallet.

'Not here. Out the back,' the youth replied, nodding in the direction of the lavatories.

As soon as the youth turned to walk towards the toilets, Snod emptied the half dozen oranges out of the hemp bag on to the seat next to him, and then wrapped one end of it tightly around his hand. Although the youth was at least a foot taller, Snod knew he wouldn't stand a chance. The second they were through the lavatory door, Snod leapt on to his back and tightly twisted the bag around his throat. He did not let go for almost a minute.

'Whose gear are you sellin'? Huh? Whose?' shouted Snod.

Slumped on the floor up against the urinals, the youth's eyes were still bulging in their sockets as his hands massaged the scorch marks on his throat.

'I can't tell you,' he croaked.

Snod kicked him in the face.

'Whose fuckin' gear is it?'

The youth shook his head fearfully. Taking the three plastic sachets of pills from the youth's inside pocket, Snod ripped them open and hurled their contents around the lavatory.

'Well, whoever the fucker is, you tell him – you tell him from me. This is Snod's patch. My fuckin' patch! You hear? I see you; I see him; I see anyone else in here, then next time, I don't let go of this? Got it?'

Ripping the twisted hemp bag from around the youth's neck, Snod turned and left the lavatory. Back in the lounge, he replaced the oranges one by one and, swinging the bag by his side, left the pub. Once outside on the pavement, he squinted up at the bright afternoon sun and began to laugh. It was a beautiful day and suddenly, in a blinding flash, he realized the full significance of those few short words that had been nagging away at the back of his mind all day long.

'Chemical synthesis – that's all I understand, really,' he shouted. 'Ha! Don't worry, Professor. That's enough. That's more than enough.'

It was nearly seven o'clock in the evening before Bill finally got through.

'Louise?'

'Yes! Bill?'

'Where've you been? I've been ringing solidly for the last hour.'

'At work, of course. I've had loads of things to catch up because of last week. How's things?'

'Bad.'

240

'Yeah?'

'Yeah. Snod showed up. And Conlon.'

'Oh, shit.'

'Exactly. But, listen, Lou, there isn't much time. You've got to get out. Leave your flat.'

'What!'

'Find somewhere else to live. Lie low for a couple of months, till I can sort things out.'

'Why on earth should I do that?'

'Louise …'

'Yes?'

'There's something I didn't tell you.'

'What?'

'It's Snod. He knows where you live. He's been to your flat before. Actually been inside it.'

'When?'

'Right at the beginning. That night, when I came down to see you in London.'

'Why did you never tell me this before?'

'I didn't want to scare you. And then, when things started to go well, I didn't think it really mattered so much anymore.'

'Bill, you are your own worst enemy, do you know that? How could you have possibly kept information like that from me?'

'Lou, Lou, I was wrong – I admit it. But, listen, this is serious. He's threatening to take it out on you if I don't find the money. Even if I do, I wouldn't put it past him to try and get at me through you. You must get out, Lou. Stay with a friend or something. I'm gonna drop out of sight, too – just for a bit – but I'll have everything sorted in a couple of weeks, I promise.'

'No.'

'What?'

'No. I'm not leaving here. No way.'

'Lou! The man's a psycho, believe me. He'd harm you. I'm sure of it.'

'I don't care. I'm not moving out of my flat – especially for someone I've never even met. Why the hell should I?'

'I told you why! Because he's dangerous! You have got to find some-where to hide.'

'No, Bill. I'm not going to – and that's an end of it.'

241

'But, Louise, what if he breaks into your flat again?'

'I'm going away tomorrow with Gail for a couple of days. And then, well, if he comes, he comes, I'll deal with it as best I can.'

'Louise! Listen to me. I am trying to tell you the man is …'

'No, Bill, you listen to me,' interrupted Louise. 'You just listen to what I have to say! There is a time to run, and a time to stop and deal with the consequences of your actions. Everyone has to face their demons sometime. I'm not going to run – and you shouldn't either.'

'Louise, I'm begging you. If you can just lie low for a bit then I'm sure I can get the money sorted and …'

'Bill. Don't you understand? You can't turn your back on things any longer. It's all over. It's finished. Libidan's over. We're …'

'We're over, too, Louise. Is that what you're trying to say?'

'Oh, Bill. My poor, poor darling, Bill. We never even really began.'

It was useless. Louise was not going to be persuaded. Ambling out into the hallway, Bill sat down on the stairs, overcome with despair. Now he had truly lost everything. Stretching out his hand and running his fingers over the smooth, hand-carved banister, he wondered what his father would have said if he could have lived to see this day: the home he had so painstakingly built with his own hands, sold off to pay for criminal debts; the family he had worked so hard to nurture and protect, estranged and divided. A long ring on the front bell broke the silence of the house. Standing up, Bill took a deep breath and began slowly to walk towards the door. Louise had been right. Of course she had. The time for running was over. With a final look back down the hallway, he wished farewell to his father and family and, twisting the catch, opened the door.

Whether it was Snod, or whether it was Conlon – the time had come to meet his fate.

Chapter 14

'Oh, good evening Dr Kennedy. I'm sorry to disturb you. I imagine you probably don't remember me …'

Utterly astounded by the sight before him, Bill felt his jaw drop open.

'No, no. I remember you very well. It's Miss Arnold, isn't it?'

'That's right. I'm sorry just to turn up like this – I'm sure you must be very busy and everything – but I wonder if I might have a word with you?'

Again Bill could sense himself beginning to gawp: Una's full length floral evening gown was in total contrast to the truncheons or baseball bats he had been expecting to have to confront.

'Er, yes, yes, of course. Please come in.'

'Thank you. I'm really sorry to disturb you.'

'No, no. Don't worry. I wasn't doing anything special,' replied Bill, standing to one side as Una glided down the hall, her underskirts hissing like a summer lawn in the breeze. 'Please, go on into the sitting room. Just on the right here.'

'Thank you. Thank you.'

'Er, please, take a seat.'

Una perched herself on the edge of the sofa, resting her sequined clutch bag primly on top of her knees.

'Would you like a drink of something? Tea or …'

'Or what?' thought Bill to himself. 'Sparkling pink champagne, perhaps?'

'No, no, I'm fine, thank you.'

Bill sat down opposite her. They both began speaking at the same time.

'So, er …'

'You see, Dr Kennedy …'

An embarrassed pause followed.

'Sorry.'

'No, no, go ahead, Miss Arnold. You were going to say …'

'It's like this, Dr Kennedy. I have a friend – a good friend who means a lot to me. And because of what I did to you, I'm worried he is going to think the less of me; if I get a criminal record, that is. And so I've come to ask if you could, well, not take things any further. In terms of a formal complaint, I mean.'

Bill stared at her dumbly for several moments. Despite clearly being a most heartfelt plea, what she had said was nevertheless totally incomprehensible.

'Er, sorry, Miss Arnold, but I don't really understand what you mean. What exactly is it that you are supposed to have done to me?'

'Break into your house, of course. Well, try and break into your house. I mean, I didn't get very far – a policeman caught me.'

'Break into my house?' responded Bill, running his hand over his jaw. 'You tried to break into my house?'

'Yes. About three weeks ago – I thought you knew.'

'Er, no. No, I didn't,' said Bill, his brow furling. 'What exactly made you want to go and do a thing like that?'

Una began to flush.

'Well, because of what you and your, er, lady friend do with the guinea-pigs I sold you. I mean, I know I'm not very broadminded about that sort of thing – sex – if that's what you call it. But all the same, I pride myself on being an animal lover and I happen to think that using living creatures for that sort of personal gratification is just plain wrong!'

That morning he had been falsely accused of dealing drugs. This evening, it was bestiality. What would tomorrow bring? Genocide? Overcome by the absurdity of the situation, Bill found himself starting to laugh.

'Miss Arnold, I've had cause to regret a lot of things I've done in my life recently, but as regards guinea-pig abuse, I can assure you, my conscience is completely clear.'

Una could feel the blush beginning to spread all the way down to her neck: nobody could simply just laugh off a charge like that – he must actually be telling the truth.

244

'But, I saw you,' she replied, her voice becoming ever more desperate, 'through the little window at the side of your house – the two of you.'

'Doing what, exactly?' responded Bill.

'You had the guinea-pig in your hand one minute and the next it was … oh, dear, Dr Kennedy, I think I've made a dreadful mistake.'

'I think maybe you have.'

'Well, then, if you weren't using them for, you know … what I mean to say is, why did you go out and buy eight guinea-pigs in the first place? I could tell straightaway you didn't want them as pets.'

It was a fair question and Bill could see little point now in continuing to hide the truth.

'I'm a scientist, Miss Arnold. A pharmaceutical researcher. I was using them to test out a new drug I've discovered.'

'You mean, you were … experimenting on them?' gasped Una in horror.

'Er, yes. Oh, dear. I suppose you probably think that's even worse, don't you?' replied Bill, watching the colour rapidly draining from Una's face. 'Right. Where do I start? OK, listen. I injected three of the guinea-pigs with a saline solution, and the other three with microscopic amounts of a hormone fragment. The hormone itself has no toxic properties whatsoever and is anyway already present in their brains in the form of a neuropeptide. The experiment lasted less than a week and they suffered no discomfort whatsoever. Quite the reverse, in fact – it lit a few flames that might otherwise have remained extinguished.'

Still Una look dubious.

'Look, come here. See for yourself,' said Bill, standing up and indicating to her to walk across the hallway, 'I've moved them into the drawing room now. You check them out while I go and make some tea. Even if you don't need a cup, I certainly do.'

Two minutes later, Bill walked into the drawing room to find a delighted Miss Arnold seated in one of the chairs with Anne of Cleves nosing her way in and out of the ruffles of her dress. Smiling, he put the tea down on the desk next to her.

'They're beautiful, Dr Kennedy, and they look so healthy! I'm amazed. You really must have been looking after them well.'

'Yes, yes. I've been pretty busy these last few weeks, but all along I've kept a close eye on their diet, tried to play with them for at least half an hour every day and that sort of thing.'

'I don't know how I can ever apologize to you enough. I've done you a terrible injustice.'

'Forget it. No problem,' replied Bill, sipping at his tea and wondering how the arrival in his house of this cranky, wildly overdressed woman could have so completely taken his mind off his cares.

'It's just that, well, ever since I can remember I have felt an empathy with animals. And whenever I see them suffer I feel like it's me and my own who are suffering. And it fills me with such ... such rage. They're our brothers and sisters, you see.'

'I know,' replied Bill, warming to her sincerity. 'All life – in all living things – is the same life. I mean, I'd always understood that as an intellectual concept – I studied DNA at University and everything – but it was only when I actually shared my home with these animals that I realized what it actually meant.'

'"All life in all living things is the same life." I've never heard it put that way before, Dr Kennedy. That's really lovely.'

'Thank you,' replied Bill, with a modest smile. 'Perhaps I should write it down.'

For a few seconds neither of them spoke, both overcome by the unexpected intimacy of the moment.

'So, did it work?' asked Una finally, reaching across and picking up her tea.

'What, the drug?'

'Yes.'

'Oh, it worked all right,' replied Bill, gravely. 'Except that it ended up deciding my fate and not the other way round. It's funny, you start out on these things meaning so well, thinking you can change the world for the better, but somehow they manage to take on a life of their own. Then, one day, you wake up and realize you're no longer in control any more. I got involved with a bad man, Miss Arnold. A violent man, I'm afraid to say. My fault. I should've known better. He's got a hold over me now, and I've only got myself to blame.'

Una sat staring at Bill, utterly mesmerized. This was her story – her predicament with Ray entirely. What an incredible irony. She had come to this house expecting to have to beg for her liberty and happiness from a pervert, and instead had found a decent, upright man, as much the victim of his good intentions as she was of her own.

246

'So, what are you going to do?' she asked quietly.

'Funny you should ask that. Just before you arrived, I came to a deci-sion. Well, not so much came to a decision as had some sense talked into me, I guess. I'm going to face up to him, Miss Arnold. Face up to myself, I suppose – and the damage my discovery could cause if it ever got into the wrong hands. And then, assuming I'm still alive and in one piece afterwards, I'm going to destroy it – consign it to eternal oblivion. Somewhere along the line I got want confused with need. The world will keep on turning just the same without my invention, I'm sure of that now.'

Drawing in a deep breath, Bill sat upright and gave Una a smile.

'But, anyway, whatever happens to me, you can rest assured the last thing I want to do is pursue a burglary complaint against you.'

Una could feel a lump beginning to form in her throat. Here was a man not only of courage, but of generosity also.

'Thank you, Dr Kennedy, you have no idea how much that means to me.'

'My pleasure.'

Una had not bargained on their conversation lasting more than a few moments, and, catching sight of her wristwatch, she realized all of a sudden that it was almost seven-thirty.

'I'm afraid I have to go now. I've got a dinner engagement in a few minutes. It's not very far from here, mind you, but I don't want to be late all the same.'

'Oh, right, well, just let me put Annie back in her cage and I'll see you out.'

As Una passed the guinea-pig across to Bill and saw him gently cradle the creature in his hands, she could feel the tears coming to her eyes. Quickly, she put her finger up to her eyelashes before her mascara could become spoiled.

'Er, sorry, Dr Kennedy, before I go, do you think I might just powder my nose?'

'Oh, sure, yes,' replied Bill, 'it's just down the hall here. Sorry about the mess inside. I've been clearing the place out – I'm going to be moving house soon.'

Inside the downstairs bathroom, Una speedily attended to her eye make-up. Thankfully it had scarcely run at all. Standing back, she gave herself a quick, critical glance in the mirror. Her eyes rested on her open neckline. After all, it did look rather bare – she really should have worn a necklace. Frowning, she stared at the small ceramic container at the end of the bathroom shelf. A splash of perfume would have been nice, too, but it had been years since she had kept any in the house. Stretching out her hand, she picked up the bottle. Dr Kennedy or his young lady couldn't possibly mind, could they? Finally, with a shake of the head, she decided against it: she had already invaded their privacy enough. Turning to walk back out of the bathroom, she caught sight of what appeared to be several dozen cartons of the exact same perfume, lying on the floor next to the bath. They must have gallons of the stuff in here! How strange. Smiling to herself, she sprayed a drop on her wrist. They would never miss such a tiny amount. Bringing her wrist up to her nose, she inhaled the aroma. It was very subtle, faint almost. Transferring the bottle to her right hand she decided to spray her other wrist, but the perfume didn't seem to want to come out. The bottle must be empty.

'Maybe just as well,' she remarked quietly to herself. 'Wouldn't want to go over the top or anything.'

Bill awoke at twenty past eight the following morning to the sound of the phone ringing. Rushing down the stairs in his pyjamas, he got to the answering machine just in time to hear Louise finishing off her brief message and hanging up. With a huge sigh of relief, he sat down on the edge of the armchair and played back the recording. The previous night he had begged her to phone him when she got safely to the office and, true to her word, that was exactly what she had done. As she and Gail were going directly from work that evening to the Cotswolds, in all probability she would be out of Snod's reach until the following week.

Walking into the kitchen, he made himself a cup of tea and reviewed his plans for the day. Having transferred all the remaining stocks of Libidan from the garage to his home, the next step was to bag them up and get them incinerated. He had meant every word that he had said to Miss Arnold. He had created an obscenity – he saw that now – taken a naturally occurring substance and turned it into an aberration. The fact that it was threatening to destroy him and everyone that meant anything to him was no unfortunate twist of fate but an absolute inevitability: he had been trading in corruption, and corruption was his payment. Still more pressing than the destruction of Libidan, however, was the need to take immediate steps to protect Louise. His only bargaining chip with Snod was the twenty-five thousand pounds and so the sooner he got his hands on it the better. Taking his cup of tea with him upstairs, Bill resolved to get changed, load up the car and drive straight to the incinerator. On the way back he could stop off at the bank and get the cash.

It took him just over half an hour to fill up the heavy-duty yellow bags and stack them in the hallway. As he went to the front door to get the car he heard the sound of tyres braking on the front pathway. Gingerly, he opened up the letterbox a fraction and peeped through.

'Shit!'

It was Conlon's car. As quickly as he could, he began hurling the plastic bags back inside the downstairs bathroom. If Conlon found him with the stuff he'd be finished. As he threw the last bag in and slammed the door, the front doorbell rang.

'Good morning, Dr Kennedy. D'you think I might have a word with you?'

Bill stared at Conlon in surprise. In comparison with the man who had marched into his house at the same time the previous morning Conlon was virtually unrecognizable. What on earth could have happened to him in the interim? The stern voice of command shrunk to a croak; the military neatness, ruffled and dog-eared. The top button had gone from his shirt and his necktie was hanging half out of his jacket pocket.

'Er, yeah, sure. Come on through.'

'Thank you.'

Shoulders slumped, Conlon hobbled painfully down the hall towards the kitchen, seemingly unwilling or unable to keep his legs together as he walked. Following behind, Bill swallowed deeply. Conlon was at least six foot two and with a chest like a heavyweight boxer. Whoever had done this to him must be built like a mountain. Easing himself into the chair, Conlon ran his hand through his dishevelled hair and turned to face Bill.

'Dr Kennedy, it seems I owe you an apology.'

'You do?'

'Yes. I met Una, er, Miss Arnold, last night, after she visited you. She told me everything. We have both misjudged you very badly indeed, I fear.'

'Well, certainly, Mr Conlon, I can absolutely assure you that my relationship with my guinea-pigs is anything but carnal.'

For some reason this last word seemed to cause Conlon to wince.

'Quite, quite. Listen, er, Mr Kennedy. Do you think I could ask you a favour?'

'Sure.'

'Have you got any food?'

'Pardon?'

'Anything to eat. A slice of bread or something. I'm rather hungry.'

'Yeah, yeah, of course. Would you like me to fix you some breakfast? Eggs, bacon … ?'

Conlon looked as though he was about to burst into tears; Bill had never seen anyone look so grateful in his life. Scarcely able to believe what was happening, Bill moved across to the fridge and took out a packet of bacon. Could it be true – were the police really off his back now? What a break! Somehow, Conlon had ended up at the same dinner party as Miss Arnold. By the sound of things there hadn't been much to eat and the two of them must have got talking.

Fifteen minutes later, the plate scraped clean before him, Conlon sat back in his seat and fixed his gaze on Bill, the sparkle and sharpness once more in his eyes.

'Thank you, Dr Kennedy. I feel much better for that.'

'My pleasure, believe me.'

'Now, William – I can call you William can't I?'

'Well, people call me Bill, actually.'

'OK, Bill. In a few moments I'm going to ask you to explain every-thing that has happened to you recently. But before you do, I have something to tell you first. Last night I made a couple of decisions in my life. Important decisions. Firstly, I have decided to leave the police force – take early retirement. And secondly, I have asked Miss Arnold to marry me.'

'Oh, wow,' replied Bill. 'Congratulations.'

'Thank you. She gave me the honour of accepting, I'm happy to say, but on one strict condition; that is, helping you out of the trouble you find yourself in. She was very impressed with what you had to say to her, Dr Kennedy, very impressed. She's been having some difficulties in her own life recently, and found your talk together quite inspirational. Now, I only got a brief outline of events – we, er, didn't quite find the time to discuss all the details – but in any case she made me promise to help you and that's what I'm going to do. Everything you tell me from now on is off the record, d'you understand? I'm Jack now. Not DI Conlon. Your friend, Jack, OK? And you're Bill, my friend and my, er … best man.'

'Your best man!' exclaimed Bill.

'Yes,' replied Conlon, looking somewhat embarrassed. 'Another thing Una decided on last night. If you would do me the honour, that is.'

'I'd be happy to'

'Good. Thank you. A week on Wednesday at St Margaret's. Formal dress if you don't mind; finger buffet in the Duke of Clarence across the road afterwards.' Conlon gave a short cough. 'Anyway, let's get started: tell me first of all how you got involved with Kevin McKenzie.'

Recalling Miss Arnold's sincerity the previous night and looking across the table into Conlon's shrewd, authoritative face, Bill did not hesitate. The time to tell all had arrived.

'I invented this drug. Not a drug in the sense you usually mean, I suppose, but a proper drug, a pharmaceutical preparation. Did Miss Arnold tell you that?'

'She did.'

'I tested it – on the guinea-pigs – and it worked and everything, but I wanted some of it made up into tablets. I just happened to mention this to Brummie, that's the man you know as McKenzie – we both worked at the same delivery company, you see – and he said he could do it for me for next to nothing.'

'Didn't you have any reservations about getting involved with a drug dealer?'

'Well, I didn't really think of him as a drug dealer, then – he was just a bloke at work. And besides, I only wanted a few pills making up. I had no intention of selling them on or anything. He told me he had access to a tableting machine belonging to a friend of his and could get them knocked up in a day or two. I paid him two hundred quid and thought that would be it.'

'But you don't know who that friend is, I suppose?'

'Oh, yes.'

'You do?' asked Conlon, quickly. 'Who?'

'A guy called Snod.'

'Snod!'

'Yes, Snod.'

'Michael Snodgrass?'

'I don't know. Might be. He just calls himself Snod.'

Conlon leant backwards in his chair, shaking his head in consternation.

'Michael Snodgrass, eh? So, our local drug baron is none other than little Micky Snodgrass. They'll love this down the station. Carry on, Bill.'

'Do you know him?'

'Snod? Oh, yeah, I know him of old. I knew his father, too. A really nasty piece of work. Have you seen this drug factory of his?'

'No.'

'D'you know where it is?'

'No idea. Brummie knew, though. Although I remember he told me it was more than his life was worth to tell anybody else.'

'He certainly never told us. The night the two of you were arrested, I interviewed him at the station. He gave us the address of a warehouse, but when we got there there were no drugs or chemicals or anything, just a sort of experimental tableting machine.'

'This is the Manesty you're talking about?'

'Yes, I think that's what it was called. How do you know about that?'

'You impounded it, didn't you?'

'That's right.'

'That was the exact same machine that Brummie used to make up my pills. Snod's blackmailing me for fifty thousand pounds to replace it.'

'Oh, I see, I see,' exclaimed Conlon. 'OK. I understand where we are now. Snod blames you for our taking his machine away, right?'

'Exactly.'

'Got you.'

'So, didn't you know Snod was manufacturing drugs, then?'

'No, we knew that someone in the area was, but everyone we ever pulled in was too intimidated to give up a name. Even Brummie just made out he was a mule – said he didn't know who the top man was. Anyway, Bill, this is very important. Have you paid Snod any money yet?'

'No.'

'Good.'

'I was going to pay him this afternoon – I've managed to raise about half of it in cash. Well, at least, I thought I had. Until he turned up yesterday and started demanding more.'

'And that was the last time you saw him, was it?'

'Yes.'

'Right then. There's no time to lose,' said Conlon, pushing the chair back and standing up. 'Let's strike while the iron's hot – get round to Snod's now and sort this out straightaway.'

'What are you going to do, Mr Conlon?' asked Bill, fearfully. 'I'm not so much worried for myself, but, well, he's threatened to take it all out on a girlfriend of mine if I don't come up with the money.'

'There is only one thing to do, Bill,' said Conlon emphatically, 'only one way to play it. I tell him you're family – that I'm responsible for you. Your fight is my fight. If he comes after you then he comes after me.'

'If you warn him like that, and if I give him the money I've made so far, will he stay away, d'you think?'

Frowning gravely, Conlon rested his hands on the back of the chair and looked down at Bill.

'Bill. You're not going to pay him any money.'

'But I don't mind, Mr Conlon, honestly. He's welcome to it.'

'The money might not matter to you, Bill, but it does to me. I can't be involved in an arrangement like that – not in my position. A police officer brokering protection payments to a drugs dealer? I'd end up in jail myself if it ever got out. But, anyway, even if I were prepared to turn a blind eye, paying him half the money would never work. Frankly, it wouldn't even work if you gave him the lot. The man's an extortioner. He'd just be back for more a few weeks later.'

'But …'

'I know you're worried about your girlfriend, Bill. But trust me, OK? You don't know Snod – I do. He only understands force. It's all the world's ever shown him. Gentlemanly compromises are all very well in nice houses like this, for nice reasonable people like you. But with Snod either you're stronger and he respects you, or you're weaker and he doesn't. It's as simple as that.'

Bill looked at the inspector's tall, imposing physique. If anyone in Harledge was a match for Snod, it was he.

'OK, Mr Conlon. We do it your way.'

'Good man, Bill. Come on, let's go.'

'Where does Snod live, then?'

'Over on Brunswick Park. He rents a town-house appartment there.'

★

The moment Conlon's car turned into the Brunswick Park estate, Bill could sense something was wrong. The large, wealthy town houses, normally so conspicuous by their lack of external activity, were bustling with life: every other residence seemed to have someone peeping out from behind the Austrian blinds, and there were even one or two people congregating on street corners.

'What is it?' asked Bill.

'There's been a fire, I think. Look!' said Conlon, pointing across the estate to where some wisps of smoke were rising up above the roofs.

Conlon was correct, for at the next turn they could see two fire engines and a police car at the far end of the street.

'Get in the back of the car!' shouted Conlon, suddenly.

'What?' asked Bill.

'In the back and stay down! It's Snod's apartment, I'm sure.'

Conlon parked and walked off down the street, returning several minutes later. As they drove away, Bill at last risked a look at Snod's apartment through the back window. The house had been completely gutted by fire.

'What's happened?' asked Bill, sitting upright.

'Someone put a petrol bomb through his letter box.'

'Bloody hell. Was he in there?'

'If he was, he's flown the coop since. From what I can gather it seems like you're not the only one in dispute with Michael Snodgrass at the moment.'

'No?'

'No. Looks like we've got a full-scale drug war on our hands.'

'What?'

'Yeah. Apparently, two days ago, a bloke by the name of Jez got practically beaten to death in a pub called the Black Dog. D'you know it?'

'I've never been in there, but I know the one you mean.'

'He's a pusher. Works for one of the out-of-town rings. If what you've said is right, then my guess is it was Snod's doing. Without McKenzie to do his distribution, he's probably lost ground and is trying to break his way back in. It looks like the competition didn't take too kindly to it.'

'So, where is he now, then?'

'I don't know for certain,' said Conlon leaning forward to make a call on his police radio, 'but I've got a pretty shrewd idea …'

As they emerged from the stairs on to the fifth-floor landing, Conlon paused for a moment and rested his hand on the balustrade. Bill watched him scan the length of the balcony, his jaw set firm in grim nostalgia.

'It feels like only yesterday, you know. Since I first came up here to put Micky away for shoplifting. I remember him laughing right in my face and saying he was only twelve. I never believed him – he was such a huge kid for his age. He got off, of course. Next time I saw him he'd got a broken nose. His father had smashed it in after he found out he'd been arrested. God. I'd forgotten how depressing this estate was. Come on. Number fifty-two. Let's get it over with.'

Walking nervously towards the door, Bill lifted up his hand ready to knock. Conlon stood with his back flat against the wall. Having looked left and right a couple of times, he gave Bill the nod. Snod opened the door almost immediately.

'You? How did you know where to find me? Eh?'

He looked fearsome, vicious – like a hunted animal.

'I, er, I …' mouthed Bill.

'Never mind, Professor,' said Snod, taking hold of Bill's lapels and dragging him into the flat. 'Come on in, I've got a job for you …'

'Hello, Michael.'

Conlon's massive frame completely filled the doorway. For the first time since he had met Snod, Bill saw a shadow of fear creep across his face, although it proved to be nothing more than a momentary lapse. Without taking his eyes off Conlon, Snod spoke to Bill in a voice that was a terrifying mixture of hostility and defiance.

'Don't think the law's gonna save you.'

'Sit down, Michael,' said Conlon, brushing past Snod and walking into the dining room.

Bill looked around the sparse, empty flat. Snod's hemp bag lay on the couch. It was empty of oranges and scorched by several black, burn marks. The petrol bomb must have gone off whilst Snod was actually inside his appartment.

'Have you got a warrant?' asked Snod, taking a cigarette from the packet and lighting up.

'Don't need one just to talk – you know that.'

Conlon sat down and indicated Snod to do the same.

'I've got nothin' to say.'

'I knew I'd find you back here, Michael. Back home.' Conlon shook his head and looked wearily around the flat. 'Home. Not what most people would understand by the word but I can't think what else to call it.'

The look of loathing that Snod gave Conlon left Bill feeling queasy with fear, but the detective remained completely unnerved and merely stared remorselessly back into his eyes.

'What d'you want?' hissed Snod beneath his breath.

'So, have you heard from your dad lately, then? No, I don't suppose you have. He moved away in the end, didn't he? Once you'd got old enough to fight back.'

'What d'you want,' repeated Snod, 'and what's he telling you I'm supposed to have done?'

'It's not what Bill's told me that matters. It's what he didn't tell you.'

'What d'you mean?' replied Snod, suspiciously, at last sitting down on the other side of the table from Conlon.

'He's family, Michael,' said Conlon, staring unblinking into Snod's eyes. 'My family.'

'He's what?'

'Family. You heard.'

'Oh, fuckin' hell,' said Snod, shaking his head in a mixture of disbelief and disgust.

'He's been stupid, I know. And if he'd've come to me first, none of this would've happened. But he didn't – and I'm not going to let you ruin his life, Michael, just because of one stupid mistake.'

Suddenly, Snod was standing back up again, shouting and angrily jabbing his finger towards Bill.

'He owes me. He fuckin' owes me fifty grand!'

'Maybe. But that doesn't change what I'm saying. If you go after him, you go after me, that's all there is to it.'

'Oh, so just like that, huh? This shit-head does me for fifty grand and I'm just supposed to walk away and forget it?'

'You've been making illegal drugs, Michael. You can't blame Bill if you get caught for that.'

'Did you tell him that?' hissed Snod, rounding on Bill.

'He didn't have to tell me! Your apartment on the Brunswick's been torched – you can see the bloody smoke from all over Harledge. You're fighting a running war with Jez and his crew. Every copper in the county knows about it now, Michael.'

Sitting back down again, Snod took out another cigarette. When next he spoke, his voice was calm again.

'So, what are you offerin', then?'

'What am I offering? I'm not offering you anything, Michael. I don't do deals. You know that.'

'And what's my name gonna be worth on the street, then, eh? If it gets out I've been turned over by a little prick like him.'

'Your name's not worth anything now anyway, Michael. Your operation's in pieces. McKenzie's done a runner. Even the girls don't want to work for you any more. Yeah, that's right, I know about them, too. We got a report from the social.'

Bill watched Snod's face twitching with discomfort. In the car he had listened as an officer from the station had read the DHSS report to Conlon over the radio.

'No. No deal. He owes me too much,' said Snod, his voice edged with desperation.

Leaning forward over the table, Conlon moved to within a few inches of Snod's face. Bill could see that he had him cornered now.

'How many times have I felt your collar over the years, Michael? Ten? Twenty? It never got personal, though, did it? Not even for a moment. I was just doing my job. But if you make me your enemy now, son, if you make me live and breathe this twenty-four hours a day, you'll discover a side of me you've never seen before. You might think you've got problems now, Michael, but believe me, you don't even know you're born …'

Snod looked up and stared long and hard at Conlon for ten, fifteen, twenty seconds. The police inspector's face was as motionless as stone. Finally, Snod's shoulders seemed fractionally to drop and with a shake of the head he stubbed out his cigarette.

'All right. If he's family.'

'Thank you, Michael,' said Conlon, standing up. 'We'll let ourselves out.'

With an urgent nod that Bill should follow him, Conlon moved towards the door. Just as they were about to leave, Snod called out across the room.

'Listen. Both of you. This was a favour. A favour because it was you, Mr Conlon. But if I ever see your face around here again, Kennedy –

ever – you're dead. No one'll save you. Not Mr Conlon. Not anybody. I'll kill you with my bare hands. That's a promise.'

Placing his arm around Bill's shoulder, Conlon ushered him carefully through the door. Smelling the fresh air on the balcony outside, Bill felt overcome by relief and turned to thank Conlon. The detective's face was grave, though, and as they began to walk away Bill knew that he should keep silent. When they reached the staircase, Conlon at last turned solemnly to face Bill.

'He meant that, you know. Stay away from this place, Bill. Never come back here. Not for any reason. Micky could well escape us yet. When all's said and done, we haven't got that much on him – we still don't know where his main factory is. Stay clear of him, Bill – I mean that. I won't be able to help you next time.'

The red Ford had all but passed out of sight before Bill finally stopped waving and walked slowly back along the driveway into his house. He looked at his watch. Five to four. It was like some sort of miracle. In the space of seven hours the burly detective had completely turned his life around. Closing the front door behind him, he looked down the empty hallway and drank in the silence. Snod – gone. The threats against Louise – gone. The need ever to sell his parents' house – gone, completely gone. Opening the door to the downstairs bathroom, he looked at the heap of yellow plastic bags. The incinerator was only four miles away. In less than an hour, Libidan, too, would be gone – vaporized into the skies above Harledge – and he could set about the task of rebuilding his life. Leaning forward, he unfastened the nearest bag and held one of the dispensers in the palm of his hand for the last time. A fine spray of mist – power beyond responsibility. With a shake of the head, he tossed the dispenser back inside the bag and walked into the living room. No, he would not miss his invention. Picking up the telephone, he dialled Louise's number.

'Good afternoon, Thomas Radley and Co.'

'Oh, hello, could I speak to Louise Schreiber, please?'

'I think you may just have missed her. Hang on a moment. Yes. I'm afraid she's already gone for the weekend.'

In a way, this was better. He knew the name of the hotel where she was staying that night, and now, at least, he had a little time to compose his thoughts before calling her.

'Oh, OK, thanks,' he replied. 'I'll, er, talk to her later.'

As Bill replaced the receiver, a frown passed across his face. He was safe. Louise was safe. Everything was safe. But ... there was something that Conlon had said – on the balcony in front of Snod's flat. A contradiction that had been niggling away at the back of his mind, and for which, all of a sudden, he realized he might have the explanation. Walking through into the front room, he began looking for his medical dictionary, but as he approached the bookcase by the window his search was cut short. In the street outside, the largest limousine he had ever seen in his life had come to a halt and its uniformed chauffeur was walking up to his front door.

'Yes?'

'Dr Kennedy?' asked the driver, respectfully.

'Yes?'

'Dr William Kennedy?'

'Yes.'

'A letter for you, Dr Kennedy. The sender has asked me to wait for your reply – if I may ... ?'

Opening the heavy vellum envelope, Bill looked down at the short, type-written message.

Dear Dr Kennedy,

I would refer you to clause 6(a) of the Contract of Employment signed by you on September 8th 1995.

' ... and, for the avoidance of subsequent doubt, it is hereby specifically acknowledged that all inventions, know-how and intellectual property of whatsoever description generated by the employee whilst in the employment of Asper Pharmaceuticals, shall automatically pass to, and become the property of the company ...'

One such invention has recently come to my attention.

May I suggest we meet to discuss this matter?

Swallowing hard, Bill put out his hand to support himself against the front door. There was no doubt what the letter meant. Sir Paul Giulani, Chairman and Chief Executive of Asper Pharmaceuticals, had somehow discovered the existence of Libidan and was claiming it for his own.

Chapter 15

Bill asked the chauffeur to pick him up at eight-thirty the next morning. When the limousine arrived outside the house just before ten past, however, he decided there was no point in pacing around the kitchen for the next twenty minutes, and so went straight out and climbed in the back. Although still nervous at the prospect of meeting the great man, he felt all the better for being on his way at last, and, as the car sped down the near-empty motorway towards London, he reviewed the events of the last eighteen hours with a measure of satisfaction.

He had arrived at the incineration company a half an hour before closing time. It was a small, local operation and it had not been difficult to persuade them to squeeze in a last-minute job; after chatting to the two overalled operators for a few minutes, he had even been allowed out on to the roof. Standing there in a borrowed hard hat, watching the whisps of smoke float languidly out of the tall aluminium-clad chimney and disappear towards the stratosphere, Bill had felt a great sense of calm settle over him: the molecule was no more – all that was left now was to destroy the equipment that had synthesized it. It had taken well over two hours to disassemble and sterilize the chromatographic column and the network of piping which fed it, but, finally, at five minutes to nine, Bill had walked to the bottom of the garden, and, with the late summer sun setting in the fields behind his house, smashed each piece of glassware into a thousand pieces. Carefully sweeping up the fragments, he had then double-wrapped them in a cardboard box and deposited them in his dustbin.

Sleep had not come easily – although, in the end, that had proved to be a blessing. For at three-thirty, as he had lain in bed turning over in his mind for the umpteenth time the events of the last three months, it had dawned on him that for all his painstaking efforts, two or three milligrams of Libidan still remained in existence. Going down to the kitchen in his pyjamas, he had unscrewed the lid of the battered tea caddy that stood on the windowsill. His memory had not played him false – the two unused experimental pills that Brummie had prepared for him were still there, individually wrapped in their cellophane packages. Having flushed one down the toilet, Bill had taken the other back upstairs and lain with it under his pillow, transferring it to the top pocket of his shirt when he dressed himself at six-thirty. In a matter of hours he was going to have to confront a man with the power to unleash Libidan on the human race: what better talisman to take with him than this, the last pill in the entire world?

The limousine arrived in Kensington High Street at half past nine. Despite the fact it was a Saturday morning and the shops and stores were all clearly open for business, the main street itself was deserted and felt strangely nervous, as though having been evacuated moments before because of a terrorist bomb warning. As the thirty-foot automobile turned into a side-road and slowed down to manoeuvre into a narrow, underground garage, Bill leaned forward in his seat and looked up at the tall granite office block above. At the top of the building, the silver reflective windows of Giulani's penthouse apartment glinted like snow on the summit of a mountain.

They emerged from the elevator into a reception area. It was a sumptuous, low-ceilinged room, filled with plush leather sofas and a dozen or so pieces of French rococo furniture. Bill felt like a fly in a gilded web – at Asper, the Kensington penthouse had been infamous as Giulani's preferred location for the ceremonial sacrifice of under-performing executives. With a respectful nod to Bill to make himself comfortable, the chauffeur withdrew discreetly through a side door. Bill guessed he doubled as Giulani's manservant. They were a good thirty minutes early.

Ignoring the newspapers and business magazines on the marble coffee table, Bill walked across the room to examine a large rosewood cabinet containing a collection of antique gold pocket watches. Each timepiece was individually held open by a perspex clasp so that its

261

inner workings were visible. Bill watched the tiny cogs and ratchets oscillating soundlessly. The watch-faces themselves had been decorated using a range of different techniques: mother of pearl insets, cloisonné panels and all manner of scrolled engravings. Bill's head swam as he imagined the row of noughts on the insurance valuation: every watch was original, and in absolutely mint condition. One piece in the centre of the display particularly caught his eye. He leaned forward to examine it more closely. The complexity of its movement was dazzling.

'Sully's escapement,' said a voice behind him. 'It's my favourite, too.'

Giulani had obviously not long emerged from the bathroom. There was a towel around his shoulders and the top button of his shirt was undone, although somehow, this appeared only to enhance his aura of aristocratic authority and charm.

'Paul Giulani, pleased to meet you.'

They shook hands.

'Pleased to meet you, too,' responded Bill.

Smiling warmly, Giulani took a step towards the cabinet and pointed at the watch that Bill had just been admiring.

'Sully was an English watchmaker, you know. Active in the late eighteenth century. His escapement was a system of counterbalances designed to reduce errors in the pendant and dial. It was his crowning achievement.'

'Oh, really.'

'Yes. It was a wonderfully sophisticated concept – but only a few dozen pieces incorporating it were ever actually made, and within ten years his French and Swiss competitors had learned from Sully's mistakes and rendered his design obsolete. Nevertheless, it is a quite beautiful object, as I am sure you will agree. Have you breakfasted yet?'

'Er, no, but I'm fine, thank you.'

'Would you like some coffee, then?' asked Giulani, inclining his head towards the rear of the apartment. 'I was just about to take some myself on the patio when you arrived. It is a lovely morning.'

'That would be nice.'

At this point, Bill expected Giulani to turn and lead him down the hallway. Instead, though, he stood quite still for several moments, scrutinizing every feature of Bill's face with his large grey eyes. Just as Bill began to feel self-conscious, he finally broke the silence.

262

'I am an anthropologist, Dr Kennedy. Did you know that?'

'Er, no, no, I didn't.'

'Yes. Pharmaceuticals may be my profession, but the observation of the human condition and human behaviour has long been my passion. Over the years, one builds up one's ideas, one's pet theories, and then, someone like you comes along. Someone absolutely extraordinary. You are twenty-eight years old, are you not?'

'Yes, that's right.'

'Phosphopenim at twenty-three. Libidan at twenty-eight. I believe you are a genius, Dr Kennedy – endowed with a more potent imagination and more creative ability than anyone I have ever met. I consider it a great privilege to have made your acquaintance.'

'Er … thank you,' gulped Bill, too stunned even to think of questioning his assertion.

'May I ask you something?"

'Please, please.'

'At any time in your life have you ever thought of yourself as such – as a genius, I mean?'

'No, no – never.'

'I thought not,' replied Giulani, with a whimsical smile. Extending his arm, he at last began to lead Bill down the hallway. 'Do you know Alistair McNeil, by the way? My head of Research and Development. He is based at Harledge, too.'

'Well, we've, er, corresponded once or twice …' replied Bill, recalling at least two acerbic memos received from McNeil during his time at Asper.

'He's fifty-five and never invented a thing. What do you think that says about my corporation, do you think? That I managed to lose you and yet still be stuck with him?'

'Er, I'm not sure,' replied Bill, nervously.

'A state of uncertainty that I, unfortunately, do not share,' responded Giulani, dryly, before suddenly dismissing the subject with a wave of his large, elegant hand. 'Please take a seat out on the patio; my lack of hospitality puts me to shame. Norman seems to have scurried off somewhere, so I suppose it's down to me to make the coffee.'

The view over central London and Kensington Park was stunning. Bill was still taking in the scenery three minutes later when, out of the corner of his eye, he saw Giulani attempting to navigate a large silver tray through the half-open patio doors. Springing forward, Bill slid them apart to let the older man pass through.

'Thank you, Dr Kennedy,' said Giulani, gratefully, placing the tray down on the patio table. 'You are most considerate.'

At this point, Bill went to close the doors, but as he did so caught sight of four television monitors racked up on the far wall of Giulani's study. He could scarcely believe his eyes, yet, palpably, it was true. Giulani really did have the Harledge site's security cameras wired back through to his home.

'Ah! I see you have espied my monitors!'

'Yes,' replied Bill, uncomfortably, conscious that he had been caught staring.

'I imagine you find the sight of them somewhat disagreeable – a sad old man indulging his twisted control fantasies. Milk and sugar?'

'No, no,' said Bill, hurriedly.

'Just black, then?' replied Giulani, leaning forward to pour the coffee.

'No, I mean yes. Which is to say, yes to the milk and sugar – but no to the, er, twisted control …'

'You are very kind,' replied Giulani, quickly smoothing over Bill's embarrassment. 'I was sincere in what I said before, though, Dr Kennedy, believe me. I do genuinely pursue a scientific study of human behaviour. I have even had one or two articles published – and in quite well-respected journals, too, if I may be so immodest as to say.'

'Really?'

'Yes. To be perfectly frank, Asper Pharmaceuticals as a commercial enterprise interests me very little these days. If it were not for the opportunity it affords of being able to watch its employees, I would probably dispose of the whole operation tomorrow. Please.'

Smiling politely, Giulani passed the cup across to Bill.

'Thank you,' replied Bill, finding himself warming more and more to the old man's peculiar combination of self-irony and erudition.

'Not that I personally spotted you and the delectable Miss Marks, by the way. No, we have Human Resources to thank for preserving that incident for posterity.'

Looking up from his coffee, Bill could see a smile forming around Giulani's lips.

'Oh, you saw that, then?'

'Twice. Although, please – I beg you – do not think me prurient. I could not bear that. No. The first time was just after you were dismissed. I found it strange viewing indeed. Spontaneous, yet at the same time oddly artificial. I had never seen anything approaching it in my life before. Later on, of course, after I had discovered the Libidan website, and learned that you were behind it, the whole performance made altogether much more sense. Although, I have to confess, the second time around, the tortured look on your face did make me smile. Poor Miss Marks. She must have inhaled clouds of the stuff. Tell me, did it take you an awfully long time to recover from her – how might one put it – attentions?'

'I've still got the scars today.'

'Surely not!' replied Giulani.

'No. Honestly. All across here – from her nails.'

Letting out a deep guffaw, Giulani placed his cup down on the table to stop himself spilling his coffee. Bill, too, felt himself wanting to laugh. Much to his surprise, he really was enjoying Giulani's company, and the incident with Angela had been the one part of the Libidan saga he had never felt able to share with Louise.

'But, anyway. The website. Let me compliment you on that before I forget. It was magnificent. Quite, quite magnificent.'

'Thank you. But it wasn't actually me who put it together. It was my, er, friend. She's in marketing.'

'Really?'

'Yes, she works for Thomas Radley – d'you know them?'

'I do indeed. They are most fortunate, Dr Kennedy, most fortunate. The dispensing technology, too, was similarly first-rate – did I recognize Advanced Aerosol Systems' handiwork there, perchance?'

'You did.'

'Ha! I thought so,' replied Giulani, clapping his hands together in glee. 'In your position it is exactly the company I would have chosen. Yes, Dr Kennedy. You achieved a great deal – and in a phenomenally short time, too. Indeed, by all rights, you should really still be in business today.'

'It was the Medicines Control Agency who closed us down in the end, you know.'

'Yes, I know, I'm sorry about that. I hope you did not find the correspondence from Dr Casey too stressful.'

In an instant, the sense of euphoria that had been building up inside Bill over the last few minutes completely disappeared.

'How did you know about Dr Casey?'

'I had some bogus complaints about Libidan fabricated,' replied Giulani, mildly. 'Letters, faxes, what have you – supposedly from concerned members of the public. The officials at the MCA had to react in the end; worried about a health scandal depriving them of their hard-earned pensions, no doubt.'

Bill stared at Giulani in disbelief. Moments before, this man had been sympathizing with Bill and Louise's endeavours, yet now he showed not the slightest regret at having personally engineered their downfall.

'So, so … you closed us down in effect?'

'Yes. Not that it was at all easy: you hid your tracks very well. I was forced to employ a professional to locate your manufacturing premises – at considerable expense, I might add – and even he did not manage to find the formula. In the end, I had to go right back to your laboratory and unearth all the original records. You erased your computer disks, Dr Kennedy, but omitted to dispose of the written documentation. It was your one oversight in this whole remarkable story.'

Mentally, Bill cursed his gullibility. How on earth could he have been taken in so easily? For all the urbane charm, Giulani was every inch the unscrupulous businessman he had spent the last eighteen hours preparing to confront. Right back on his guard again, Bill blessed his foresight in having returned to the laboratory and created an experimental protocol for a different hormone fragment. Whatever happened now, though, he had to try and keep the conversation off the subject of the document that he had so hurriedly forged. If Giulani were once to revisit it, it would not stand up to scrutiny a second time.

'Well, then, if you've found the formula, why did you ask me here this morning?'

'We haven't found it – not yet – although I am assured it is only a matter of time. I have a small team of chemists in Switzerland working to reproduce your experimental conditions. There are only a limited number of derivatives that can be produced from the original hormone fragment, as I'm sure you are aware.'

'So, what do you want from me, then?'

'Well, firstly the formula – I see little point in paying to reinvent the wheel. And, secondly, Dr Kennedy, I want to offer you a job. Alistair McNeil's job, in fact. You will be the youngest person in the history of the pharmaceutical industry ever to have succeeded to such a position, I believe. As for McNeil – please don't worry about him. He has other talents that can be put to good use elsewhere.'

Bill swallowed deeply, struggling to comprehend what he had just heard.

'Let me get this straight. You are offering to make me head of Research and Development at Asper, in exchange for the formula for Libidan – is that what you're saying?'

'In a nutshell, yes.'

'And what if I don't?'

'Don't …'

'Don't give you the formula – don't take the job.'

'Well, then … nothing,' replied Giulani, inoffensively. 'I am not a vindictive man, Dr Kennedy, despite what people may say about me. If, after consideration, you feel this role is not for you, then you are perfectly free to go on your way. That is, as long as you do not attempt to recommence marketing Libidan, of course: I may derive little personal satisfaction from running Asper Pharmaceuticals, but it would be willfully negligent of me to abandon its interests in the case of a molecule as important as this. Without a shadow of legal doubt, Libidan is Asper's intellectual property. Were you to infringe it again, I could not allow myself to show such clemency a second time.'

Bill stared out over the balcony. The gardens and palaces of London stretched out before him as far as his eyes could see. Even as recently as twelve weeks ago the position he was being offered would have seemed like a dream come true. Giulani was speaking again.

'But let us not dwell on such an unpleasant eventuality. This is a wonderful opportunity for a young man such as you, Dr Kennedy. If you take it, I will of course allow you complete discretion in your choice of associates. You mentioned your lady friend earlier. If you wish to employ her as brand manager for Libidan, then I would have no objections. Indeed, on the basis of her efforts and experience hitherto, she would appear to be the ideal choice.'

Placing his coffee cup back on the table, Giulani looked across at Bill and raised his eyebrows in expectation. The time had come for Bill to make his reply. His palms felt wet with perspiration. In his top pocket he could feel the tiny pill pressing against his chest. He was glad he had brought it with him.

'Well, Mr Giulani. First of all, thank you for your tremendously generous offer. I am deeply, deeply flattered. But if the last three months have taught me anything, it's that our job as scientists should be to develop therapies that benefit the human race as a whole: drugs that cure people, as opposed to drugs that just allow us to line our pockets. Libidan doesn't fall into that category. Not by a long way. At best it's of questionable therapeutic value, at worst it's just scientifically-assisted rape.'

Bill felt genuinely elated. The sleepless night of soul searching had not been in vain. He had never felt himself to be a particularly articulate person, but this time, when it had really mattered, he had been able to explain exactly what he meant. For several moments he watched Giulani staring at him impassively. Surely, now, this would be it. Having been accused of greed and a lack of ethics, the old man could do nothing else but throw him out. However, to Bill's complete surprise, his face broke into a broad smile.

'I thought you might say something like that. Ventures such as these are not without their ethical dilemmas, I am all too well aware of that. May I pour you some more coffee?'

Bill nodded, unable to make a verbal reply – clearly, the old man neither gave nor took anything in the least bit personally. Having leant forward and poured Bill a second cup, Giulani composed his thoughts for several moments and then began speaking again.

'All right, Dr Kennedy. It seems to me you have two major reservations: firstly, the charming, albeit naïve notion that technological innovation either can, or should, be directed towards the benefit of the human race as a whole, and secondly ...'

'I don't think it's naïve at all,' interrupted Bill, annoyed all of a sudden by the tone of patrician disdain in Giulani's voice. 'I think it's a perfectly civilized principle.'

'Really? You do surprise me,' replied Giulani, coolly, 'since when you were given the opportunity of upholding that principle, you elected so completely to flout it.'

'What d'you mean?'

'Well, I seem to recall that when you first introduced Libidan, you priced it at nineteen pounds ninety-nine a pack. In less than a week, though, you had increased it to practically two hundred! Now, in all honesty, let me ask you, was that price rise anything to do with an increase in your production costs?'

'No, but …'

'Of course it wasn't. Rather, it was a recognition on your part that a tiny élite paying a high price will always provide the drug manufacturer with greater revenue than ten times their number paying a small one. And my word, you caught on quickly, didn't you? Scant concern for the greater good there – if you don't mind my saying.'

'Yes, but it was different for us. I had a debt to pay off. I had only a few weeks to do it, and …'

Bill left the sentence unfinished, suddenly conscious of how hollow his protestations were sounding.

'Exactly. At the first sign of a cash-flow problem your philanthropic ideals went right up the chimney like a childhood Santa Claus. And that's my point. You would never have made a success of your business if you had done otherwise: innovation has its price – someone has to pay it. Take any other novel therapeutic compound in the world today. Take HIV. Effective drug substances have existed for over ten years now, yet how many of the world's sufferers are actually receiving them?'

'I don't know, a fairly small number, I imagine,' replied Bill, fighting down a rising sense of shame. How had the deeper significance of the price rise so completely escaped him at the time?

'Less than zero point one. Under one tenth of one percent – and for precisely the same reasons that you pitched the price of Libidan where you did. And it's not just medicine, either. The same pattern manifests itself across the entire spectrum of technological development. Look at the telephone – a perfect example: invented nearly a century ago, yet six out of ten of the world's population have never even seen one, let alone used one! The fact is, Dr Kennedy, technology benefits individual human beings, it can even benefit particular groups of human beings, but it seldom benefits the human species as a whole. On the contrary, just like any other adaptation, it is much more likely to render the non-adapted majority extinct.'

'That's frightening. It's worse than that – it's fascist.'

'Nature is fascist, Dr Kennedy. The strong, the rich and the wily adapt to new situations; the weak, the poor and the feckless do not. I would be insulting both our intelligences if I suggested anything otherwise.'

269

'So what are you saying, then?' cried Bill, angrily. 'That we should just let Libidan happen? Wash our hands of all responsibility? Let a rape drug out on to the market?'

'Which was the second of your two objections, I believe,' replied Giulani, calmly. Folding his hands together, he leaned back in his chair and eyed Bill shrewdly. 'The compound you have discovered is a peptide, isn't it? We deduce that from the raw materials you were working with. Correct?'

'Yes,' said Bill, stiffening involuntarily. The faked experimental protocol again. He had to be careful.

'Which means there is a receptor somewhere. A receptor which, when stimulated, gives rise to a specific, reproducible neurochemical response.'

'I imagine so, yes.'

'Do you think it possible that the same pathway may be accessed or influenced by other means? By other compounds? By genetic modification?'

'In theory ...'

'In theory, fiddlesticks!' exclaimed Giulani. 'Within two generations the human genome will be mapped out in the minutest detail. You are as much aware of that as I am. Every receptor analysed, every pathway determined, every protein characterized. The mechanics of the human sexual process will be laid flat out on the table like the blueprints for some new washing machine. That is no theory! It's an absolute inevitability.'

'I suppose so.'

'And, equally inevitably, the information will fall into the hands of people like you – and people like me. I think your work with Libidan amply illustrates what will happen next.'

Bill stared at Giulani, horrified not just by the old man's arguments but by the fact that his own behaviour seemed so completely to validate them.

'And are you happy to contribute to that process?' he gasped. 'Do you feel no reservations at all about perpetuating that system?'

'Do I feel happy contributing to the understanding of human physiology? Yes, I do. Do I feel happy contributing to the continued evolution of our species? Yes, I do. Let me remind you of what Stephen Hawkings said in 1998, an epoch-making observation if ever there were one. He said, 'The human race is in need of competent engineering.' Those were his exact words. Our DNA is a mess, Dr Kennedy. Haphazardly designed, cluttered with extraneous and redundant information, utterly catastrophic in its genetic aberrations. The sooner it is disassembled and competently reconstructed the better.'

'Unless, of course, you happen to be weak or vulnerable. Because there's no place for people like that in this brave new world, is there? They're not members of this, this ... élite super class of yours who get to keep all the benefits of new technology for themselves!'

'My dear Dr Kennedy. How can I make you understand?' replied Giulani, throwing his hands up into the air in exasperation. 'It is not simply that class and evolution go hand in hand. Class is evolution. Without class, human society does not develop. Art cannot proceed beyond basket-weaving, medicine beyond crushing up roots into pots of boiling water. Individuals cannot bypass that process, and more to the point, individuals cannot change it. In forty years – with or without the consent of William Kennedy – the human race will have its Libidan, to use and, yes, abuse, along precisely the same lines as every other one of its discoveries. And having done so ... will pass on to the next stage in its evolution.'

Staring out over the balcony again, Bill began to feel a terrible feeling of hopelessness welling up inside him.

'Dr Kennedy,' Giulani's voice had suddenly become gentle again. 'I can see you have found this discussion distressing. Please, come with me. I have something for you that will perhaps illustrate my point more eloquently.'

Bill followed Giulani along the corridor in a state of rising despair. He was losing control of Libidan – he could feel it. Back in the reception area, Giulani extracted a key from his trouser pocket and opened up the rosewood cabinet. Taking the Sully watch off its stand, he passed it to Bill.

'I want you to have this.'

Bill stared at Giulani dumbly for several seconds.

'I couldn't, no.'

'Please. It would mean a great deal to me. I meant what I said earlier: you are a man of immense natural genius, I am certain of that. But what you lack, I believe – and this is as much a function of your years as anything else – is a sense of perspective. You have made some great discoveries, and you will go on to make more. But, ultimately, they will all be subsumed into a broader tradition of human knowledge and human history. As was Sully's work.'

Holding out the timepiece, Giulani pressed it firmly into Bill's hand.

'Take this watch. Look back over the last two hundred years since he made it. And then look forwards, two hundred years from now into the future. The human race is on the verge of discovering its biochemical and genetic make-up. A process which you cannot change, but to which you may contribute, if you feel it is your destiny.'

Putting the watch in his pocket, Bill looked into Giulani's face and watched him smile. Within moments, though, the gentleness began to drain from his features and his air of aristocratic command returned once more.

'Thank you for your time this morning, Dr Kennedy. My chauffeur is at your disposal for the rest of the day.'

The air in the underground garage was stale and suffocating and Bill was overcome by a claustrophobic desire to get out of the building as soon as he could – to walk under the sun and to breathe in the open air. Mumbling to the chauffeur that he might be back later, he staggered up the stairway and, dragging his shirt collar apart, spilled out onto the pavement outside. The main street had now filled with shoppers, but as Bill wandered amongst them, every man seemed to have Giulani's cold, uncompromising eyes, and every woman Louise's distraught face, blank and haunted as he had seen it through the rain-streaked taxi window. All along, he had been certain of his ability to protect the world from his invention, certain of his power to put the genie back in the bottle. But even if his bogus paper trail was never uncovered, simply by letting Giulani know that Libidan existed, Bill had virtually guaranteed its subsequent rediscovery at some point.

After walking aimlessly for almost an hour, he found himself on the edge of Hyde Park. Slumping down onto a bench, he ran his hands through his hair, digging the tips of his fingers into his scalp. All his life he had basically maintained an optimistic view of the world and his fellow humans, but the image of the future that Giulani had painted was bleak indeed: an élite group of technocrats, empowered by their own sense of superiority, manipulating and distorting the human genome, piling up aberration after aberration; while men and women of good

272

will were either powerless to resist, or unwittingly contributed to the process – as he and Louise had done with the invention and launch of Libidan. He could never, ever accept Giulani's offer – he would rather take his own life than do that – but how was he now to atone for the terrible process that he had started?

'Spare us a few pence for a cup of tea, guv?'

Bill looked up. The tramp was standing almost right in front of him, his hand extended plaintively.

'Er, yeah, yeah, sure, mate,' replied Bill, digging into his pockets for some change. Finding none, he opened up his wallet. He only had a ten-pound note. Taking it out, he handed it to the tramp. The man's eyes opened wide in surprise and, clearly expecting Bill to retract the offer at any moment, he leaned quickly forward and plucked the note from his hand. Bill looked into his dark, unshaven face. It had probably been quite handsome once, but now, blotchy from vitamin deficiency and alcohol excess, it was painfully worn and haggard.

'Thanks,' said the man with a grateful nod, retreating quickly. Before he had got six feet away, Bill called out after him.

'No, no. Thank you.'

The tramp turned, looked at Bill uncertainly and then carried on walking: the strange young man on the park bench was obviously some sort of weirdo. Bill, however, had meant every word. For in the instant he had looked into the man's face, he had known exactly what he now had to do.

Catching a number nine bus, Bill was back in Kensington High Street in under fifteen minutes. Hopping off at the traffic lights at the junction of Kensington Church Street, he went into the homeware store on the corner and made his way straight to the cutlery section.

'How much is that one?' he asked the assistant, pointing to a large, wooden-handled knife in the centre of the display cabinet.

'Er, thirty-six pounds. It's not a general purpose kitchen knife, though, it's for Sushi.'

'How strong is the blade?'

'Oh, really strong – molybdenum tipped. Incredibly sharp, too'

'OK, I'll take it.'

'I'll wrap it up for you.'

'Thanks. Listen, do you have a phone around here?'

'Yes, over by the lifts.'

Directory enquiries gave him the number straightaway. As it rang, he slipped the knife out of its plastic sheath and lightly ran his finger along the blade. It was as sharp as a surgeon's scalpel.

'Hello?'

'Hello, is that Lester? Lester Mold?'

'Yes.'

'It's Bill Kennedy here.'

A stunned silence.

'Oh, hello.'

'Long time no speak. How are you?'

'Er, fine. Fine.'

'Surprised to hear from me, I suppose.'

'Well, er, yeah ...'

'Listen, I've got something for you,' said Bill, sliding the knife slowly back inside its sheath. 'Can we meet up, do you think?'

'What?'

'It's all a bit complicated. I can't explain now – I'm in a call box and the money's just about to run out. Can you meet me at Asper?'

'Well, I suppose so, but ...'

'This afternoon?'

'What! It's closed today. It's Saturday.'

'I know. Meet me in the contractors' car park at the back. Three o'clock. Can you make that?'

'What's all this about?'

'I'll explain everything then. It's important, though, honestly. Don't let me down, Lester, please.'

Hanging up, Bill made his way back to the front of the store and stood on the pavement outside trying to decide how to travel back to Harledge. He could go by train, but as Giulani's apartment was only five minutes away, he decided to take him up on the offer of his chauffeur.

If his life was going to end that afternoon, then it seemed only fitting that for his last few hours he should travel around in comfort.

When Bill had gone to the housing estate with Conlon it had been early afternoon and the children must all have been at nursery or at school. Today, as he parked his car in front of the post office at around five o'clock, he could see a huge group of them playing football on the central grassy area. There looked to be around twenty-five in total, girls as well as boys, aged between about five and eleven. Locking the car door, he rested his arms on the roof and watched them laughing and yelling as they hurtled around after the ball.

A bunch of kids. Competition without rancour. A beautiful sight to behold before dying.

Turning away from the game and walking towards the tower block, he ran through his mind how Conlon had behaved the previous day. Respect would be crucial. More than crucial – it was his only hope. Arriving at the fifth-floor balcony, he stopped for a breather, resting his hands on his thighs and staring unseeing at the livid splashes of graffiti around the entrance to the stairwell. Even before he had fully recovered his breath, though, he forced himself to stand back upright again and march straight towards the front door of the flat: he dared not risk a moment's hesitation, a moment of self doubt.

'You! What the fuck are you doing …'

Before Snod could finish the sentence, Bill stuck his foot through the door, and putting all his body weight into his arms, shoved Snod as hard as he could inwards into the flat. Hours of nervous anticipation were transmitted into the push, and, taken completely by surprise, Snod flew across the living room like a rolled-up newspaper. Slamming the front door behind him, Bill marched straight across to the table and stood there, watching Snod pick himself up.

'We've got to talk. Sit down.' he said, quietly.

'I told you, if you ever …'

Before Snod could finish, Bill extracted the knife from his belt, raised it high above his head, then swung it downwards, burying the blade deep into the surface of the table. 'We have got to talk!' he roared, his face contorted with rage, his voice echoing around the flat.

It worked.

Slowly, Snod picked himself up and, walking warily around to the opposite side of the table, took a seat. The moment he had lowered himself into the chair, Bill yanked the knife back out again and slammed it down on the surface of the table. Instinctively, Snod threw himself back-wards, falling out of the chair on to the floor. Half crouched, ready for the fight, he looked up, only to see Bill slide the knife across the table towards him and then take a seat himself. A look of astonishment passed over Snod's face. Bill had deliberately positioned the handle of the knife inches from Snod's hand, with the tip of the blade facing back towards Bill himself.

'I want a minute of your time. That's all. One minute. If you don't believe what I've said by then, you can use the knife – use it on me. I won't fight back.'

'What is this?' hissed Snod suspiciously, not shifting out of his crouch, 'What d'you want?'

Drawing in a deep, deep breath, Bill slowly began to speak.

'They first appeared when you were about ten or eleven. The spots. They told you not to worry – said it was puberty come early. It felt strange all the same, though, didn't it, with hair on your chest and under your arms three years before all the other kids in the class? And you sprang up so tall. I bet they looked like babies to you.'

Watching Snod's jaw drop open and seeing the anguished look of recollection spread across his face, Bill knew that he was right.

'But then, of course, you didn't grow any taller, not after you were twelve. Not that anyone was very worried about that either: the others were catching up and you were just average again. Except that the spots didn't go – even when you were in your early twenties.'

'How do you know?' rasped Snod, his voice hoarse, his eyes rolling. 'How d'you know all this?'

'It was something Conlon said to me. He said he couldn't believe you were only twelve when he first tried to arrest you – because you were so incredibly tall for your age. But you're the same height today, aren't you, Snod? What? About five foot one or two? You've never grown an inch since you were twelve years old, have you?'

'What d'you want?' asked Snod, raising himself from his crouch, a look of vengeance and loathing on his face.

'I know what's the matter with you, Snod. I'm the only person in the world who does. You have a condition called Bullman-Sachs. It's very rare. Very, very rare indeed – maybe only fifty or sixty people in the whole country have it besides you. Your body lacks a particular enzyme, called alpha-hydroxylase. Its absence advances puberty in exactly the way I've just described. Exactly in the way it happened to you.'

'You're lying. It's just a skin condition. They checked me out.'

'Then how come nothing worked? All those lotions and creams and steroids? Bullman-Sachs was only identified a couple of years ago. No one knew of its existence when you were in your teens. But there's a

276

treatment now, Snod. You have to believe me. A treatment that works.'

'No, no!'

Picking the knife off the tabletop Snod advanced towards Bill. With every ounce of self-control he possessed, Bill forced himself to stay still, not to move by even so much as an inch.

'I told you I wouldn't fight and I won't. Kill me if you want to, but before you do, you should know that if I'm right – and I'm almost sure I am – you have got to get help, and you have got to get it quickly.'

Bill could feel his voice beginning to falter – Snod was holding the blade right under his throat. He had to keep talking.

'I think, I think, you may be about to enter the third and final stage of Bullman–Sachs. Metastasis. The spots become cancerous. If you don't get the treatment soon – you'll … you'll be dead. Possibly in less than two years.'

They stared at each other eye to eye. Finally, without lowering the blade, Snod spoke.

'If it's true. If I've got it. This … disease. What's it to you? Why should you care about me?'

'Because I'm a doctor,' replied Bill.

Finally, after what seemed to Bill an eternity, Snod let the blade fall to his side, moved slowly backwards and sat back down. For several seconds Bill remained unmoved, unspeaking, watching Snod's blank expression and imagining the thoughts that were passing through his head, the piecing together of great swathes of his life which hitherto had been a mystery to him.

'Snod. Can I examine you?' said Bill, finally. 'I'm not an expert, but I talked to someone this afternoon who knows a lot about what you've got. He told me what I need to look for, to be absolutely certain. Hold on to the knife if you want to, I don't mind.'

Moving around to the other side of the table, Bill crouched down and brought his hands up to Snod's face. At first he flinched, but as Bill slowly probed the red, scaly marks, he closed his eyes and seemed to relax, soothed by the touch of the cool, gentle fingers on his brow.

'You're not stage three, Snod. Not as far as I can tell. There would be lumps underneath the skin, but it still feels very soft. But all the same, we've got to go.'

'Go? Go where?' asked Snod.

'St. Margaret's Hospital in London. My friend has talked to the

Professor of Medicine there. They'll admit you tonight, take blood samples tomorrow and your treatment can begin in a couple of days. They're looking forward to seeing you. You're quite a find, you know.'

'Now? I can't go now.'

'Yes, you can. I've got my car outside. We'll be there in an hour.'

'But …'

Again, Bill knew that he had no other option than to stand absolutely firm.

'No, Snod. No running away. Not any more. Your life has just changed – you have to recognize that. But for the better, I think. Come on. Pack a bag and some things. I'll wait for you out on the balcony.'

Snod emerged five minutes later, a sports hold-all in his left hand. Locking the front door, he stared at the outside of the flat as though seeing his childhood home for the first time. Again Bill wondered what life must have been like for him, thrust unprepared into early puberty and then held there ever since, dangling in suspension between adolescence and adulthood. Finally, Snod turned and looked at Bill.

'Why? Why did you come back?'

'I told you – I'm a doctor. Well, a doctor of sorts, anyhow.'

'But what do you want?'

'Nothing, Well, no, that's not actually true – there is one thing.'

Snod stiffened. Had this, after all, been just a cruel trick to lever some advantage from him? Bill's relaxed smile quickly set his fears at rest.

'It's all right. It's not money or anything. Just a small thing you can help me with – a bit of professional advice, I guess you could call it. Come on. We'll talk in the car.'

A footfall. A muffled click of the kitchen door, and Una knew that the moment she had been anticipating for over a week had at last arrived. Sprinkling a pinch of feed on to the placid surface of the fish tank, she watched the small particles of grain float down through the water. She was in no hurry. Let him come to her this time. She had all afternoon – she had the rest of her life.

'It's on. Next Wednesday. Have the van ready from three.'

'No. It isn't,' said Una, without looking up.

'Don't disappoint me, Una. You can't pull out now. Not at this late stage.'

'Oh, yes I can,' she quietly replied, watching intently as the tank's solitary angel-fish emerged suspiciously from its hiding place among the ornamental rocks and began moving slowly across towards the food.

'What d'you mean?'

Ray was on the other side of the tank now, only inches away. She could see his belt-buckle through the water. Still she stayed crouched down, not looking up at him.

'I mean it's not going to be next Wednesday. Or the one after that. Or ever, in fact. They've been tipped off.'

'Who have?'

'The animal testing laboratory.'

'How d'you know?' he asked, quickly.

'I know because it was me who made the call.' Finally, she looked upwards, and, just as Jack Conlon had told her, met and held his gaze. 'I share your objectives, Ray. I always will. But not your means. I couldn't stand by and see that old man hurt.'

'What did you tell them? You didn't mention any ...'

'Don't worry,' interrupted Una. 'I didn't give any names away. They have no idea who or when.'

They stood staring at each other face to face. His features remained immobile but his cold blue eyes flickered from side to side. Looking into his face, she wondered why it had taken her so long to recognize him for the cynical manipulator that he really was.

'You do realize the position this puts you in,' he said, at last, turning and sauntering lazily across towards the front window of the shop. 'I can't be responsible for how the other members of the group will take this, you know – how they will react.'

'I said I didn't give away any names. Not that I'd forgotten what those names were.' He turned and looked at her. Again she held his gaze. 'I know you've always been one for democracy, Ray, but perhaps this is the time for you to start exercising a little more authority over the group – showing some leadership. If you still want to have a group left to lead, that is.'

A muscle in his right cheek twitched – just momentarily and just once – but all the same, in that instant, Una knew she had him. Crouching back down, she began observing the angel-fish again, utterly absorbed within moments by its silent, careful passage back across the tank and into the camouflage of the ornamental rocks.

The next time she looked up she was completely alone, save for a faint draft around her neck telling her that the kitchen door needed closing.

As soon as Louise put her foot over the threshold, she could tell that someone had been in her flat. Letting her heavy weekend bag fall silently to the floor, she quickly thrust out her free hand to stop the front door from squeaking on its hinges. Standing completely still for almost a minute, she strained her ears to detect any sound that might indicate the intruder's continued presence. Nothing. Sliding the bag across the carpet to ensure the door stayed jammed open, she crept down the hallway step by step, ready at any moment to turn on her heel and dash back out into the street: if Snod was even half as dangerous as Bill maintained, she had no intention of confronting him within the narrow confines of the flat.

The bedroom and living room doors were both slightly ajar. What had he done to her home in the two days that it had been unoccupied? Trashed the furniture? Left some vile bodily deposit between her sheets or under her pillow? Coming to a halt outside the living room door, Louise tried to stoke up her courage. He was almost certainly long gone, and, in any case, she couldn't stay cowering in the hallway all day long. Taking a deep breath, she gripped the door handle and marched purposefully into the living-room.

But her intruder had not gone.

Rather, he was standing at the window, looking out over the park, casually drinking coffee from her favourite mug.

'Bill! What are you doing here?'

'Sorry, Louise, I didn't hear you come in. Are you OK?'

'Am I OK? Am I OK? No, I am not OK!' gasped Louise, 'You scared me half to death. How on earth did you get in here?'

'Sorry. I was miles away there. You didn't think I was Snod, did you?'

'Well, yes, I did, actually!' exclaimed Louise, resting her back against the living-room door in a mixture of relief and annoyance. 'What's going on? We called you about ten times yesterday. Are you on the run or something?'

'No, no, nothing like that. Don't worry. There's no need for either of us to hide from him – not now, not ever again.'

'Why? What's happened?'

'You told me to face up to him – so I did. He was just a kid, Lou. A sick, frightened kid, kicked and beaten into a corner and then cheated

280

out of ever growing up. I've got him into a specialist hospital – about a mile away from here.'

'A hospital?'

'Yeah. St. Margaret's in Westbourne Grove – I drove him over there myself. They're going to start him on a course of remedial drugs tomorrow. It's fantastic news, don't you think?'

'Well, yes, I suppose so, – but what about the money? The money you owed him for the machine?'

'Settled, sorted. Debt cleared.'

'What? How?'

'Conlon – of all people.'

'The policeman?'

'Yeah, DI Conlon. I'm gonna be his best man next week, too.'

'His what?'

'It's bizarre, isn't it? God knows what I'm gonna say if they ask me to make a speech: we've been the best of friends ever since he beat the crap out of me down at the nick. Sorry, Lou. I'm probably not making much sense here. Maybe you'd better sit down.'

As Bill walked across the room towards her, Louise stared at him in puzzlement: something in his demeanour seemed subtly to have changed. Perhaps it was because she hadn't seen him for a couple of days, but somehow his physical presence appeared more substantial, more solid.

'How did you get in here, anyway?' she asked, allowing herself to be manoeuvred into the armchair.

'Snod taught me a trick with your lock. That's how he broke in before. Worked first time it did – I couldn't believe it. I've been here since yesterday evening.'

'What, you stayed here all night?'

'Yes, I hope you don't mind,' replied Bill, walking back across the room and sitting down on the broad window sill. 'It's a terrible intrusion into your privacy, I know, but I've been, well, sort of soaking up your presence around the flat. I knew we wouldn't be seeing each other again after today so I just couldn't stop myself.'

'Why won't we be seeing each other again?' asked Louise, frowning. 'I mean, if it's all finished like you say, then that's great, isn't it? Surely, we can go back to …'

'It's not all finished, Louise,' interrupted Bill. 'Not until you know everything. Not until you know the whole truth.'

It was more than a subtle change. He was a different person. The Bill Kennedy she had known before could never have looked at her with such candour.

'Know what, Bill?'

'That night, when you came to Wyburn – after your course in Warwick – it wasn't the Libidan in the atmosphere in my house. I lied to you, Louise. About an hour before you arrived, Brummie brought around three experimental pills. I put one in your water. I spiked it – on purpose – I wasn't drunk. I knew exactly what I was doing. And I had no excuse.'

Closing her eyes, Louise's mind went back to the morning she had awoken in the bed next to Bill, racked with guilt and self-disgust. Completely at a loss to understand her behaviour the previous night, she had eventually charged herself with an act of stupidity as shameful as any she had perpetrated in her life before. But, if anything, the explanation she had now been given was even more degrading. It had been no moment of recklessness of her part. She had been used – cynically and callously used.

'So, I was a guinea-pig, then. Is that what you're saying? Just like the laboratory animals you kept in that room behind the stairs.'

'Oh, no, Louise. It wasn't science. Never for a moment.'

'So, what was it, then – sex?'

Turning, he looked out of the window over the park. Despite the confession he had just made, she could see a smile once again passing across his face.

'Do you remember when we first met? You probably don't, do you? I do. Like it was yesterday. On Harledge East station. I stood there by the barrier, watching you and Gail walk down the platform, laughing and smiling together.'

'Yes, I remember.'

'I fell in love with you then, Louise, the very first moment I saw you. But instead of trying to win you over, persuading you of how I felt and trying to make you feel the same, I tricked you. I drugged you. That's what was wrong with Libidan, you see: being able to take something you haven't earned and don't deserve. It was what was wrong with me, too, I suppose.'

'Bill, I …'

'No, don't, Louise, please – let me finish what I have to say – I've been standing in front of this window for hours preparing this speech. These last three months, working with you at the garage, seeing you nearly every day, have been the happiest and most fulfilling time of my life. I've never felt better than this – as a person, as an individual – and I don't think I ever will. And that's why I want you to marry me.'

'What did you say?'

'I want you to marry me.'

Louise stared at Bill in complete consternation. He really meant it. The room went deathly quiet. Outside she could hear a taxi drive past in the street.

'Bill. I'm only twenty-three. I don't want to get married yet. I … I've got so many things I want to do.'

'I know. I know.'

'I've got my career – I mean I've only just left college. I wasn't planning to settle down with one person for years yet, if ever. You can't expect me to …'

'And I want to have children with you, too.' interrupted Bill.

'Bill, don't do this, please. I can't marry you. I'm not ready for a lifetime relationship yet. Not with you, not with anyone.'

'Louise, Louise. Listen. I'm not saying marry me now, OK? I realize you haven't thought about settling down yet. And that's fine – I didn't want to either until, well, a few weeks ago, I suppose. What I am saying is that one day you might feel this way as well, and when you do – if you do – I'll be waiting for you.'

'But Bill, you can't hang around forever waiting for me. It's not fair on you. And, more to the point, it's not fair on me, either – I can't be saddled with that sort of emotional responsibility.'

'And that's why I said we can't see each other again. Don't worry, I'm not going to spend the whole time moping around after you, looking all lovelorn. You need to be free to live your life and arrive at the point I am now in your own time. I mean, more than that, it's what I actually want you to do. And when you're ready. Just call.'

Suddenly, she too, was back on Harledge East, surprised to discover that the shy, awkward-looking man in the purple tie was her best friend's big brother.

'Maybe … maybe you should be looking for someone else who's ready now. Someone who feels just the same way you do.'

With a smile, Bill turned and looked back out over the park again.

'I've got this vision, running through my brain. I've had it for days now. I come home from work. Park my car in front of the house. I mean, it's just so corny and conventional, I know – happy families – God! I walk through the front door. And there are the kids, all sitting on the carpet, smiling back up at me. And it's you with them. Not someone else. You. It's what I've got to offer, Louise. A house and garden somewhere. It might not be much. But it's there for you, if ever you want it.'

'But what if I don't want it, Bill? Or if I want it … with someone else.'

The instant she spoke, Louise hated herself for the pain her words might cause him, but instead of looking hurt, Bill slowly slipped his right hand into the top pocket of his shirt. Taking out a thin cellophane package, he held it up to the light.

'D'you know what this is, Louise? It's the last pill. The last Libidan pill in existence. D'you know what it means for the man who owns it? What it really means? I'll tell you. Any woman in the world, that's what.'

Without taking his eyes off Louise, Bill slowly tore open the package and took out the tiny white sphere.

'Except I don't want any woman in the world. I only want you. I know you'll get other offers after I'm gone – because you're so intelligent and beautiful. And OK, maybe I'm being stupid, hoping that someone like you could ever want someone like me. But when the other men turn up, remember all those hours we spent in the garage side by side. Remember how we shared together, and worked together, and laughed together. And remember this, Louise. Remember this.'

Placing the pill on his tongue, Bill took a sip from the dregs of his coffee and, swilling the two around in his mouth together, swallowed them down.

The mid-morning sunshine was brilliant beyond belief and, as he stood on the pavement outside the flat looking up at the sky, he had to shield his eyes with his palm to protect them from its radiance. At the very last moment, just as he had been about to close the front door, she had sprung out of the armchair, hurled herself down the hallway and thrown her arms around his neck. It would be how he would remember her. Somewhere, a bicycle bell sounded and, turning to his left he saw a young girl, about twelve years old, riding down the street towards him.

Holding an apple in her left hand and steering the handlebars with her right, she flashed him a smile as he stepped backwards to get out of the way. A simple act of politeness and a simple gesture of thanks – what more wonderful start to the rest of his life could he wish for than this? Smiling, Bill thought of Snod, lying there in his hospital bed. It was a lovely day – perhaps he would walk over to St. Margaret's and pay him a late morning visit. Letting the young girl pass in front of him, Bill felt the faintest of breezes from her slipstream brush against his face. Just as he was about to walk off, he was surprised to find that the draught did not seem to be decreasing, the further she moved away, but somehow getting more powerful. Puzzled, he looked down the street after her. The current of air was really quite strong now. Where on earth was it coming from? No sooner had the question occurred to him than a blast of wind practically blew him off his feet. All around him a gale was springing up – vicious and untamed – that howled about his ears and tore through the veil of the summer morning.

And, all at once, it was a winter's day.

The sun had gone. The sky was a churning black mass of cloud that lashed rain against his face like a flail. He was running. Running down the pitch towards the goal. From the corner flag a ball had been hoisted high into the air, and he knew that if he were to take his chance, he would have to fly to the very heavens to meet it. And so he began to rise. To rise upwards in a leap of such magnificence and athleticism that every man, woman and child in the crowd would remember the sight until their dying day. Soaring neck, head and shoulders above the other players, he ascended ever higher, until, at the supreme apex of his flight, he held himself in suspension above the earth – a man defying nature, a man made more than human by the strength of his will and the power of his mind.

The ball was bouncing crazily around inside the net. Arms flailing, he landed, caught it and in a single movement turned backwards on his heel. Fighting off the congratulations of his fellow players, his jaw set rigid in determination, again he began to run, not stopping until he had slammed the ball down on the centre spot. And, as he stood there – hands on hips, lungs straining for oxygen, looking left and right for the stadium clock – a tiny voice, so quiet and measured that it could only be his own, began to speak to him above the cries of the still roaring crowd. It said, 'Don't worry about the time left for you now – the hours and the minutes that may remain on the clock. The time has come for you to start enjoying the game. You may go on to win. You may go on to lose. It doesn't matter either way any more.

'Because, now, you are free.'

Slowing down to throw her apple core into a waste-bin, Paula Gilbert dismounted, and, as she did so, felt overcome by the desire to turn and look back down the street, so strange and serene had been the expression of the man she had seen standing outside the apartment block. But, by the time she was able to manoeuvre her bike around to get a good enough view, the street was empty and the man had gone.